LAURA RESNICK

VAMPARAZZI

An Esther Diamond Novel

DAW BOOKS, INC.

DONALD A. WOLLHEIM, FOUNDER

375 Hudson Street, New York, NY 10014

ELIZABETH R. WOLLHEIM
SHEILA E. GILBERT
PUBLISHERS

http://www.dawbooks.com

First Printing, October 2011
1 2 3 4 5 6 7 8 9

DAW TRADEMARK REGISTERED
U.S. PAT. AND TM. OFF. AND FOREIGN COUNTRIES
—MARCA REGISTRADA
HECHO EN U.S.A.
PRINTED IN THE U.S.A.

Prologue

Belgrade, 1733

It was late at night when the two men met at a modest inn that sat in a narrow street of the oft-conquered "white city" which lay along the Sava River where it flowed into the Danube. Here in the heart of the Habsburg Empire's restless eastern provinces, which had been claimed as a war prize from the Ottoman Turks in recent years, the men met as allies—as friends, in truth. After concluding their secret business, they would part company for the last time, never to meet again.

And what they accomplished tonight in this obscure Serbian inn, by the flickering light of cheap tallow candles that smoked unpleasantly, would affect the fate of many individuals, human and otherwise, on more than one continent, for centuries to come—though only a few select people would ever know about it.

Jurgis Radvila had arrived in Belgrade the previous day and had been waiting inside the inn since then. So he was dry and relatively comfortable—though this private back room's amenities did not extend to a hearth fire—when Dr. Maximillian Zadok arrived, dripping wet and shivering from the miserable weather of early spring.

As Max issued a breathless greeting to his colleague, a cocky servant boy helped him remove his wet cloak and hat. The innkeeper and his wife were already abed, but the boy, perhaps identifying this courteous foreigner as a gentleman likely to reward him with a few extra coins for good service, proposed bringing him some bread, cheese, and ale. Max accepted the suggestion, and he offered to pay handsomely to have his weary horse fed, rubbed down, and stabled for the rest of the night.

Radvila told the boy that he would not be using his own bed tonight, for which he had paid in advance; his colleague could have it. He added that his own horse would need to be saddled and ready to depart within the hour.

The boy looked puzzled, since traveling so late at night was decidedly eccentric—as well as dangerous. The men dismissed the lad. They felt no inclination to explain to a curious servant that they both had unusual means of defending themselves against the usual perils.

Nonetheless, Max warned, "Traveling conditions are abysmal tonight, my friend."

"I have a very long journey ahead of me. The sooner I leave, the sooner I will be in Vilnius." The Lithuanian shrugged, his heavily lined face revealing no dismay about enduring the wet, windy night. "And I am restless after two days in this inn. You know how inactivity vexes me."

"I do apologize for my late arrival," Max said. "I had thought to be here several days ago. But the boat I was on foundered. And the condition of the roads . . ." He shook his head.

"I was growing concerned. I am relieved to see you."

"And I you," Max replied. "I gather that the, er, work was completed successfully?"

"Of course," said the gray-haired man.

"I had no doubts, but nonetheless, I am relieved. It was a daunting and dangerous endeavor. As I well know."

"It was necessary," Radvila said simply. After a brief pause, he said, "You have come alone, Maximillian?"

The two men spoke to each other in Latin, as was their established habit; although they were both fluent in multiple languages, it was their only common tongue. Of necessity, they had each learned to speak a little Serbian during their sojourn in this region, but their fluency in it stopped well short of intelligent conversation. Their syntax in the local language relied primarily on phrases such as, "Where is the vampire?" and "Open the grave."

Max was about to respond to Radvila's question when the door opened and the servant boy carried in a modestly loaded tray. He set it down, then told them he would go awaken the groom and deliver the instructions about their horses. The boy closed the door behind him as he departed.

As soon as they were alone again, Radvila asked, "Does your solitary arrival mean you have been unsuccessful in securing the necessary support for the treaty?"

"On the contrary. I am alone, as you observed, but not empty-handed." After a brief, longing glance at the food and ale, Max picked up the leather satchel he had been protecting from the weather by shielding it under his traveling cloak. He opened it to reveal documents inside, kept safe and dry during his long, eventful journey from the imperial court in Vienna to this weary city in the Balkan Peninsula.

"What is this?" Radvila asked, watching as Max withdrew the documents from the satchel.

"This is the result of my negotiations with the Magnum Collegium and with the Austrian government. My efforts did not produce precisely the results that you and I discussed—"

"They won't sign the treaty?" Radvila's gray brows swooped down in sudden anger. "If my comrades and I had not intervened—"

"Calm yourself, my dear fellow," Max said. "The treaty will be ratified tonight. The Magnum Collegium and the imperial court of Charles VI have each provided official letters authorizing me to sign it on their behalf. These are your copies of those documents."

With a courtly gesture to honor the historicity of the occasion, Max presented the documents to Radvila, saying, "As the designated representative of the Magnum Collegium, which esteemed body recognizes the wisdom of your proposal to them, and as a temporarily appointed envoy of the Habsburg monarchy, which government expresses its gratitude for all that you and your comrades have done to help stabilize its newly acquired provinces in this volatile region—"

"We did not do it for the Habsburgs," Radvila said brusquely.

"I hereby present you with these documents which guarantee that my signature on the Treaty of Gediminas will bind these parties to this sacred agreement, as surely as your signature will commit the Council of Gediminas to it."

Radvila accepted the documents and looked them over. "I can't decide whether their Latin is very weak or very good."

"I don't understand."

"These letters are oddly phrased."

"Are you saying they're unacceptable?" Max asked with concern.

"Oh, *I* find them acceptable," the Lithuanian said dryly. "But do *you*?"

"Oh. Yes. Well, er . . ." Max cleared his throat. "Although agreeing to this treaty was seen as prudent when I explained what I had experienced here in His Majesty's eastern provinces . . ."

"Yes?"

"The treaty was also perceived as controversial and potentially a source of great embarrassment," he concluded uncomfortably.

"Ah. I see. And thus if anything goes wrong . . ." Radvila waved one of the letters at his colleague. "You will be held responsible."

"Yes. I will." Max spoke with resolve as he added, "I accept that risk. I have seen too much to turn back now."

Radvila extended his own hand to clasp Max's with warm approval. "I knew the night we met that you were a man with the courage to see this through. Indeed, I have often been amazed to find such wisdom in one so young."

"Oh . . . I'm a little older than I look," his companion replied. "Now, since you must depart soon, I suggest we proceed."

"Of course." Radvila added with a touch of concern, "And then I urge you to eat and get some rest. If I may speak candidly, you look terrible."

"I have no doubt of it," Max said wearily.

Radvila laid out upon the wooden table three copies of the treaty he had brought with him. Max reviewed the elegant text, acknowledged that the terms were exactly as they had discussed, and accepted the quill that Radvila handed him.

A few moments later, all three copies were signed.

The two men stood silently, looking down at their signatures, and recognized the significance of what they had wrought.

Then the Lithuanian smiled and slapped his companion on the back. "Your vampire hunting days are over, Maximillian."

"Indeed," Max said. "I pray that I have done the right thing."

1

Everything you think you know about vampires is wrong.

I learned this while being harassed by vampire fanatics, bitten eight times a week by a self-proclaimed creature of the night, and attacked by a real vampire. So I speak with some authority on the subject.

Much of my education about vampires came from my friend, Dr. Maximillian Zadok, a 350-year-old mage who protects New York City from Evil. You would think (I certainly did) that ridding the city of the bloodsucking undead would be included in that job description, but it turns out that confronting vampires is a little more complicated than a simple equation of Max versus Evil. Among those of the exsanguinating persuasion, there is a wide range of behavior, from "evil monster" all the way across the spectrum to "law-abiding and fully integrated member of society."

Who knew?

Something else I learned is that vampires are exactly like vegetarians, in the sense that you can spend a lot of time with one and not have the faintest idea—until it's mealtime.

I speak from experience about that, too.

My name is Esther Diamond, and I'm an actress. My reluctant familiarity with vampires of all varieties—real, fictional, and pretend—began when I was cast in *The Vampyre,* a new stage play based on the nineteenth-century story by Dr. John Polidori. The author is mostly remembered in our time because he accompanied Lord Byron on a trip through Europe in 1816, serving as the mercurial poet's personal physician. Polidori was with Byron, Mary Shelley, and Percy Bysshe Shelley at the rented villa in Switzerland that summer where, in response to a challenge set by Byron that they should each write a ghost story, Mary started work on her famous novel *Frankenstein*.

Dr. Polidori was soon fired by Byron—who was reputedly the inspiration for Lord Ruthven, the title character in Polidori's "Vampyre;" Ruthven is an alluringly sinister aristocrat who uses and abuses others without compassion or conscience. Published in 1819, the story was a commercial success in its era, igniting the reading public's enduring love affair with vampires. It was the first vampire fiction written in English, and also the first characterization of a vampire as seductive and sophisticated. Although the work is little-known today, Polidori's vision of the vampire was innovative in its time, and it influenced other fiction writers of his century—including Bram Stoker, who came along several generations later and wholly eclipsed Polidori's tale with *Dracula,* which has dominated our image of vampires ever since.

Polidori died two years after the initial publication of his story, when he was only twenty-six years old—one year younger than I was when I was cast in the play.

I had never heard of "The Vampyre" (or Polidori) until I learned about this planned production. Since no copies of the brand-new stage adaptation were available, I read Polidori's story when preparing for the audition. And I immediately realized why its popularity these days is limited to ardent students of nineteenth-century gothic literature. Although mercifully short, its flowery language and flimsy characterization don't translate well to modern tastes.

The story's protagonist is an apple-cheeked young Englishman named Aubrey who is befriended by the dissipated Lord Ruthven. They travel together to Europe, where Aubrey falls in love with the ravishingly beautiful and innocent Ianthe—who happens to be obsessed with vampire folklore. Aubrey doesn't take her quaint fears seriously until after she's found dead, with telltale teeth marks on her neck. By the time he realizes that Lord Ruthven is the quaint fear that killed Ianthe, Aubrey has already made a sacred promise, sworn under duress, not to reveal what he knows. So, naturally, he can do nothing thereafter but wring his hands in helpless despair. Aubrey returns to England, where he soon falls ill, and he's incoherent with fever by the time he discovers that his beloved sister's new fiancé is none other than—yes!—Lord Ruthven. The young man dies without managing to warn his sister what a fine mess she's getting herself into. The aristocratic vampire slakes his thirst on his new bride (can you spot the metaphor?), then he disappears, leaving behind her corpse. The end.

Only the lucrative popularity of vampires in contemporary culture, I thought, could explain the resurrection of this storyline for an off-Broadway play.

Indeed, as I soon learned, the popularity of one *particular* vampire explained it: Daemon Ravel.

Though the atmospheric play was (to be candid) mediocre fare, Ruthven was an ideal role for this Byronic leading man who played only vampires—and who, indeed, claimed to *be* a vampire. *The Vampyre* was being produced as a showcase for him. I had never heard of Daemon Ravel, but I kept my happy ignorance to myself during the initial audition. During the callback, when Daemon was brought in to read opposite me, I pretended to know who he was and to be an admirer of his work, since I shrewdly sensed that admitting otherwise might cost me the job.

Sure, I have principles. But I also have bills to pay. Most of all, I have an ardent desire to work in my profession.

Anyhow, I got the job. No, not the job as the ravishingly beautiful Ianthe; that role went to a ravishingly beautiful actress. I was cast as Aubrey's sister. She has no name in Polidori's story, where the two female characters are little more than a means for Lord Ruthven to torment Aubrey. For the play, though, the sister was named Jane—Miss Jane Aubrey. In the story, she's a delicate ingenue, barely eighteen years old. In the play, to differentiate her from the young and innocent Ianthe, she became a twenty-four-year-old spinster, a doting older sister who had been managing Aubrey's household since their parents' deaths, and who was considered past praying for, in terms of marriage, until Lord Ruthven came along.

I initially thought that playing a nineteenth-century spinster meant I'd be wearing something warm onstage when the play opened in late September in Greenwich Village's drafty Robert Hamburg Theater. However, I realized during the initial costume fittings that the clothing in *The Vampyre* would be as sexed-up as I had already discovered the dialogue and the direction were. Thus it was that eight shows per week, my breasts were in perpetual danger of falling out of my Regency-era gown. Not because I'm so busty (I'm not), but because my extremely low neckline, combined with my diaphanous push-up corset, created a precarious situation. The delicate fabric of my gown also ensured that the shadowy outlines of my legs were often exposed to Lord Ruthven's gaze, as well as to the rapt audiences watching him seduce and devour me.

I did suggest to Fiona, the wardrobe mistress, that a sensible spinster from a respected family of that period would perhaps dress a tad more modestly. Rather than earning me a warmer costume, my suggestion merely ensured that Fiona, who fervently believed that actors should be seen and not heard, went from disliking me to openly loathing me. From then on, I was pretty much on my own with my costume problems—the difficulties included getting into and out of it, since it was authentic enough to fasten via lacing down the back. And woe betide me if I got the gown a little dirty before it was scheduled for cleaning.

To my surprise, my parents had proposed coming to New York to see the show. They weren't unsupportive of my acting career, but they'd also never been particularly interested in it. It just wasn't something they understood. Even though I had by now been pursuing my profession in New York for over five years, they still vaguely thought of it as a phase I'd get over. So their threat to come all the way from our family home in Madison, Wisconsin, to see *The Vampyre* caught me completely off guard (and I privately harbored dark suspicions that my mother was a closet fan of Daemon Ravel). Fortunately, the show's short run (eight weeks) made it pretty easy to talk them out of this plan. I was still recovering from my parents' previous visit two years earlier, so I thought it was too soon for another one.

I also felt uncomfortably self-conscious about the notion of performing this play in front of them. Although Polidori's text refers to "sin," "violent excitement," and vampires enjoying "nocturnal orgies," his story is very tame stuff by modern standards. The new stage adaptation, by contrast, sought to appeal more to contemporary tastes—and, in particular, to the tastes of Daemon Ravel's fans, who were its target audience.

Consequently, the whole show was a heavy-handed, two-act bout of erotic titillation. The dialogue was full of sexual innuendo and double entendres. Daemon's delivery was relentlessly sultry and smoldering, and his scenes with me were smotheringly seductive. Miss Jane Aubrey, a respectable (though scantily clad) spinster and standard stereotype, was drawn to Lord Ruthven like a moth to a flame . . . and behaved just about as intelligently. There was also some semi-explicit touching and grabbing of my person in the scene where Ruthven convinced Jane to marry him, as well as in the sinister depiction of their wedding night, where the usual vampire metaphors of pleasure and pain, penetration and piercing, orgasm and death were all maxed out.

None of this was stuff I particularly wanted to do in front of my parents.

Moreover, since Daemon liked to "improvise," the explicitness of his touching and grabbing was sometimes more than just semi. I'd had stern words with him about that a few times. I'd also spoken sharply to him the other night about his growing tendency to employ actual suction, occasionally with a grazing of teeth, when he was supposed to be *pretending* to bite me and drain my blood in the wedding-night scene.

Daemon responded by assuring me he was a lover, not a killer, but claimed it was hard to control himself when he was so close to the throbbing pulse of a tempting woman's hot blood, blah blah blah.

Throughout rehearsals, as well as during the weeks we had been performing the show, Daemon steadfastly maintained the pretense that he was a real vampire and that he stuck strictly to playing vampire roles as a matter of ethnic pride, so to speak. He even kept little bottles of what he claimed was human blood inside a minifridge in his dressing room at the theater. He told fans (among whom he included his fellow actors) that his role as Ruthven was so spiritually demanding for him, he needed a restorative drink between shows when we did two performances back-to-back. (The rest of us usually had a restorative pizza on those nights.)

Daemon had reputedly started his career in the East

Village by appearing as a vampire in a series of performance art pieces. This led to him being featured in a popular rock video, which increased the size of his cult following. Then he was cast in a series of national commercials and print ads as the vampire icon for Nocturne, a brand of blood-colored beverages. (His famous tag line was, "I don't drink . . . wine. I drink red wine coolers.")

Those Nocturne ads, which he was still doing, had elevated his standard of living to its current level. He inhabited a Soho loft whose windows he had paid a fortune to have replaced, in a highly publicized renovation, with heavily tinted glass that blocked the sun's rays. He could also afford a chauffeur-driven limousine that transported him everywhere. When he had to go anywhere by day, he insisted on being shielded from the sun by a large black umbrella when making the "potentially terminal" transition between building and car.

I envied him that car when I was wearily hauling a tote bag full of my stuff toward the subway station after the show each night, or calling for a cab when it was too late for the subway to be a wise choice for a woman alone. Because of the vampire theme of the show and the night-dwelling target audience, we added a second performance to our schedule every Friday and Saturday night, and it started at midnight. On those nights, I didn't get out of the theater until three o'clock in the morning. So I had certainly been tempted, more than once, to accept Daemon's occasional offers to give me a lift home—but I always declined. Walking to the subway or waiting for a cab inevitably seemed simpler than being alone with Daemon in the cozy backseat of his opaque-windowed car. He already took too many physical liberties with me when we were onstage; I didn't want him feeling encouraged to take any more.

Which is not to say that Daemon was interested in me. He wasn't. The actor was already deeply, obsessively in love with someone else: himself. He was just eager to get others to share his passion.

Daemon's D-list celebrity status had led to him getting his own cable TV series in which he played a brooding, misunderstood vampire with a heart of gold. While solving deadly problems for the troubled mortals who kept stumbling into his life, he struggled nobly with his innate bloodlust, chastely wooed a plucky girl reporter, and played surrogate parent to a cocky kid whose widowed mother was eaten by Daemon's wicked vampire arch-nemesis in the pilot episode.

I watched part of one disc from the DVD set of the show, *He of the Night,* which Daemon gave me as a "welcome aboard" present after I was cast in *The Vampyre.* Mostly it left me with the impression that he would have been wise to heed to the age-old advice to actors to avoid working with children. He probably should have avoided working with bad scriptwriters, too.

Daemon's fanatically loyal fans weren't numerous enough to boost the ratings for his inane series, and *He of The Night* was canceled halfway through its first season. The actor's resolute and oft-repeated determination only to play his "own kind" limited his opportunities thereafter, much the way mine would be limited if I were only willing to play middle-class Jewish girls. And his persistent attention-seeking as a self-proclaimed vampire ensured that he wasn't taken seriously in our profession. Go figure.

However, as a gifted self-promoter, Daemon was able to convince a producer that featuring him in the limited run of a sexually charged adaptation of a neglected gothic classic would be profitable—and so this production of *The Vampyre* was mounted in time to open in late September, ensuring a handy seasonal theme for the show's publicity in the weeks leading up to Halloween. We were scheduled to run through mid-November and shut down before Thanksgiving week, when a show with a markedly differently target audience would move into the Hamburg Theater for the holiday shopping season.

For Daemon, starring in *The Vampyre* was primarily a way to keep his profile high while reframing his image enough, he hoped, to secure a film deal. He was no longer just an advertising model whose lame cable series had flopped; now he was the star of a sold-out off-Broadway play, and an actor who had proved he could handle the demands of a period piece.

Whatever.

For my part, despite being cold and getting fondled and bitten in every performance, I was happy to be working, glad to add a high-profile off-Broadway production to my résumé, and pleased to be playing to packed houses.

Sure, the audiences only came to see Daemon, and I doubted they'd care (or necessarily even notice) if I were replaced halfway through a performance by an animated stalk of broccoli. But I still enjoyed playing to full houses so deeply absorbed in the play that no one ever coughed, rustled candy wrappings, or answered a cell phone during a performance. They also invariably gasped, sighed, and clapped in all the right places; and they never raced to the exits the moment the play ended, too rude to stay for the curtain call.

I had to admit, Daemon's fans were a great audience.

Which is not to say that they were always well-behaved. In fact, one of his ardent followers had given me the black eye I was sporting this evening.

The show was in the sixth week of its run when Halloween weekend arrived, and the size and hysteria of the crowds surrounding the theater had increased noticeably in the past few days. On Thursday, Halloween night itself, we'd added an additional midnight performance to the weekly schedule. Even so, the street outside the theater that night was full of frustrated fans who couldn't get a ticket to a performance. Many of them had seen the show already (indeed, some of them had seen it *multiple* times), but the burning desire to watch their favorite vampire performing live on All Hallows' Eve clouded their judgment, such as it was. So when the scalpers ran out of exorbitantly priced tickets, a mini-riot started.

Consequently, last night the police cordoned off the street that the Hamburg Theater was on, assigned extra patrolmen to keep the crowd under control, and made some arrests when fans got too rowdy. To my annoyance however, they did not arrest the woman who attacked me.

I *told* the cops to arrest her. But did anybody listen to me? No, of course not. *I* was only the victim. *I* was only the actress lying on the filthy cement ground outside the stage door with a throbbing eye at three o'clock in the morning because some lunatic girl had just slipped past a distracted patrolman, flung herself at me, and started pummeling me while screaming, "You bitch! Stay away from him! He doesn't want *you!*"

I assumed she was referring to Daemon. I might have been willing to tell her that, despite the high-voltage sexual tension between our characters onstage, Daemon and I hardly knew each other—and, in fact, I made a *point* of staying away from him.

But she didn't give me a chance to say so. No, she just spat in my face, punched me, and wrestled me to the ground.

And did she get locked up for assault, as she damn well deserved? No. Since I wasn't "too badly hurt," the cops on the scene, though they spoke sternly to her, suggested that I let bygones be bygones. I think the police were tired of the whole circus and just wanted everyone to go away and leave them alone.

Cops.

Fuming about this as I studied the damage in my bathroom mirror at home before leaving for the theater the following evening, I resolutely did not let myself think about one particular cop. One who had *not* been at the theater. One whom I hadn't seen in more than two months. Not since that stormy August night in Harlem when I had realized that, despite how I felt about him, we couldn't see each other again. Because I'd nearly gotten him killed. *Twice.*

There wasn't going to be a third time.

No, I ordered my battered reflection in the mirror over my bathroom sink. *Don't think about Lopez. Just don't.*

It was something I'd had to remind myself at least once a day since that dark, terrifying night in Harlem when we had both nearly died. Thinking about Lopez was a bad habit. But it was one I'd have to break, since seeing him again was out of the question.

He called me a few times after that night, even though I had told him not to do so. The first time he left a message for me, it was pretty clear he didn't really think I'd meant it. It had been a wild and strange night, I was frightened and upset, and he obviously assumed I'd feel differently once things had calmed down. He also obviously assumed I would call him back. I didn't.

The second time he left a message, he sounded hesitant. He hadn't heard from me since we'd parted company in the middle of a citywide blackout, he said, and he was a little worried. Realizing that he wouldn't let it rest until he was sure I had arrived home safely and was all right, I called back that time—and was relieved to get his voice mail. I left a quick message saying I was fine, and I was glad he was fine, too, good-bye.

He left me one more message, saying he'd like to see me and talk. I must have picked up the phone twenty times during the following week, but I put it back down every time. In the end, I stuck to my resolution and didn't call him. And he left me alone after that.

It was the right thing. If not precisely what I *wanted,* it was nonetheless the way I knew things had to be. So I was glad he had accepted my decision. I didn't want him to keep trying to see me. It was good that he hadn't called again since then. Not even once.

Jerk.

I glanced irritably at the silent cell phone lying on the broad rim of the old porcelain sink.

And Lopez wasn't the only man who hadn't called me lately. I'd left several messages this week for my agent, Thackeray Shackleton, and I still hadn't heard back from him.

Men.

I took a calming breath, ejected Thack and Lopez from my thoughts with grim determination, and started applying makeup to cover up my black eye.

In normal circumstances, I wouldn't bother doing this, since I was going to put on stage makeup for the performance as soon as I got to the theater. Then again, in normal circumstances, I wouldn't have been spat on, punched in the face, and knocked down by a crazed fan outside the stage door.

There had been a few dozen of Daemon's fans (and also some of his detractors) hanging around the theater every night since we'd begun our run in September. But in recent days, their numbers had swelled to hundreds. It was by now a challenge just for me to get into and out of the theater each night. The heightened lunacy surrounding the show this weekend also ensured that paparazzi were hanging around out there nightly, too, snapping photos of anything they found interesting. Daemon loved the attention and actively courted it. He lived by the philosophy that no matter what was said about him, being talked about was better than *not* being talked about. I, on the other hand, didn't want my black eye featured in some cheesy tabloid, so I was concealing it before leaving the safety of my apartment this evening.

We were doing two shows again tonight—for the third night in a row. Every audience deserves an actor's best work no matter when they see a play, so I wanted to remain centered and sharp all the way through the end of the second show tonight. Therefore, I was trying to conserve my energy and my focus when I was offstage.

Which is why it was probably a good thing that no one told me until after the second show that night that I was being stalked by a murderous vampire.

2

I was still in my bathroom, applying makeup to my black eye, when my buzzer rang.

I went to my front door and pressed the button that would let my visitor into the building. I didn't bother to use the intercom, since I knew who my guest was. I opened my door so he could let himself into my apartment.

I was back in front of the bathroom mirror when Leischneudel Drysdale came bounding up the stairs of my building, paused to knock courteously on my open door, then entered the apartment in response to my invitation—which he could hear easily, since my bathroom was only about four feet away from my front door.

"Hi, Esther. How's your eye?" Leischneudel stuck his head into the open bathroom door and took a good look at me. "Hey, I can hardly see the bruise."

"Good," I said. "That's the idea. Want something to drink before we go?"

"I'll help myself," he said genially. "You finish what you're doing."

He went to search my refrigerator, having become comfortable in my modest home during the weeks we'd been working together. Leischneudel, who came from a small town in Pennsylvania, had evidently doted on his grandfather; having inherited the old man's name, he had decided not to change it upon becoming an actor and moving to New York.

He was well-cast as the apple-cheeked and perpetually helpless Aubrey in *The Vampyre*. A blond, blue-eyed, prettily handsome young man, Leischneudel was only a couple of inches taller than my 5 foot 6. Although as fair-skinned as he, I'm brown-haired and brown-eyed, and we really didn't look like siblings. Nonetheless, the casting seemed to work well onstage. Perhaps because offstage, I had quickly developed an older-sister sort of relationship with him.

Although he was a good actor who'd gotten some work in the two years he'd been in the Big Apple, Leischneudel was unprepared for all the attention *The Vampyre* was getting, and he felt overwhelmed by it. He was intimidated by the volatile fans outside the theater. *Inside* the theater, he was also intimidated by our cranky wardrobe mistress, our bipolar stage manager, and our melodramatic fellow actors.

For the past few days, he had insisted on escorting me to and from work each night because of how unpredictable the crowds outside the theater had become—though, given the frightened way he clung to me, I thought it was questionable who was escorting whom. However, I had appreciated his company last night, shaken as I was after being mauled by one of Daemon's crazed fans. Leischneudel had accompanied me home, stayed with me while I iced my sore eye, and chatted with me until I had felt calm enough to bid him good night and then go straight to sleep.

From the kitchen, he now called, "Is it okay if I finish this juice? It expired yesterday."

"Go ahead," I said absently, dabbing gingerly at my tender skin.

Leischneudel returned to the bathroom a few moments later and watched me make the finishing touches to my eye as he sipped from his glass of juice.

Glancing at him, I noticed that he was unconsciously making a strange face and tilting his head at an odd angle. "Is something wrong?" I asked.

"Oh. The humming." He gestured to the fluorescent light over my bathroom mirror. "It sets my teeth on edge."

I didn't hear any humming. But I knew that Leischneudel had suffered from delicate health for much of his life, and I'd certainly realized by now that he was more sensitive than I—in multiple ways. With that thought in mind, I realized there were dark circles under his eyes today. "You look tired. Is this schedule killing you?"

Although Daemon Ravel as Lord Ruthven was the star of the play, Leischneudel's character was the protagonist of Polidori's story, and he went through the most dramatic changes during the course of the show: Aubrey falls in love, grieves heartbrokenly over his sweetheart's death, comes to realize that his trusted friend is a monster, has a nervous breakdown, succumbs to a raging fever, goes mad with grief and guilt when his sister is murdered, and dies just before the curtain comes down. It was draining to do so many performances of a role like that in just a few days.

Leischneudel waved aside my concern. "It's not the show. It's Mimi." When I stared at him blankly, he reminded me, "My cat."

"Oh! Right." I went back to applying makeup. "What about her?"

"She woke me up *really* early this morning, crying. Her face was all swollen and tender. Abscessed tooth."

"Did you take her to the vet?"

He nodded. "We were there for *hours*. Then I decided I'd better leave her there overnight. She'll need someone to keep an eye on her, and we'll be working most of the night again."

"Will she be all right?"

"Yes," he said. "But the bills for her treatment may kill *me*."

I smiled. I recalled that Leischneudel had found Mimi starving on the street soon after he'd moved to New York. This wasn't his first anecdote about the expense of caring for her, but he obviously doted on her.

"Anyhow, that's why I didn't really get any sleep." Seeing my concerned expression, he made a dismissive gesture. "I'll be okay."

Like most actors, he was interested in makeup and costume, so he asked what I was using on my bruise, and he studied the combination of colors I had applied to conceal the purple-blue discoloration.

As I peered at my reflection, he said to me, "It looks fine. Add a little mascara and a touch of blush, and no one will notice." He added with an envious sigh, "You're so lucky, with those cheekbones."

They were my best feature. And fortunately, they could be emphasized enough to distract from an eye which, despite Leischneudel's assurances, still looked a little discolored. I'd have to apply my stage makeup heavily tonight. "I'm just glad it's not swollen," I said. "That would be hard to conceal. You were right about applying ice last night."

"Does it hurt much?" he asked sympathetically.

I shrugged. "A little sore. Not too bad. Luckily, Jane punches like a girl."

My attacker had been dressed like my character, Miss Jane Aubrey. One of the eccentricities of this show was that many of the people in our audience were in costume. There was a wide variety of goth and vampire outfits each night, as well as a significant number of people in Regency costume. A few of the male fans dressed up like the fashionable Lord Ruthven—and those tight, high-waisted Regency trousers were an ill-advised choice for some of them. Hardly any of the fans came dressed as Ianthe or Aubrey, presumably because those characters were victims rather than vampires. To my surprise, though, many female fans dressed up like my character. Leischneudel and I referred to those fans as "the Janes." I had grown used to them by now, but I had found it a little unnerving at first to keep bumping into carbon copies of myself (some of them less recognizable than others) every night. The girl who'd punched me last night looked more like me than most of them did.

"I hope she's not there again tonight," Leischneudel said.

"Me, too," I agreed. "She hurtled at full speed straight across the thick dark line that separates rude from crazy. I'd much rather we didn't meet again."

Satisfied with my makeup, I left the bathroom and headed for my bedroom. Leischneudel trailed behind me. I live in the West Thirties in Manhattan. It's a convenient location, if not an elegant one. The apartment, which was in perpetual need of maintenance that seldom got done, had certainly seen better days; but it was rent-controlled, which was a huge advantage to a struggling actress. It was also spacious by Manhattan standards, in the sense that I had a second bedroom; granted, it was only the size of a walk-in closet (which was essentially what I used it for), but it was an enviable luxury for a person of my limited means. The apartment was furnished and decorated with things I'd found at thrift stores and inherited from friends fleeing New York for a saner, more affordable life elsewhere. It was home, and I was comfortable there.

Leischneudel sat on my double bed while I puttered around the bedroom, filling my tote bag with various things I'd want with me at work for another two-performance shift that wouldn't end until the wee hours of the morning.

"I can't believe Daemon took that Jane home with him after she attacked you!" Leischneudel said, still scandalized by last night's events.

Recalling the insolent way Daemon had winked at me when he loaded my overwrought look-alike into his limousine last night renewed my irritation with the celebrity vampire. "*I* can believe it," I grumbled.

Indeed, that had a lot to do with why the cops had resisted my innovative suggestion that they arrest my attacker. Daemon had volunteered to take charge of her, and everyone but me considered that a perfectly satisfactory solution to the problem. (Leischneudel missed all of this, having gone in search of the cab we had called. I was attacked when exiting the stage door about a minute behind him.) If the star of the show could soothe the crazed fan (and, indeed, Jane calmed down as soon as Daemon put his arm around her and cooed sweet nothings into her ear), then the cops wouldn't have to arrest and book yet another girl who wasn't exactly dressed right for the lock-up, and that suited them just fine.

No one present pretended not to know exactly what "soothing" the young woman would entail. Daemon had a well-earned reputation for picking up female fans for casual sex. It was one of the reasons so many of them waited outside the stage door for him each night.

At three o'clock in the morning, having just performed two shows back-to-back, I was too exhausted to do much more than glare irritably at the cops with my remaining good eye while they waved Daemon off as he bundled the clinging Jane into his waiting car, under the envious gazes of dozens of other fans—some of whom were also dressed just like my character.

This job was a little surreal.

"When Daemon does things like that, he just encourages that sort of behavior," Leischneudel said. "Now other unbalanced girls hanging around the theater will think the way to, er, meet Daemon is to attack *you*."

This hadn't occurred to me before. I paused in my packing as I realized that Leischneudel might well be right. "Great. Thanks to Daemon rewarding a fan with sex for punching me, more lust-crazed vampire groupies are bound to attack me before our run is over. That's just wonderful."

I'd like to kill the Nocturne-swilling creep for this. I

pictured opening the coffin he reputedly slept in, inside his sunless Soho loft, and driving a wooden stake right through his narcissistic little heart.

"I won't let it happen," my companion assured me.

"Huh?" Indulging in my satisfying vision of Daemon's startled expression when I staked him, I'd lost track of the conversation for a moment. "What?"

"I'll stick right by your side outside the theater from now on. No one else will hurt you, Esther. I promise."

"I appreciate that, Leischneudel." I stuffed a few more things into my bag and said grumpily, "But, good grief, why me? I'm playing the plain spinster in this show, not the ravishing young beauty. I should be fully clothed and pitied by the audience, not envied and assaulted. Why *me?*"

"Because you're playing Jane," Leischneudel said. "And she's the woman Ruthven really loves."

I gave him an incredulous look as I picked up my tote bag. "He *kills* her on their wedding night."

"Ah, but he *marries* her," Leischneudel pointed out, following me as I exited the bedroom.

"Marrying her doesn't make murdering her more romantic." I went into the kitchen, which was basically the same room as the living room, separated from it by a counter.

"But *why* does he marry her?" Leischneudel argued. "He doesn't marry Ianthe, after all."

"He marries Jane to torment her brother. And probably to get his hands on her money." I opened the refrigerator and pulled out a couple of water bottles to pack in my tote. "Want one?"

"No, thanks. I brought my own." He nodded toward the daypack he'd left sitting by my door when he arrived. Then he said, "You're so cynical about love, Esther!"

"Oh, come on. Ruthven seduces and lies to a naive woman, he destroys her weak-minded brother, and then he murders her." I shook my head. "You're calling that *love?*"

"Well, no," he admitted. "But the *fans* are calling it love. They think Ruthven has reluctant feelings for Jane."

"According to Daemon—who plays him, after all— Ruthven has hunger pangs for her. That's not the same thing." I packed a few protein-rich snacks into my tote, along with the water, then closed the bag. "Ready to go?"

Leischneudel nodded, and I picked up my keys and put on my jacket. He scooped up his daypack and preceded me out the front door, then paused and waited while I locked it behind us.

I followed him down the stairs as he said, "The fans think Ruthven proposes marriage to Jane because he wants to change."

"It's not an emotional scene," I pointed out as he held open the front door of the building for me. "Not in that sense, I mean. He's seducing her in the proposal scene. Also dominating her. Jane is as intimidated as she is aroused. She's too scared to say no."

Early November now, it was dark and chilly as we set out for the theater.

"He doesn't have to offer her marriage," Leischneudel said, walking down the windy street toward Ninth Avenue, where we would catch a cab heading downtown. "It's clear from Jane's behavior in that scene that Ruthven could have whatever he wants, then and there."

I didn't disagree, since that was indeed the way the scene was written and the way we played it.

"But he doesn't feed on her or sleep with her then," my companion continued. "Sure, it's what he did with Ianthe when he had the opportunity—"

"Then killed her." I thought the theme of Ruthven *murdering* every woman he seduced seemed to be getting glossed over in this interpretation.

"But when he could ruin Jane, even kill her . . . instead, he convinces her to commit to him. To agree to marry him."

"Completely different situation. Jane's got money and no boyfriend," I said. "Whereas Ianthe's got no money and a boyfriend—you."

Leischneudel said, "But we know Ruthven has used and discarded plenty of other women besides Ianthe. *Jane* is the one he decides to marry, though. The one and only!"

"*That's* why there are so many girls dressed like me—like Jane—at the theater every night?" I said in amazement, never having thought of it this way. "Because Ruthven *marries* her before he rips open her neck and dumps her exsanguinated corpse on the stage?"

"Yes."

"Okay, those fans aren't just lustful, they're crazy," I said, hunching inside my jacket as the wind whipped down the street. "Is that really what they want in a lover?"

"Well, maybe not the 'rips open her neck' part," Leischneudel conceded. "Though there's definitely a lot of interest in the way he bites you in the final scene."

"And he'd better watch his step. That's been getting a little too real lately." Fortunately, though, despite his vampire persona, Daemon didn't have fangs.

"But female fans identify with Jane," Leischneudel said, "because she's the one woman who finds a place in Ruthven's tormented heart."

"Which doesn't stop him from *killing* her," I reminded him as we reached Ninth Avenue.

Leischneudel stepped up to the curb and stuck out his arm to hail a cab. Until recently, I had taken the subway to the theater every evening. But walking through the throng of people outside the Hamburg had become too chaotic and stressful over the course of the past week. So now I arrived at work by cab, getting dropped off as close to the stage door as possible.

Raising his voice to be heard above the roar of the cars careening down the avenue, Leischneudel continued, "Ruthven reaches a turning point, a fork in the road when he falls for Jane."

I rolled my eyes. "He doesn't *fall* for—"

"He thinks he can change course, find a new path. But then Aubrey returns to England, sees them together, and loses his mind. Ruthven realizes he was wrong. He is what he is, and he *can't* change. He destroys everything he touches. That's his curse. That's what it means to be *The Vampyre*. So he accepts his destiny to destroy Jane, too."

"Accepts it, embraces it, and sails full steam ahead with it," I said as a cab pulled up to the curb.

"But it's not what he wants in his heart. Not deep down." Leischneudel opened the car door for me. "That's what the fans think, anyhow."

I climbed into the cab. Leischneudel gave instructions to the driver, then got in next to me and closed the door. The taxi leaped back into the flow of traffic, wheels screeching dramatically as we raced to catch the next green light on Ninth, heading down to the Village.

I said to Leischneudel, "Are you serious? The fans are reading all that into the play?"

"Some of them are." He added with a smile, "The ones who dress up like Jane, anyhow."

"That interpretation is quite a stretch. I mean, I'd like the play a lot better if it were actually that interesting."

"Me, too," he agreed.

"But honestly, I still think it's just a gothic melodrama about three not-very-bright people who get preyed on by a hungry, oversexed vampire."

"I know," said Leischneudel, who had struggled hard in rehearsal to understand why his character fell into a self-destructive decline and let his sister be victimized, rather than exposing Ruthven as a lecher and a murderer. "But wouldn't it be nice if we were in a play as good as the one the fans think they're watching?"

"Indeed." After a moment it occurred to me that Leischneudel was so terrified of the fans that (despite the touching promise he had made this evening to protect me from them) he usually hid behind me whenever we saw them. So I said, "Wait a minute. How do you know what the fans are saying?"

"Fan blogs," he said. "I took my laptop to the vet's today. And I had a *lot* of time on my hands while they treated Mimi."

"*This* is what the fans talk about online? Ruthven's hidden depths?"

Leischneudel laughed at my incredulous tone. "Among other things. They talk a lot about Daemon, too, of course. About his lifestyle, about his career, and about wanting to, um, meet him. They also talk about us—the other actors in the show—which is sometimes interesting . . . and sometimes embarrassing."

"Let me guess," I said dryly. "Your trousers?"

"Sometimes." He cleared his throat.

Leischneudel was well-proportioned, and his costume fit him like a second skin.

He continued, "Mostly, they talk a lot about being vampires, or wanting to be vampires, or what they think vampires are like. They also talk about wanting to, um, get personal with a vampire."

"No kidding?" I said dryly.

"They parse every scene in the play, particularly the ones with Daemon, analyzing every line, every movement, and every glance to a degree that's either scholarly or obsessive—I can't quite decide."

"I'm voting for obsessive," I said.

"And some of them talk about wishing they were Jane."

"Not that I'd want to spoil a good blog discussion with finicky details," I said, "but Jane gets murdered at the age of twenty-four."

"Maybe some of the fans think it would be worth dying young, to get bitten by Ruthven—or Daemon—in the final embrace." Leischneudel shrugged. "Or maybe they fantasize that he'd turn them, and they'd become his undead true love."

"Good grief." I thought over everything he had said.

"Well, if those fans are so hot for Daemon—or the 'vampire lifestyle,' or whatever—that they're idealizing a one-dimensional villain like Ruthven and interpreting him as a complex and tortured character . . . I guess that explains a lot about the show's popularity."

Leischneudel leaned forward to peer ahead, through the cab's windshield. "Speaking of which . . ."

"What's going on here?" the driver asked as we approached the street the theater was on.

I rolled down my window to look ahead and saw that the crowd was even bigger tonight than it had been on the previous two nights. As our cab pulled up to the police barricade blocking the side street, flashbulbs started going off in my face—making me glad I had taken the trouble to apply makeup to my bruised eye.

A thick crowd of people gathered around the taxi as soon as it came to a halt. Some of them were wearing ordinary street clothing, but others wore costumes so elaborate they would need special assistance to maneuver their butts into their theater seats later—if they'd been able to get tickets to one of tonight's sold-out performances. Some of the costumes were professional-looking creations that included fanciful wings, spiderwebs, hooves, or talons. Other fans were wearing all-purpose goth or bondage outfits—some of which were less than perfectly flattering to the wearers.

Our cab driver flinched and uttered a startled curse when two people whose costumes were disturbingly realistic imitations of bloodless corpses flung themselves across the windshield of the car to peer inside at all of us. I hastily rolled up my window when a toothy monster tried to reach into the car to grab me.

Another flashbulb went off in my face as someone tried to capture the moment. Since the fans surely knew the sight of Daemon's car by now, I supposed they were rushing our cab because they were just eager to catch a glimpse of anyone associated with the show.

A cape-clad creature with a rotting face thudded its fist on the hood of the car.

The cab driver sputtered, "Who are these . . . these . . ."

A growling, hissing vampire suddenly tried to open Leischneudel's locked door. My startled companion scooted closer to me.

Our agitated driver said, "*What* are these . . . these . . ."

"These," I said wearily, "are the vamparazzi."

3

"They're *what?*"

"Vamparazzi," I repeated.

It was the name that Leischneudel and I had given to the combination of paparazzi and vampire groupies that swarmed around Daemon Ravel and *The Vampyre*.

Our disoriented driver said, "I'm going to have to let you folks out here."

"No, tell that cop who's coming this way now that we're cast members," I said. "He'll let you through."

Leischneudel said anxiously, "We'd like to be dropped off as close to the stage door as possible." After another look at the bizarre crowd pressing their bodies up against the cab, he added, "If you could drive up onto the sidewalk and get right next to the door, that would be good."

A uniformed cop approached the cab, making his way through the excited throng of wannabe vampires, tabloid photographers, and young women dressed as Miss Jane Aubrey.

"This is crazy," said our driver.

"No one in this car is disputing that point," I said.

A young woman wearing white body paint, a skimpy red outfit that had to be very uncomfortable on this chilly autumn night, and big red wings smiled at me through the window, revealing a row of sharp fangs. Ahead of us, a good-looking man dressed exactly like Daemon's character in *He of the Night* was escorting a woman across the crowded street, heading in the direction of the theater. His companion was wearing a long, hooded cloak. Although she tripped on her hem, she nonetheless seemed more sensibly garbed than the two women who crossed the street next, both wearing black corsets, fishnet stockings, and not much else.

The cab driver spoke to the cop, who recognized me and Leischneudel and agreed to let the car through the barricade. As we rolled slowly down the street, traveling toward the stage door, we passed far more people than could fit into the theater tonight—even over the course of two performances.

"The Janes look chilly tonight," Leischneudel observed, nodding toward a group of bare-armed young women whose white Regency gowns were as low-cut as the one I wore onstage.

"Well, yes. It's *November*," I said. "I think this is an example of natural selection in action."

"Do you see her?" he asked. "The one who attacked you?"

I studied the women in the bright glow of the lights along this crowded street. "I don't know."

It was hard to tell, since they all looked roughly the same—like me in my costume.

After a moment, I added, "Ah, but I do see some familiar faces."

The vamparazzi didn't consist solely of Daemon's ardent fans. A few of them were his vehement detractors. My favorites among these were earnest protesters from the Society for the Scientific Study of Vampires (SSSV). The same three people from SSSV showed up outside the theater about once a week, and I suspected the bespectacled trio was the society's entire membership.

Spotting their picket signs in the crowd, Leischneudel said without enthusiasm, "They're back? I kind of hoped they had gone away for good."

"Oh, I would be so disappointed if they did that," I said.

The SSSV protesters challenged Daemon's claim of being a real vampire and demanded that he submit to scientific testing. Personally, I liked the idea of Daemon spending a couple of days being poked and prodded by skeptics. However, he brushed off their demands with a combination of smug dismissal and vapid vagueness that evidently satisfied his fans—who verbally abused the SSSV protesters whenever they showed up at the theater (which was perhaps why the trio didn't come more often).

I had originally supposed that, as critics of Daemon's behavior, the SSSVers would be natural allies with another group of detractors whom our taxi crept slowly past tonight.

"Hey, look, Vampire Recovery is here, too," I said to Leischneudel, pointing them out. "It's a full house tonight. All the misfits are on board."

Vampire Recovery (greater New York metropolitan area membership: seven) wanted to help Daemon transition to "inactive/dormant status" and thus embrace a lifestyle free of active vampirism (though not, I noted from their outfits, free of the ubiquitous black clothing).

Despite condemning Daemon's vampire lifestyle, VR had actually turned out to be the SSSV's most bitter enemy, since the former insisted that the actor's vampirism was a serious affliction while the latter declared it was baseless nonsense. This ideological chasm had led to a short-lived rumble between the two tiny groups on our opening night. It ended when one of the recovering vamps got a nosebleed and fled down the street, pursued by mad scientists eager to test his blood for proof of vampirism. Since then, both groups had been intimidated into somewhat subdued behavior—not by the exasperated cops, but by vamparazzi who insisted, with leather-clad aggression, that Daemon had every right to remain an active vampire and also to refuse to be scientifically tested like some lab rat.

Seeing several Vampire Recovery reps hovering near the theater, presumably planning to heckle Daemon when he arrived, Leischneudel said wanly, "I wish we could just beam into the theater via a transporter device, like they do on *Star Trek*."

He was always fine once he was in costume, in character, and waiting in the wings for his first cue; onstage, he was a consummate, focused professional. But he found all *this* stuff a nerve-racking ordeal. I found it a distraction and a nuisance, but as long as I wasn't, oh, being *physically assaulted,* the bizarre nightly commotion didn't unravel my nerves the way it did Leischneudel's.

Then again, I'd been living in New York longer than he had. In this city, a person got used to almost anything after a while.

When the cab came to a halt outside the stage door, Leischneudel said to the driver, "Can you get closer to the door? I mean, *really* close?"

But the cabby, whose nerves were also frayed by now, emphatically refused to drive onto the densely populated sidewalk. Especially not in plain view of the cops assigned to crowd control tonight.

Then I saw Daemon's car pulling up behind us, and I squeezed Leischneudel's hand. "Hang in there. We'll slip inside when they all make a bee line for the vampire."

"*Which* vampire?" the driver muttered.

"The real one."

"*What?*"

"Don't worry," I said as I paid the fare. "He never eats eat right before a show."

We waited until we saw Daemon's car door swing open, and then we made a dash for it. Leischneudel clung to me like a bad prom date as I shoved my way through the milling crowd.

"Daemon! Daemon! Over here!" a tabloid photographer shouted *right* into my ear.

His flash went off six inches from my face, momentarily blinding me. I stumbled a little, trying not to fall down as Leischneudel's feet tangled with mine. Seeing nothing but swimming spots, I reached for whatever support I could find, and I wound up clutching a tall, skinny man.

"Are you okay?" he asked.

While trying to regain my vision and my balance, I squinted up at my rescuer as Leischneudel panted anxiously in my ear. I saw spectacles, a beard, and brown hair, and then I saw the picket sign overhead: UNDEAD—OR JUST UNTRUE?

"Science guy?" I blurted.

"Dr. Hal, with the Society for the Scientific Study of Vampires," said my rescuer.

"Hi. Um, sorry." Still blinking and seeing spots, I tried to extract myself from his embrace. "Esther Diamond. With *The Vampyre*."

"I know."

He helped me regain an upright posture—no easy task with half of Leischneudel's weight leaning against me now—and kept a firm grip on my shoulders.

"Close your eyes completely for a few seconds," Dr. Hal instructed. "That'll help."

Leischneudel's grip around my waist tightened while I did as the doctor suggested. "Esther?" he said nervously.

"Just a minute." When I opened my eyes again, my vision was indeed better.

A busty Jane immediately thrust a hanky under my nose. "Can you give this to Daemon for me?"

"Huh?" I said.

"Not *you*." Her hot glare of hatred made me remember Leischneudel's warning that obsessed female fans might now believe that punching me was the way to get laid by Daemon. But caught between Dr. Hal and Leischneudel, I couldn't move.

To my relief, Dr. Hal pushed the buxom Jane away. Then he said to me, "Miss Diamond, we need your help."

"Huh?" I said again.

Miss Busty Jane shoved Dr. Hal aside and pressed her unwelcome bosom against me as she simpered at Leischneudel, who was clinging to me so tightly that I thought we might need medical assistance to be pried apart once we got inside.

"Personal bubble," I said to Busty Jane as she smooshed her breasts into me while leaning closer to Leischneudel. *"Personal bubble."*

Ignoring me, she said sweetly to my companion, *"Please,* will you give this to Daemon for me? A token from a lady?"

I saw writing on the handkerchief and realized she'd scrawled her phone number on it. I could also tell that Leischneudel was starting to hyperventilate.

"We can end this madness, with your help!" cried Dr. Hal, trying to shove Busty Jane again.

She was made of tough stuff. She pushed back—so hard that Dr. Hal's picket sign fell on his head as he stumbled sideways.

"Ow!"

Leischneudel's terrified grip tightened reflexively, to the point that I suddenly had trouble breathing.

This turned out to be a blessing, since Busty Jane's hanky was directly under my nose when she said to Leischneudel, "Tell Daemon it's saturated with my feminine essence. I've rubbed it directly on my—"

"Oh, good God!" This time *I* shoved Jane. With a little more force than Hal had used. She fell backward into a photographer, who cursed loudly when his camera fell out of his hands and skittered across the pavement. He turned on Busty Jane, shouting in venomous anger. She started trying to climb over him, shrieking at Daemon, who had emerged from his car, and urging the actor to accept her handkerchief.

"Come on," I said to Leischneudel. "Let's get inside!"

I felt him nod against my hair and shuffle his feet in the direction of the stage door.

"Miss Diamond, wait!" cried Dr. Hal, physically seizing me by the shoulders again.

Leischneudel tried to pry the scientist's hands off me, but seemed too overwhelmed to speak or protest.

"You can help us!" Hal said.

"I don't want to help you," I said. "I want to go inside and do my show."

Leischneudel grunted in support of this plan.

Hal said urgently, "He claims he keeps blood in his dressing room."

"Daemon? Yes, I know. *Everyone* knows. He makes a point of mentioning it in every interview. If you'll just let me go now . . ." I joined Leischneudel in trying to loosen the doctor's viselike grip on me.

"You need to get me a sample!"

That made me pause. "Pardon?"

"We need to know if it's human blood!"

"Oh, come on, it's Nocturne wine cooler," I said dismissively. It was the exact same color as blood, and I knew that Daemon got cases of the beverage for free.

"You're undoubtedly right," Hal said. "Let's prove it!"

I shook my head. "Forget it, Hal."

"*Doctor* Hal, if you don't mind."

"I wish you luck, but there's no way I'm getting involved in this."

A roar of excitement arose from the crowd around us, and I assumed that if I looked over my shoulder, I'd see Daemon striking a pose or kissing a fan.

My bearded captor said, "Don't you even care about the travesty that this charlatan is perpetrating?"

"Don't *you* realize that proving he's got Nocturne instead of blood in his minifridge won't make the slightest bit of difference to his fans? They *choose* to believe his ridiculous claims. *Facts* don't enter into it."

"His behavior is a reflection on you!" Hal said.

"Stop right there," I said irritably. "I work with him. That's *all*."

"You help him get away with this! By allowing him to fake exsanguination of your body every night, you assist him in his—"

"Oh, get a grip! It's a *play*, Hal." I pulled myself out of his grasp with such force that Leischneudel lost his hold on me and staggered back a few steps.

"All right, if you won't bring me the so-called blood," Dr. Hal persisted, "can you at least get me a sample of his semen?"

"*What?* How do you think I'm going to get a sample of his— No, never mind. Let's not go there." I shook off the mad scientist when he tried to grab me again, then said, "Come, Leischneudel!"

I turned and stomped toward the stage door, pushing people out of my way. I felt Leischneudel's hand clutch my jacket, and I dragged him through the crowd to the door—where I said something unkind to the cop on duty about his inability to keep this area clear for us. Then we went inside.

Once the door was safely shut behind us, I turned to examine my companion. He was as white as a ghost, his pupils were dilated, and his nostrils were flaring with emotion. I decided we *did* need to find out if there was Nocturne in those bottles in Daemon's refrigerator. Although I never drank alcohol before a performance, and Leischneudel didn't drink at all, I thought we both needed a bracer after that too-eventful arrival.

"Come on." I took his elbow and guided him down the hall to Daemon's dressing room.

When we got to the door and he realized I intended to enter, he balked. "We can't go in there!"

I turned the knob. "Sure we can. They've unlocked it." It would get locked again in the wee hours, after we all left.

As the star of the show, Daemon had the nicest dressing room among *The Vampyre*'s four cast members. The one I shared with the actress who played Ianthe was drafty and had no comfortable chairs. Leischneudel had his own dressing room by default, since Daemon's contract had required a private one. In any case, all the dressing rooms were pretty much bare bones, which was typical of New York theaters. Most of the little luxuries in Daemon's room, such as his minifridge, were his personal possessions, temporarily installed here to ensure his comfort.

Timidly following me as I entered the star's lair, Leischneudel said, "Aren't we intruding?"

"I'll tell Daemon it was an emergency. I know you don't normally indulge, but I think we could both use a quick drink, don't you?"

"Oh, I don't know, Esther . . ."

"Well, *I* could, anyhow." I opened Daemon's fridge and peered inside, where there were, as I had glimpsed a few times before now, about half a dozen vials full of ruby red liquid. The decorative little bottles looked as if they had been designed to hold cologne.

I pulled one out of the fridge and said, in a decent imitation of Daemon, "I don't drink . . . wine cooler."

Leischneudel smiled, starting to relax a little.

"But any port in a storm," I added in my own voice.

He came closer. "You really think it's Nocturne?"

I gave a derisive snort. "Of course." I opened the small bottle, sniffed its contents, then took a cautious sip, expecting to taste mediocre red wine diluted by fruit juice and soda.

Leischneudel drew in a sharp breath. "Esther."

Instead, I tasted salt, iron, and something altogether *much* too biological. I gagged, spat, dropped the little bottle, and covered my mouth with my hand as blood splattered on the nice area carpet at my feet—which was Daemon's personal property.

"Oh, my God!" I blurted.

A sultry voice in the doorway said, "So *you're* the one who's been pilfering my supply."

Leischneudel and I whirled to face Daemon as he entered his dressing room, an expression of amused surprise on his face as he looked at me.

"Ugh! *Blegh!*" I made unattractive gestures with my tongue as I tried to chase away the disgusting taste and texture I had just sampled. "You *do* keep blood in these bottles!"

Daemon blinked. "What were you expecting?"

"I was hoping for Nocturne."

He looked skeptical. "Seriously?"

"Well, 'hoping,' would be an exaggeration," I admitted. "We got roughed up on the pavement out there. *Again.* I wanted a drink."

Daemon grinned wickedly. "Be my guest."

"A drink of *alcohol.*"

"An insipid substitute."

Leischneudel stood motionless, his nostrils quivering as he stared wide-eyed at the puddle of blood soaking into the carpet at my feet.

I looked down at it, too. "That was revolting. But I'm sorry about the mess, Daemon."

He shrugged gracefully. "These things happen. Especially with virgins."

I'd been around him long enough to know that "virgins" meant people inexperienced in "vampire sex," which I gathered involved blood ingestion—a sexual practice that struck me as roughly on a par with jumping off a cliff if it did not include exchanging recent blood-test results with one's partner. I had always assumed

Daemon was lying about it. Now, as I fumbled in my tote bag for a bottle of water to wash the sickening taste of blood out of my mouth, I wondered if there was some truth to those claims after all.

Yes, I understood that *saying* he kept blood in his dressing room was part of his schtick. But why was there was *actual* blood in here?

Then a more important question occurred to me.

"Is that blood safe?" I asked anxiously. "I mean, has it been tested?"

"Shhh." Daemon put a gentle finger over my lips. "You're perfectly all right."

I brushed his hand aside. "*Please* tell me it's not human."

He looked down at his finger, and I noticed that it was smeared with blood. "It looks like you didn't even swallow," he said wryly. Holding my gaze with sensual intensity, he licked the blood off his fingertip. "Mmmm."

I took comfort in the conviction that he probably wouldn't do that unless he knew for certain the blood was indeed safe.

I wiped my mouth with my hand and realized there was blood on my chin from when I had reflexively spat. "Blegh."

Leischneudel bent over to pick up the bottle I had dropped, which he set gingerly on the makeup counter. Then he looked at my face. "Oh! Here, Esther. Let me." He picked up a towel, held it briefly under the tap in the corner sink to dampen it, then wiped my mouth, chin, and hand.

I said, "I'm really sorry about your carpet, Daemon. I'll clean it up." I opened my water bottle and drank a big sip.

While I was swishing water around in my mouth and trying not to think about the texture of the hemoglobin I had just tasted, Daemon said, "No need. Victor will be along any moment. He'll see to it."

Daemon had a personal assistant who did everything

for him but wipe his bottom. And for all I knew, maybe Victor did that, too.

I felt myself gagging again and decided to avoid nauseating mental images until after I had recovered from tasting blood.

"No, I'm the one who spilled it," I said. "I'll clean it up."

"Nonsense," Daemon said dismissively. "Leave it to Victor. He'll know what to do."

"Well . . . I'm sorry about it. And also about coming in here without asking."

Leischneudel added, "We were a little stressed out."

Daemon sat down in front of his makeup mirror and studied his reflection with satisfaction. "The fans *are* excited tonight, aren't they?"

Although he embraced and perpetuated various familiar tropes of vampirism, Daemon refuted the popular notion that vampires didn't have reflections. He described it as a fictional embellishment that conflicted with the laws of physics. This explanation satisfied his fans while eliminating practical challenges that he couldn't realistically overcome. Apart from the obvious impossibility of managing to avoid reflective surfaces at all times wherever he went, he also needed to be able to look into the mirror, like any other actor, to prepare for performances.

His black hair already looked sexily windswept, but he evidently decided it needed some preparation for tonight. Daemon reached for a brush and some hairspray and started working on it.

Seeing an opportunity to voice his concerns, Leischneudel stiffened his spine and raised the subject of my safety, in view of what had happened last night.

While Leischneudel talked and Daemon ignored him, I grabbed some tissues from Daemon's makeup table and tried scrubbing my tongue. Then I drank more water.

"Oh, lighten up," Daemon said after a while. "It was

just some harmless fun. And Esther looks fine." He sent me a darkly flirtatious glance. "Ravishing as always."

Leischneudel explained that I had a black eye which was well concealed by makeup, and he persisted in warning Daemon that his ill-advised actions of last night might have dire consequences for me.

Daemon tilted his head this way and that, his attention fixed on his reflection as he styled his hair. His gaze only wavered for a moment—when I gargled some water. Both men turned to look at me.

"Sorry," I said.

"You should embrace new sensations, Esther," Daemon advised. "Not try to obliterate them from your being."

"Whatever." I gargled some more, hoping it would irritate him.

Daemon merely shrugged and shook his head, still looking amused about catching me red-handed with his blood supply.

I imagined the disappointment on Dr. Hal's face, if we met again, when I had to tell him it really *was* blood.

Then I remembered the semen request and felt a tad queasy again. However, if a woman didn't actually know Daemon, I realized as I watched him set aside his hairbrush and open his makeup box, the thought of getting that personal with him would probably seem more appealing than nauseating.

For all that he was vain, self-absorbed, and full of absurd pretensions, there was no denying that nature had blessed Daemon with physical allure. He was about 6 foot 2, with a lean, graceful build, square shoulders, slim hips, and firmly muscled legs. His black hair was thick and wavy, and his dark eyes and brows were intensely dramatic in his pale, handsomely hawklike face. His age was a closely guarded secret, but I thought he was probably in his midthirties.

He had an attractive speaking voice and good stage

articulation, but he had dodged my questions about whether he'd had formal training. I thought he probably had, though; after playing the lead role in a demanding schedule for the past six weeks in a good-sized theater, Daemon's voice was still as clear as a bell, not worn or hoarse. That level of vocal stamina suggested he was a trained stage actor, like the rest of us. But he was habitually vague about his past, and he never admitted to anything as mundane as taking acting classes or attending drama school.

He was also never very clear about how he had supposedly become a vampire. There were occasional allusions to being debauched by a seductive older woman when he was a lad, but "being turned" was an "intensely private experience" that Daemon preferred not to talk about. I wondered if the tabloid reporter to whom Daemon had lately agreed to grant an exclusive and very expensive in-depth interview would get a more detailed version of the tale out of him.

As if my thoughts had summoned him, Al Tarr, the writer who was Daemon's constant shadow these days, appeared in the doorway. His cynical blue gaze swept the room, taking in everything, and then he nodded in the general direction of the stage door as he said to us, "Did you hear that the cops have arrested a real vampire out there tonight?"

4

I frowned. "What?"

Leischneudel, who was still jumpy from the full court press we'd gotten outside the theater, gaped at Tarr. "They've arrested a real vampire?"

"Actually, about a dozen of 'em." Tarr chuckled and gave Leischneudel a friendly little punch in the stomach.

I repressed an irritated sigh. Of course the cops were arresting unruly vamparazzi. They'd been doing it for the past two nights.

Annoyed that I'd fallen for another of Tarr's juvenile gags, I said, "What a droll wit you have."

"Hee hee!"

When he tried to pat my cheek, I tried to bite him.

"Whoa, I think we've got a vampire right *here*," Tarr said cheerfully.

"Now, now, children," Daemon admonished.

"I like a woman with spunk," said Tarr.

"I only appear spunky," I said. "Really I'm timid and vaporous."

He shrugged. "We could still go out."

"No, we couldn't."

A staff writer for *The Exposé*, Tarr had been tagging after Daemon this past week, following him everywhere but the bathroom; and I gathered this would probably go on for a few more days. He was, he said, determined to get the real truth about the man behind the mask, the victim behind the vampire, the cuddly creature of the night behind the celebrity facade.

Tarr was in his early forties, stocky, and short. He had a receding hairline, a ruddy complexion, and big teeth. I found his perpetual grin annoying and somehow sleazy. His unabashed nosiness, combined with his terrier-like persistence, made it clear how he'd become a top tabloid reporter. As he told anyone who failed to flee his presence quickly enough, he had a long résumé of in-depth feature stories about major Hollywood stars and was on a first-name basis with half the celebrity parolees in Tinseltown. I gathered this was his way of saying that Daemon should be flattered Tarr was covering him.

"To return to the subject . . ." Leischneudel said to Daemon. "It might be a good idea for you to issue a statement condemning violence against your fellow actors—and, in particular, against the ladies in the cast."

Tarr said, "This is about last night, right?"

"Once again, those razor-sharp journalistic instincts zero in on the obvious," Daemon said, starting to apply base to his face, as he continued creating the dissipated-yet-sexy appearance of Lord Ruthven.

"Were you hurt?" Tarr said to me.

"It's nice of you to ask, Al," I said. "Some sixteen hours *after* you got into the limo with my attacker and Daemon without asking me that."

Tarr held up his hands as if to proclaim his innocence. "Hey, they were leaving, and I gotta stick with my boy. You know that."

"*Must* you call me your 'boy'?" Daemon said.

I shrewdly sensed that Tarr's 24/7 companionship was wearing on the vampire's nerves. Good. Daemon should have to work hard for his money, like everyone else. *The Exposé* was reputedly paying him thousands for this exhaustive profile. And in addition to the money, he'd get what he valued most—even more attention.

"Jeez, everyone's so touchy tonight." Tarr shook his head as he ambled all the way into the room, heading toward a chair. He paused at the spilled blood. "Hey, what's this? Did I miss a little bloodletting?"

I realized in that instant why the little bottles in the refrigerator contained blood. *The Exposé*'s crafty reporter was sticking his nose into every aspect of Daemon's existence. The actor had undoubtedly supposed that Tarr would investigate those bottles. I recalled Daemon saying something, when he caught me with a bottle a few minutes ago, about his supply being pilfered. Tarr must have stolen one of the bottles so he could get its contents analyzed.

I gagged again when I realized that if Daemon had been thorough enough to anticipate that possibility, then the blood in the bottles might well be human.

"You're *sure* that blood was safe?" I asked faintly.

Daemon glanced at me in the mirror. "You'll be fine. Stop worrying."

"You had some of that stuff?" Tarr asked in surprise.

"Quite by accident," I said. "That'll teach me to poke around in a vampire's fridge."

Daemon's gaze returned to his own reflection as he purred, "But if you'd like to poke around in something else of mine, I have a few suggestions . . ."

"Oh, give it a rest, would you?" I was tired of him already tonight—and he hadn't even fondled me yet.

I turned to leave the room and walked straight into Daemon's assistant, Victor, who was rushing through the doorway. Victor rushed everywhere and seemed to exist in a perpetual state of semipanic. I found him courteous but fatiguing. An effeminate, plump, completely bald man in his late thirties, Victor had a tendency to over-react to everything—which always made me wonder how he'd wound up working for Daemon, of all people.

When I explained about the bloody carpet and apologized, Victor had a moment of near hysterics over the stain. Then he manfully pulled himself together, patted my shoulder, and told me not to worry about it.

"We can probably save the carpet. And even if we can't, I don't want you to feel bad about it," Victor said warmly to me. "It's only a *thing*. And people matter more than things, don't they? So I just thank God you weren't hurt when this happened, Esther."

"Thanks."

"How would she have been hurt?" Tarr asked in puzzlement.

"I don't want you to beat yourself up over this," Victor continued. "I want you to try to put it out of your mind. You've got two performances to do tonight, and the show must go on."

I hadn't actually planned to think about the carpet ever again, so I was able to assure Victor with all sincerity that I would refrain from engaging in distracting self-condemnation over this incident.

"Good for you!" He patted me again, then pulled out his cell phone. "Now I'm just going to call the dry cleaner and see if he can deal with this tonight."

"You know a dry cleaner who works on Saturday nights?" I asked.

The assistant stage manager knocked on Daemon's door. "Forty-five minutes to curtain, people." When he saw me, he paused. "How's the eye, Esther?"

"I'm fine," I said.

"See? She's fine," Tarr said to Leischneudel.

"That's not the point," the actor replied.

Daemon ignored us all.

"Come on," I said to Leischneudel. "Let's go get ready for the first show."

We left the dressing room and walked down the hall. Victor's voice, talking urgently on his cell with the dry cleaner, echoed behind us.

Then I heard Tarr call out, "Hey, Esther!"

I looked over my shoulder and saw him exit Daemon's dressing room and come after us. "You and me, we have to talk!"

"No, we don't," I said firmly.

"You're the only cast member I haven't interviewed yet."

I was aware of that. And given my druthers, I'd like to keep it that way. "I don't have anything to say."

"Oh, come on, I gotta have *you* in the article! You're *Jane,* the girl Ruthven really loves."

I blinked and looked at Leischneudel.

"I told you," the actor said. "It's what everyone's talking about."

"And those scenes between the two of you are hot, hot, *hot!*" Tarr let out a low whistle and waved his hand as if he'd just burned it. "Everyone wants to know what it's like to get initiated by Daemon Ravel."

"Initiated?"

"Into vampire sex."

"*What?*" I blurted. "Are you kidding? I've *never—*"

"I'm talking about the wedding night, sweetie." Tarr added, "You know—in the *play?*"

"Don't call me 'sweetie,' " I snapped. "And *here's* what I can tell you about being 'initiated.' I have absolutely no idea what it's like to be touched, embraced, or bitten by Daemon Ravel. I *only* know how Lord Ruthven does those things." I grabbed Tarr's polyester-blend collar and said between gritted teeth, "Are we clear now?"

"That's a cute take, toots," Tarr said. "But my readers are going to want a lot more than that."

"Then they will have to live with the dull ache of disappointment." I turned away and headed toward my dressing room.

"So we'll talk later, right?" Tarr called after me. "Maybe over a drink somewhere?"

"You have to admire his persistence," Leischneudel said to me.

"No, I don't."

He halted outside his dressing room and opened the door. "If you need help with your dress, you know where I'll be."

I nodded and kept walking. The wardrobe mistress, who didn't like anyone but Daemon, rarely helped me. And Mad Rachel, the actress who shared my dressing room, couldn't always be counted on.

As I approached our dressing room, I heard Mad Rachel's voice booming forth from the other side of the closed door, and I realized that this was probably one of those nights when I would need Leischneudel to lace up my gown.

"Fuck you, you fucking cocksucker!"

I opened the door and entered the room. As expected, Rachel was on her cell phone.

"No, fuck *you*, you cocksucking fucker!" she shrieked.

She was already in costume, having evidently gotten Fiona, the cranky wardrobe mistress, to help her. Rachel Manning was about twenty-five, petite, and extremely pretty. She looked like someone who should be on TV, though the tremendous carrying power of her voice made her a natural for the stage.

"Go fuck yourself, Eric!" she hurled into her cell phone.

I was used to this sort of thing after so many weeks of it; but I had found it disorienting at first to see this fine-boned woman in her demure Regency gown screeching vicious obscenities into a cell phone.

Rachel lived with her phone glued to her ear. Her boyfriend, Eric, was usually the person at the other end of the call, though sometimes she gave him a break and talked to her agent or her mother. And she seemed physically incapable of lowering her voice. Whether obscenely angry, as she was now, or just conversing, Rachel always yammered into the phone with the same well-supported volume that she used onstage; she did this no matter how many times the stage manager or Daemon read her the riot act about it—which they did often, since her backstage bellowing had disrupted the performance a few times.

When she saw me enter the room, she turned away without acknowledging me and shouted into her phone, "I *hate* you, Eric, you fucking cocksucker!"

Half the time, she chatted to Eric about minutiae; the rest of the time, the two of them fought hysterically while Rachel cursed, at top volume, like a drunken stevedore handicapped by a sadly limited supply of obscenities.

"Go to hell, you fucker!"

It was already clear what kind of night tonight would be. Suppressing a sigh, I walked over to the makeup counter and set down my tote bag.

Rachel looked startled by this. She held the phone away from her ear for a moment and bellowed at me, "Do you *mind?*"

"Huh?"

"This is a private conversation." Her tone and facial expression suggested that I had the IQ of chewing gum. *"Private."*

I felt an overwhelming urge to throttle her. But if I did that, we'd have to cancel the show. And then the vamparazzi would riot.

So, in the interests of public safety, I mastered my perfectly understandable impulse to kill Mad Rachel, and said, "Then you should take it somewhere else. I have to get ready for the show, and this is my dressing room, too."

Looking outraged, she complained to Eric, "This place sucks so bad. I can't believe what I have to put up with!"

"Ditto," I said sourly.

Since the men had private dressing rooms, Rachel and I, who had disliked each other from the start, had requested the same consideration. Bill, the bipolar stage manager, had refused our request. Multiple times. The reasons he gave us varied, depending on whether he was in a manic or a depressive phase of his cycle; but the bottom line was that Daemon was a star, and neither of us was. I had never had a dressing room to myself and wouldn't normally have made such a request; but Mad Rachel pushed the limits of what I could put up with night after night.

"This fucking place!" she bellowed as she stormed out of our dressing room. "The *theater,* Eric. *That's* what place!"

Rachel slammed the door so hard the room shook. I could hear her yakking into her phone for another fifteen seconds, until she was finally far enough away that the sound of her voice no longer penetrated the thick walls and closed door of this dressing room. When merciful silence at last descended, I took a few deep, steadying breaths, trying to calm myself and start focusing.

I took off my street clothes and my bra, and I donned the foundation garments for my costume: white stockings, pretty garters, and a translucent, strapless, push-up corset that, being wholly modern, fastened in front. Then I styled my shoulder-length brown hair into a simple Regency-era topknot, with loose tendrils framing my face. Ruthven took down Jane's hair on their wedding night, so I never used hairspray for this show; I didn't want lacquered strands sticking out like porcupine quills in that scene.

I cleaned off the street makeup I had worn to get past the tabloid photographers tonight, then started applying my stage makeup—more heavily than usual, since I needed to make sure the bruise around my eye wouldn't show up under powerful stage lights. Because I was dressing a little later than usual tonight, I started doing

my breathing exercises and vocal warm-up while applying my makeup, so that I could deliver my dialogue
without stumbling over words, straining my voice, or
failing to be heard by half the audience. When my face
was done, I gave it a generous dusting of powder, and
then I moved to the center of the room and started doing my stretches and physical warm-up exercises. The
corset wasn't ideal garb for that, but since I wore it the
whole time I was onstage, I preferred to wear it while
preparing, too.

Then I pulled on Jane's gown, careful not to let it
muss my hair or smear my face, and settled it into place
over my body. It was a plain white gown, high-waisted,
with a blue sash. Jane wore it for the whole play, not
even changing for her wedding day; since her brother
was deathly ill at the time of her nuptials, Jane got married quietly in a private service, without fanfare or festivities. I finished dressing by adding Jane's jewelry to
my ensemble: a broach and a pair of earrings.

Preferring to avoid Mad Rachel when she returned to
give her face and hair a final touch-up, I left my dressing
room and went down the hall to Leischneudel's room,
which I entered after a brief knock on the door. He was
still working on his makeup, so I did some more warm-up
exercises while waiting for him to finish that and then
lace up my gown.

Glancing at me in the mirror, he said, "Good job with
the eye. I don't think the bruise will show up at all."

I paused to say, "Good," then returned to breathing
and vocalizing while I repeatedly bent over, stretched,
and rolled up slowly, warming up my spine—and ignoring the way the wires of my push-up corset poked and
squeezed me.

After a few minutes, Leischneudel asked, "Any word
yet on when Thack is coming to see the show?"

I decided I was prepared enough, and I slumped into
a chair. "No."

He winced at my dispirited tone. "Sorry I asked."

Leischneudel's agent was quitting the business, and I had promised to introduce him to mine, Thackeray Shackleton (not his real name, I suspected—but then, doesn't everyone come to the Big Apple to reinvent himself?).

"Six weeks we've been running," I said, "and Thack still hasn't come, and still prevaricates when I ask what night to hold a seat for him. In fact, this week, he hasn't even returned my calls." I sighed and leaned back, staring at the ceiling.

Knowing what I was thinking, Leischneudel said, "He's *not* planning to dump you."

"Of course he is," I said morosely. "What else would explain this? Thack is conscientious. He always watches his clients working. It's part of his job, and he takes it seriously."

"Maybe he's really busy and just hasn't had time—"

"Six weeks, Leischneudel! Something's *wrong*. We're closing in two weeks, I don't have another job lined up, I haven't had an audition for anything . . . He's barely even spoken to me since I got this part!"

"You *got* this part," he pointed out, "and your reviews are excellent."

"When they bother to mention me," I grumbled.

This show was a vehicle for Daemon; the reviews mostly focused on him. After that, Leischneudel got the most attention, since the male roles were better developed than the female roles in *The Vampyre*—following the pattern of Polidori's story.

Leischneudel persisted in his doomed effort to cheer me up. "And you were great in that episode of *The Dirty Thirty* that aired a few weeks ago. Didn't you tell me Thack said so, too?"

"He didn't say 'great.' He said I 'did very well.' Talk about being damned with faint praise."

"Esther."

"Besides, the size of my role in *D-Thirty* got reduced after Nolan's heart attack, so it wasn't as good a part as we'd originally thought it would be."

The paycheck had been as much money as originally expected, though, thank God. In addition to the usual bills, I'd had to replace my bed and paint my bedroom after my mattress had spontaneously burst into flames one night in August. While I was *on* the bed. With Lopez.

There's nothing like unexpected conflagration to ruin a moment of passion.

At the time, I thought the spontaneous combustion of my bed was an attack on me by an evil sorcerer in Harlem. Since then, though, I'd begun to suspect . . .

Don't think about Lopez, I reminded myself. *Don't.*

I welcomed Leischneudel's intrusion on that distracting train of thought when he said, "It was still a good role, Esther."

"Yeah, but . . ." I shrugged.

The Dirty Thirty was the latest spin-off series in the *Crime and Punishment* empire of prestigious police television dramas. I'd been cast in a meaty guest role for one episode. My scenes were all with Michael Nolan, one of the lead actors on the show, and he'd had a heart attack while filming the episode. Nolan wouldn't be able to work for quite some time, and when they wrote his character out of the remaining scenes of that episode, they wound up writing me out, too. So my character had less screen time than I'd hoped.

On the other hand, this was at least better than the scenario my mother (who wasn't thrilled about the prospect of me portraying a homeless bisexual junkie prostitute on national TV) had hoped for, which was that they would pay me but never air the episode.

"Stop brooding and stand up so I can lace you up," Leischneudel said as he rose from the makeup table.

He was right. I was brooding. *Two* men not calling me—even though, I reminded myself, I *didn't want* one of them to call—was too disheartening. One way or the other, I needed to resolve my fear that Thack no longer wanted me as a client.

He was a young agent who had a respectable client list and was rising in his profession. Although he was flamboyant in an uptown yuppie way, he was originally from a middle-class family in Wisconsin, like me. He was also hardworking and polite, which I had so far found to be rare qualities in New York theatrical agents.

I would be sorry to lose him; but if that's what was on the horizon, then I wanted to get it over with rather than fretting about it any longer.

"I'm going to call him again," I said with determination. "He needs to commit to seeing the show or else he needs to tell me what's wrong. I can't keep chasing my tail about this."

"Good," my companion said with approval.

"Where's your cell? I don't want to risk going back to my dressing room now."

Leischneudel didn't bother to ask why. Although he and Mad Rachel were believable onstage together as innocent young lovers, when they were offstage, Leischneudel avoided her at all costs.

He pulled his phone out of his daypack, handed it to me, and started doing up the back of my gown while I dialed Thack's cell phone number.

It occurred to me that when Thack saw an unfamiliar number on his phone's LCD screen, rather than mine, he might actually answer, instead of letting the call go to voice mail . . . And I was right.

"Hello?" he said after the third ring.

"Thack, this is Esther Diamond. When are you coming to see *The Vampyre?*" I said in a rush.

"Esther?" He sounded surprised. And not thrilled. "Uh . . ."

"We only have two weeks left. When shall I reserve your seat?"

"I thought every performance was sold out," he pre-varicated. "The show's a hot ticket. I heard some of the scalpers are getting three hundred dollars per seat."

"For *this* show?" I blurted. "The vamparazzi really *are* crazy."

"The who?"

"Never mind. When are you coming?"

"Oh, I don't see how you could even get me in, if—"

"I can get you in," I said firmly. "Daemon's contract allows him access to a couple of VIP seats for any performance. I'll make him give one to me." I figured Daemon owed me for my black eye. "How about tomorrow?"

"Well, er, I don't have my calendar with me, so I'm not sure . . ."

"Look, if you don't want me as a client anymore, just say so!"

In the silence that followed, I realized this was a tad more confrontational than I had intended.

Then he said, "What?"

In for a penny, in for a pound. "Is that why you're not coming to the show? Because you're getting ready to dump me?"

"Dump you?"

"If that's the case, I'd rather you just tell me right now, in a straightforward way."

"*Dump* you?" he repeated, sounding aghast.

His tone opened the door on a tiny glimmer of relief.

"Oh, my God," he said. "Is *that* what you've been thinking? That I was planning to . . ." He sighed, then said heavily, "*Actors.*"

Leischneudel gave a final tug as he finished fastening my gown, then circled me to meet my gaze as I said hesitantly into the phone, "So you're *not* planning to drop me?"

Leischneudel smiled and gave me a thumbs-up.

"No, of course not," Thack said soothingly. "Put the thought out of your head. It never entered mine."

"Then why have you been avoiding me for weeks?" I demanded.

"Because you keep asking when I'm coming to the show!"

"But you *always* attend your clients' shows!"

"Yes, but in this case, I just . . . just . . ."

"What?" I said. "You just *what?*"

"I just . . . *hate* vampires," he grumbled.

I blinked. "*That's* the problem?"

Leischneudel's eyes widened. "Thack hates vampires?"

I whispered to Leischneudel, "You *heard* that?"

"Yes!" Thack cried, unburdening himself with gusto now. "I hate vampires!"

"Oh." After a moment, I said with weary commiseration, "I know the feeling."

5

"But, Thack," I continued, "haven't you had other clients in vampire shows?"

"Not so far," he said. "I've been lucky."

"Oh."

"Look, I could cope with sitting through a stage adaptation of a gothic classic that a more merciful culture than ours would have let remain neglected," Thack said. "I really could. After all, I've sat through worse things. Many times."

"Uh-huh." I recalled now that Thack hadn't been enthusiastic about getting me an audition for this play. He'd done so only at my insistence, after I'd heard about it from another actor.

"But a neglected *vampire* gothic, with a leading man who claims to *be* a vampire, and an audience of people who dress *up* in vampire costumes?" He made a sound of physical pain. *"It's obscene!"*

Thack shouted so loudly that I jerked the phone away from my ear for a moment.

Leischneudel asked, "Is he all right?"

"Who *is* that?" said Thack.

"Leischneudel Drysdale," I said. "He plays Aubrey."

"Oh, yes," Thack said, recovering his composure. "He's been getting very good notices, hasn't he?"

"So have I," I snapped. "When they bother to mention me."

"Yes, I know you have," my agent said soothingly. "I have been following the show in the press, Esther. But I . . ." He made a muffled sound of disgust. "I *loathe* vampire plays."

"Yes, I think I've grasped that."

"*And* vampire movies. And TV shows. And vampire novels! And *wine cooler ads!*" He was really warming to his theme. "I just *HATE* them!"

"I want you to take a deep breath and calm down," I said firmly.

"Sorry," he said. "*Sorry.* It's a thing."

"I can tell."

After a moment, Thack sighed and added, "But you're right, of course. You're a client, and I should have come to see you in *this* vampire play well before now. And I apologize for being so obtuse that you thought I was planning to drop you. So . . ." He stifled a little groan. "Get me a seat for tomorrow. I'll be there."

"You're not going to have anti-vampire hysterics during the performance, are you?" I asked anxiously.

"No. Of course not." After a moment he added, "I don't think so."

"Look," I said, "maybe this isn't such a good idea, after all."

"No, I'm coming," he said. "I will not neglect a client on the basis of mere . . . good taste."

"Oookay. I'm glad. I think." Realizing it would be kind to throw him a bone at this point, I said, "By the way, Leischneudel Drysdale needs a new agent."

"Oh?"

I could practically *hear* Thack sitting up straighter. Lots of actors wanted a new agent, of course; but not many of them were employed actors getting good reviews in a high-profile show.

"Yes," I said. "His agent is quitting show business to go raise goat cheese."

"Goats," Leischneudel whispered, still standing right in front of me.

"Well, not everyone loves agenting," Thack said magnanimously.

"Or vampires," I noted.

"It's a thing," he repeated. "Don't even get me started."

"So we'll expect to see you tomorrow?"

"Yes."

"There'll be a ticket waiting for you at the box office."

After ending the call, I decided I would claim *both* of Daemon's VIP seats for tomorrow's performance. I called Maximillian Zadok, who lived and worked only a few blocks away from the Hamburg, and invited him to the show, too. He accepted my invitation with pleasure. Max had wanted to come sooner, but he'd been unable to get a ticket to the sold-out run. And, well, what with all the groping and pawing my inadequately clad character endured onstage, I'd been a little recalcitrant about securing a seat for him before now.

As I ended the call and returned Leischneudel's cell phone to him, we heard Bill, the stage manager, say over the backstage intercom system, "Places for Act One. Curtain in five minutes. Please take your places for Act One." He sounded depressed.

"That's us," said Leischneudel, donning his elegant Regency frock coat as I opened the door to exit the dressing room. He followed me out into the hallway.

He and I opened the show each night. The play's first scene portrayed the two of us exchanging letters which established that Aubrey was traveling in Europe with the mysterious Lord Ruthven, whom he'd met at a party in London, while Jane managed her brother's household back in England. Correspondence between the siblings was one of several ways that this stage adaptation restructured Polidori's story to make it thriftily accommodate a cast of only four people, as well as minimal scene changes.

As we made our way to the wings, Leischneudel asked me about the man whom I had just used his cell phone to invite to tomorrow night's performance. "Is Max a friend?"

"Yes, a close friend."

"A potential boyfriend?" he prodded.

Leischneudel had a sweetheart in Pennsylvania whom he usually saw twice a month, and he was eager to improve his income to the point where he felt he could propose marriage to her. I had met Mary Ann briefly a few weeks ago; a nice, level-headed girl, less pretty than Leischneudel and every bit as polite. Happy in love, Leischneudel wanted to see me having a happy love life, too.

However, given the way that had been going this year—I met someone I really liked, then nearly got him killed *twice*—I had decided to put romance on the shelf for a while.

"No, Max isn't boyfriend material," I said. "He's, uh, more like an eccentric uncle."

"He's older?" Leischneudel guessed.

You have no idea.

"Yes," I said. "A senior citizen, I guess you'd say—though I rarely think of him that way."

In fact, although he didn't look a day over 70, Max was closer to 350, thanks to accidentally drinking a mysterious and never-replicated alchemic potion in his twenties—back in the seventeenth century. The elixir hadn't made him immortal, but it ensured he'd been aging at an unusually slow rate ever since. Fighting Evil for the past three centuries or so had kept him fairly fit, and constant study and extensive travel had expanded his agile (if sometimes befuddled) mind. His courtly manners, however, did not seem to have changed a great deal since the powdered-wig era.

I thought again about Max seeing Daemon fondle me onstage and figured, oh, well, it was too late to *un*invite him. Besides, he was a man of the world, after all—albeit the Old World.

Leischneudel asked, "Will he be all right, rubbing shoulders with the vamparazzi?"

"Oh, he'll be fine," I said confidently. "Max has dealt with stranger things than vamparazzi."

Come to think of it, so had I.

I added, "Thack, on the other hand, sounds like he'll be a bit perturbed by the whole scene."

"I really appreciate you mentioning me to him."

"It's my pleasure, Leischneudel."

We stopped talking when we reached the darkened wings and started preparing mentally for the performance. After a few moments of silence, we gave each other a quick "break a leg" hug, then took our places onstage.

We wound up waiting there for about fifteen minutes. The frenzy outside on the street spread into the lobby as people who'd been unable to get tickets tried to force their way into the theater. We later heard there were some more arrests. However, despite that distraction and the late start, the first show went fine.

Between performances, I repaired my hair and makeup in my dressing room while waiting for our usual pizzas to be delivered, then I joined Leischneudel in his dressing room to eat. We used towels as bibs to avoid staining our costumes while we ate our late supper, trying to satisfy our hunger without getting so full we'd feel sluggish onstage afterward. Back in my dressing room, Mad Rachel was picking at her own pizza while whining loudly to her mother, who apparently didn't mind being telephoned so close to midnight.

Daemon, as usual, retreated alone to his own dressing

room. Despite the pretense that the star replenished his strength with a bottle of blood between shows, I assumed that Victor discreetly slipped some food (or at least a protein shake) into his room when everyone else was onstage. I also assumed this was why one of the few restrictions on Tarr's access to Daemon was that he wasn't allowed in the vampire's dressing room during or between shows, though Daemon claimed (reasonably) that it was because he needed to focus and recharge in solitude.

Unfortunately, rather than simply leave the theater and go live his life, this meant that Tarr often prowled around backstage, bothering the rest of us. Tonight he barged into Leischneudel's dressing room to try to get me to answer some questions, as Daemon's "costar" in the show. (Actually, Leischneudel was the costar; and Tarr had already cornered and interviewed him.)

I was about to decline again when I realized that if I just gave Tarr his damn interview, he'd finally leave me alone. So, finishing my supper, I nodded in acquiescence and gestured to the only unoccupied chair in Leischneudel's small, stark dressing room.

To my surprise, Tarr had done his homework and was familiar with my career, including my stint as a chorus nymph this past spring in the fantasy-oriented *Sorcerer!*, a short-lived musical staged at a theater only a few blocks from here. He also complimented me on my recent appearance as a prostitute on *D30* (which was what fans of *The Dirty Thirty* affectionately called the gritty crime drama).

"You were really convincing as a streetwise crack whore," he said.

"Thanks," I said, pleased—after all, it was my *job* to be convincing. "The writing on that show is so good, I really enjoyed that role."

Surprising me again, because it was a better question than I had expected of him, Tarr asked, "So what's it like to go from that role to playing Jane, a virginal, sheltered woman living two hundred years ago?"

So I talked for a little while about how I had prepared for a historical role, and the different choices I employed in body language, diction, tone, attitude, and facial expressions when playing a genteel Regency lady, as compared to playing a drug-addicted hooker living on the streets of New York's 30th Precinct.

And then Tarr decided to stop humoring me. "So fans are wondering, as you must know, how real is the sexual heat between you and Daemon onstage? And does it extend to your offstage lives?"

"There *is* no sexual heat between me and Daemon onstage," I said firmly. "It's between Jane and Ruthven. Offstage, Daemon Ravel and I are colleagues and scant acquaintances, nothing more. Which you already know, Al, since you're with him day and night!"

"Yeah, but I gotta ask the question," he said with his perpetual grin. "So how *about* onstage? What's going on between the two of you there? And don't say 'nothing,' because everyone in the audience already knows better."

"Well, Jane is completely ensnared by the handsome, worldly aristocrat who's wooing and seducing her. And since Daemon's performance is so good, that's easy for me to play, of course," I lied.

Actually, I thought Jane should have her head examined. Ruthven's courtship of her was openly predatory and nearly sadistic at times, he was almost certainly a fortune hunter, and his conversations with her consisted of nonstop sexual innuendo. If I were on a date with this guy, I'd feign an attack of appendicitis after the first half hour.

But I wasn't reckless enough to say any of this to Tarr, whose article would be read by Daemon's volatile (and occasionally violent) fans.

Tarr proceeded to ask more "probing" questions about the heavily eroticized tone of Daemon's interaction with me, which I continued deftly (and accurately) reframing as Ruthven's interaction with Jane.

"I know Daemon likes to improvise," Tarr said after a few minutes. "And I've heard the two of you, uh, discussing it backstage. How do those unscripted moments come about between the two of you, and how do you feel onstage when he fondles your—"

"Please stop right there," said Leischneudel, who'd been listening silently until now. "You'll need to change the subject, Mr. Tarr, or else leave my dressing room."

Sure, he was scared of vamparazzi; but he was quite capable of standing up to Daemon or Tarr on my behalf. I was capable of it, too, but I appreciated the support. I smiled at him to let him know.

"Whoa," said Tarr, his gaze flashing gleefully back and forth between the two of us. "Looks like I've been barking up the wrong leading man. So the two of you are an item?"

"No," we said in unison.

"I'm practically engaged!" Leischneudel added.

"Ah, so you don't want your girl to find out about you and Esther," Tarr surmised, grinning.

"Mary Ann knows about Esther," Leischneudel said. "I mean, she's met Esther. I mean, there's nothing *to* know!"

Obviously enjoying himself, Tarr said with mock sincerity, "You mean, you and Miss Diamond are just *good friends?*"

Leischneudel's jaw dropped at how sleazy Tarr made the phrase sound, then he looked to me for help.

I shook my head, indicating we should just ignore it. Then I said to Tarr, "I think we're done here, Al."

"Just one more question!"

"No."

"A real one this time," he promised.

I sighed. "Fine. Then the interview is finished, over, *done.*"

"Okay." He paused, apparently trying to build suspense, before saying, "What's it like to work with a vampire?"

I blinked. "*That's* your 'real' question?"

He shrugged. "I gotta ask it."

I thought it over, then said truthfully, "Actually, it's pretty much like working with anyone else." After all, it wasn't as if I had never before worked with someone who had a few pretensions or eccentricities.

"You gotta give me more than that," Tarr said.

"Why do I have to give you more than that? In one sitting, you've implied that I'm sleeping with each of my male costars. Throw in Mad Rachel as my lesbian lover, and you'll achieve a perfect trifecta of slander."

"You call her Mad Rachel?"

I said to Leischneudel, "Oops. I should have kept my mouth shut."

"No, no," Tarr said, waving his notebook in the air as if to assure me he wouldn't use that slip of the tongue in his article. "It suits her. And she drives Daemon *nuts*. Remember a few nights ago? He's onstage alone, rising from the dead by the light of the moon, replenished and renewed after drinking Ianthe's blood, and the audience is so absorbed in the moment you could hear a pin drop in that theater—"

"And then everyone heard Rachel yakking into her cell phone backstage," I said dryly. "Oh, yes. I remember."

Leischneudel caught my eye and giggled. We *all* remembered. Daemon had gone on a rampage that night. But despite his star status and the fact that he was dramatically impressive in his rage, Rachel had blown him off like a cheap attempt at a pick-up in a hotel bar. Her crass indifference to the show, the audience, and his anger left Daemon sputtering and discombobulated. It was the one time in our entire acquaintance when I sympathized with him.

I consoled myself with the knowledge that, with behavior like that, Rachel's career in our profession would be short-lived, despite how pretty she was and how well her voice carried to the back row. However, that knowledge wasn't much of a comfort while I was still nightly sharing a dressing room with her.

"Speaking of lesbian lovers," said Tarr, "when I was out in Hollywood—"

"*Were* we speaking of lesbian lovers?"

"Yeah. You and Mad Rachel."

I said in exasperation, "We're *not*—"

"Hah! Gotcha! Just kidding." Tarr winked at me. I found that quite grotesque for some reason. "Anyhow, when I was out in Hollywood, there was this *big* star I covered who was a secret lesbo. So one night—"

"I've got a second show to go perform," I said quickly, feeling like a cornered animal as Tarr began one of his Hollywood anecdotes. "We're finished here, Al."

"Wait, no, seriously. What's it like to work with Daemon?"

"He's a fine actor, a true professional, and a great guy to work with," I said, removing my towel-bib and standing up.

Tarr frowned and said to my companion, "That's exactly what you said when I interviewed you, Lei-guy."

Leischneudel winced at the nickname.

Tarr repeated, *"Exactly."*

Leischneudel looked guiltily at me.

Tarr saw that, and his habitual grin broadened. "Ah, so the kid got that line from you, huh?"

"Let's just call it a consistent reaction among the cast, shall we?" I checked my appearance in the mirror, expecting to hear Bill's five-minute warning over the intercom at any moment.

Tarr chuckled and closed his notebook. "Okay. How about off the record, in that case?"

"Off the record?"

He nodded. "Yeah. What's it like to work with Daemon?"

I realized Jane's lips needed a touch-up after my meal. I borrowed Leischneudel's makeup kit for that. "This is completely off the record?"

"Yep."

I found the color I wanted. "Off the record . . . He's a fine actor, a true professional, and a great guy to work with." I applied the lip rouge.

"Hey, you don't *trust* me?" Tarr feigned wounded feelings.

"Go figure." I blotted Jane's mouth. "We're finished *now,* right?"

"Yeah," he said. "So now that we're done with business, maybe we should go out sometime. Just you and me."

"No, thank you," I said. "Leischneudel, time for Act One places?"

"Yes." He recognized this cue and responded with alacrity. "Absolutely. Let's g—"

"No pressure," Tarr said to me. "Just a drink. We'll see how it goes."

I sighed. So much for the tabloid prince leaving me alone now that I had given him his interview. Determined to nip this in the bud, I said, "I want you to listen carefully to what I'm about to say to you, Al."

"Uh-huh."

"You and I will not be going out together." I enunciated clearly. "It will never happen. *Never.*"

"Hey!" He grinned wolfishly. "Do I have a rival?"

Involuntarily, I thought of Lopez.

Looking at (I was appalled to realize) my current suitor, an ill-mannered hack with the sensitivity of a bulldozer, I was suddenly swamped with longing for the attractive police detective whom I had refused to see again.

Actually, Lopez had dumped me first (or, as he put it, he had given me up); and I tried to keep that fact in mind whenever I wanted to surrender to impulse and phone him. But when circumstances (or, rather, Evil) had reunited us after he broke up with me, he evidently reconsidered his decision . . . or at least wanted to talk about reconsidering it.

"Is there another guy in picture?" Tarr prodded.

By then, though, I knew that Lopez had been right in the first place; we mustn't keep seeing each other.

I said, "Um . . ."

Now, as I gazed in bemusement at the man who was grinning sleazily at me, I was sharply reminded of my ex-almost-boyfriend, precisely because of all the ways in which he was nothing like Tarr.

"I mean, if you're not seeing Daemon or the kid . . ." Tarr said.

"Esther doesn't date actors," said Leischneudel.

Not that I thought Lopez was perfect. Far from it. For one thing, he thought I was crazy and probably felonious (although, admittedly, he had his reasons for the former and was not entirely wrong about the latter). He could be a little cranky and rigid. He was also critical, and some-times he was too cynical—though I supposed that this was a natural result of his profession. And I had a feeling I'd rather try to disarm a bomb than meet his mother (whom he clearly loved—though their mutual affection mostly seemed to express itself in exasperated arguments).

"Well, I'm not an actor," Tarr said cheerfully. "So we're good to go."

But Lopez was fun to be with, easy to talk to (well, most of the time), brave and reliable, shrewd about hu-man nature, full of engaging quirks, very smart, and more patient that I usually gave him credit for. And when he looked at me a certain way, I felt sexier than the highest-paid screen temptress in Hollywood.

Whereas with Tarr looking me right now, I just felt underdressed.

"I know this piano bar where they play oldies," the tab-loid reporter said, apparently interpreting my awkward silence as a sign that I was weakening. "You'd like it."

I self-consciously tugged my barely decent neckline upward while I avoided his gaze, feeling depressed and dismayed by how much I still missed Lopez after more than two months of trying so hard not even to think about him.

Tarr added, "And I have a coupon. I can get drinks half-price there if I bring a woman."

My powers of articulation returned to me. "Tempting though that invitation is, Al, I must decline, on the grounds that I am studying to become a nun."

"I thought you were Jewish." Then his perpetual grin widened in appreciation of my sly wit. "Oh, I get it! Good one."

Over the intercom, Bill called for Act One places.

"Oh, thank God," I muttered.

"Esther and I have to go." Leischneudel simultaneously slipped into his frock coat and herded Tarr toward the door of the dressing room. "We open the show."

"I know," said Tarr. "I'm here every night, after all. Watching this goddamn play over and over. Wondering why anyone would pay three hundred dollars to see it, let alone to see it *again.*"

Leischneudel briefly froze in astonishment. "The scalpers are getting three hundred a seat? For *this* play?"

"There's no accounting for taste," said the reporter as we all exited the room.

Out in the hallway, we encountered Victor—or, rather, we *frightened* Victor. He was pacing with his back to us and whispering frantically into his cell phone. When he turned around and saw us, he shrieked in surprise, dropped his phone, and clapped a hand over his mouth.

"Jeez, pal," said Tarr. "You really need to cut back on the caffeine."

"Are you all right?" Leischneudel asked in concern.

Victor closed his eyes for a moment, then nodded. He lowered his hand and said, "You startled me."

His voice was faint, and he didn't seem to be breathing. He looked pale. Although the theater was (as I had good reason to know) drafty and cool, there were beads of sweat glinting on his forehead.

"Victor, you don't look so good," I said as Leischneudel retrieved the older man's phone from the hard cement floor and handed it to him. "And I really think you should breathe."

"Yes, *breathe*," Leischneudel urged, patting Victor on the back.

Victor suddenly started panting like a nervous dog. His voice still faint, he squeezed out the words, "It sounds like something . . . something *terrible* may have happened."

"Your call was bad news?" Tarr asked.

Victor panted, "I think so. It might be. I'm not . . ."

"Breathe a little more *slowly*." Leischneudel demonstrated what he meant, encouraging Victor to imitate him.

"Anything to do with Daemon?" Tarr asked.

Victor flinched. "You can't say anything to him!"

The reporter opened his notebook. "Why not?"

I took away Tarr's notebook. "Surely that's none of our business."

"Just keep breathing." Leischneudel glanced at me, aware that we needed to get to our places.

"Don't say anything to Daemon," Victor said frantically. *"Please."*

"Don't say anything about *what?*" Tarr prodded, trying to retrieve his notebook from me.

"It might turn out to be nothing. An ugly prank or a mistake . . . God, I hope it's nothing! It's *got* to be nothing," Victor babbled. "And even if it's something, there's nothing we can do about it right now, and I mustn't distract Daemon."

But distracting the rest of us was fine, apparently.

Rachel came out of my dressing room and saw us all. "God, what are you still doing here?" she said critically.

"Didn't you guys hear Bill call Act One places? Am I the only professional around here?"

She shoved her way through our little group, oblivious to me and Tarr wrestling for his notebook, and to Victor panting and sweating while Leischneudel patted his back and urged him to keep breathing.

I gave up my struggle with Tarr, let him have the notebook, and said to Leischneudel, "She's right. We have to go right now."

"We really do," the actor said. "I'm sorry, Victor. Um, I'm sure everything will be fine."

"You won't tell Daemon, will you?" Victor said urgently. "The show must go on!"

"No," I promised, "we won't tell him."

"Tell him *what?*" Tarr persisted.

"I have no idea. And *you,*" I said to the reporter, "leave this man alone."

"Of course," Tarr said with pellucid innocence. "Absolutely."

Poor Victor.

Leischneudel took my arm, and we scurried toward the darkened wings to start the second show. From that moment forward, I had no room in my head to spare a thought for Victor or whatever he'd been babbling about. Also no room, thankfully, to dwell on Tarr having asked me out on a date (so to speak).

During intermission, I saw Victor backstage, but he was so artificially bright and bubbly, I assumed that the crisis, whatever it was, must have passed. Given his tendency to overreact, I assumed it was nothing—an assumption which seemed to be confirmed when he bent my ear, at length, about the carpet on which I had spilled blood hours ago, assuring me the dry cleaners thought they could get the stain out completely.

I brushed him off and found a quiet spot backstage to rest in solitude for the remainder of the intermission. This was my sixth performance in three days, I was feeling the burn, and I would be onstage for much of Act Two. Ianthe had been eaten by Ruthven in Act One, but she appeared briefly several times in Act Two, when a feverish, guilt-ridden Aubrey imagined his sweetheart haunting him for failing to save her from Ruthven. Apart from those moments, Mad Rachel would be wandering around backstage until the curtain call, complaining of boredom because too few of her acquaintances were available for phone chats this late at night. I wondered how Leischneudel, who had an exhausting part, was getting through this second show, given that he'd gotten so little sleep last night, thanks to Mimi the cat.

When the curtain rose on Act Two, though, I didn't feel the fatigue anymore, nor did I see it in my two leading men as we performed scene after scene. That's the magic of the stage and the synergy of actors with a live audience. I knew I'd be exhausted as soon as the show was over, but I felt energized and alert as I waited in the wings to go back onstage for my final scene, Jane's wedding night.

Once I was onstage, face-to-face with my groom in the golden light of our private sitting room at night, and nervous about adjourning with him to the adjoining conjugal chamber, I spoke about my poor brother, who was too ill to attend the small, intimate wedding breakfast which had followed the private marriage ceremony this morning. A little while ago, my delirious sibling, openly horrified to learn my marriage was now a fait accompli, had said strange things to me about my groom, bizarre comments that were unquestionably a symptom of his brain fever . . . but which nonetheless made me uneasy enough that I now tried to broach the subject of those incoherent accusations with my new lord and master.

My husband brushed aside my questions with sinister half-answers and boldly explicit physical flattery as the two of us began circling each other like swordsmen in

the early moments of a mortal duel. Slowly, almost lan-
guidly, he pursued me around the room, drawing ever
closer, his intense gaze, silken voice, and erotic predation wearing down my reticence until, finally, I stopped
fleeing and let him touch me, claim me, *own* me. He
spoke to me of life, death, blood, innocence, pleasure,
and pain, all the while taking down my hair, stroking my
body, and exploring portions of my anatomy that no
man had ever touched before.

Including portions which I had specifically told Daemon *not* to touch *again*.

I found the vampire's lengthy speech about life, the
universe, and everything rather tedious and derivative,
but Jane found it provocative and enthralling—as did
the audience. Tarr had described the fans' absorption
well; when Ruthven stopped speaking long enough to
press several slow, sultry kisses against Jane's shoulder
and neck, you could have heard a pin drop in that theater. Then when he ran his hands over my body and
reached inside my dress to cup one of my breasts, I heard
sighs throughout the audience, and an audible moan
from someone sitting close to the stage.

My uncomfortable but flimsy push-up corset was not
much protection against this sort of intrusion, and I was
annoyed. Daemon's hands, as he well knew, were supposed to stay *outside* my dress at all times.

Ruthven droned on for a while longer, toying with his
bride, alternately seducing and terrorizing her. Although
Jane by now wanted to lie down on the floor and fling up
her skirts for him, *I* was incensed when Daemon slid his
hand down to the juncture of my thighs and cupped me
there. I writhed and moaned with feigned passion, which
activity I used to conceal my firmly moving his hand to
my hip while I stomped on his instep.

He wanted to improvise? *Fine*. Two could play that
game.

Daemon grunted in surprised pain then snorted a

little with laughter, which reaction he concealed by burying his face in my tumbled hair.

He had his revenge, though. As Ruthven swept Jane into their final embrace, his long, hard, taut body pressing against her supple and yielding one, and lowered his mouth to her unresisting neck . . . Daemon bit me.

I mean, *really* bit me. Like he was actually trying to get blood from my veins. I uttered a stifled sound of pain as my knees buckled and I clutched his shoulders.

I heard more sighs and moans, the audience responding to Ruthven's ruthless sexual domination and what they thought were my expressions of orgasmic ecstasy.

Then Daemon started sucking intensely. Without thinking, I gasped and reflexively shoved at his shoulders. He clutched me tighter, I lost my footing, and we began sinking to the floor together—which was not how the scene had been choreographed. The audience, a number of whom had previously seen the play and probably realized we were going off course, seemed to collectively hold its breath as our unrehearsed wrestling took us both down to our knees, pushing, clutching, and writhing.

I suddenly remembered the little bottles of blood in Daemon's dressing room. The tinted windows of his Soho loft. His insistence on avoiding direct sunlight. As he bore me to the floor, his teeth and tongue working on the tender flesh of my throat, I panicked.

I'm being murdered by a vampire, I thought, *right in front of hundreds of people!*

Then I thought, *And some of them paid three hundred dollars to see this show. Unbelievable!*

I felt the spotlight on us intensifying and growing brighter; the effect was supposed to make Jane's body look whiter, drained of blood as she died. I realized that if I gave a death rattle and went limp, Daemon would have to stop biting me and carry on with the scene. I tried it and, sure enough, it worked.

Daemon rose to his feet and uttered a few lines as I

lay dead, my neck throbbing while I plotted his evisceration. Next, Leischneudel entered, found my corpse, and went mad with grief. Then the vampire, exercising hypnotic power over Aubrey, convinced the young man to take his own life. Leischneudel plunged a prop dagger into his torso and collapsed, staying well outside the spotlight that made me look pale enough to have been exsanguinated. The two of us lay motionless onstage as Daemon gave his final speech, a dark little homily about the price of messing with a vampire.

Two things happened as soon as the curtain came down. The audience exploded into thunderous applause and noisy cries of rapturous adulation. And I leaped to my feet, sought Daemon in the dark, and kicked him as hard as I could.

"Ow!" Leischneudel howled, flailing and stumbling backward.

"Oh, no!" I cried, realizing I had miscalculated. "I'm sorry!"

With my pupils contracted in response to the spotlight shining on Jane's dead face, I couldn't see anything when the stage went dark.

Leischneudel must have stumbled into Mad Rachel as she was coming onstage for the curtain call. I heard her bellow, "Oof! Goddamn it! Watch where you're going!"

Someone touched me, and I swatted the hand away.

"It's *me*," Leischneudel said, shouting to be heard above the roar of the crowd.

"Oh! Are you okay?" I shouted back.

"Come on, hold hands!" Rachel said. "Why is everyone in the wrong place?"

"I think she tried to *kick* me!" Daemon sounded shocked.

"Come *on*," Rachel said.

I still couldn't see anything, but when I felt Daemon grab my hand, I shoved him. "I'm *not* holding your hand!"

"Here, *I'll* do it." Leischneudel shouted, "Daemon, give me your hand!"

"No! I'm not holding a *guy's* hand in the curtain call!"

The curtain rose on us all standing there bickering.

We immediately fell into line for our bows, but I didn't accept Daemon's outstretched hand, and when he tried to grasp mine, I stepped out of reach as I smiled at the audience—who were all on their feet, shouting and applauding wildly.

We did four curtain calls, the most we'd ever done. The audience was still applauding and shouting for another one when the curtain came down again and I turned on my heel and stalked offstage, followed by Leischneudel.

"Are you okay?" I asked him, relieved to see he wasn't limping.

"I'm fine," he assured me.

"I'm *so* sorry," I said. "I meant that kick for *him.*"

"So I gathered. What's wrong? What happened?"

"I swear, I will *kill* him before this run is over."

Daemon was onstage, taking another curtain call alone. Afterward, as soon as he exited into the wings, I walked up to him and slapped him so hard my hand stung. He staggered backward, his eyes watering.

He shook his head a couple of times, as if to clear his vision, then said, "Oh, come on, Esther. They loved it! *Listen* to that applause. *Five* curtain calls!"

"If you *ever* do that again," I shouted, "I will hit you that hard onstage, in the middle of the performance. I mean it!"

"Hey, great show, guys," Tarr said behind me. "Whoa, Esther! Daemon! You guys really took that scene to a whole new level!"

I resisted the urge to slug Tarr, too, and stormed down the hallway toward my dressing room. Behind me, I heard Daemon accepting Tarr's congratulations.

"What a jerk!" I muttered. "Leischneudel?"

He was right behind me. "Yes?"

"I'm exhausted. I want to go home. Please get me out of this gown. Right now!"

"Of course." He started undoing my laces, trotting to keep up with me. "What happened, Esther?"

"I think he's started to believe his own bullshit." And for a moment there, with Daemon's teeth sinking into my throat, *I* had believed it, too. Feeling sticky, tired, and cranky, I added, "*God,* I want this dress off."

"Halfway there."

"Good." I reached my dressing room, flung open the door—and froze when I saw Detective Connor Lopez there.

6

Lopez was sitting slumped in a stiff-backed chair next to the makeup table. His face was turned away from me, but I could see it clearly reflected in the brightly lit mirror that ran the length of the table. His legs were stretched out in front of him, his arms and ankles crossed, his chin resting on his chest. His eyes were closed and his long, dark lashes lay against his cheeks in peaceful repose.

He was . . . dozing? Here?

He flinched and lifted his head abruptly when Leischneudel, hot on my heels as he unlaced the back of my costume, bumped into my suddenly immobile body, inadvertently smashed his pert nose against the back of my head, and exclaimed, "Ow!"

"Oops!" I said.

Lopez's dazed gaze flew to us as he sat up, blinking in startled surprise. I stepped through the doorway and turned to face Leischneudel, whose hand was clasped over his nose while his eyes watered.

"I'm sorry! I'm so sorry. You should get danger pay for working with me tonight. Is it bleeding?" I said in a rush, more flustered by the sight of Lopez than of my fellow thespian staggering backward in pain (again) because of me. "Come on, Daemon might not be far behind us. Get in here before he sees it." After what had just happened, I wasn't as certain as I used to be that Daemon's appetite for hemoglobin was just an act.

I dragged Leischneudel into my dressing room, slammed the door behind us, and tried to pry his hand away from his face.

"Let me see it," I said, using the firm tone I often found it expedient to employ with him.

He removed his hand and gave a little sniff as he reached for the pocket of his elegant Regency waistcoat.

"It's not bleeding," I said with relief. Unlike a certain D-list celebrity who reveled in his gothic antics (my neck was really smarting, and I knew there'd be a telltale mark there by tomorrow), I had no desire to see my colleagues' blood.

Behind me, I heard Lopez rise to his feet and shove the chair away.

Leischneudel pulled out a neatly folded handkerchief and used it to dab at his eyes. "It's all right. It just really hurt for a second there." He sniffed again and shook his head. "I thought things like this wouldn't happen anymore."

"Things like walking into me?" I said.

"Pain."

"I'm sorry," I said again. "I forgot you were right behind me."

He stuffed his handkerchief back into his pocket, touched his nose tenderly, and said, "I'm fine. It feels better already. And it's a lot easier to get this thing off you when you're standing still, anyhow." He put his hand on my shoulder to turn me slightly as he shifted position to get his hands on the back of my dress again. That's when he saw Lopez.

"Oh!" Leischneudel froze in surprise, his hands on the laces of my gown, as he stared at the strange man in my dressing room.

Taking in the detective's uncharacteristically grubby

appearance tonight, I suddenly realized how disreputable Lopez looked. Even intimidating. Particularly to someone who had no idea who he was or what he was doing here.

Come to think of it . . . "What are you doing here?" I blurted.

"You know him?" Leischneudel asked anxiously.

"We need to talk," Lopez said to me.

"We do?"

"Right away," he said, his gaze riveted on the sheer foundation garment exposed by my half-undone laces. Then his blue eyes shifted coldly to Leischneudel. "Hi."

"Er . . . hello," the actor replied, obviously wondering why Lopez looked ready to kill him.

My heart pounded with mixed emotions.

I had struggled with my desires but had remained resolute and strong since the last time we'd seen each other, that stormy night in Harlem more than two months ago. Why did Lopez have to come here now and make this even harder for me?

I had missed him so much. Why hadn't he come sooner, damn him?

Wow, he came! He couldn't stay away from me.

Okay, *stop*, I thought.

Recognizing the awkward silence that was filling the room as I stared in smitten fascination at Lopez while he and Leischneudel eyed each other, I realized that I should make introductions.

I said to Lopez, "This is Leischneudel Drysdale, one of the actors in the show."

Calling on his good manners, Leischneudel released my laces and stepped forward to offer Lopez a courteous handshake.

I said, "Leischneudel, this is—"

"Hector," Lopez said, giving Leischneudel's hand a quick, curt shake. "Hector Sousa. I'm a friend of Esther's."

I gaped at Lopez, stunned by his use of a phony name and having no idea what to say next.

Leischneudel looked down at his hand with a slight frown, rubbing his fingers together as if trying to remove an unpleasant substance.

This caused Lopez to rub his own hand self-consciously down the front of his sweatshirt. "Um, sorry."

Always the gentleman, Leischneudel quickly said, "No, no, not at all." But since the cat was out of the bag, he pulled out his handkerchief again and wiped his hand. I noticed that the white fabric came away darkly smeared, which would make Fiona even crankier than usual.

I glanced at Lopez's hands and noticed that they were rather dirty, as if smeared with crude oil. Like everything else about his appearance this evening, that was unusual for him. While not fastidious, he was generally a clean, tidy guy. Tonight, though, he looked like a street thug. Or, alternately, like a laborer at the end of a long, hard overtime shift.

An NYPD detective assigned to the Organized Crime Control Bureau, Connor Lopez (who didn't look like a "Connor") was in his early thirties, slightly under six feet tall, and lithe and lean, like a soccer player. The youngest of three sons, he had inherited rich blue eyes from his Irish-American mother; and maybe his lush, full lips had been another of her hereditary gifts to him. Otherwise, he (I had always assumed) resembled his Cuban-born father; his straight, shiny hair was coal black, his skin was a burnished golden olive hue, and his facial features were strong and distinct.

When on duty, he usually wore conservative, budget-conscious suits (I suspected he was a regular customer of Banana Republic). Off-duty, I had mostly seem him dressed like any regular guy trying not to scare off a woman: casual, but not sloppy.

Tonight, though, he was in a hooded gray sweatshirt that had seen better days. There was an odd yellow stain around the bottom hem, a hole in one elbow, dark smudges all over the sleeves, and more smudges on his chest and stomach, as if he'd wiped his dirty hands there a number of times before now. The rounded neckline of a T-shirt was visible above the zipped-up V-neck of the sweatshirt, and I could see, even with this limited view, that the garment was ragged and old. His legs were covered by slightly baggy military khakis—the kind of bile-colored trousers that have lots of pockets and pouches. He wore lace-up work boots that came up to his shins. They looked waterproof, sturdy, and well-made; but like the clothing, they, too, appeared to have been in his life a long time and subjected to hard use.

Lopez looked very tired, and his eyes were bloodshot. He also needed a haircut and a shave. If not for the rolled-up bandana around his head that was holding his hair off his face, it would be hanging in his eyes; and he looked as if he hadn't used a razor in at least three days. The heavy shadow of facial hair made me notice something else: he was unusually pale. The last time I had seen him, in late summer, he'd been tan and sun-kissed. Now he looked rather sallow, as if he hadn't been outdoors in weeks.

Wondering at the changes in him in the months since I had last seen him, a horrible thought struck me. Had he been kicked off the police force—which I felt sure would devastate him—because of me? Or because of what happened that night in Harlem? Did unemployment and depression explain his grubby, unkempt appearance?

I was appalled. I had given up Lopez because I didn't want to ruin his life—along with the far more pressing concern of not wanting to get him killed. Had I ruined his life anyhow?

Oh, *no*.

"What's *happened* to you?" I asked in despair.

Both men looked startled by my tone.

"Is something wrong?" Leischneudel asked uncertainly.

"He never looks like this," I said, shaking my head.

"No?" Leischneudel said.

"No, of course not," I replied. Lopez normally looked like the sort of man you could bring home to your mother, if your mother weren't Jewish.

"Oh. But it's kind of a good look for him, don't you think?" Leischneudel said generously. "Sort of . . . the Jersey docks meet the Meatpacking District."

"Maybe when it *was* a meatpacking area," I said dismissively. "But not now, all trendy nightclubs and gay bars."

"Well, yes, the grime might be a little much for the club scene," Leischneudel conceded. "Even for rough trade."

"You do know I'm standing right here?" Lopez said to us.

"Oh, I'm sorry!" Leischneudel giggled nervously. "Esther and I talk about makeup and costume so much, I guess it's become an unconscious habit. We didn't mean to be rude."

"I'm not in cos . . ." A faint look of surprise crossed Lopez's face, then he smiled wryly. "That's okay."

"Are you all right?" I asked him. "I mean . . . you haven't been kicked off—"

"I'm fine. Everything's fine with me. Okay? It's you I'm worried about." Lopez brushed self-consciously at his ratty clothes. "I just didn't have time to clean up before I came here."

"So this look isn't a whole new lifestyle for you?" I said in relief.

"Not exactly. I was in a hurry."

"And you rushed to the theater at three o'clock in the morning from where?" I prodded. "A wildman wilderness camp near an oil refinery?"

He smiled again. "Good guess."

I frowned and started to say, "Lop—"

"I needed to talk to you." He glanced at Leischneudel, then gave me a meaningful look. "It's important. I didn't think it should wait for a shower and a change of wardrobe."

"Why? What's wrong?" Leischneudel asked in concern.

We both looked at him.

"Oh!" Leischneudel giggled nervously again. I thought he was blushing, but the heavy stage makeup made it hard to tell. He started backing toward the door. "That was my cue, wasn't it? Sorry. I'll leave you two alone to talk." He opened the door and backed into the hallway. "Take your time."

"Thanks. We will." The moment the door closed, Lopez said tersely to me, "Why was he taking off your clothes?"

There was a soft knock and the door reopened. Lopez looked at Leischneudel with an expression of exaggerated patience as the actor stuck his head back into the room.

"Er, Esther. I'll wait for you in my dressing room?"

"Okay," I said.

"You won't leave without me?" Leischneudel prodded, his face briefly twisting into an expression of hunted dread at the prospect of facing the vamparazzi alone tonight.

"Of course not," I said.

As soon as the door closed again, I said to Lopez, "Why did you give him a fake name?"

"Let's get back to *my* question. Are you sleeping with that guy?"

"With *Leischneudel?*" I felt like he'd just asked me if I was sleeping with Bambi or Winnie-the-Pooh. "Of course not."

"Then why were his hands all over you?"

"He was helping me with this costume." I gestured

with irritation to the laces on my back. "It's so authentic, I can't get out of it by myself."

Lopez choked on a startled laugh. When I gave him an exasperated look, he tried to stop.

"Sorry." He cleared his throat and said again, "Sorry." Then he ruined his apology by laughing some more.

"Very funny," I said sourly. "You're not the one who has to get into and out of this gown six nights a week."

"Speaking of your costume—"

"No, now we do *my* question. Why did you use a phony name when I introduced you to Leischneudel?"

He was about to respond when we heard Daemon's voice in the hall right outside my dressing room. "Is she in there? Ah, good!"

"But she's got a visitor, and they don't want . . ." Leischneudel protested as the door was flung open and banged against the wall. ". . . to be disturbed."

"What?" Daemon sashayed through the door as he casually shook off Leischneudel's awkward attempt to restrain him. I turned to face Daemon, annoyed by the intrusion. He came to an abrupt halt when he saw Lopez. "Oh! A visitor? *Oh.*" Daemon's glance flicked past me for a moment, then he met my eyes and smirked. I felt a slight draft on my back and realized he could see in the mirror that my gown was half-unlaced. Obviously concluding that he had interrupted my visitor in the middle of undressing me, Daemon now included Lopez in his smirk. *"Ohhhh . . ."*

I said to my companion, "Meet Daemon Ravel, the vampire onstage."

"And offstage, too," Daemon added, always quick to present his creature-of-the-night credentials.

Lopez folded his arms across his chest. "I trust you have a good reason for barging into a lady's dressing room without knocking?"

"Ooh!" Daemon grinned lasciviously at me. "You've found a spicy one."

"If whatever you want isn't really, *really* important," I said to Daemon, "then it'll have to wait until tomorrow."

"And rugged," Daemon added, giving Lopez an appraising look. "But maybe a *touch* overdone on the gutter-rat theme."

"What do you want?" I asked wearily.

"Just returning your earring, darling." He held up the dangling object up for me to see. I touched my earlobes and realized one earring was indeed missing. Daemon said, "It came off when I bit you."

With my attention divided between playing my role, wanting to gut Daemon for the way he was taking advantage of me onstage, and physical pain as he actually bit and sucked, I hadn't noticed the earring falling off—go figure.

"Thanks. If there's nothing else . . ." I nodded toward the door as I took the earring from him.

All three men watched me put it on. Then Lopez frowned, came closer, and touched the sore spot on my neck. The skin was tender, and I flinched a little.

"What happened here?" Lopez asked me as he cast a dark glare at the two men.

Realizing he could see it, I turned around and went to look at the hickey in the mirror. Sure enough, the welt wasn't waiting until tomorrow to become visible. It was already mottled and pink, the skin inflamed and irritated, with little dots of purple bruising starting to appear, thanks to Daemon's teeth.

"Goddamn it, Daemon. Do you know how much makeup I'm going to have to put on this tomorrow?" I said. "Not to mention how much it *hurts*."

"Did I get a little too carried away?" Daemon asked with sultry amusement. "Sorry. You bring out my hunger, Esther."

"*He* did that to you?" Lopez said to me.

"You *bit* her?" Leischneudel exclaimed, scandalized. "That's what happened out there tonight? Daemon! You shouldn't *really* bite her."

"He did that to you in the *play?*" Lopez said.

I nodded. "And if he does it again, I'm going to castrate him." In the mirror, I met Daemon's gaze with a cold glare.

"Surely you're not going to pretend you didn't enjoy it even a *little?*" the vampire icon purred. "The audience certainly liked it. And I must admit, so did I."

"Out," said Lopez. *"Now."*

Daemon said, "It's that warm, pulsing jugular vein right under my mouth that I just can't resist when we're—"

"That's her carotid artery." Lopez shoved Daemon through the door.

"Wait, I knew that," said Daemon, stumbling backward.

"And if your teeth ever touch it again," Lopez said, "I'll remove them all. Are we clear?"

Daemon staggered into Leischneudel, who was asking if I was all right as Lopez slammed the door in their faces.

"This show is really taking its toll," I grumbled, studying my reflection. "I've got a black eye, too, under all this makeup. One of Daemon's crazed fans attacked me last night."

"Yeah, I heard."

"You heard?" I said in surprise.

"And to think my mom worried that police work would be dangerous," he said dryly. "I guess she should just be glad that none of her sons became actors."

"Hmph."

Lopez crossed the room to stand behind me and look at my welt while I studied it in the mirror. "He didn't break the skin. But disinfect it when you get home, anyhow," he said. "I doubt that guy's had all his shots."

"You should have punched him," I said grumpily. "He should be punched."

"He should be," Lopez agreed, meeting my eyes in the mirror. "But the cops will make him plenty miserable tonight without my help. And if we can avoid it, I'd rather they didn't know I was here. If I break his nose, well, word might get out."

"The cops?" I turned around to look at him directly, disquieted again. "Are *you* still a cop?"

"Of course." His surprised expression changed as realization dawned. "*Oh.* I get it. You thought I'd lost my job and become a derelict? Do I really look *that* bad?" When I nodded, he grinned. It made him look a lot more like his usual self. He gazed over my shoulder, assessing his reflection in the mirror. "I guess I've gotten so used to it, I didn't realize."

"What's going on?" I demanded. "Why do you look so scruffy? Why are you using a phony name? Why can't the cops know you were here tonight? Why . . . Oh! *Oh.* Oh, my God." I had seen enough episodes of *Crime and Punishment* to make an educated guess. "You're working undercover?"

He nodded. "And I shouldn't tell you. So let's not tell anyone else. Understood?"

I had also watched enough episodes of *C&P* to know that working undercover was dangerous—and being exposed while working undercover was *particularly* dangerous.

"I won't tell anyone," I assured him. "So you're still a cop. But in *theory,* you're not a cop right now?"

"In theory, I'm also not even here right now." He picked up a makeup sponge that was lying on the table, examined it briefly, then took it over to the sink in the corner, where he turned on the water.

I turned to look at my welt again in the mirror, wondering just how much trouble it would be to conceal it for tomorrow's performance.

As Lopez rinsed the sponge under the running tap, he said, "So don't talk to your, um, colleagues here about me. If they ask, just say I'm an old friend and then change the subject. Okay?"

"I don't understand," I said as he returned to my side with the damp sponge and started dabbing gently at the welt on my neck. "If you're not here, then what are you doing here?" I drew in a sharp breath at the feel of the cold water on my tender skin.

"This will be all right," he said soothingly. I felt the warm clasp of his hand on my other shoulder, steadying me. The heat of his body warmed the flesh of my half-naked back as he stood close behind me. "But it'll hurt for a couple of days."

"Uh-huh."

"Does he do this to you eight shows a week?" Lopez asked darkly.

"No. I mean, he likes to push his luck a little." I sighed and half-closed my eyes, guiltily enjoying the touch I had missed. "But tonight he went way out of bounds."

"You're right," he said. "I should have punched him."

I could feel his breath on my neck.

I said, "He was . . ."

"Was . . . ?" he murmured.

"Was feeling his oats tonight . . . But most shows, he just . . . just . . ."

Lopez heard the breathless distraction in my voice, and our eyes met in the mirror. My chest rose and fell with sudden vigor inside my push-up corset. His gaze drifted down to the low-cut bodice of my gown, and I felt a flush of pleasure warm my whole body as his hands tightened on me—until the pressure of the cold sponge against my welt made me wince, startling him.

"Ouch."

"Sorry." He gentled his touch, dabbing tentatively again. "I, uh . . ."

I think we both remembered in that moment that I had told him we shouldn't see each other any more, and that I hadn't returned his last phone call, the one asking me to meet him so we could talk. At any rate, I felt awkward and self-conscious now, and he didn't look at my cleavage again. After a couple of more cold dabs at my neck, he put down the sponge and said matter-of-factly, "After you disinfect it, maybe put some ice on it for a while."

"I will."

"Make sure you tell the cops how you got that," he added. "They'll be interested."

"The cops?" I said blankly.

"Yeah. I'd rather they didn't find out I was here, so don't volunteer anything about me."

"The *cops?*" I repeated.

"But I don't want you to *lie* to them when they question you. Do you understand? If they *ask* you about me, tell the truth. Just don't talk about me in front of the other people being questioned. I'll deal with—"

"Whoa! Back up a step. Why are the cops going to question me?"

"It's all right," he said. "You're not under suspicion."

"Of what?"

"Murder."

"Murder?" I bleated. "Someone's been *murdered?*"

Lopez blinked. "Oh. I didn't tell you that part yet, did I?"

"No," I snapped. "You left that part out while giving me first aid advice."

"I'm sorry. I meant to explain this to you in an orderly, unalarming way."

"Why am I going to be alarmed?" I asked suspiciously.

"But I'm a little tired, and this has been kind of a confusing conversation so far, what with Licenoodle—"

"Leischneudel."

"—the Vampire Ravel, your earring, your neckline. Er, I mean, your neck." He repeated with emphasis, "Your neck."

"Uh-huh."

Lopez sighed and ran a dirty hand over his beard-shadowed face. "This is not going the way I intended." He glared at me. "Which is par for the course when I'm with you."

"Who's been murdered?" Fear seized me. "Oh, my God! Not Max?"

"*No.* Not Max," he said firmly. "This has nothing to do with Max."

"Oh, thank God." I took a steadying breath. "No, I suppose not. I mean, I just spoke to him tonight."

"So you still see him regularly?"

"Yes, of course. But I haven't stopped by his place lately, even though it's near here. The show's been kind of exhausting."

"I'll bet."

"He's coming to see it tomorrow night."

"Oh? Good."

I looked at him in surprise. Lopez had always disapproved of my friendship with Max.

In response to my expression, he said, "It might not be a . . . a *completely* terrible idea if . . ." He took a breath and concluded with obvious difficulty, "If Max kept an eye on you for a while."

"Really?" I blurted. "Wow. That's a sea change." When he didn't respond, I prodded, "I was . . . surprised when he told me that you went to him for help when I was missing during the blackout this summer."

"Uh-huh."

"What changed your mind about him?"

"Nothing. But when I suspected you might be trapped with a killer, I was desperate." Lopez avoided my gaze. "I'd have gone to Satan for help, let alone Max."

"That's an absurd compar—"

"And when he and I talked, I realized that, whatever else I may think about him, I could count on him to step in front of a moving train to protect you."

"Well, yes." Actually, although Max and I had become close friends, I knew he would risk his life for *most* people, not just me. That was his calling—protecting people from Evil.

Realizing the weight of what Lopez had just acknowledged, though, I smiled and said warmly, "So you finally approve of him?"

"No, of course not," he said, spoiling the mood. "I think he probably leads you into trouble a lot more often than he protects you from it."

"That's not tr . . ." Well, there might be a *little* truth in that. So I changed the subject by pointing out, "He saved your life that night in Harlem."

"I have a lot of questions about what happened."

"You sound so ungrateful!" I said critically.

"Of course I was grateful. I thanked Max very nicely, *and* I overlooked a bunch of things I could have arrested him for."

"Arrested? But—"

"I also bent over backward to keep both of your names out of what happened that night."

"Oh?" I had suspected as much, since no cops ever contacted me about it. "Thank you."

"That doesn't mean I don't have questions about whatever *did* happen. A *lot* of questions."

"You wouldn't like the answers," I said morosely. Lopez and I had waded through that kind of discussion before. Multiple times. It never went well.

"You're probably right." His shoulders slumped, and he suddenly looked exhausted.

I recalled that it was the middle of the night, I'd just done two shows, and he was so tired he'd dozed off while waiting here for me.

And he'd mentioned *murder*.

"Why are you here?" I asked. "What's going on?"

"We got off track again, didn't we?" he said wryly. "Sorry. Look, there's something you need to know, and I wanted to . . . to . . ." He paused and frowned in distraction as the stentorian echo of Mad Rachel's voice penetrated the closed door of the dressing room.

"You didn't call me after the first show, Eric!" she shrieked. "How can I *trust someone who doesn't even call me WHEN HE SAYS HE WILL?*"

Lopez stared at the door with a bemused expression as Rachel's voice approached this room. He asked me, "What is *that?*"

"Mad Rachel," I said wearily. "The other actress in the play."

The door opened and Rachel entered the room, still in makeup and costume, bellowing into her cell phone, "Fuck you, Eric! That is *not* what you said today!"

"This is unbelievable." Lopez flung himself into a chair, crossed his arms over his chest again, and said to me, "Don't you have *any* privacy in this place?"

"It's a public theater," I pointed out. "What were you expecting?"

Rachel paused momentarily in her tirade when she saw Lopez, then said into the phone, "A strange man is in my dressing room. Yes! Right now! Where am *I?* In my dressing room, *Eric.*"

"I *thought,*" Lopez said to me, "that the 'public' nature of the place would stop at the door of your dressing room. A room where you—you know—*undress.*"

It was a reasonable assumption in the normal world. But in the theatrical world, dressing rooms tend to be pretty public places, and actors lose most of our modesty pretty early in our training. I had worked on any number of shows where actors and actresses all shared a large communal dressing room and had very few physical secrets left after the first few days. I had also worked various venues and gigs where I changed clothes in public rest rooms or utilities closets. When doing Shakespeare in the rain one summer, I had made my changes behind a curtain, so that the audience couldn't see me, but where I was nonetheless in plain view of anyone who happened to be spying on us from the woods behind our set.

"I don't *know* who he is, *Eric*." Mad Rachel gestured to Lopez and said to me, "Do you know this guy?"

"Yes. It's fine. He's an old friend of mine." After a pregnant pause, I said to Lopez, "I can't remember your name."

He sighed in exasperation. "Hector Sousa."

"Well, this is *my* dressing room, too, Esther, and I don't appreciate finding a strange man hanging around in here," Rachel said. "We *share* this space, you know. You need to be more considerate."

"What?"

"You shouldn't always be thinking about just yourself," she said primly.

"What?" I'd had *enough* for one night. This was a bridge too far! "*What* did you say to me?"

Lopez muttered, "Fire in the hole."

"You have the *nerve*—the utter unmitigated *gall*—to lecture *me* about being considerate?" I snarled. "You shrieking, whiny, loud—"

Lopez slid off his chair, seized my elbow, and started dragging me toward the door. "We're getting sidetracked again."

"You *shrill*, nagging, noisy—"

"I don't know," Rachel said into her cell phone. "Esther's having a cow about something. Esther Diamond. You know, that actress who they put in my dressing room."

"*Your* dressing room? *Yours?* Why you little b—"

Lopez clapped a dirty hand over my mouth, hauled me forcibly out of the dressing room, and dragged me some distance down the hallway. He didn't let go of me until after I stopped struggling.

I was panting hard, my blood heated with rage. He kept his hands on my arms, as if afraid I might bolt.

"Take a deep breath," he said. "And another. That's good. Keep breathing."

"Sorry," I said. "Sorry. I guess I snapped. It was just one thing too many, you know?"

"I get it." After a moment, he asked, "Eric is her husband?"

I shook my head. "Boyfriend."

"Wow. Imagine what the fights will be like when they're *married*."

I remembered that, as a cop, he sometimes thought of marriage in terms of domestic violence statistics. "You think they'd ever get married?" I said doubtfully.

"Sure. People just like them get married all the time," he said. "Ain't love grand?"

"Okay, I'm better now. Really." I sighed. "She just gets on my last nerve."

"I can see why." He smiled. "But I'll bet people in the very last row can hear every word she utters in the play."

I gave a puff of laughter and nodded.

"Let's just hope she doesn't turn up dead," he said seriously. "If anyone besides me knows how you feel about her, it won't look good."

Recalling what we had been talking about before Mad Rachel interrupted us, I said, "Lopez, you're scaring me. Who *has* turned up dead? What's going on?"

"Okay, here it is." He paused, then warned me, "This is disturbing stuff."

"Go on." I braced myself.

"The body of Adele Olson was found this afternoon."

"Who?" I said blankly.

"In the, uh, vampire community, she's known as Angeline."

I shook my head. "I don't think I know anyone named Angeline *or* Adele Olson."

"She's the fan who attacked you outside the theater last night."

"*What?*" When he nodded, I said, "Jane's been *murdered?*"

He frowned. "You knew her as Jane?"

"Huh? Oh. No. I didn't know her at all." I briefly explained about the Janes. "So that's what I call anyone who dresses up like my character."

"*Exactly* like your character." He looked me over. "Right down to the shoes, earrings, and hair. She didn't have quite the same build as you, and I don't think her face looked anything like yours—then again, I never saw her when she was alive."

"You mean you've seen her *dead?*"

"No, I've seen some postmortem photos."

"Oh." That sounded grisly, too.

He continued, "But despite the differences, to a casual observer, she was pretty much a ringer for you. When you're both in costume, I mean."

Seeing how troubled he looked, I realized why he'd come to the theater in the wee hours to speak to me, evidently against orders, and without pausing to clean up first. Appalled by what I suspected was on his mind, I said slowly, with great reluctance, "You think the resemblance is significant."

"It might have nothing to do with you," he said. "Initial investigation suggests she was a mixed-up girl with dangerous tastes and not much sense."

Recalling the way she had attacked me, I wasn't inclined to argue with that description.

"So maybe she just ran into some fatal trouble last night. But, well, yeah, I'm a little worried," he admitted, "Someone who hung around this theater, who superficially resembled you, and who dressed *exactly* like you when you're onstage has been murdered." He nodded. "The possible implications bother me."

I shivered. "*This* is your attempt not to alarm me?"

"Sorry. This all went much better in my head than it's going in person."

"Ah," I said. "That *never* happens to *me.*"

He smiled briefly, then got serious again as he said,

"There's something else I need to tell you about this. Something . . . a little weird."

"Oh, goody."

"You're going to hear about it, one way or another. So I'd rather you hear it from me."

"Because you're so good at not alarming me?"

"Okay, if you'd *rather* learn about it from the tabloids . . ." Lopez said a little crankily.

"The tabloids?" I repeated with dread.

"The department won't be able to keep this quiet." He gave a disgusted sigh. "That would've been for the best, but too many people already know. If it's not on the Internet yet, it will be any minute now."

"What?" I asked anxiously.

"The victim was exsanguinated." He added, as if thinking that I might not be familiar with the term, "Drained of all her blood."

I gaped at him in horrified astonishment. "You mean she was killed by a vampire?"

7

Lopez said with forced patience, "No, of course not."

I frowned in confusion. "But you just said . . ."

"She was exsanguinated, Esther," he said. "Not bitten by an immortal creature of the night."

"How do you drain all of someone's blood?" I wondered. A scant familiarity with vampire fiction was my only source of information on the subject.

"Details probably aren't a good idea."

"Who besides a vampire *exsanguinates* people?" I demanded.

"I should have guessed," Lopez said wearily. "You believe in vampires."

"No," I said. "No . . . Well, actually, I don't know." I had seen too many strange things (such as zombies, animated gargoyles, evil spirits, doppelgängers, and mystical vanishings) to dismiss the possibility outright. "Let's say I don't believe in the pop culture stereotypes of vampires."

"Like your leading man?" Lopez cast another dark glance at the welt on my neck.

The leading man, I realized, who had been feeling his oats tonight. Who had, for a few moments there onstage, scared me into believing he might actually be what he claimed to be.

"He keeps blood in his dressing room," I blurted.

"Yeah, I heard. I gather *everyone's* heard. We'll find out soon what it really is."

"Oh, it's blood, all right." I felt a little queasy again.

My companion was skeptical. "What makes you so sure?"

"I drank some of it."

"You *what?*" He reflexively grabbed my shoulders.

"It was an accident. I thought it was Nocturne wine cooler."

He looked shocked. "You drink Nocturne?"

"*No,*" I said. "But it was the only thing available at the time."

"Even so . . ." He let go of me, his expression suggesting that he was completely rethinking his opinion of me.

I said, "To return to the point, those bottles in his fridge are filled with—"

"What were you doing, having a cocktail in that guy's dressing room?" my ex-almost-boyfriend demanded.

I sighed and explained. I tried to keep it brief but, as was often the case, Lopez had a lot of questions, so I wound up telling him almost everything that had happened in Daemon's dressing room. While we talked, we drifted toward one of the theater's darkened backstage alcoves, both tired and wanting to get off our feet. He used his dirty sleeve to dust off a packing crate for me, then we sat on it together. I could hear occasional familiar noises and voices echoing through the backstage area as the stage crew reset everything for tomorrow's performance and various people milled around.

When I finished my account, Lopez was silent for a few moments, mulling it over—probably looking for possible links with information he wasn't sharing with me.

"What are you thinking?" I asked, shifting uncomfortably. I'd been in this push-up corset for hours, and it was starting to feel like diabolical torture.

"If it's human blood," he answered, "whose is it and how did the Vampire Ravel acquire it?"

"Those are creepy questions."

"But the answers aren't necessarily criminal. He claims in public that he indulges in blood play, so—"

"In what?"

"Blood play. Sexual practices that involve shedding, sharing, and/or ingesting blood."

"Oh, vampire sex. Right. He makes claims about it in private, too. I assumed he was lying until I took an innocent swig of his wine cellar."

"I can't believe you were going to drink Nocturne," Lopez muttered, clearly still disillusioned with me.

"Can we stick to the subject?"

"Okay. Right." After a moment, he asked, "What was the subject again? Sorry, I'm a little tired. I haven't been to bed since . . . Actually, I can't remember."

"Ah. So *that's* why you fell asleep in my dressing room."

"Yeah. I was listening to the show on the intercom for a while after I snuck in. You sounded really good, Esther. I wasn't even sure it was you, at first—*very* much the proper English lady," he said. "But then there was a scene with the vampire yammering at the half-wit brother about a vow of silence and the meaning of honor . . . something like that, anyhow. And I guess it lulled me right to sleep."

I laughed. Lopez smiled as he removed his bandana, stuck it into a pocket, and ran his fingers through his overlong hair, rubbing his scalp as if trying to soothe a fatigue headache. I suddenly wanted to do that for him, so I folded my hands tightly together on my lap.

Returning to the subject, I asked, "If the blood in Daemon's refrigerator turns out to be human, will they arrest him?"

"No, not necessarily. Not if he can produce the consensual adult whose blood it is, for example."

"So you don't think it's . . ." Remembering that I had *tasted* some of it, I couldn't manage to finish my sentence.

"The victim's blood?" Lopez shook his head. "I doubt it. It would be very convenient for the cops if Daemon were dumb enough to stock his fridge with evidence of a homicide. But we don't get that lucky in most investigations."

"He picks up fans for casual sex, so I suppose he could have blood samples from multiple partners," I mused.

"Maybe . . ."

Hearing his doubtful tone, I prodded, "But you don't think so?"

"I think he might not still be alive and healthy enough to do eight performances a week if he didn't make a point of knowing exactly whose blood he's playing with and that it's safe."

"He told *me* it was safe." I felt anxious again.

"And I'll make sure we get a definite answer from the lab about that tomorrow," Lopez promised firmly.

"They'll analyze it that soon?"

He nodded. "This case will be a feeding frenzy for the media, so the department wants to clear your costar or else charge him—one or the other—as soon as possible. They'll start processing the physical evidence as soon as they collect it."

"Maybe the blood isn't even human." I liked this theory, because it meant that I had not sipped human blood tonight.

"Oh, I think it probably is." Lopez absently rubbed the black stubble on his jaw while he mused aloud, "I have a feeling you were right. Daemon Ravel's been so rigorous about cultivating his vampire image, he wouldn't neglect a detail like that after giving a tabloid writer access to every corner of his unlife. He's invested years in this masquerade, after all."

"And a lot of money, too," I added, thinking of the famous sun-blocking windows he'd had installed in his Soho loft.

"So he's probably been thorough enough to stock that fridge with human blood, knowing the reporter would pilfer some of it. I'll bet the cops will find more of it in his home, too."

"You think the police will search his loft?"

"They might be there already." Seeing my surprise, he explained gently, "The victim went home with Daemon late last night, Esther. Based on what's known right now, that's the last time that anyone saw her alive. And the body was dumped only about eight blocks from Daemon's address. The investigating officers were getting a search warrant while I was being briefed. Cops will be arriving *here* any minute, too."

"Oh." I remembered that he had said so earlier. My head was spinning. After a moment, I realized what had probably upset Victor between shows. I asked, "You said too many people already know about this?"

He nodded. "By the time the police arrived and secured the scene, locals were talking, and a couple of journalists were asking questions."

"I think someone phoned Daemon's assistant around midnight and told him about it." Perhaps a reporter asking for a comment or quote about the murder? If so, no wonder Victor had been so unnerved. "I'm sure he didn't say anything to Daemon before the second show was over, but he might be telling him right now."

Lopez shrugged. "It's all right. No one involved in the case seems to think there's any risk of Daemon Ravel trying to run away. He'll lawyer up, but he won't go into hiding."

"Oh. Good point." I thought it likely that, if forced to choose between the two things, Daemon would prefer a prompt public hanging in Times Square to disappearing and eventually falling off the radar. "I guess the cops will question all of us—everyone who works with Daemon?"

"Probably. In any case, they'll definitely want to talk to you, due to your connection with the victim."

"We weren't connected," I said irritably. "She dressed like my character, and she punched me in the face last night outside the stage door. That's not a *connection*."

"It is now that she's been murdered," Lopez said. "Listen to me. I want you to stay away from Daemon. Depending on what happens in the next few hours, he might be in custody by morning, anyhow. But if not, then until he's either arrested or cleared, *stay away* from him. Do you understand me?"

"You really think he's the killer?"

"I don't know. And until I do, you shouldn't go anywhere near him."

"But I do eight shows a week with him," I pointed out.

"Stay away from him *offstage*," Lopez clarified patiently. "However badly Daemon behaves onstage, I'm pretty skeptical he'd commit a murder there."

"I really don't know about this." I shook my head. "Sure, Daemon's a jerk with bloodsucking pretensions. And tonight he actually scared me onstage. For a minute there, I thought . . . you know."

I touched the welt on my neck, remembering the reckless enthusiasm with which he had bit and sucked while I wrestled with him in front of the audience. Was he reliving what had happened in private with the demented fan he'd taken home last night? Had she struggled, too, before dying?

"I really *should* have punched him," Lopez muttered.

With my wits recovered, though, I recognized that Daemon had let go of me as soon as the lighting changed and I played Jane's death. He hadn't even missed his cue, never mind losing his head while holding me in his arms and gnawing on my neck. What had excited Daemon tonight, *far* more than biting me, was the audience's captivated reaction during that scene, followed by the wild applause, the standing ovation, and the curtain calls. That was what he was after, and being too rough with me was just a means to get it. My neck was a prop, not the real object of his appetite. His actions had been a narcissistic performance, not a seduction or an attack. And that was in keeping with all my other experience of him.

"Despite everything, I have a hard time seeing him as a murderer," I said. "I mean, murder is serious. It's for real. Whereas Daemon is such a poseur. He's just so . . . *absurd.*"

My companion, more experienced than I with such things, pointed out, "You know what a serial killer's neighbors and coworkers usually say when he's arrested? 'He seemed like such a harmless guy.'"

"Oh." I felt a chill, and I wasn't sure if it was because my neckline invited pneumonia in that drafty theater, or because of what I remembered next. "Uh, did I mention that I hit Daemon and threatened him tonight?"

Lopez gave a startled laugh. "After he bit you? Good."

"Maybe not so good," I said uneasily.

Realizing I was unnerved, he covered my clasped hands with one of his and squeezed gently. "Keep in mind that when a man preys on a lone woman, he's usually looking for an easy, vulnerable target. He wants a victim who'll be terrified and submissive, not someone who'll fight back, verbally challenge him, and turn his attack into a struggle that he risks losing."

"Oh." I was slightly reassured by this. "Daemon probably knows that leaves me out."

He grinned and released my hands. "Anyone who's ever *met* you knows that leaves you out."

"Look, you met Daemon tonight. Sort of. Did he strike you as dangerous?"

"No, he struck me as pretty absurd, too," Lopez admitted. "But impressions can be misleading, so that doesn't mean it's safe for you to be around him. Besides, his being the killer is just one of the possibilities that got me sneaking in here to talk to you now instead of going home to sleep off a thirty-hour shift."

"I have a feeling I'll regret asking this, but what other possibilities are you thinking about?"

"Well, even if Daemon's not so convinced by his own act that he went nuts and tried to be a real vampire, killing a woman in the process . . ." Lopez's hair fell into his eyes. He brushed it away. "That doesn't mean that no one *else* felt convinced enough by Daemon's crap to try it. It might be someone Angeline knew, someone she hooked up with sometime after leaving here with Daemon. Or maybe the killer is someone who's obsessed with Daemon. In which case . . ." He paused before saying, "One of the patrolmen who's been on duty here thinks that some of Daemon's fans would like to take your place—or take your character's place."

"Yeah, I'm hearing that a lot tonight."

"Some of his fans see the chemistry between you and Daemon as—"

"It's *not* between me and Daemon," I said sharply. "It's between Ruthven and Jane!" After a moment, I added, "Sorry. Sore spot."

Staying on point, he continued, "For a fan obsessed with Daemon, the *perception* of his attraction to you—or to your character—could make you a target. The person who killed a Jane look-alike, after Daemon singled her out in public last night, might be working his—or her—way up to killing the real Jane. So to speak."

"Well. I'm really glad I asked you to specify your worries for me," I said sourly. "I feel so much better now."

"It's just a theory," he said, trying to soothe me.

"It's a *theory*," I said, my voice a little shrill with anxiety, "that got you rushing over here after a thirty-hour shift, in the middle of the night, when we haven't even seen or spoken to each other for months—"

"And whose choice was *that?*" he snapped.

There was a moment of tense, surprised silence between us.

"Sorry." Lopez took a steadying breath and repeated, "Sorry. That's not what I meant to say."

"I *told* you why . . ." I felt flustered. "I mean, I *think* I told you why—"

"Let's not get sidetracked again," he said. "I didn't come here to . . . I don't want you to . . ." He let out his breath in a rush and concluded, "We need to stay focused."

"Okay." I didn't know what else to say.

Like a seasoned actor slipping back into character for the next scene, Lopez deliberately shifted gears into cop mode. "Have you noticed anyone strange hanging around the theater lately?"

I gave him an incredulous look. "Uh, *yes.*"

"Oh. Right. Let me rephrase that." He brushed black hair out of his eyes again. "Has anyone recently made you feel threatened or uncomfortable? Or seemed to be paying too much attention to you?"

"Yes," I said. "The murder victim."

"Anyone *else?*" he prodded.

"Of course." I gave him a few examples by describing the gauntlet I'd run outside the theater to get to work tonight.

"How did the mad scientist expect you to collect a sample of Daemon's semen?" Lopez demanded. "Wait. Never mind. I'm pretty sure I don't want to know."

"And when Leischneudel and I came to work *last* night," I said, "some guy dressed in a black cape jumped right into our path when we were trying to get into the theater and threatened to drink our blood. I might be able to identify him if I saw him again. His fangs didn't fit so well—they kind of wobbled, and he had a bit of a drooling problem."

"You're making me really glad I deal with criminals instead of theatergoers," Lopez said.

"These aren't theatergoers," I said. "They're vamparazzi."

"Whatzi?"

I explained the phrase, which he liked, and then I concluded, "I don't think the odds are very good of being able to spot a crazy killer in that particular crowd."

"You've got a point," he said dryly. "All right, let's talk instead about your safety. There are some rules I want you to follow until the killer is in custody."

"You mean guidelines," I said.

"No, these are *rules*, Esther. And if you break them, I promise you, we'll have the worst fight we've ever had. Because I don't want the investigating officers on this case to brief me about *your* death." When I didn't respond, he said, "Are we clear?"

He did not sound patient or soothing now. And, well, he had a point. So I said, "Yes. What are the rules?"

The list was pretty much what you'd expect. In addition to avoiding contact with Daemon when we weren't onstage, I mustn't go anywhere alone; I must be extremely cautious with vamparazzi, strangers, and mere acquaintances; and I couldn't let anyone into my apartment whom I hadn't known since before I auditioned for *The Vampyre*. Lopez agreed that Leischneudel could be an exception to this rule, since the actor wasn't a suspect and his insistence on escorting me to and from work each night dovetailed well with the "don't go anywhere alone" rule.

Lopez also suggested, with obvious ambivalence, that I consider staying with Max for a while. "Just until the killer is arrested."

I shook my head. "No, there's no place for me to sleep there."

"So bring a sleeping bag. His place is huge, isn't it? You could probably have the whole top floor to yourself."

"Ugh, no! I couldn't possibly sleep up there. That's where . . ." I froze and stopped speaking. For a moment, I stopped breathing.

"That's where *what?*" Lopez prodded.

The third floor of Zadok's Rare and Used Books, in the West Village, was where Hieronymus had lived. Max lived on the second floor and kept his laboratory in the basement. The bookstore was on the main floor.

Hieronymus had been Max's apprentice. And we had killed him.

Well, *Max* had killed him, along with the help of an out-of-town mage named Lysander. But I had helped. A lot.

It had been necessary, and I didn't regret it. Hieronymus had been malevolent, power-mad, and practically genocidal. I felt a little haunted by his death, but not sorry about it. I had also taken pains to make sure Lopez never knew what we had done. There was too much about it that he wouldn't understand—too much that the legal system, of which he was a part, wouldn't understand, either.

"What's on the third floor of Max's place?" he asked suspiciously.

Hieronymus' third-floor living quarters were sparsely furnished, and there was a bed there. But I couldn't sleep in a bedroom vacated by someone I had helped kill. I just couldn't.

I also couldn't explain the situation to Lopez. So I gave myself a mental shake and said simply, "I don't want to impose on Max."

"I don't think he'd regard it as an impos—"

"I have three locks on my front door at home. I'll use them all. I'll keep all the windows locked, too. Leischneudel will search my place at night when he takes me home. And I'll follow all your rules. Okay?"

"Call nine-one-one if there's any trouble," Lopez instructed. "*Any* trouble. And call my cell if anything at all seems a little odd or out of the ordinary to you."

"Ever since opening night, things seem odd and—"

"I mean, if you think someone in the subway is staring at you, or if you see a stranger loitering outside your apartment, or if you hear a noise at night that's probably just the building settling, *call me.* Do you understand?"

"Yes. I understand that. But there's something I don't understand," I said. "Why were *you* briefed about this case?"

He was in the Organized Crime Control Bureau. Unless Angeline's death was mob-related—and nothing Lopez had said to me indicated this—I didn't understand why an OCCB detective would be involved in this investigation. Unless . . .

I asked suddenly, "It is because of me? Because the cops know that you and I are . . . friends?"

That wasn't precisely the right word, but calling him my ex-almost-boyfriend seemed like a bit of a mouthful. And I supposed what was between us was indeed a kind of friendship.

"They *didn't* know we're . . . friends," he said, obviously unable to think of a better word, either, for our strange relationship. "But when they briefed me, I disclosed. So hopefully they'll keep in mind, when they question you, that I know you."

"So if that's not why, then why *have* you been briefed?"

"They called me after someone realized this murder could be related to the case I'm investigating," he said carefully.

Still not seeing the potential organized crime angle, I asked, "Why do they think that?"

"There are some similarities. Such as where the body was found." He shook his hair out of his eyes. It promptly fell back over them.

"Where was it found?"

He hesitated, then said, "Okay. This part's bound to be in the news, too. The body was found underground."

8

"What do you mean, underground?" I asked with a frown. "Was Angeline killed on a subway train?"

"No. She was found on an old abandoned subway platform downtown. At a station that closed about fifty years ago."

"Fifty years ago?" I blinked. "What was she doing there?"

"Nothing. There's no blood at the scene. She was killed somewhere else."

"But if she was exsanguinated . . . I mean, there wouldn't *be* blood, would there?"

"Oh, there would be a fair amount. It wasn't done with surgical tidiness." Obviously not wanting me to dwell on that, he continued, "Transit workers found her. It was just dumb luck that she was discovered so quickly. Workers seldom have a reason to access that site, and no one else is supposed to go there at all. Hardly anyone even knows the place exists. The body could have been there for weeks or months, completely decomposed—or even eaten by rodents—before anyone found it."

I gave a startled gasp of revulsion.

"Sorry." He touched me briefly in apology and gave himself a shake. "I didn't mean to . . . You know."

I realized he'd spoken so frankly because he was too exhausted to self-edit well.

"Anyhow," he continued, "this play you're in has been such a headache to the department for the past couple of nights that the officers on the scene thought of it right away when they saw the historical costume the victim was wearing. And, of course, it turned out that she'd made quite an impression on the patrolmen outside the stage door last night."

"Then they also called you because this might be connected to . . ." Even though we were alone, I lowered my voice, "To your undercover case?"

"Well, calling me was a professional courtesy. So to speak," he added, rubbing his bloodshot eyes. "Mostly, they were being thorough. Daemon Ravel's involvement will put this investigation under a microscope. The department doesn't want some telegenic celebrity lawyer to create reasonable doubt by claiming we failed to exercise due diligence or cross-reference similar cases."

With his long hair, grubby clothes, and beard-shadowed face, Lopez looked kind of scary when he scowled darkly over the prospect of that happening.

Then he continued, "But the cops who caught this case *really* like your costar for the murder. Failing that, they really like an as-yet-unknown obsessed fan for it. And their third favorite theory is that Angeline just made one bad choice too many last night. Murder is usually pretty simple, you know. So, with all those juicy possibilities right in front of them, they're inclined to think any similarities to my case are probably just . . ." He shrugged. "Coincidence. A distraction."

"What do you think?"

"I don't know yet. They need to interview Daemon and to get forensics results. And I need to go over their case more thoroughly tomorrow. Tonight, I was, uh, caught flat-footed. I only really heard what was said up until the point where they named the actress who Angeline attacked last night, and I realized *you* were the person she was dressed up like when she was killed. After that . . . everything else was just kind of a roaring in my ears."

"Oh." Despite my skimpy clothing and a noticeable draft, I felt a welcome warmth slide gently over my skin.

"So I thanked them for the information, and I asked to be updated tomorrow," Lopez said. "I also agreed to follow orders, maintain my cover, and not interfere in this investigation."

"But then you came here."

"Then I can straight here," he confirmed.

The glow was spreading all through me now. "Thank you."

He held very still while I brushed his hair out of his eyes.

"You're welcome."

My hand lingered for a moment. He closed his eyes with a soft exhalation, turned his head, and pressed his cheek against my palm.

I smiled as the stubble on his jaw tickled my skin. "You *really* need a shave."

He smiled, too, and opened his eyes. "Yeah, I guess I do."

Sitting together in the shadows, our eyes held for a contented moment.

Then Mad Rachel's voice, echoing through the whole backstage area, broke the spell. "What do you *mean* I can't leave?"

We both turned our heads to listen. I heard an unfamiliar male voice arguing with Rachel near the stage door. I couldn't make out his words. His tone was polite but firm, despite Rachel's growing hostility.

"The police? Why do the police want to talk to *me?*" After another brief interchange, she said, "Fine, *all* of us! Whatever. *Why?*" When she didn't get an explanation that satisfied her, Rachel started shrieking for our stage manager. "Bill! *Bill!* **BILL!**"

I heard more voices. Agitation began spreading through the cast and crew now. Leischneudel sounded confused and anxious. I heard Bill's voice, too. He sounded depressed.

"I think that's my cue," Lopez said wryly. "I'd better go."

"They'll see you," I said with concern. He'd had trouble at work in the past because of me; I didn't want to cause him more problems. "The cops, I mean."

"No, they won't." Looking more alert now, he rose and took my hand. "Come on. There's something I need to show you."

"Now?" I got to my feet.

"Yes. Hurry." He tugged me with him as he moved along the shadowy corridor, heading away from the commotion generated by Mad Rachel.

"Not this way," I protested softly. "It's a dead end."

"Not exactly."

"But—"

"It's the way I came in."

I frowned. "How?"

He turned the corner and, as I'd predicted, we entered a dead-end alcove. There was some cleaning equipment, a broken vending machine, and a scarred door that led down to the basement. Lopez opened the door, turned on the stairwell light, and pulled me after him.

"You came in via the *basement?*" I asked.

"And if *I* can, then maybe someone else can, too," he said.

I felt cold again. "Such as the killer?"

"I'd feel better if this building were more secure while you're working in it," he said, descending the stairs rapidly. "I'll show you how I got in, so you can show the stage manager—or whoever's responsible for this kind of thing around here—and have him seal it up."

"Slow down," I said anxiously. "This dress isn't made for scrambling up and down staircases."

"Oh, sorry." He let go of my hand so that I could use it to lift my skirts as I descended the rest of the way. I felt air on my back and realized I was still half-unlaced.

"I've never been down here before," I said as we reached the bottom of the stairs. It turned out to be pretty much what you'd expect of the basement of a sixty-year-old theater: big, dusty, industrial, shadowy, and full of air ducts, water pipes, and machinery that powered the Hamburg.

Lopez led me across the length of the large basement, into a dark alcove behind piles of junk and ancient, rusted-out machinery, and down a few more stairs— smoothly worn and slippery with time. At the bottom of the small flight of steps, set deep in this seemingly forgotten corner under the theater, there was a big, heavy, very old door. I noticed stains and rusting on its lower portion, as if there'd been occasional flooding at this level over the years.

If I weren't with someone I trusted, I'd be very nervous by now. Actually, given that a woman who was a ringer for me had recently been murdered, I would be balking and shouting for help. But since I was with Lopez, I was just surprised and curious, as well as puzzled. What did these obscure portions of the Hamburg Theater have to do with either of us?

He opened the heavy, creaking door, and I saw that it led into a pitch dark corridor. Lopez paused and bent down to pick up something—a small backpack that was sitting on the floor, next to the door. I didn't realize it belonged to him until I saw how easily the thing slid into place as he slipped the straps over his shoulders.

"You really did come in this way," I blurted.

"I thought I might be conspicuous upstairs, carrying a backpack, so I left it here. I wanted to slip in and out of the theater without anyone but you noticing I was there." He grinned at me. "Little did I know that your dressing room is as busy as Grand Central Station."

Looking at our subterranean surroundings, I said, "Sneaking into the theater from underground seems a little elaborate."

"Well, I thought I could probably get in this way."

"Why did you think *that?*"

"And it seemed easier than trying to slip discreetly past a few hundred crazed vamparazzi and a team of patrolmen who've been alerted by now to keep a sharp eye out for anyone who looks suspicious."

"Such as a scary-looking undercover cop?"

"Fine, I get the message, I'll shave," he said.

"And change your clothes?"

"That, too," he agreed absently. "Come on, we need to hurry. They'll start looking for you soon."

He reached into one of the Velcro-flapped pockets of his military-style pants, from which he pulled out a small flashlight with some straps hanging from it. Using this for illumination, he led me through the door where he'd collected his backpack, and down a long, dark corridor with a low ceiling. I tripped on the rough ground, and he took my hand again, holding onto it to steady me as we proceeded. As my eyes adjusted to the dim light, I realized that the walls were rough and unfinished, and the low ceiling was slightly curved. This wasn't a corridor, it was a tunnel.

"Where *are* we?" I asked, clutching his hand tightly.

"We're going under the street." His voice was calm, despite the eerie surroundings. "Don't worry. The structure is solid here."

"Uh-huh."

At the end of the tunnel, we emerged into a small chamber with a very high ceiling and a crumbling iron spiral staircase which, bizarrely, led nowhere. There was just a sealed wall at the top of those stairs. On our level, behind the staircase, there was a low, rusty, iron door set deep in the wall.

"Your crew could seal off the door we came through back there," Lopez said, "but I think this one would be a better choice." He rapped his knuckles on the thick, old iron door. "It's the only way into this whole area, and a little welding would seal this thing so tight, no one and nothing would get through there."

"I'll tell Bill," I promised.

"Make sure you do. It's important."

I glanced around at the strange place we were in. "I'm not likely to forget."

He smiled at that. "True."

"But this seems . . . well, kind of an improbable way for anyone to try to get into the theater."

"*I* got in this way," he reminded me.

I gestured to our underground surroundings, dark and spooky in the faint illumination of his little flashlight. "How did you even know about this?"

"That's not important right now. What *is* important—"

"Is that I tell Bill to seal up this door. Yes, yes, I know."

Lopez grunted a little as heaved open the heavy door under the spiral staircase, an effort that was accompanied by a long, loud, echoing screech of rusted hinges.

I flinched at the noise, and I thought the jarring racket would surely be heard. But then I realized we were too far away from the theater for that.

"Where exactly are we?" I asked, after the door was open and the screeching had stopped.

"Under Eighth Avenue."

"Why did someone build a cellar under Eighth Avenue?"

"This isn't a cellar," he said. "Or it wasn't, back then."

"Back when?"

"The nineteenth century." Lopez pointed to the spiral staircase. "This was originally an access chamber to the water system under the Village. For maintenance workers. The entrance from above ground was sealed off decades ago. Probably to prevent curious kids or pedestrians from getting down here and getting hurt."

I peaked through the rusted door he had pried open and looked into the stygian darkness beyond. "This was the water system?"

"Part of it. Abandoned more than a century ago. Here, have a look."

He came closer to me and raised his flashlight to my head. The straps I had noticed dangling from it touched my hair, and then he settled the light on my forehead, tightening the straps around my head to keep it steady.

That's when I realized what the device actually was. "This is a headlamp!"

"Uh-huh." He finished adjusting it on my head, then fastened the strap around my chin. "As long as we're here, you might as well see."

"See *what?*"

Lopez grinned. "A glimpse of the hidden world under the city." He took my hand again and led me to the threshold of the ancient door, leading into pitch darkness. As we ducked our heads to pass under the doorway, he said, "Watch your step. There's a little water in here."

"How much water?" I hung back, tugging against his hand.

"Not that m . . . Oh, you're worried about your costume?"

"Fiona will kill me if I ruin these shoes."

"Fiona?"

"The wardrobe mistress." The light on my forehead shone on Lopez, who was standing in pitch darkness. I could see a curved wall behind him, made of long, narrow bricks. It looked very old. Intrigued, I took one cautious step forward. "What *is* this?"

"Watch your feet," he said, gently halting me with a hand on my shoulder. "I forgot for a minute you're in

some Regency lady's shoes. Here, try this. Lean on me."
He shifted position and claimed both my hands, holding
them so that our palms were pressed together, our fingers linked. "Go ahead, lean in."

"This is like a trust exercise in acting class."

"And the fact that you're bound to fall out of that
dress if you lean forward one more inch has nothing to
do with my suggesting this."

"Oops." Realizing he was right, I hunched my shoulders a little to prevent that from happening.

He sighed. "Oh, well."

Leaning forward in this awkward posture, I let Lopez
take a lot of my weight as I turned my head this way and
that, trying to illuminate the parameters of this mysterious place with the headlamp.

The forgotten underground tunnel stretched out
darkly on either side of me, its smoothly cylindrical
shape carrying on in a straight line as far as I could see
in this faint light, gradually disappearing into complete
and intimidating blackness in both directions. The
curved ceiling was only a little higher than Lopez's head,
and a narrow, very shallow stream of water flowed
through the gently rounded brick floor at his feet.

"This is amazing!" My voice echoed eerily through
the long, empty tunnel, prompting me to call, "Helloooo!" Then I listened to the echo that bounced along
the brick walls and disappeared into the distance.
"Cool."

Lopez encouraged me to lean further in, still using his
hands for balance, so that I could see more.

I flinched a bit when I spied something creepy dangling from the tunnel ceiling in the syrupy darkness
some distance to my left. "What's *that?*"

He peered in the same direction. "Tree roots. Over
the years, they force their way through the mortar of
these old underground constructions." He added, "Even-

tually that affects structural stability and can cause problems."

"But since the tunnel's not in use anymore . . ." I started to shrug, then realized that my precarious balance, as well as my low neckline and partially undone laces, made that an unwise gesture.

"It's still not good for public safety to have things collapsing under Eighth Avenue—or anywhere else," Lopez said. "And people down here can get hurt in cave-ins."

"Who comes down *here?*" I demanded.

"Well, urban explorers, for one."

"Oh, people who explore tunnels, bridges, abandoned shipyards, and stuff? I've seen some TV programs about them."

I thought urban exploration seemed interesting—but also like a hobby I was content to know about *only* via my television. It looked dirty, uncomfortable, and dangerous, and I suspected that anyone who did it regularly probably had to get a lot of shots, since it seemed to bring people into frequent contact with garbage, sewage, rust, used syringes, industrial waste, rats, and other things I didn't want to get close to. I gathered from my TV viewing that urban exploration was also not strictly legal, since it often involved trespassing or going into places where public access was prohibited. I wasn't in a position to be smugly critical about breaking the law; but the possibility of being arrested did strike me as an additional disincentive for crawling around in polluted storm drains.

"Here, look this way," Lopez said, gesturing with his head and shifting his weight to reposition me and point my attention in the other direction, away from the eerily dangling tree roots. "Look at what I found when I was coming to see you."

I was about to ask again why he had chosen a route through abandoned underground water tunnels, rather than a more conventional path to the theater, since even trying to sneak past vamparazzi and cops struck me as less trouble than coming via this eccentric entrance, but then my attention was captured by what he was trying to show me, as he instructed me exactly where to point the light that was fastened to my head.

"Oh!" I said with surprised pleasure, leaning heavily against his supporting hands as I strained to see farther down the length of the tunnel. "Look! What *is* that?"

About thirty yards away from us, a series of long, shiny-white spires hung down from the sloping ceiling. Some of them were perfectly straight; others twisted and twined into weird, fantastic shapes. Some were very short and thick, while others were slender and almost long enough to touch the tunnel floor. They gleamed beautifully in the faint light of my headlamp, glistening like stony icicles, as if dotted with glitter or tiny shards of crystal.

"They're stalactites." I could hear in his voice that he was pleased with my enthusiastic reaction to this surprise. "There's a lot of stuff under the city that's abandoned or forgotten, but none of it is stagnant or dead. It's constantly changing. Those crystal formations developed over decades down here. They'll keep growing for centuries if they're left undisturbed."

"Growing how?" I tilted my head from side to side, enjoying the way the shifting light made the dangling formations glitter.

"Water drips down from the street and the ground above us, through layers of soil and sediment, picking up mineral deposits along the way," he replied. "Those stalactites are formed by years and years of that water creating tiny cracks in the tunnel ceiling and leaving behind microscopic deposits from every drop that falls. Until you get *that*."

"*Wow.*"

"Yeah." After a moment he added, "And it's all right

under our feet every day, while we're walking around the city."

I looked at the beautiful shapes for another moment, then asked, "If you came here this way, where did you come *from?* How did you get into this tunnel in the first place?"

"Oh, there's a whole maze of entrances and exits. This tunnel hasn't been in active use for over a hundred years, but it links up that way—" He nodded in one direction. "—with the steam tunnels under New York University." Then he nodded in the other direction. "And it connects that way with a portion of the old covered canal under Canal Street. If you know where you're going, you can link up with the storm drains for this part of the city, too, or with part of the old sewage system."

"Ah. With attractions like *that,* no wonder you didn't just use the street entrance to visit me."

Lopez smiled. "Well, apart from not wanting to be seen, since I'm not supposed to be here, I wanted to check this out. To see if it looked like anyone else has been using this entrance."

"And what's your conclusion?"

He shrugged, which made me lose my balance. Preventing me from falling, he helped me stand solidly on my own feet again. Then he stepped out of the tunnel and joined me on dry ground in the access chamber. "I can't tell whether anyone's been here. But I'd have felt better if the door had been rusted shut when I tried to get in tonight."

"This really doesn't seem like a place where you'd want to find the exit blocked," I said as I removed the headlamp and returned it to him.

"Oh, I could have just doubled back until I reached a different exit. And then I'd have tried to slip into the theater some other way." He shook his head. "But the fact that the door's still working . . . Well, it doesn't really tell me anything. Except that I want you to make sure it gets welded shut."

"I still don't understand how you even knew this door was here. I mean, I work here, and I didn't know any of this underground stuff was attached to the theater. And I'll bet when I show it to Bill, he'll be surprised, too. So how did *you* . . . Oh."

I looked him over head-to-toe again as it all started coming together in my mind. Lopez had just revealed an unusual level of familiarity with the physical underbelly of the city, and he had come here via abandoned underground tunnels. I remembered him telling me this past summer, when we had visited a crumbling nineteenth-century watchtower together in Harlem, that he'd always been interested in such places and was prone to poking around in them. And tonight, I now realized, he was dressed and equipped much like the people I saw on TV programs about shimmying down manholes and crawling through forgotten drains and sewers.

"Does your undercover case have something to do with urban explorers?" I asked slowly.

"Something," he said.

"So you . . . you . . ." I gestured vaguely to the tunnel. "Do *that?*"

"I used to. In high school and college. I pretty much gave it up when I became a cop, since it's not exactly legal—especially not since the attacks of nine-eleven. There's been heightened security ever since then." He started leading me back the way we had come here. "We've stayed down here too long. They've probably looked all over the theater for you by now."

"So now you're doing this as undercover work?" I persisted.

"Well, I'm not a creeper anymore, but Hector Sousa is."

"Creeper?" I repeated, following him into the dark but dry tunnel that had led us to this access chamber.

"Someone who goes where he's not supposed to go."

"Like an urban explorer?"

"Uh-huh. Here, watch your step." He took my hand to lead me back through the dark tunnel that ran under the street the Hamburg was on, using the headlamp as a flashlight again. "My first assignment after I got out of uniform was on an antiterrorism task force, working undercover. There was a lot of anxiety at the time about urban explorers wandering around abandoned sites and installations, both underground and above ground, without supervision or authorization. Who exactly were they? What were they doing? What were their intentions? Had they been infiltrated by anyone whose intentions *weren't* innocent? And so on. So the department created an identity for me—"

"As Hector, a man with no razor?"

"—and I made contact with urban explorer groups in the city, going into the field with them—which mostly meant going underground at night—and looking for terrorist activity."

"Did you find any terrorists?"

"That's classified."

"Oh. Of course."

"But it was a big waste of time." He added, "Don't ever tell anyone I said that, though."

"Who would I tell?"

"At first, it was kind of fun, since I was getting paid to do things that I used to do as a hobby. But I don't really like undercover work. You're isolated from other cops, and you have to lie to everyone all the time—the people in your real life, as well as the people you're investigating." We exited the tunnel and entered the Hamburg's basement through the heavy door at the bottom of the short flight of old steps. "And since my investigations weren't finding anything worth reporting, I felt pretty silly and useless after a while. So I started pressing for reassignment, until I finally got it."

"But now they've convinced you to do it again?"

"I was approached a few weeks ago and asked if I could re-establish some of my old contacts and activities in the urban explorer community. Same identity, different kind of case. And the OCCB agreed to, um, loan me out for a little while."

So evidently Lopez's changed appearance since the last time we'd met was the result of spending a lot of time underground in recent weeks, as well as assuming Hector's identity.

"You're not looking for terrorists this time?" I asked.

"I'm not supposed to discuss what I'm looking for," he said as we passed through the basement, heading toward the big staircase that would lead me back up to the theater—where NYPD cops were probably already questioning my fellow actors.

"But your case has similarities to last night's vampire victim?" I prodded.

"Vampire victim," he repeated, looking pained. "You just couldn't resist using that phrase, could you?"

"Well, she did have all her blood dr—"

"You've been hanging around the vamparazzi too long."

"I *don't* hang around with them."

"Then maybe *playing* a vampire victim every night has affected your judgment."

"My judgment is . . ." I realized that he had just deliberately steered me away from the subject of his investigation—and was trying to irritate me enough that I wouldn't notice the ploy. Which made me even more curious, naturally, about what he was investigating that might be related to Angeline's death. "You said one of the reasons they briefed you on last night's murder was because of where the body was found."

"You should go upstairs now," he said firmly. "They'll be looking for you."

"Underground."

"Your friend Licenoodle will be worried."

I ignored this obvious attempt to distract me. "What are you investigating underground that—"

"Esther."

I gasped as the most horrifying possibility occurred to me. "There've been other victims, haven't there?"

For a moment, his expression went so carefully blank that I knew he was considering lying to me. Then his shoulders sagged and he said, with obvious reluctance, "Maybe."

"Maybe?" I repeated shrilly.

He sighed in weary resignation. "In the past couple of months, three bodies have been found in . . . unusual underground locations."

"Three murder victims?" I exclaimed.

"One may have been natural causes."

"*May* have been?"

"There, uh, aren't enough remains for us to be sure."

"Oh." I queasily recalled what he had said earlier about the effects of decomposition and hungry rodents. Then I demanded, "And the other two bodies?"

He hesitated, then nodded. "Murder."

"Were they exsanguinated?" Seeing that he didn't want to answer me, I prodded sharply, "Well?"

"Try to stay calm."

"Lopez!"

"We've kept this out of the press. No one knows the details. And it has to stay that way. Do you understand?"

"Yes, yes, go on," I said impatiently.

"The bodies of two missing urban explorers have been found at other abandoned underground locations."

"Drained of all their blood?" I asked anxiously.

"Not exactly."

"What does *that* mean?"

Looking very tired again, he said, "Only *some* of their blood was drained."

9

"**Y**ou weren't going to tell me this, were you?" I said accusingly.

"I'm not *supposed* to tell you this," he pointed out, obviously clinging to his fraying patience.

"You've got vampire victims littering the landscape, I could be next, and you weren't going to *tell* me about this?" I was working up a head of steam now.

He rubbed his forehead as if it ached. "I should never have tried to talk to you when I haven't slept in . . . I don't know how long. That was my first mistake—thinking I could deal with you when I'm half-dead."

Warming to my theme, I demanded, "And what's wrong with your colleagues, that they're doubtful about the connection between exsanguinated murder victims recently found underground and last night's murder? Are they gibbering idiots?"

"My next mistake was thinking I could talk to you at *all*," Lopez said with morose self-condemnation. "Even if I'd gotten some sleep first. At what point did I think this might go *well?* Where was my head?"

"A vampire's stalking the city, and you didn't think this was worth mentioning to me?"

"Why would I mention it to you?" he demanded,

his volume rising. "Just because you're in a vampire play?"

"Well . . . Um . . ." Actually, when he it put it that way, I realized there might be a flaw in my logic. Which didn't stop me from saying, "You should have told me!"

"Told you *what?*" He clutched his skull as if it was really pounding now. "Esther, there is *not* a vampire stalking the . . . There's no such *thing* as . . . Just because the victims have been . . ." He scrubbed his hands through his hair. "No. Wait. *Stop.*" Lopez took a very deep breath. And another. Then he lowered his hands and said with almost epic calm, "We can't talk about this now. You have to go upstairs and answer police questions. And I have to go home and die."

"What?"

"Or at least get some sleep."

Actually, he did look ready to keel over. I took a deep breath, too. "Okay. Yes. You're right. I'll go talk to the cops. And pretend we haven't had this conversation. You go home and . . . shave. Seriously."

"You don't get to nag someone you're not dating," he snapped.

"We'll talk again tomorrow."

"I can't tell you how much I'm looking forward to it."

I overlooked his needlessly sarcastic tone and turned my back to him. I said over my shoulder, "Since I have to go face your colleagues now, could you please lace me back up? I don't want the rest of the NYPD to become this familiar with my underwear."

"Fine." He came closer.

"It works pretty much like shoelaces," I said helpfully.

"Uh-huh." He yanked the sides of my gown together over my chilly back and started tightening and pulling on the laces, his touch impatient and impersonal.

"Careful," I chided. "If you tear something, I'll get in big trouble. The wardrobe mistress doesn't like me."

"Oh?" He yanked again, obviously still annoyed with me. "Why ever *not?*"

"The first time I wore this costume, I asked for more clothes."

That startled a laugh out of him. His touch gentled, and I could hear a modicum of good humor returning to his voice as he said, "Well, I have to admit, given what you're wearing, I can't understand why there aren't a lot more *men* coming to see this show."

"Daemon is onstage a lot more than my neckline is," I said dryly as Lopez finished tying the back of my dress.

At the mention of my leading man, he put his hands firmly on both of my shoulders and gave me a gentle squeeze. "It's so late," he said. "After they question you, make sure the cops send you home in a squad car, okay?"

I felt his breath on my neck as his hands stroked down my bare arms. I closed my eyes. "Okay."

"I'm . . ."

"Hmm?" I leaned back a little, trying to get closer to him without doing anything overt.

"I'm sorry. About . . ." His hands moved on me. Comforting. Arousing. "I didn't want to scare you. I just want you to be safe."

"I know." My voice felt weak. So did my knees. I sank against him, my back melting into the sturdy wall of his chest.

It was only for a few seconds, I promised myself. I'd move away from him in an instant. But first, I needed . . . Well, it had just been too long since I had been near him like this.

Lopez lowered his head to rest his cheek against my hair as he tightened his grip on me. He released his breath on a long, slow exhalation. We stood together silently, his body solid against mine as I gratefully soaked up his heat . . . and felt dizzily aware of a growing desire to soak up a lot more than that. Remembering that I had decided to give him up rather than get him killed was a lot easier to keep firmly in mind when he wasn't touching me. Or speaking to me. Or within a mile of me.

I was trying to summon up the will to pull myself out of his grasp when he turned me slightly toward him. My breath trembled in my throat, my blood humming in anticipation of what he might do next. He moved one hand from my arm so that he could trace a finger alongside the rising welt on my neck.

I drew in a sharp breath, excited by his touch.

"Does this still hurt?" His voice was low and soft.

"Um . . ." I'd forgotten about the bite on my neck. And now that Lopez had reminded me of it with his gently tickling touch . . . All I could think about, actually, was the feel of his hands on me, his body warming me, the soft caress of his breath on my hair . . . and the quickening rise and fall of his chest as he held me. I had no idea if my neck hurt, but the exultant pounding of my heart sure did.

The heavy thudding in my chest brought me to my senses. The sound of my own heartbeat reminded me that I wanted *his* heart to go on beating, too.

"Be honest with yourself, Esther," the vicious killer had said to me that fatal night in Harlem, having left Lopez to die alone in the dark. *"Would he be lying in agonized paralysis awaiting his death now if not for you?"*

Fueled by remembered horror, guilt, and grief, I summoned every bit of willpower I possessed, and I stepped away from him. "I have to go upstairs."

In an effort to conceal my chaotic feelings, I wound up sounding curt. He heard it and immediately removed his hands from me.

"Right. Yes." He cleared his throat. "Remember what I said. Don't lie to the cops about anything, but be discreet about what we've discussed."

"I will." I met his dark-lashed eyes, blue and bloodshot and a little brooding now. Then I looked away again. "Thank you for coming here to warn me even though you weren't supposed to get involved."

He didn't say anything. Maybe he was remembering,

as I was, that he'd done more extreme things than this for me in the past—including lie to his superiors, conceal evidence, and falsify reports. Which had a lot to do with why he'd broken up with me in the first place. That wasn't the kind of cop he wanted to be, and seeing himself as an honest and honorable police officer was closely entwined with how he saw himself as a man, too.

Finally he said, "I'd better leave."

When he turned around and went the way we had just come, I said, "You're really going back there?" I knew he didn't want to be seen, but the underground passages still struck me as a dark, scary, and damp way to make his exit.

"I like the tunnels," he said, walking away without looking back, his shoulders slumped with fatigue. "It's quiet down there."

"Sure," I muttered, lifting my skirts as I turned to climb the stairs back up to the theater. "Very quiet. Except for a vampire prowling around, draining people of their—"

"I *heard* that," Lopez said irritably.

I exited the basement without encountering anyone. As soon as I closed the door softly behind me, though, I heard a terrible wailing that seemed to penetrate the very walls of the building. Someone was sobbing and screeching with the uninhibited passion of a toddler, but this person sounded a little older than that, if not necessarily more mature.

Following the tooth-jarring noise of Mad Rachel's wails of rage and anguish, I made my way toward the dressing rooms. I arrived to find that the area was jammed with people; the cast, the crew, Al Tarr, Victor, and a number of cops were all present.

Mad Rachel was inside our dressing room with the door closed. Between sobs, she screeched, *"I want Eric! I want my mamma!"* And also: *"Don't touch that!"*

I heard someone else in the room trying to reason with her; someone who sounded stressed-out and exasperated. A cop assigned to the hapless task of questioning her, I guessed. Whatever he said, it was followed by full-volume ranting from Rachel, the gist of which seemed to be that the police were horrible people and she hated them.

Bill was standing in a corner, deep in conversation with a uniformed cop, his face morose. Victor was pacing just outside the closed door of Daemon's dressing room, wringing his hands and muttering to himself. Leischneudel was with him, trying to persuade Victor to take a sip of water. The actor dropped the water bottle when he saw me. It hit the floor with a thud, startling Victor, and rolled away.

"Esther!" Leischneudel cried with obvious relief. "I thought you'd left without me."

"Ah, there's the missing actress," Tarr said casually, to no one in particular.

Leischneudel ran toward me, but a tall stranger in a dark coat got in the way, saying, "Esther Diamond?"

Behind him, Leischneudel was waving his arms and grimacing at me.

"Yes," I said.

"We've looked all over for you." Without even glancing behind him, the man moved smoothly to block Leischneudel's path when the actor tried to get around him to reach me. "Where have you been?"

"Who are you?" My gaze flashed to the gold badge he was wearing in plain view. "And what's going on here?"

"Esther, you won't believe what's happened!" Hovering behind the tall detective, Leischneudel's face and tone reflected appalled shock.

"I'm Detective Branson, NYPD." The cop's gaze fastened on my neck, and I realized he was looking at the bite mark Daemon had left there. "I need to ask you some questions."

I looked around with an air of alarmed bewilderment. "About what?"

"Esther!" Leischneudel exclaimed. "Jane has been m—"

"Please wait over there, sir," Detective Branson interrupted him, pointing to a chair about ten feet away without taking his gaze off my neck. "I need to speak with Miss Diamond."

Leischneudel was hopping around behind him, trying to get my attention. In a moment of lapsed judgment, the actor clutched his throat, stuck out his tongue, and crossed his eyes.

Branson turned around and looked at him. Perhaps due to his years on the police force, he didn't react to Leischneudel's grotesque pantomime. "*Now,* sir."

"Jane's been murdered!" my friend cried, abandoning his attempt at simulating violent death. "The one who attacked you last night!"

"Murdered?" I repeated.

"She hath been most foully slain!" Seeing our expressions, Leischneudel forced himself to taking a calming breath. "Sorry. That just slipped out."

"Is there somewhere private we can talk?" Branson asked me. "Such as your dressing room?"

I pointed at the door that was practically vibrating under the assault of Mad Rachel's shrieking wails. "She and I share that room."

A spasm briefly crossed Branson's face. "Okay, not in your dressing room then."

"Jane's been *murdered?*" I said.

"Her name wasn't Jane," Branson said wearily, evidently having already learned why we called the victim that.

"But she's been murdered?"

"She's been found dead." Branson used the dogged tone of one trying to get control of the conversation. "And I have some questions for you. Starting with, where have you been for the past twenty minutes?"

"The bathroom."

He shook his head. "We looked for you the bath-room."

"The one in the lobby," I specified, hoping they hadn't searched that far afield for me.

The cop frowned. "Why were you *there?*"

The volume of Rachel's sobs increased until I could have sworn the door was rattling. I nodded toward it. "I was avoiding *her.*"

My explanation evidently satisfied Branson, since he moved on. "I understand that you and Adele Olson met last night?"

"Who?"

"The victim."

"She's been *murdered?*" I repeated.

"Please answer the question, Miss Diamond."

"What was the question?"

"Did you meet the victim last night?"

"Not exactly. And you know," I said seriously, "she might not be dead now if you people had arrested her, the way I asked you to."

I thought I saw a vein pulsing in Branson's forehead as he said, "Tell me about your encounter last night with Adele Ol—"

"Oh, my God!" Leischneudel gasped, startling both of us. He pointed toward my heels. "What happened to your dress? Fiona will kill you!"

Branson frowned. "Remind me who Fiona is."

"Something's happened to my dress?" The last thing I needed, considering everything else that was going on, was trouble with the wardrobe mistress. "Oh, *no.*"

"Miss Diamond—"

"Here, look." Leischneudel lifted the back of my skirt while I twisted around to see what he was trying to show me. I discovered that my recent subterranean sojourn had left a dark smudge on the hem of my white gown. Fortunately, it didn't look like a permanent stain; but Fiona would snark at me about it, even so. "Damn."

Bending to look at the damage reminded me of how tortuously uncomfortable my corset had become by now. I said absently, "I need to take off my clothes."

"What?" said Detective Branson.

"The worst part, Esther," Leischneudel said urgently, "is that the cops think Jane was killed by a vampire."

"We do *not* think—"

"You can't keep me here!" Rachel screeched inside our dressing room. "Equity will hear about this! You'll never work in this town again!"

"Actors." Branson looked like he had inherited Lopez's headache.

The door to Daemon's dressing room opened, and all eyes turned in that direction. The *Vampyre* star emerged, preceded by a uniformed cop and followed by a female detective.

As soon as he saw me, Daemon said, "Esther! Tell them I didn't really mean it!" His pale face was tense and strained, his normally seductive voice taut and panicky. "Tell them it was just part of the play! *Tell* them."

My hand flew to my neck, my palm covering the telltale welt there. The melodramatic gesture was reflexive, not intentional. But everyone in the hallway stopped speaking and stared at me. I could feel all eyes fixated on the bite mark I was instinctively covering with my palm. Obviously, the incident onstage had already been a subject of interest in the police interviews.

"Esther," Daemon said desperately.

I looked at my handsome costar: vain, self-absorbed, ambitious, and deeply mired in his fame-seeking masquerade. Even if I could picture him murdering a girl (and I still didn't see it), could I imagine him prowling around in dark, dank, dirty underground tunnels to hide her body? Or to prey on other victims?

I stared mutely at Daemon, simply unable to envision him in that role.

Yet another cop came out of Daemon's dressing

room. He held up one of the little bottles from the refrigerator and said to the female detective near Daemon, "It sure *seems* like blood. The same stuff's in the
other bottle that's in the fridge, too."

"Oh, it's blood, all right," said Tarr, taking notes. "I
could've told you that."

Daemon snapped at him, "You're not helping, Al."

The female detective looked at Tarr with open dis-
like. She did not, however, confiscate his notebook. Tarr
was presumably a witness in the case, since he'd left here
last night with Daemon and Angeline. And Lopez had
said that Daemon's involvement would put this investigation under a spotlight. So maybe the cops figured that
trying to prevent Tarr from writing about tonight would
just be a fruitless effort. It would also presumably ensure that he wrote incendiary commentaries about the
police stifling freedom of the press in an attempt to conceal how they were bungling the investigation.

No wonder Lopez liked the underground tunnels.
There were no tabloid reporters, photographers, or
groupies down there.

"When will you release pictures of the stiff?" Tarr
asked the policewoman, still writing in his notebook.

"We won't." She raised her voice to be heard above
the sound of Rachel's persistent screaming and crying.
"Can't someone convince that woman to calm *down?*"

"Lotsa luck with that," Tarr said. "Noisiest broad in
the world. High-strung, too."

The policewoman said to Branson, "Maybe we should
send her home."

Everyone in the hallway nodded vigorously in response to this suggestion.

Except for Detective Branson, who shook his head with
manifest regret. "We haven't been able to get a statement
yet. Well, not one that's of any use. And I think we really
need it tonight. *Before* tabloid goons have a chance to start
planting absurd ideas and false impressions in her head."

"Hey, I take that as an insult," said Tarr.

"Good," said Branson.

"I want Eric!" Rachel screeched.

"Will getting ahold of this Eric person calm her down?" the frustrated lady detective asked, also looking a bit headachy now.

"Not that I've ever observed," I said.

"When I was in Hollywood," Tarr said, "this *really big* star I was covering—I probably shouldn't say who, since he was married—was sleeping with a girl like Rachel, and there was this one time—"

"Not now, Mr. Tarr," the policewoman said.

"Come on, you *gotta* release photos of the corpse," Tarr said without missing a beat. "I mean, this is great stuff!"

We all glared at him with varying degrees of revulsion.

"What?" he said, looking around at us. After a moment, he shrugged. "Just doing my job." He went back to scribbling in his notebook.

The Exposé would have a field day with this murder. The case was one more reason, I realized, that I (and anyone else with taste or sound judgment) should avoid Tarr.

"I hear that freelancers were at the scene, anyhow," Tarr said. "So we're gonna run photos from *someone,* even if you guys won't play ball."

Ignoring the reporter, the detective said to her colleague, "Get those two bottles from the fridge over to the lab. We need both of their contents analyzed as soon as possible."

"Both?" I repeated with a frown. "Two?"

There'd been about half a dozen bottles in that fridge at the start of the evening. I had dropped only one, so there certainly ought to be more than two bottles still in there now. Unless . . . My gaze flew to Daemon and my jaw dropped.

"My God," I said in disgust. "You really *do* drink blood between shows!"

"You're not helping, either," he said darkly.

Detective Branson gestured to my neck. "How exactly did you get this bite mark, Miss Diamond?"

I met the cop's intent gaze as Rachel howled from behind the closed door, *"We're all going to DIE!"*

Branson's cell phone rang, and he reached inside his coat pocket. "Excuse me for moment."

He winced at Rachel's next piercing shriek and put one hand over his ear as he pressed his cell phone against the other ear. He spoke with his caller only long enough to tersely exchange some information. Then he nodded to the female detective as he ended the call. "They've found more of those bottles at his home. They've also found, er, a coffin."

She absorbed this, then said to Daemon, "All right. Let's go, sir."

I looked at Daemon again. "Are you under arrest?"

"Not yet," he said wearily. "But the night is young."

"Actually, it's nearly four o'clock in the morning," said the lady detective. "And we still have quite a lot to talk about. So let's get moving."

Daemon's shoulders sagged. "Victor."

"Yes?" The hand-wringing personal assistant looked like he was trying not to cry.

"Call my lawyer."

"Of course! Right away."

"No, better still, go to his place, get him out of bed, and bring him to . . . to . . ." Daemon looked at the detective.

"Manhattan South." She handed a business card to Victor as she said, "Your employer has declined to answer any more questions without a lawyer present. The sooner the attorney meets us there, the sooner we can proceed." Then she gestured in the direction of the stage door. "Is it still a madhouse out there?"

"*Yes,*" Branson and a uniformed officer said simultaneously.

"Is there a less conspicuous exit from this place?" she asked with a touch of exasperation.

I thought of the tunnels, but I doubted that was the sort of exit she meant.

Bill offered to show her to the fire exit, which was on the other side of the stage. She spoke into a police radio, asking for an unmarked car to come collect Daemon outside that door. For the first time since I'd met him, the celebrity vampire seemed to favor a discreet departure, too. Although not under arrest—not yet, anyhow—he nonetheless looked like a prisoner as he was escorted out of here by the woman detective and two stern-faced patrolmen.

As Rachel continued sobbing at full volume, I squirmed uncomfortably, trying to relieve the irritation of the corset wires poking into my breasts. I turned toward my dressing room, anxious, exhausted, and eager to go home. Then I saw Detective Branson's face and realized I'd be here a while longer.

Indeed, another hour passed before Leischneudel and I finally made our way to the stage door, wearing our street clothes and carrying our belongings. Detective Branson had agreed, at my request, to have a squad car take us home. My bruised face was scrubbed clean, and I was limp with fatigue. Leischneudel was still so overwrought by the news of the murder, he was hollow-eyed and babbling nervously.

Detective Branson had asked me a lot of questions about Daemon, his behavior, and the biting incident onstage. He'd also asked me a lot about the murder victim, focusing so much on my "interaction" with her and my "attitude" to her that I got exasperated. I discovered, not for the first time, that I was less sensitive and caring than a man expected me to be. For all that I readily acknowledged that the murder of a young woman was a dreadful tragedy, I nonetheless found the detective's implications that I ought to feel more emotionally invested in Angeline's death nonsensical—and also annoying.

"My entire 'relationship' with the victim," I'd wound up snapping at him, "consisted of her knocking me down and punching me. Yes, *obviously,* I'm sorry that she died young, and I find the manner of her death extremely disturbing. But, no, of course I'm not *upset,* detective. Why would I get emotional over the death of total stranger who assaulted me during the two whole minutes that I was acquainted with her?"

Well, after that outburst, the rest of the interview was tense, even hostile. I sincerely hoped Branson wouldn't follow through on his threat to question me again at a later date.

With my nerves frayed, my eyes stinging with fatigue, and my shoulders drooping, I followed Leischneudel through the stage door and was immediately greeted outside by the staccato brightness of flashing bulbs and the excited cries of vamparazzi.

I squinted against the camera lights going off in my face and making my tired eyes water. "They're still here? It's nearly five in the morning!"

"Where's Daemon?" someone in the crowd shouted. "We want Daemon!"

A uniformed cop approached me. "Miss Diamond?"

"Yes."

"There's a squad car coming to take you home. It'll pull up to the curb any minute now."

"Thank you, officer."

There were police barricades blocking off this area now, providing us with a mercifully clear path to where the car would collect us. Eager fans leaned forward, hanging over the barricades, some of them smiling and shouting at Leischneudel, clamoring for his autograph. He seized my arm, clutching me tightly and avoiding eye contact with the vamparazzi.

Despite the predawn chill of early November, many of the women out here were in revealing outfits, with deep V-necks, slit skirts, bare shoulders, and lacy sleeves. I wondered if their ghostly white faces and dark-blue lips were due to goth makeup or to hypothermia. Predictably, there were also a number of Janes waiting out here—but at least one of them had given in to a shred of common sense and donned a coat over her flimsy white gown. There were also scary-monster creatures, guys in leather jackets, women in velvet capes, photographers, and more cops than usual. I looked around for Dr. Hal's little trio, but they seemed to have gone. All things considered, that was a relief.

Neither of the uniformed cops stationed at the stage door looked familiar to me. They weren't the two officers who had declined to arrest Angeline last night. I wondered if those men had been taken off this assignment because of the tragic outcome of that decision. However, for all that Angeline might indeed still be alive now if she'd been locked up after assaulting me, the cops on the scene couldn't possibly have foreseen what would happen when they let her go. No one could.

No one but the killer.

I shivered as a dark chill swept through me.

The crowd was now chanting, "Dae-mon! Dae-mon! Dae-mon!"

The cop who had previously spoken to me said, "We tried to tell these people that Mr. Ravel is gone." He shook his head. "Like reasoning with the sea."

"Welcome to my world, officer," I replied. "I don't suppose you've seen the play?"

"At three-fifty a ticket? Are you kidding?"

Leischneudel, who was still clinging anxiously to me, heard this. "*That's* what the scalpers are getting now?"

"It was, as of midnight tonight." The cop added cynically, "If the show doesn't close, the price will go even higher."

Leischneudel and I exchanged a glance, both suddenly realizing that *The Vampyre*'s remaining run depended entirely on whether Daemon was arrested or released. This obvious fact hadn't occurred to me before now. We didn't even know if we still had jobs.

"Ah, here's your ride," said the cop as a squad car pulled up to the curb. He took my elbow to escort me to the vehicle, while Leischneudel stuck like a burr to my other side.

"Wait, Aubrey!" someone cried.

"They're leaving!"

"*Aubrey!* Over here!"

In their eagerness to claim his attention before he got into the car, several shouting fans leaned precariously far over the police barricade while reaching for Leischneudel. Then one of them, perhaps so sleep-deprived by now that all sense of reality had deserted her, started trying to climb over the dense crowd, apparently intent on hurdling the barricade. She flung herself forward, her weight and momentum carrying the whole mass of bodies beneath her forward, too. The angle of their combined, top-heavy weight toppled the barricade, which fell over with a thunderous crash. The noise was accompanied by the shrieks and howls of tumbling vamparazzi, some of them probably in a bit of pain now, others just startled or alarmed.

The two cops with us rushed forward to help the fallen fans and sort out the writhing heap of arms, legs, wings, fangs, and leather. While their attention was wholly focused on that, several Janes scrambled over the pile of bodies and rushed straight at me with maddened expressions on their faces.

"Esther!" Leischneudel cried in alarm. "Watch out!"

I barely had time to drop my tote bag and cover my head with my arms before the well-dressed Regency ladies started pummeling me. Too stunned to scream for help, I uttered breathless grunts of fear and confusion as

I fell to the dirty ground and curled up in a defensive ball while they punched and kicked me.

I heard Leischneudel shouting, and I sensed he was scuffling with the Janes. I risked opening my eyes and peeking through my elbows, which where positioned to shield my face. I saw more daintily slippered feet running toward me—and then I felt even more weight piling on top of me.

"Stop!" Leischneudel shouted at them. *"Stop!"*

"Get her! *Get* her!" one of the Janes cried.

Get me? Why? WHY? What have I *done?* I thought.

"Out of my way!" To my relief, a sturdy Jane plucked a skinny one off me and shoved her aside. But then Sturdy Jane took her place and started pummeling me.

"Go away! She's mine!" another Jane cried. "*I'm* the one going home with Daemon tonight!"

"No, *I'm* going home with him!"

Sitting on top of me, these two Janes starting shoving furiously at each other.

Oh, good God, Leischneudel had been *right*. After last night's incident, now these girls thought that attacking me was the way to get laid by Daemon! Maniacally deluded about the link between cause and effect, *that* was why they had suddenly jumped me when they saw their chance tonight.

This was all Daemon's fault. If he wasn't arrested for murder, then I would have to kill him.

But I could only do that, it occurred to me as someone tried to pound my head into the pavement, if I lived through this.

"*I'm* going home with him!" another Jane shrieked, trying to bite my left knee.

I found it hard to believe that sex with *anyone* could be worth all this, let alone sex with a self-absorbed actor.

I kneed that girl in the face—and I found that I felt much better when I heard her shriek in pain.

Okay, my interval as a cowering victim was officially *over* now.

"*Off!* Get off!" I barked at the Janes. Or I tried. I could barely breathe.

Utterly enraged now, and finding this feeling vastly preferable to being frightened and bewildered, I started trying to uncurl from my defensive posture so I could fight back and give these lunatic girls the black eyes and bloody lips they damn well deserved. However, getting out of my fetal position was harder than I had anticipated, since I was by now at the bottom of a pile-on that, as near as I could tell, consisted of half the female population of New York.

I still couldn't breathe, and I realized that I was going to faint—or worse—if I didn't get some air pretty soon.

The prospect of suffocating to death beneath a bunch of squealing, lust-crazed vampire groupies all wearing *my* costume was so appalling, it lent unholy strength to my limbs. I started heaving, kicking, and elbowing the girls, grunting with effort, desperately sucking in quick gasps of air when possible, as I struggled to fling the Janes off me.

"Ow! She's like an *animal!*" one of them complained when my elbow hit her in the gut.

"Off!" I snarled—though it came out more like an inarticulate gurgle.

"Help! Officers!" Leischneudel shouted, still trying to fight off my attackers. Then I heard a fleshy thudding sound. Leischneudel grunted in pain, collapsed, and fell down next to me, his hands clutching his groin reflexively as he lay on his back. *"Ow."*

"Lei . . ." I croaked breathlessly.

A plump Jane fell on top of him, her butt landing squarely on his solar plexus. He appeared to black out then.

To my relief, I heard a shrill police whistle pierce

through the cacophony. Then male voices shouted with reassuring force and authority. I saw large, sensibly shod feet approaching me swiftly, then I felt heavy weights being removed from my body. I was gratefully drawing in huge gulps of air when a pair of strong hands seized me by the shoulders and helped me sit up.

"Miss Diamond! Are you all right?" the rescuing cop asked me anxiously.

I nodded, still gulping down air.

"Are you sure?" he prodded.

Able to speak now, I said, "I want them arrested! *All* of them! Do you hear me?"

This wasn't an attempt to prevent them from following in Angeline's tragic footsteps. I just wanted them all to stew in jail while they contemplated the sin of attacking an innocent actress.

"Arrested!" I repeated. "I want them to have criminal records! Rap sheets! Legal expenses!" I realized I was shouting. I took another breath and said less hysterically, "They deserve to be arrested for this."

"Yes, ma'am. Absolutely. We're taking care of it."

Then I gasped as I recalled that my gallant defender was lying wounded on the pavement. "Leischneudel!"

I turned and scooted over to him. Another cop was tending him. His eyes were open, but the cop was advising him not to sit up just yet. I glanced around and saw that other cops were getting the chaotic scene under control. I was glad to see that quite a few of the vamparazzi obviously disapproved of the Janes assaulting me, and they seemed to be helping the police round them up. The rest of the fans were voluntarily retreating back behind the barricades, noisy but orderly. Some of them started calling out concerned questions, wanting to know if Leischneudel and I were okay.

"Maybe you shouldn't get up just yet, sir," said one of the cops as Leischneudel began trying to rise.

"No, no, I'll be all right." He reached for me, and I

helped him climb slowly to his feet. He stood there for a moment, using me for balance, his posture a little bit hunched over. His face was still strained, but he nodded after a moment. "I'm okay. It's just always kind of a shock to the system when that happens. You know what I mean?"

The two cops nodded vigorously.

Leischneudel took a deep breath and smiled wanly. "I'd really like to go home now."

"Of course."

As we helped Leischneudel walk gingerly toward the squad car, the cop who'd spoken to me earlier said, "With such an exciting show out here, I don't know why anyone would pay three-fifty just to see the *play*."

"Indeed." Another flashbulb went off in my face. "Heigh ho, the glamorous life."

10

Lopez was nibbling delicately on my neck, the wet heat of his mouth seductive and sultry. His lush lips caressed my sensitive skin, and his teeth nipped just hard enough to hurt me a little—in that *good* way.

"I missed you," I whispered, wanting to weep with longing. "I tried so hard to be strong, but now that you're here, I . . ."

I . . . actually, I couldn't remember how he had gotten here. Or why he was here. I also didn't know where "here" was.

But I didn't really care. His arms were around me, his hands moving over my body, his tongue stroking and teasing me . . .

I gasped when he shoved me down onto the bed. He followed me down to the mattress, his solid weight deliciously heavy on me, his touch rough and ruthless as he imprisoned my hands over my head and started kissing me with reckless hunger.

"He's really not *the altar boy he pretends to be, is he?"*

"What?" I said, startled by the sound of a woman's voice here in my bedroom—ironic, cold, a little malicious.

"Hmm?" His breath was warm and sweet as he nuzzled me, suddenly gentle again.

"Who said that?" It had sounded so familiar. I'd heard those words before. In exactly that voice. "Who's here?"

"You remember." Lopez looked down into my face. Even though it was dark, I could see how blue his thick-lashed eyes were. I could see, I realized, because there were flames all around us. Illuminating everything. The bed was on fire!

He murmured softly against my lips, "She killed me."

"This is dangerous." I looked around at the burning bed. "We should do something about this. Don't you want to know what to do?"

"Because of you," he said. "She killed me because of you. Remember?"

I did remember! I had asked for his help one hot summer night in Harlem, and now he lay near death in a dark ritual space, a secret room consecrated to Evil, where no one would know to look for him.

"I went there for *you*," he whispered.

"I know." I started crying.

"The Lord of Death is dancing around your lover," she said with unholy glee, *"waiting to escort him to the cemetery!"*

"No!" I wailed.

Lopez was standing behind me now, and we were in a long, dark, echoing tunnel underground. Stalactites hung down around us, creating a shimmering upside-down forest of beautiful, tortuously twisted crystal formations.

"You like it here," I mused. "I didn't know that about you."

He was trying to unlace my Regency gown. "The girl was a ringer for you in this dress. You should take it off."

I felt him pulling on the fastenings of my gown. I also saw him lying in front of me, on the cold, damp floor of the tunnel. He had been given an ordeal poison and was dying of slow paralysis. Sweat beaded his face. He could barely breathe. He was looking at me, silently imploring me to do something about this.

"I did what I had to!" I said desperately. "You should go now!"

"Let's get this dress off you first," he said behind me.

"Am I really in danger?" I asked.

"I wanted to show you this."

"What?"

Still lying on the floor, his neck was bleeding now. He showed me the fang marks on his jugular vein.

"No, it's my carotid artery," he said.

"This is your *doing," his killer said to me. "You have no one to blame but yourself."*

"You're an evil bitch," I replied.

"But she got in here, even so," Lopez whispered, tugging at my gown.

I felt impatient now, wanting him to finish undoing my laces and take off my clothes. To shed the layers between us so we could embrace, naked and uninhibited. I yearned for that. But the more he yanked and tugged and tried to free me, the more knotted and tangled the laces got, and the heavier and thicker the layers of cloth became.

"Maybe I *have* to wear it," I said at last. "Maybe this is just how it is."

"It looks good on you," he said judiciously.

I looked at the teeth marks on his neck as he lay dying on the filthy floor of the tunnel.

"There's more to this, isn't there?" I asked.

"You know the answer to that by now."

I touched my neck and felt bite marks there. "Yes, I know."

When I pulled my hand away from my wound, I saw there was blood on my fingers. "Is it safe?"

"Ask them."

I turned in the direction of his gaze, and I saw a horde of vamparazzi stampeding through the tunnel, coming in this direction. I recognized Daemon among them, dressed as Lord Ruthven. He was surrounded by grinning goth girls and mean-looking guys in black leather. There was also a woman in white body paint, with a low-cut red dress and elaborate red wings. When she smiled, I saw a row of sharp teeth. She was with a guy who had wobbly fangs and a slight drooling problem.

"They think a vampire did it," Leischneudel said, standing beside me. He looked hollow-eyed and frightened.

"Is it really blood?" Dr. Hal shouted, stampeding with the other vamparazzi. He waved a placard overhead that I couldn't quite read. "How do you *know*?"

"I just *hate* vampires," Thack said to me.

"Should you be wearing a white suit down here?" I asked, looking at his outfit.

"Don't be absurd," he replied. "I never wear white after Labor Day."

"But—"

"Get her! *Get her!*" the Janes screamed, racing toward me with maddened expressions.

I gasped in fear and fell back a step, then turned to ask Lopez for help. But I saw him lying there, dying because of me, and I changed my mind. Instead, I turned and ran in the other direction, leading the swarm away from him. But I didn't know where I was going. I was just staggering around in the dark, my legs heavy and unresponsive, the thick blackness of the tunnels closing in on me.

I tried to shout for help, but my voice didn't work.

I looked over my shoulder and saw the vamparazzi coming for me, their flashbulbs going off, illuminating the tunnels. In the elusive light of their flashes, I could see an escape route, but my legs wouldn't *move*. The Janes were stalking me now, their fangs drooling, blood dripping from their pouty pink mouths.

"Hey, can I get some photos of this?" Al Tarr asked me.

I found my voice. "Go away!"

Tarr pulled out his notebook, poised his pen over it, and asked, "So that's my rival?"

He nodded toward Lopez, who leaned casually against a tunnel wall nearby, wearing grubby clothing, his hair too long, and in need of a shave. He looked dangerous and sexy.

"What's he doing here?" the reporter asked, scribbling in his notebook.

"He's always here," I said. "You know that."

"Does he know any good songs?"

"What?"

Tarr shook his head and kept taking notes.

I frowned when I saw that Lopez's neck was still bleeding.

"What if there really *is* a vampire lurking around here?" I asked Tarr.

The tabloid writer looked surprised by that. "If there is . . ." He thought it over. "Well, then we gotta get some pictures."

I shook my head. "I don't have a camera."

"Me, neither." He prodded, "But you know who does, right?"

"Yes." I looked over at the wall again, but Lopez was gone. I watched a Jane stalking past me and Tarr, her eyes glowing, her fangs dripping. I stood very still, not even breathing, hoping she wouldn't notice me. After she moved on to another prospective victim, I nodded and said, "I know who has a camera."

"Can you get it?" Tarr asked.

"Get it?" I repeated.

Get it . . .

The sharp ring of the telephone jerked me out of a sound sleep. I flinched, my heart pounding, my brain disoriented and befuddled. I looked around in confusion as I pressed a hand against my thudding chest.

The phone rang again.

Get it.

I groaned as I rolled over in my bed and glanced at the clock on my nightstand. It was a little after noon. So

I'd had almost six hours of sleep. I scrubbed my face with my hands as the phone rang again. Squinting my stinging eyes against the sunlight that was filtering through the blinds on my bedroom window, I picked up the receiver and croaked, "Hello?"

"How did you manage to turn yourself into a suspect?" Lopez demanded.

Since I had seen him only moments ago in my dreams (where I had done a little more than just *look*), hearing his voice on my phone confused me. As did his opening salvo.

I said, "Huh?"

"When I left the theater last night, you were a witness and maybe a target. Now you're also a suspect," he said in exasperation. "How *do* you manage these things?"

"Huh?"

He backed up a step. "Are you awake, Esther?"

"I am *now*," I said irritably. "I think I liked you better in my dreams."

"What?"

"Why did you wake me?"

"I didn't know you'd still be asleep." After a moment, he added, "Sorry. It probably should have occurred to me. I know they kept you at the theater until nearly five. And I also heard about what happened when you left. How are you?"

I winced as I sat up. "*Ow* . . . A few aches and pains, that's for sure. I wonder how many women were in the pile-on?"

"Five were arrested."

"It seemed like more," I said wearily, sliding out of bed and stumbling down the hallway. "So you've talked to the cops today, I gather?"

"Yeah. Branson and I connected by phone a couple of hours ago. Which is how I know that you're a suspect now."

"I don't understand." I went into the kitchen to open

a bottle of painkillers and pour a glass of water. "How? *Why?*"

"Funny, that's what *I* said."

"Well?"

"Apparently you made a poor impression on Detective Branson when he interviewed you."

"Oh, good grief."

"I've only seen a little of your work," Lopez said. "But I've seen enough to know you're a very good actress."

"Yeah?" I perked up. "Did you see—"

"So why can't you at least *fake* sensitivity and womanly emotion when the situation calls for it?"

"Whoa. Branson thinks that because I'm not distraught over the victim's death, that means I might have *killed* her?" I swallowed three painkillers with a gulp of water.

"Something like that," Lopez said dryly.

"You're not going to disagree with me when I say he's an *idiot,* are you?" I decided that caffeine was the essential chaser for my ibuprofen breakfast.

"Apparently he expected better of you, Esther," Lopez said solemnly. "But then, he doesn't know you like I do."

"Hmph." I started pouring water into the coffee machine. "Wait a minute. If I'm a suspect, that means . . . They still don't know who the killer is?"

"Right again."

"Daemon's not under arrest?" I blurted in surprise. It had seemed like a sure thing last night.

"No. They sent him home a couple of hours ago."

"Hey! So I still have a job!" That made me feel energized, even without the caffeine.

"Well, for tonight, anyhow."

I paused while measuring scoops of coffee. "You mean they still might arrest him?"

"If they think they can make a case," Lopez said.

"They can't right now. But they still like him for this, so they'll be trying. While also looking at other suspects. Such as—oh, for example—*you*, now that you've alienated Branson."

"Oh, surely I'm not a *serious* suspect?" I switched on the coffee machine.

"No, but you did feasibly have a beef against the victim, who attacked you and then went home with your boyfriend."

I gasped in revulsion. "He's *not* my—"

"I know. But that's one possible interpretation of the murder. And it's one that Branson's entertaining, now that you've pissed him off." Lopez added critically, "That wasn't smart, Esther."

"Bullshit," I snapped. "My whereabouts are accounted for. Leischneudel brought me home in the cab waiting for us outside the theater, and he stayed here until nearly four. Then we called for a taxi to come take him home. If Branson doesn't believe me or Leischneudel, then he can check with the taxi cab company."

"Oh, he will. But Branson thinks one possibility is that as soon as you were alone, you went back out by yourself—"

"At that time of night?"

"—and you found, confronted, and killed Angeline."

"I wasn't *homicidally* angry about my black eye." I stretched a little, trying to wake up my stiff muscles. "I just wanted her arrested for assaulting me."

Lopez said, "His theory relies on a level of ruthlessly effective time-management that I told him definitely doesn't apply to you."

"How thoughtful of you to stick up for me," I said sourly.

"But it's a theory that does fall within range of the estimated time of death—which is never as conveniently precise as they make it seem on *Crime and Punishment*."

"Oh, for God's sake." I decided to redirect the conversation. "While you were listening to Branson theorize that I'm a *murderer*—"

"Okay, look, I told him there was no way—"

"Did you happen to notice anything *else*, detective?"

"Such as?"

"He never mentioned *you* being at the theater. Or Hector Sousa. Or a scary-looking guy in desperate need of a barber."

"Oh. Right."

"The cops have no idea you were there last night."

"And I owe that, no doubt, to your shrewdly evasive and cunning conversational skills."

"Okay, the subject never came up," I admitted.

"That was going to be my next guess."

"Things were so bizarre and chaotic when the cops were there—"

"Branson did mention *that*."

"—that I don't think any of the other actors even remembered they'd met you."

"On the other hand, I think the cops who were there last night will remember for years to come that they've met all of *you*."

"For all the good it did them. Why can't they make a case against Daemon?" Realizing from the silence that followed that he was debating whether or not to tell me, I pointed out, "You know that Daemon will tell me if I ask him."

"So go ask him."

"But then I'd have to talk to him," I objected, as the aroma of brewing coffee filled my little kitchen.

He laughed. "All right. That tabloid reporter who follows him everywhere will probably squeeze a lot of this out of him and make it public, anyhow."

"Count on it. Tarr is persistent." For no rational reason, I added, "He asked me out."

"Tarr did?"

"Uh-huh." I felt my face flush and wished I hadn't mentioned it.

After an awkward pause, Lopez said, "I guess even tabloid writers get lonely."

"I don't like him," I said quickly. "I turned him down."

Another pause. A longer one. "Why are you telling me this?"

I really had no idea. Nor could I have explained why I asked, "Have you gone out with anyone? You know, since . . ."

"Adele Olson was seen leaving Daemon's loft," he said, retreating safely into cop mode. "Alive and alone, healthy and on her own two feet."

I was embarrassed and appalled at my own behavior. The last thing I wanted was for Lopez to think I was playing games with him. Which was probably exactly what he did think now.

Fortunately, his information was surprising enough to distract me from my mortification. "She was seen leaving his place? Who sees someone at *that* time of night?"

"There were still some people on the streets. It was barely thirty minutes after she attacked you."

I snorted involuntarily. "*That* was fast."

I heard his puff of laughter and felt relieved that we were getting back on an even keel, as if my odd little outburst hadn't just happened.

"I gather that Angeline turned out to be too crazy even for Daemon's taste," Lopez said. "He insists nothing happened between them."

"They didn't sleep together?" I said in surprise.

"He says no. Which happens to be consistent with the medical examiner's findings," he said. "Meanwhile, a thorough—*very* thorough—investigation of Daemon's loft hasn't yet uncovered any evidence to contradict his story."

"What *is* his story?" I asked. "He just gave her a lift somewhere?"

"No—though he did give one to your friend, Al Tarr."

"He's not my fr—"

"After leaving the theater that night, Daemon's car swung by the *Exposé*'s offices on Houston Street to drop off the reporter."

The fact that Daemon had given Tarr a lift somewhere made more sense, I realized, than my vague assumption at the time, which was that Tarr was accompanying Daemon and his groupie home, and would watch TV or something in the living room while they . . . I stopped there, realizing these were mental images I didn't want to pursue now any more than I had on the night I'd seen the threesome drive away from the theater.

I poured myself a cup of coffee and asked, "Tarr went to work at three in the morning?"

"Sleaze never sleeps," Lopez said dryly. "The tabloid is a twenty-four-hour-a-day operation. So Tarr checked in, did some work, then slept there. I guess they have a few cots on the premises, in case a hot new scandal—like this murder case, I suppose—requires their crack journalists to be on hand around the clock."

"If Tarr makes a habit of sleeping at work, it certainly explains a lot about his appearance."

"Doesn't *he* shave, either?"

"Then Daemon went home?" I prodded, steering the conversation back on track.

The ride to Daemon's Soho loft took only a few additional minutes, especially at that time of night. He dismissed the driver, then took Angeline inside with him. Within a few minutes of entering Daemon's home, she damaged a twelve thousand dollar glass sculpture. She sulked about his distressed reaction to the incident, then got angry when she couldn't drag his attention away from the damage.

"Apparently this sculpture wasn't just something an interior decorator had picked out for him," Lopez said. "Daemon described himself to the investigating officers as a serious art collector."

"So vampirism isn't his only pretension?" I sipped my coffee.

If Angeline's casual destruction of a treasured work of art hadn't already switched off his libido, then (as Daemon later told the cops) the tantrum that followed certainly would have done so. Just wanting to get rid of the girl now, he told her he wasn't in the mood for company anymore and asked her to leave. She was insulted and offended, ridiculed him, and threatened to expose him as sexually impotent and incapable.

"But apparently he's slept with so many women that he had no concern this would be taken seriously. Or, at least, that's his story, and he's sticking to it," Lopez said. "And he got rid of her after a few more minutes. With some shouting and foul language, but without any violence—well, except for a little more damage that she did to his sculpture before leaving."

That was the last he saw of her, according to Daemon. Investigation of his home revealed that the sculpture was indeed damaged, and Angeline's fingerprints could be found on a few things in the living room, which is where she had spent her entire brief visit. So far, the police had found no evidence that she'd ever entered any other portion of the dwelling. Nor were there any signs of violence apart from the broken items accounted for in Daemon's story (the sculpture and also the glass Angeline had been drinking from).

Two witnesses had already been found who saw her alive after that, when she left Daemon's building and then walked up West Broadway. It was late; but it was a Friday, and a few people were coming home from nights out on the town. And apparently a woman on the street in a Regency gown was memorable, even on Halloween weekend in New York City.

"But no one knows yet what happened after that," Lopez said. "One possibility, of course, is that Daemon followed her."

"But he had just thrown her out," I said, pouring a second cup of coffee.

"Maybe he's lying. Maybe she walked out, for whatever reason. Then he followed her, trying to get her to come back, and things got ugly. Or maybe he did throw her out, but then he felt uneasy about her threats to expose and embarrass him, so he decided to go after her." After a moment, he added pensively, "If so, though, he didn't take her back to his place."

"How do you know?"

"Even if Daemon spent hours cleaning and scrubbing his loft—which somehow strikes me as even less likely than his being a vampire—forensics would have found *something* if he had committed the murder there. There's a lot of blood in the human body." I heard a touch of frustration in his voice as he continued, "It happened somewhere else. I'm sure of it. And finding out *where* would be a big step forward."

"You really don't think Daemon's the killer." I could tell from his tone.

"No, I really don't," he admitted. "But it's not my case."

"It's connected to your case," I protested. "It's probably the same killer."

"Maybe."

"Oh, come on. Exsanguinated murder victims found under—"

"Maybe," he repeated firmly. "I'm about to head over to Manhattan South to read their reports, review Daemon's interview, and examine their evidence. And I'll see what I think then." He added, *"No one* has more fun on a sunny Sunday than I do."

"Did you go to Mass today?" I asked.

"What are you, my mother?"

"There's no need to be insulting," I said. "It was a friendly question."

"Well, yes. That's where I was before I called you."

He waited, apparently expecting me to comment. I didn't. I gathered from things he'd said in the past that his parents were fairly religious Catholics, and I knew from our . . . friendship that he attended Mass regularly. (And that his mother nagged him if he didn't.) By contrast, I was a secular Jew who only went to Temple twice a year, at most (and only if my mother *really* nagged me). I probably shouldn't be interested in his private spiritual convictions, given that I was trying to exorcise my fascination with him, but I was curious about just how religious he was and how much his faith affected his worldview.

I was also aware of the irony that, of the two of us, I was the one who believed in various mystical phenomena (with good reason), while he, who attended the Eucharist each week, was the steadfast skeptic.

Deciding I should stick to the business at hand, I dropped that topic and said, "I assume you've got an alternative theory about who the killer is?"

"I've got a few," he said. "But I try not to fall in love with a theory when I don't have any evidence to support it."

"You think that's what *they're* doing," I pounced. "You think the cops investigating Angeline's death are so in love with their theory that the celebrity vampire killed her, they're not even—"

"Don't," he said. "Branson's already mad at *you*."

"Oh, Branson's a—"

"Let's not make him mad at me, too."

"But if the cops are overlooking—"

"Stop," he said.

"They could miss—"

"Don't you want to know about the blood?"

"What blood?" I asked blankly.

"That was the first thing I meant to tell you when I called."

I recognized what he was doing. "Don't change the sub—"

"The blood you *drank,*" he prodded. "Thinking it was—God help us—Nocturne wine cooler."

"That blood? Oh!" Actually, I did want to know. "Yes! What about it?"

"Well, it's definitely human."

"Ugh." My hand reflexively covered my mouth. "I *think* I spat most of it out. Maybe all of it . . ."

"And there's nothing wrong with it. I mean, it's healthy. You're absolutely fine."

"Oh, good," I said with relief. "Er, I guess it's not . . . not . . ."

"The murder victim's blood? No." I could hear amusement entering his voice. "But it does belong to someone you know. Someone who, you'll be pleased to learn, eats lean proteins and whole grains, has never smoked, and takes a multivitamin every day."

"Who?"

"I've really been looking forward to telling you this . . ."

"Well?"

"It's Daemon's own blood."

"You're kidding!"

"No, I couldn't make up something this good."

"He extracts and bottles his own blood?" I said incredulously.

"And then pretends he got it from sexual partners in, er, unconventional practices."

"Why?"

"I wish I could see your face right now," he said.

"It's contorted with amazement."

"Apparently he's been doing this for years." Lopez was laughing as he said, "Daemon increased his, uh, production of snack food in preparation for having Tarr living in his pocket. He evidently thought that sheer quantity would convince the *Exposé* that his act is for real. Or something."

"Maybe that's why he looks so pale." I had thought

the actor had naturally dramatic coloring, but perhaps he instead had an iron deficiency due to frequent phlebotomy. "What do you call blood play if you only do it with yourself?"

"I don't know. I'm wondering if it can make you go blind or grow hair on your palms."

"So, with women, Daemon just, uh, does standard stuff?"

"I'm not sure anyone had a strong enough stomach to ask him for specifics about that. But whatever else he may or may not do, he doesn't drink any blood other than his own." Laughing again, Lopez added, "And he only drinks his own when he can't get away with substituting Nocturne."

"Talk about dedication to building an image," I said in amazement. "He couldn't just study acting and audition for roles, like the rest of us?"

"Hey, his masquerade got him a nice loft in Soho, a chauffeur-driven limo, some starring roles, and lots of tail."

"Well, when you put it that way . . . I wonder what sort of exotic, commercially viable creature *I* could pass myself off as?"

"I think you're an exotic, commercially viable creature just the way you are."

I cradled the phone against me ear and smiled. "Thank you."

"What I've just told you is confidential, by the way."

"Yeah, I guess *so,* considering how much trouble Daemon went to in order to convince the world that he habitually drinks blood and has 'vampire sex.'"

"And what you and I talked about last night still goes," Lopez said seriously. "Stay away from him."

"But you don't think he's the murderer," I argued.

"No, but that's my *opinion,* not an established fact. And a bunch of homicide cops *do* still think he's the killer."

"What do they—"

"Daemon says he went to bed alone after Angeline left, and he didn't see or speak to anyone until his personal assistant showed up around noon. That's at least eight hours without an alibi. So the cops will be looking for proof that he's lying and that he *wasn't* innocently at home in bed for the rest of the night."

"Instead of doing that, they should be looking for the real killer," I said.

"They're doing *both*." Lopez sounded a little cranky. "Even if the investigating officers *weren't* a little too in love with their current theory, they'd have an obligation to follow up on a suspect's statement—especially a suspect who doesn't have an alibi for the estimated time of the crime. That's part of a cop's *job*, Esther. Because, shocking as this may sound, suspects lie to the police. All of the time."

"Ah. I see your point."

"In that case, I should mark this date on my calendar," he grumbled. "Sunday, November third, the day you saw my point about something."

"I don't think you got enough sleep last night," I said.

"Until the cops on the case are absolutely sure about Daemon," he said firmly, "I want you to view him as dangerous and treat him with sensible caution."

I wondered how much higher ticket prices would go when the tabloids, fans, and scalpers all realized that Daemon, having been released without being arrested, was still under intense police scrutiny.

"And, as you may remember," Lopez continued, "I didn't get enough sleep last night because of a different theory. One which is, if anything, even more plausible today: The killer may be someone obsessed enough with Daemon to kill a woman who seems to be the object of his interest."

Nearly being smothered beneath a pile of lust-crazed Janes ensured that I was taking that theory very seriously, too.

"That's another good point," I said encouragingly. "You're doing very well."

"Thank you so much."

"Note how I am taking the high road and ignoring your tone."

"Uh-huh."

Thinking of last night's attack made me realize that if I was going to do a show today, I should probably assess the damage to my appearance. Carrying my coffee cup, I went into my bathroom while I listened to Lopez reiterate the safety rules he wanted me to follow until the killer was in custody.

As soon as I saw my reflection in the mirror above my sink, I sucked in my breath on a horrified gasp.

"What's wrong? Esther!"

Hearing the sudden alarm in his voice, I realized just how worried about my safety he really was. I said quickly, "Sorry. I'm fine. It's nothing. Well . . ." I grimaced. "Not *nothing*. I just looked at myself in the mirror."

"Oh." His sigh of relief was clearly audible over the phone. "Did you grow fangs overnight or something?"

"It's going to take a lot of effort for me to look presentable enough to do a show today."

My black eye—Angeline's legacy to me—felt better today, but it *looked* much worse, an ugly blossom of black, purple, and sickly yellow. There was a swath of stinging mottled red across my cheek, an abrasion made by someone shoving my face into the pavement last night. My complexion was ghastly pale with fatigue, and there were dark circles under my eyes.

"How's your neck?" Lopez asked.

I pushed aside my sleep-snarled hair and took a good look in the mirror. "I think there's an old *Star Trek* episode where people on an alien planet are dying of mysterious welts that look just like this one."

"Let's pause a moment to enjoy the fact that the guy

who did that to you has just spent *hours* being questioned by over-tired cops who think he's a murderer."

Leaning closer to the mirror, I used my fingertips to gingerly explore the inflamed flesh, which was various shades of pink and blue, speckled with angry little puce dots. I said in appalled wonder, "You know, if he did have fangs, like a real vampire, this would be a serious wound. I'd probably be in the hospital now."

"A real vampire?" Lopez repeated.

"You know what I mean."

"No. I don't. And we'll have to leave it that way, since I need to go to work now." He ended the call by saying vaguely that he'd be in touch again, then he hung up.

I held the phone against my chest for a moment, filled with mixed emotions. Then I went back into the bedroom, put the receiver into its cradle, and pulled my cell phone out of my tote bag to check for messages.

As expected, Bill had recently sent a text message notifying everyone that the show would go on and advising us to be at the theater at the usual time for a Sunday performance. *The Vampyre* bowed to tradition in that respect, keeping early hours this one day of the week. Our 5:00 P.M. start, though later than most other matinees, ensured that there were still plenty of restaurants serving dinner and trains running to the suburbs when our Sunday performance ended.

Bill had sent an additional text message to me. It said that Fiona wanted to speak to me about a stain on my costume. I deleted the message and wondered how good my chances were of avoiding the wardrobe mistress completely again today.

I took off my nightgown and put on my terrycloth robe, intending to go take a shower, when the land line rang again. My caller was Thack.

"I've read the news," he said. "So I wasn't sure whether I would still have to—er, would still be able to see *The Vampyre* today."

I explained the latest development and assured him the curtain would indeed rise.

He prodded, "So Daemon Ravel has been questioned by the police in connection with *murder?*"

"Yes." I assumed that most of the facts (as well as plenty of fabrications) were all over the Internet by now. So I said candidly, "The cops questioned everyone at the theater, but they were particularly interested in Daemon. They seemed to consider him a suspect."

However, my candor stopped short of telling Thack that *I* was both a peripheral suspect and a potential target in this case. My agent was prone to overreaction, and I saw no productive purpose in mentioning those looming clouds to the man whose job it was to think optimistically about my future.

"Well, I certainly hope all those groupies whose adulation keeps Daemon Ravel employed are paying attention. *This* is what happens when you go around posing as a vampire," Thack said censoriously. "Pretending to be an undead creature of the night. Wearing fangs and capes. Claiming to suck blood from the necks of virgins and—"

"I don't think virgins are a key element in Daemon's schtick."

"*Nothing* good comes of playing with these appalling stereotypes. And I hope this will be a lesson to Mr. Ravel."

"I don't know, Thack." I thought of Lopez's recent enumeration of the professional and personal benefits Daemon enjoyed as a result of his masquerade. "He may view a scandal like this as just the cost of doing business."

"When the music stops, the band has to be paid, Esther. The only respectable thing Daemon Ravel can do, now that he's involved in a murder, is express public contrition over his revoltingly clichéd behavior and retire into quiet obscurity." Perhaps remembering then that our show still had two weeks left to run, he added, "Er, after *The Vampyre* closes, of course."

"Of course." Since it was clear that Thack could easily be pushed over the edge into a lengthy rampage, I also decided not to mention that I'd been physically attacked by some of Daemon's fans—including the murder victim. "I have to go, Thack. I'll see you backstage after the show?"

"Yes. And if I have any appetite left after sitting through this play, I'll take you to dinner."

As soon as I hung up, I realized that I had forgotten to reserve Daemon's VIP seats for tonight, so I called the box office and did it now.

"Yes, Daemon and I discussed it, and Victor was going to phone you to authorize it," I lied cheerfully to the staffer who took my call. "You're saying Victor hasn't called? Really? Hmm. Do you think that his employer being questioned by the police on suspicion of murder could be why he forgot?"

I got the seats.

Next, I called Leischneudel.

At my request, he and the cops who'd driven us home before dawn had searched my apartment when they dropped me off. Though exhausted, I was following through on my promise to Lopez to take safety precautions. And given that I had just received news of the murder *and* been attacked outside the stage door, the cops seemed to consider my anxiety normal and my request reasonable. Leischneudel had offered to spend the night here, but I declined. I felt a little guilty about sending him home alone, knowing that Mary Ann wasn't visiting him this weekend and Mimi was at the vet's; and I sincerely appreciated his heroic struggle to protect me from the maddened Janes. But he was so overwrought with nerves and tension, he was making *me* jumpy, and I just felt too wrung out by then to cope with him bouncing off the walls of my apartment for the next few hours.

"Did you get any sleep after you got home?" I asked him now.

"Not really." His voice sounded a little raspy over the phone, which was unusual for him and obviously a sign of his fatigue. "I was too wired, after everything. So I finally gave up, got out of bed, and called Mary Ann. Luckily, I caught her before she went to the library this morning. She's working on a backbreaking research paper."

His almost-fiancée was a graduate student, on a full scholarship, with a 4.0 GPA. Leischneudel was very proud of her.

"Is that why she hasn't visited lately?" I asked. "Too much work?" Leischneudel had mentioned that Mary Ann had a heavy course load this semester.

"Yes. I haven't seen her in three weeks. We talk almost every day, of course, but it's not the same thing." He sighed. "It was going to be hard for her to get away this weekend, because of this paper she's working on. And I knew we'd be doing additional performances here for Halloween weekend, so I wouldn't be able to spend much time with her, anyhow . . ." He made a rueful sound. "The way this weekend has turned out, I can't decide if I'm glad for her sake that she stayed home, or sorry for my sake that she's not here with me."

"I know the feeling," I said morosely.

"Anyhow, I'm glad I called her. Because, of course, when I told her everything that's happened, Mary Ann knew exactly what I should do."

"Oh?"

"Bring Mimi home!"

I smiled. "Of course."

"So I went and picked her up a little while ago."

"How is she?"

"She's a lot . . ." He cleared his throat, and his voice started to sound more normal as he continued, "A lot better today. But temperamental about taking the medication they sent home with us."

"Ah, but a man who fought off lunatic Janes last night can certainly confront one small cat today."

"She has claws *and* fangs," he pointed out.

"Fair point. And speaking of fangs, the cops let Daemon go."

"I know. I saw Bill's message." Leischneudel said hesitantly, as if broaching a shocking subject, "I really don't think he's a vampire, you know. Daemon, I mean. Not Bill."

"Well, I admit to a moment of terrifying belief in the Vampire Ravel when he was gnawing on my neck onstage last . . ."

"He should *not* have done that! That was so *wrong*." Despite everything else that had happened since then, Leischneudel was obviously still shocked by that solecism.

"But otherwise," I said, "yeah, I know he's not a vampire."

"And I really don't think he could have killed that girl," Leischneudel said pensively. "Not the way . . . the way it was done."

"No, I don't believe he did it. And now we know he hasn't been arrested for it." Well, not yet, anyhow.

"After all that's happened, can you do the show today?" Leischneudel asked with concern. "Will you be all right?"

"Yes," I said firmly. "I'll need to put antibiotic ointment on my abrasions, and slather pain-relieving liniment all over my aching body, and possibly get a rabies shot for the bite on my neck. As well as put a vat of stage makeup on my face. But I'll be okay. And the show must go on."

"There's something you should probably know."

I was surprised by how tentative his voice sounded. "Yes?"

"There are pictures of you on the Internet today. Photos. From last night—or very early this morning, I guess."

"Hey, can I get some photos of this?" Al Tarr asked me.

I had a sudden memory of flashbulbs going off in my face. Both in reality and in my dreams, casting light in the darkness . . .

Leischneudel said, "They're not the most flattering photos ever taken of you."

"No, I suppose not," I said absently. I hadn't been at my best by 5:00 A.M., even *before* being physically assaulted.

Flashes of light illuminating the way . . .

What if there really *was* a vampire preying on people?

"If there is . . . Well, then we gotta get some pictures."

"Pictures," I murmured. What did *that* mean?

"I can hardly recognize you in some of them," Leischneudel said, "and I know you, after all."

Lopez had two victims, maybe three. Angeline was probably number four. All exsanguinated and left in underground locations.

Daemon's involvement as a suspect ensured that Angeline's murder would be complicated to prosecute successfully—impossible, perhaps, if the police took so much as a single misstep. Of course Lopez was being cautious and thorough. He had to be. It was his duty.

But I knew someone every bit as capable and dedicated as Lopez who didn't share the constraints of his world.

Photos. Pictures. A clear image to analyze.

I shook my head. "I don't have a camera."

"But you know who does, right?"

"Yes, I know who has a camera."

Yes, I thought with relief, I knew who could give me some clarity on the big picture here.

"So I'll come by for you a little before four o'clock?" Leischneudel said.

"No," I replied. "I won't be here. We'll have to go to the theater separately today."

This suggestion met with a noticeable lack of enthusiasm. "Separately?"

"It'll be okay." Trying to sound confident, I said, "All things considered, I'm sure there will be plenty of policemen on crowd control today."

"But where will you be? I could meet you somewhere, and then we could—"

"I'm not quite sure where I'll be," I lied, not wanting to bring Leischneudel along while I asked a 350-year-old mage about vampires. "And I don't want to make you late for work, if I'm running behind schedule."

"Esther, are you all right?"

"I'm fine. I just have to go see a man about a camera."

11

"**W**ell, there is one obvious question I must ask immediately," said Dr. Maximillian Zadok (Oxford University, class of 1678), gazing at me intently as he considered the events I had just related to him in full. A short, slightly chubby man with innocent blue eyes, longish white hair, and a tidy beard, he spoke English with the faint trace of an accent, reflecting his origins in Central Europe centuries ago. "Are there any Lithuanians involved in this matter?"

"Lithu . . . Oh. Um."

As long as I had known Max (which had only been six or seven months—but it often *seemed* much longer), he'd had a . . . a *thing* about Lithuanians. He had never explained it, and I had never really pursued it; but as near as I could tell, he and Lithuanians seemed to be like two Mafia families. Not necessarily enemies, but separate and wary; and if you belonged to one, then you couldn't belong to the other.

His raising the subject again sparked my curiosity; but with more urgent questions at hand, such as whether a vampire was stalking the city, this didn't seem the time for me to insist on an explanation about Max's complicated relationship with the people of a small Baltic nation.

"Er, no, to my knowledge, there are no Lithuanians involved," I said. "I haven't gone around specifically asking everyone's ethnicity, but no self-identified Lithuanians have stepped forward."

"No?" Max frowned. "I find that surprising. Even puzzling."

I blinked. "Really?"

"Hmm." He stroked his beard, a thoughtful expression on his face. "Tell me, were the victims' intestines consumed?"

"By *consumed*, you mean . . ."

"Eaten."

"Yeah, I was afraid that was what you meant," I said. "I have no idea. I suppose it's possible. Even though Lopez was so tired that he said more than he meant to, that's the kind of detail I'm pretty sure he would deliberately omit when talking to me." If only to spare me from having nightmares.

"Oh, I meant to ask, how *is* Detective Lopez?"

I had come to Zadok's Rare and Used Books, located in a townhouse on a side street in Greenwich Village, after showering, dressing, eating, and packing my tote bag with everything I'd need to get me through the day. If anyone in New York could shed light into the dark corners of this situation, it was surely Max—talented mage, long-lived alchemist, ardent student of magic and mysticism, and local representative of the Magnum Collegium, an ancient worldwide (albeit obscure) organization dedicated to confronting Evil wherever it lurked. Max's help and guidance had saved my life (and the lives of others) on previous occasions, and it was through our friendship that I had discovered that there are more things in heaven and earth, Horatio, than were dreamt of in my philosophy.

"How is Lopez?" I said. "If you mean, did anything weird or mysterious happen while he was with me, the answer is no."

There had been previous . . . incidents.

I'd been in deadly danger one night when Lopez was trying to rescue me, in a pitch-dark church where the electricity had been disabled; my life was saved when the lights inexplicably started working again, apparently in response to his will. On another occasion, he had experienced possession by a fiery Vodou spirit. And then there was the memorable night my bed caught fire for no apparent reason . . . while he was in it.

Lopez barely even acknowledged it as a noticeable coincidence that the church lights that night had started working when he wanted them to. He didn't remember the spirit possession at all (which, Max had told me, was a common reaction among those who'd been possessed). And he thought something was wrong—*really* wrong—with my mattress, so he wanted an arson investigator to examine it. (However, like most things left outside in my neighborhood, the ruined mattress promptly vanished.)

Max wasn't sure what to make of these episodes, but he thought it was possible that Lopez possessed unconscious, unwitting mystical talent of some sort. I knew without asking that my ex-almost-boyfriend would find such a theory only slightly less absurd than Daemon's claims about being a vampire. And I . . . I really didn't know what to think.

"Actually, I was just asking after his health and well-being," Max said. "I haven't encountered him since that ferocious night in Harlem when death came uncomfortably close to embracing him."

"*Too* close," I said. "Much, *much* too close. I can't get him involved in anything like that again, Max."

"He seems to be deeply involved in *this* matter already," my friend pointed out gently. "As is his way when there is danger afoot."

"Well, I guess the one thing we can all agree on is that there's *danger*," I said. "The question is, is it the sort of 'mundane' danger that the police are equipped to deal with—such as a serial killer with, um, exsanguination equipment? Or is the killer—despite Lopez's undisguised contempt for this theory—an immortal creature of the night sinking its fangs into people's necks to drink their blood?"

"Oh, I very much doubt it's *that,*" Max said, shaking his head.

"Really?"

"Indeed, no. I share Detective Lopez's conviction that such a theory is too outlandish to entertain seriously."

"Oh, thank goodness," I said, feeling relieved and very glad that I had come here and told Max everything. *Vampires.* What had I been thinking? I laughed a little. "It must be the atmosphere I've been living in lately. You know—this gothic play, our bizarre leading man, the vamparazzi. I guess it all got to me. I really worked myself into a state of nerves by the time I got here."

"Perfectly understandable," Max said kindly.

He patted my hand, then offered to pour me more tea. I accepted. We were chatting in a pair of comfortable old easy chairs next to the little gas fireplace in the bookstore. Nearby was the small refreshment station that Max kept stocked with coffee, tea, cookies, and other treats for his customers. There was also a large, careworn walnut table with books, papers, an abacus, writing implements, and other paraphernalia on it. Along the far wall of the shop there was an extremely large wooden cupboard that happened to be possessed; although the cupboard was prone to alarming displays of smoke, noise, shrieks, and agitated rattling, it seemed to be silent and dormant today—as it often was for weeks at a time.

The shop had well-worn hardwood floors, a broad-beamed ceiling, and dusky rose walls. Its layout was defined by a rabbit warren of tall bookcases stuffed with a wide variety of books about the occult, printed in more than a dozen languages. The stock ranged from recent paperbacks to old, rare, and very expensive leather-bound tomes.

The bookstore had a small, fiercely loyal customer base, and it got some foot traffic from curious passersby. But the shop was primarily an innocuous front for Max's real work, which was protecting New York and its inhabitants from Evil. I didn't know whether fighting Evil paid well (did the Magnum Collegium dole out fiscal rewards and bonuses?) or whether Max had invested wisely over the course of his three and a half centuries of life; I just knew that he seemed to have a comfortable income, and I rather doubted it came from the desultory business that the bookstore did.

After Max poured me another cup of tea, he also offered me a cookie. I declined, but the mere mention of something edible caused Nelli to wake up, lift her head, and look at us imploringly, her expression suggesting that she was only moments away from dying of starvation.

"No, Nelli," Max said firmly. "We've discussed this before. The veterinarian says that sugar will wreak havoc with your delicate metabolism."

She gave a little groan of disappointment and laid her head back down on her paws.

Nelli was Max's canine familiar. I had been present on the chaotic occasion when she transmuted from an ethereal dimension and assumed physical form in this one, in response to Max's supplication for assistance in confronting Evil in New York City. Although she was (despite Max's objection to the word as inaccurate and inadequate for a being of Nelli's complex mystical nature) a dog, she was nearly as big as a Shetland pony. Her massive head was long and square-jawed, framed by two floppy, overlong ears. The fur on her paws and face was silky brown, and the rest of her well-muscled physique was covered by short, smooth, tan fur.

I leaned back in my chair and sipped my tea, realizing that I had let myself get carried away. "What with all the craziness surrounding the show, I guess the pump was really primed, so to speak, when Lopez told me about the exsanguinations." I shook my head. "I talked myself into thinking there's a vampire prowling the city."

"Oh, that could very well be the case," Max said, matter-of-factly. "Although vampires are not the *only* beings who consume the blood of their victims, exsanguination is such a prevalent feature of vampirism that it would be foolhardy not to consider the possibility of a vampire being responsible for these slayings."

"*What?*"

"But we can certainly rule out *imaginary* creatures."

Confused, I sputtered, "But you—you . . . *Vampires?* You just said . . . Lopez . . . too outlandish . . ."

"Oh, dear. I see." Max made an *tsk-tsk* noise while shaking his head. "Fiction writers have a *great deal* to answer for. The absurd misinformation they have encouraged people to believe about a truly dangerous phenomenon is inexcusable! I don't wish to sound unduly critical or censorious—and no one enjoys a good yarn more than I do—but I consider perpetration of such absurd falsehoods to be unconscionably irresponsible."

His round, bearded face was creased in a disapproving frown, and there was a steely tone of offended principle in his normally warm, gentle voice.

"Huh?" As was often the case, I had no idea what Max was talking about.

"I hadn't intended to say anything, since I've no wish to appear unenthusiastic about your participation in a popular theatrical production, let alone ungrateful for your kindly securing me a ticket to see it. And I assure you, the inaccuracies which I anticipate encountering in *The Vampyre* do not in any way mitigate the eagerness with which I contemplate seeing your performance today!"

"Uh-huh." I knew that he would get to the point if I waited long enough.

"But . . ." He sighed. "I read Dr. Polidori's story nearly two centuries ago, when it first became all the rage. And there's no denying that his acquaintance with the facts was extremely scant, at best—"

"The facts about *what?*"

"Vampires," Max said. "It was evident to me, when I read 'The Vampyre,' that Dr. Polidori's interest was not in conveying an accurate rendering of such beings, but rather in metaphorically exorcising his grievances against his former employer Lord Byron. As well as exploring his own ambivalent feelings about, er, other things."

"So vampires aren't undead creatures who prey on the living and survive by draining our blood?" I asked hopefully.

"Oh, he was more or less accurate in that respect," Max said dismissively. "But, as I tried so fruitlessly to explain to Stoker many years later, the undead are *not* articulate, well-dressed aristocrats."

"Stoker?" I said blankly.

"However, Dr. Polidori's enduring vision of the vampire as an elegant, intelligent seducer had by then already taken too firm a hold of Stoker's imagination. Perhaps he should not be blamed—he was Irish, after all, and they are a poetic, fanciful people. And the result of *his* vision is still with us today, alas."

"Wait a minute, *Bram* Stoker?"

"Which is not to say, by any means, that I would ever imply that his work was careless or slipshod. No, indeed. He was a dedicated, almost obsessive researcher."

"Bram Stoker, the author of *Dracula?*"

Max nodded. "Moreover, his interest in the subject of vampires was unquestionably sincere and serious. I must also confess that I was genuinely flattered by his inquisitive enthusiasm with regard to my own experiences as vampire hunter."

"Whoa! Max, you're a *vampire hunter?*"

"Oh, not anymore, certainly. That would be completely inappropriate."

"It would?"

"But before ratifying the Treaty of Gediminas, yes, I battled the undead in Serbia for nearly three terrible years."

"Serbia?" I said. "Wait. No. We'll come back in a minute to battling the undead. Max, you knew Bram Stoker?"

"Yes. And I would just like to clarify that despite the claim that he based the character of Dr. Van Helsing on me, my English was *never* that bad."

"Oh." I had read *Dracula* in college, and I vaguely recalled skimming over Van Helsing's dialogue, too impatient to wade through the stilted, awkward syntax that Stoker had assigned to the novel's foreign-born vampire hunter. "No?"

"I attended Oxford University, for goodness sake!" Max sounded a trifle exasperated. "I had been speaking English for more than two hundred years by the time I met Stoker. Oh, I still had a bit of a continental accent then, as I do now, but I was never *unintelligible.*"

"Of course not," I said. "Wow! He really based Van Helsing on *you?*"

"Well, I suppose Oscar could have fabricated that merely to test my reaction. He could be quite devilish that way."

"Oscar?"

"Wilde."

I sat bolt upright. "You knew *Oscar Wilde?*"

"By the time *Dracula* was written and published, I had not seen Stoker in many years, and I never had the opportunity to ask him myself. Oscar claimed Stoker had told him that I was the inspiration for the character." After a pause, he added, "Oscar also claimed that the resemblance was unmistakable. Hmph."

Recognizing my cue, I said, "Well, it *is* unmistakable, Max. Oh, never mind Van Helsing's awkward dialogue. That's just dramatic license. And the character is, er, Dutch, after all. But he's the hero of the story! Van Helsing arrives on the scene when the other characters are lost and frightened, preyed upon by Evil, and have no idea what's going on or what to do. And *he,* in his wisdom and experience, gives them a clearer picture of the situation, organizes them, and courageously leads them into victorious battle against their powerful adversary." Realizing I meant it, I said, "Of *course* you were the inspiration for that character, Max."

"Oh," Max was blushing bashfully. "Oscar was probably just teasing me when he said that. We shouldn't take it too seriously."

Although it was a distraction from the problem at hand, I nonetheless had to ask. "Max, what was Oscar Wilde like?"

"Hmm." He thought back to his memories of a man who had died more than a century ago. "Brilliant in some ways and surprisingly foolish in others. Very good company when the occasion was right and rather trying company when it was not." Max smiled and shook his head. "We were acquaintances rather than friends."

"And Stoker?"

"Well, like so many novelists, he was often more engaged by what was inside his head than by what was right in front of him. He was a decent, civilized man, and on the occasions we met, we found a great deal to talk about—mostly because of his interest in vampires and my experiences in hunting them." Max added with another touch of exasperation, "So, really, considering our interviews, you would think he would have gotten *something* right in his novel."

"Er, just how inaccurate is it?"

"So inaccurate that its far-reaching influence as an authoritative tome on vampirism has misled generations of the living about the nature of the undead," Max replied sadly.

I began to realize that when we each used the word "vampire," Max and I weren't even talking about the same thing. I was apparently talking about something that didn't exist; and I had no idea what he was talking about.

"Then Hollywood filmmakers subsequently took up the story," Max said. "At which point, even the faintest remaining resemblance to reality entirely vanished."

"That's what usually happens in Hollywood," I noted.

"Thus we have long since reached the point where people actually think, *incredible* as this seems, that a vampire is an immortal, befanged, elegant creature of the night who tidily drains people's blood by biting them in the neck." Max snorted, making his white moustache flutter. "It would almost be amusing if it weren't such a deadly serious matter."

"Let me make sure I understand," I said. "Vampires are real, but everything I know about them is wrong?"

He beamed at me. "That's an admirably succinct summation, Esther!"

"Thank you," I said. "Now that I know what a vampire is *not*—i.e. Lord Ruthven, Count Dracula, and the like—can you be equally succinct in explaining what a vampire *is*?"

His face scrunched up briefly as he sought a way to reduce his normally loquacious descriptions to as few words as possible in this case. "A vampire is a mystically animated undead individual driven by mindless, voracious survival instinct to prey upon the living for sustenance."

"Ah. So Polidori and Stoker did get that part right."

"In essence," Max conceded. "But unlike their portrayals, the vampiric undead are not beings whom you'd ever meet at a social gathering. And they certainly don't make engaging quips about not drinking . . . wine."

"I gather they'd stand out in a crowd?"

"Being undead isn't just a matter of lacking a pulse," Max said. "An undead vampire is always in some stage of decomposition, and this is, er, quite noticeable."

"Without going into detail about that," I said quickly, "do you mean they gradually disintegrate and return to the elements? Like dead people who are *actually* dead?"

"Not necessarily," Max said. "Well, not *soon,* anyhow. Blood is the essence of life—the mysterious internal river of our own animation, if you will. The more human blood the vampire consumes, the slower the rate of decay and the longer the creature can prolong its existence. The undead aren't consciously aware of this equation. They are consciously aware of very *little,* in fact. But it does mean that they are primally driven to attack and consume prey. It also means that the most violently aggressive vampires are consequently the most enduring ones."

"So I guess you also wouldn't find one of them running an estate in Transylvania or hiring a British solicitor?"

"Indeed, no."

"It sounds like they're essentially rabid animals," I said.

"Another succinctly accurate summary, my dear. But they are far more terrifying and dangerous than that. Infused with dark mystical power, they are ferociously strong, instinctively cunning about hunting and being hunted, and very challenging to dispatch. They are also," he said with a shadow of dread that I sensed had followed him across the centuries, "horrifyingly prolific. Their numbers multiply with appalling rapidity."

I gasped in revulsion. "As in . . . vampire sex?"

Max blinked. "Good heavens, no. I didn't mean—However . . . Hmm. I did occasionally observe, er, physiological phenomenon among vampires which would certainly support a theory that they are capable of sexual activity. But I never saw or heard any evidence that they were interested in it, let alone that they were capable of procreation."

"Oh. Good." I added, "Based on your description, it really doesn't sound like a vampire could get a date, anyhow, never mind get lucky."

"They are truly repellant creatures," Max said with feeling.

"Quite a stretch from my posturing, womanizing, leather-clad costar who claims to be a vampire," I said. "Also quite a distance from Lord Ruthven's flowery monologues about honor, betrayal, pleasure, pain, yada yada."

"Oh, the undead don't make speeches," Max said seriously. "They're not capable of it."

"I was amazed before now that posing as a vampire got Daemon Ravel laid so much. After what you've told me, now I'm flabbergasted."

"Yes, the eroticization of the undead has always puzzled me," Max said. "Then again, I suppose I am the only person alive who actually experienced the Serbian vampire epidemic during the reign of Emperor Charles VI."

Although I had no idea who Charles VI was, I said, "Yes, I'd say that's certain, Max. But if they don't breed and make little vampires, then how does their tribe increase?"

"Their fatal predation—which sates their hunger, extends their existence, and kills the living—*also* infects their victims with the same dark magic, turning them into vampires, too."

"*Whoa.* That *is* efficient," I said, realizing why he dreaded even the memory of his vampire hunting days. "In other words, as soon as you've got one vampire in the neighborhood, you're well on your way to having an infestation of the things."

"It takes a little time, of course," he said. "A vampire doesn't rise the moment the living person dies. There's a process of mystical transformation. It can take anywhere from a single night to several days for the deceased to rise as a vampire."

"Hang on." I thought over what he had told me, then said with relief, "In that case, we *don't* have a vampire on our hands. The cops have found exsanguinated murder victims, not vampires. I know Lopez can be a little rigid about these things, but I think he would definitely notice and be interested if any of the deceased had risen from the dead."

Max disappointed me by saying, "Oh, I should have been clearer in my explanation. The victims *can* rise from the dead, and all too often do so. Well, too often for *me,* anyhow. But mystical transition to undeath is not a certainty. In many instances, and for a variety of reasons, the vampire's victim stays dead. Vampiric transformation is inhibited, for example, if the exsanguination was more or less total at the time of death."

"Oh." I thought of Adele Olson, aka Angeline.

"Or if the vampire consumed major organs or body parts upon committing the murder. Particularly if the creature ate the head, the liver, the intestines, the feet, the—"

"I don't need the whole list," I said faintly.

"No, perhaps not," he agreed. "However, this knowledge turned out to be significant in vampire hunting, since the undead, for reasons which have never been quite clear, are particularly attracted to the consumption of intestines."

"Oh. *That's* why you asked about that." I rather wished he hadn't explained it to me.

"While this habit leaves behind a dreadful mess for the living to clean up—"

"I can imagine."

"—it does have the benefit of ensuring that the victim doesn't become a vampire."

"Oh. If so, then why don't vampires, you know, control themselves and skip dessert? So to speak."

"Infecting their victims with vampirism isn't a conscious goal or intent. It's merely a diabolical side effect, if you will, of the vampire sating its mindless craving for human blood."

"Ah. Right. Driven by instinct. Not self-aware." How *did* such creatures morph into the objects of erotic desire in popular culture?

"Mind you, it's not as if a victim's corpse is left intact even if the vampire does not consume parts of the body. Indeed, the undead are such messy eaters, it can often be difficult to ascertain what, if anything, is missing from the victim's remains."

I felt my gorge rise and recalled that Lopez had said the exsanguination wasn't done tidily. I swallowed, took a steadying breath, and said, "Obviously, we're not talking about a couple of delicate fang holes in the neck."

"Indeed, no. Vampires don't have fangs." He paused and added, "Well, rarely. Apart from being in some stage of decomposition and decay, their outward physical features usually don't change a great deal in undeath. So they primarily rely on strength and viciousness to access a victim's blood. The results are . . ." Max cleared his throat. ". . . something no one should ever have to see."

I decided to move quickly past that point. "What about the trope that drinking a vampire's blood turns a person into one?"

"Ah! That actually happens to be true. But it's rarely advisable."

"Based on your description of the undead, I doubt that people are often tempted," I said. "What happens to victims who get attacked but not killed?"

"Vampirism seldom affects an individual who lives through the attack—though not many people *do* survive. Interestingly, vampirism is also less likely to infect a victim who is killed during a full moon."

"Really?" I said in surprise. "I would have thought it was the other way around."

"It does seem peculiarly counterintuitive, doesn't it?" Max said. "And, of course, when in doubt, there are thaumaturigical measures one can take to prevent the deceased from rising again."

"*What*-ical measures?"

"Thaumaturgy," Max said. "Magic."

"Ah. Such as . . ."

"Oh, placing garlic in the mouth and around the head of the deceased, for example. Along with the proper incantations, of course."

"Hey, garlic! That really works?" I was glad that *something* I knew about vampires was applicable.

"Only sometimes," Max said with regret. "All magic is notoriously unpredictable, after all."

"As I have had occasion to notice."

"Thrusting a stake through the heart of the deceased is only an effective measure if it really secures the individual to its grave. If the vampire which subsequently tries to rise is particularly strong, or if it's capable of problem solving, or if the soil is sandy, or if the grave is too shallow . . ." He shook his head. "Well, so many things can go wrong, staking the corpse is almost not worth bothering to do. Especially given what an exceedingly unpleasant task it is, as well as how much it upsets the loved ones of the deceased."

"But wouldn't driving a wooden stake through its heart solve the problem once and for all? I mean, doesn't that kill—I mean, dispatch—a vampire?"

"Alas, no," Max said. "And this common misconception is a particularly persuasive example of why misleading people about vampires is so dangerous. Thrusting a wooden stake into the heart of an undead attacker, aside from requiring more physical strength than most people possess, would accomplish nothing more fruitful than bringing you into close contact with a diabolically strong monster that wants to drain your blood and eat your intestines."

"That is a warning," I said, "that I definitely won't forget."

"A misinformed person would almost certainly wind up as a vampire victim by attempting to eliminate the undead in combat by that method. Though it was, I suppose, a convenient way for Stoker to dispatch the villain of his novel," Max added judiciously. "One must remember, in all fairness, that he was a sensitive person who abhorred violence, and he would probably not have been comfortable writing about vampire slaying with more veracity."

I thought of *myself* as a sensitive person who abhorred violence; but apparently this wasn't a unanimous view of my character.

Max continued, "After all, Stoker had no way of knowing that his wholly ineffectual method of dispatching a vampire would be taken as gospel for more than a century after his novel was published."

"No, I think Bram Stoker really couldn't have foreseen *anything* that's happened as a result of *Dracula*." Though, now that I knew the truth, I was rather tempted to blame the Irish novelist for Daemon Ravel. "But if a wooden stake doesn't work, then what does? *Something* must, or I guess you wouldn't have survived the, uh, Serbian vampire epidemic."

"Yes, fortunately, several methods are effective for slaying vampires. As well as for disabling them."

I blinked. "How do you disable a vampire?"

"Ah. The undead vampire is a mystical creature of dark forces, but it is not regenerative. It can be neutralized by dismemberment."

"That sounds even more unpleasant than staking corpses to their graves."

"It's also much more difficult, since vampires don't hold still for the process."

"No, I suppose not."

"And they are dauntingly fierce combatants. Although neutralizing a vampire may be a pragmatic solution to dealing with multiple attackers, it's a fatal mistake to assume that a vampire has ceased to be dangerous before it's terminated." His expression seemed haunted by memories as he continued, "I learned this through bitter experience. Which is also how I learned to dispatch them. I had never seen a vampire before I arrived in Serbia in 1730, and I knew very little about them. We *all* knew very little. Learning how to combat them was a trial and error process. One which, to my great sorrow, few of my fellow vampire hunters survived. It was a very dark time in my life, Esther."

I asked, "Were the other vampire hunters friends of yours? Or colleagues from the Magnum Collegium?"

"Yes. Like me, two other members of the Collegium were on that mission at the request of His Majesty's government."

"His Majesty?"

"Charles VI, the Habsburg ruler of the Austrian Empire. He also sent soldiers with us, to assist in our investigations. Fine young men who had no idea what they were getting into. Too many of them fell bravely in combat, never to rise again. As did one of my colleagues. The other . . ." As Max remembered his other colleague, his blue eyes clouded with a mist of tears, even after such a long passage of time. "He became one of the undead, and I had to dispatch him myself."

"Oh, Max," I said sympathetically.

"I carried out my duty by reminding myself that, had he known the fate that awaited him, he would have instructed me to do so."

"Of course." Imagining the horror of it, I said, "The creature who took his place was not your friend and not what he wanted to become. You did what must be done."

He cleared his throat and retreated safely into a more academic tone. "Decapitation and fire are the effective means we had by then discovered for slaying the undead. Fire, however, was often impractical. It is, as you know, my weakest element as a mage—and was even more so, all those years ago. I was particularly ineffectual at generating fire of any kind when I was under stress or frightened, as I usually was when confronting vampires. And in the 1730s, the mundane means of generating an impromptu fire were very limited and unreliable. Nor did we have always have fuel to maintain one. Conditions were often marginal."

I tried to picture Max as he must have been in those days. Already well into his seventies in 1730, his unusually slow aging process would have ensured that he still looked like a relatively young man. In that long ago era, he was still within the range of a biologically normal lifespan, and the world in which he was living then was not yet very different from the one in which he had been born and raised.

"So you mostly defeated vampires by decapitating them," I surmised.

"Yes. Decapitating the animated undead in combat is a bit more difficult than it might sound—"

"Oh, it sounds pretty difficult."

"—but it was the only reliable method of dispatch I found until . . ."

"Until?"

"Until the Lithuanians came," he said.

"Max!" I almost leaped out of my chair. "*Lithuanians?*"

He nodded.

I gaped at him.

He sighed and his gaze grew distant and distracted, as if remembering the encounter vividly now, across the span of centuries.

After a long moment, I said, "Well, you can't stop *there*, Max."

He looked startled, as if having momentarily forgotten where he was. "Ah. Yes . . . They came to Serbia because of the vampire epidemic. Because of our failure to contain it and end the outbreak." He added heavily, "Because of *my* failures."

"Oh, Max."

"There were three of them," he said.

"Only three?" For some reason, I had pictured an invading army. Or at least a large wagon train.

"More arrived later. But the three of them were a very effective force," Max said. "They were led by an elder named Jurgis Radvila, who was one of the most remarkable individuals I have ever known."

"Go on," I prodded.

"With Radvila and his comrades came the first ray of hope I had glimpsed during my terrible sojourn in Serbia," he said. "To understand why I made the choice I did, you must understand what that terrible vampire epidemic was like. And you must also learn, as I had to, that—"

"Yes, Max?"

"That vampirism is a good deal more complicated than I had realized when dealing only with the undead."

12

Medvegia, 1732

As his weary horse plodded into yet another humble Serbian village to which the vampire epidemic had recently spread, Max immediately recognized the apotropaics he saw—the methods by which the locals were attempting to shield themselves from Evil.

Bulbs of garlic hung in doorways and windows of homes throughout Medvegia. Crucifixes were prominently displayed on doors, and protective symbols were drawn over thresholds and on rooftops in white chalk. Some homes had a profusion of iron nails pounded into the outer walls around every window or entrance; this was a serious expense for such poor families, but less costly than losing a life to a vampire intruder. Directly outside of one cottage, a very large, ornate cross stood upright on its own, pounded into the ground.

Max heard two of the soldiers in his small escort exchange a few quiet words, speculating that the cross had been stolen from the local Orthodox church. It was clear from their tone that they were merely observing, not criticizing. These two young men had been serving in the region for six months; they had seen far too much to be

shocked by something as mundane as stealing sacred or-
naments from a church. They had also seen enough by
now to realize why a God-fearing family had done such
a thing, and why the other villagers evidently accepted
it.

His back ached, his eyes felt gritty with fatigue, and
his stomach rumbled irritably with the nervous digestive
disorder he had developed in recent months. He knew
he still seemed like a young man to others, with a smooth
face, thick brown hair, and a trim, upright figure; but for
the first time since his aging process had mysteriously
slowed decades ago, he was feeling the true weight of his
seventy-five years. Vampire hunting aged a man.

Lieutenant Hoffman, a young officer who had arrived
in the region only recently, was riding on Max's left. A
courteous, slightly shy fellow, he had been silent so far.
Now he pointed to a tumbledown home as they passed
it and asked, "What is that, Dr. Zadok?"

Max's gaze followed the direction of Hoffman's gesture. He saw thick, wide streaks of brownish-red all
around the cottage's doorway and its two windows. The
same rusty color was splattered on the ground in front
of the door

"It's the blood of a recent victim," Max explained.
"Someone who was a member of that household, or at
least a frequent visitor there. The family collected the
blood from the remains they found after the person was
killed."

"Mein Gott!" Hoffman exclaimed. "Is that some
ghastly mourning ritual?"

"No. The people inside that house think that warding
their home this way will prevent the victim from returning there as a vampire." He paused. "They are mistaken.
The odor of blood will *attract* vampires—including the
one which they specifically fear."

"Should we not warn them?" the lieutenant asked.

"Yes," Max said. "We will do so."

But he knew from experience that the locals probably wouldn't heed his advice. Unable to defeat their ghoulish adversaries, the people of this region clung fervently to their beliefs in various ineffectual wards and remedies. And Max increasingly accepted this. If he couldn't eliminate the threat or protect these people, then what right did he have to take away their false sense of comfort in empty measures?

There were too many vampires in the region, and their numbers were increasing too rapidly. Locating them or devising protections against them took too long and was too often ineffectual. Fighting them led to too many human casualties while diminishing the vampire population only slightly.

Max felt increasingly helpless—even useless. And he hated the feeling.

Meanwhile, almost as if life were still perfectly normal in this vampire-infested village, local people began emerging and appearing, as if from nowhere, drawn by curiosity to this small group of foreign soldiers and one modestly dressed civilian riding slowly toward the main square. Strangers were uncommon in rural areas, and usually a welcome diversion if they came in peace—though strangers often did *not* come in peace here. This region had been repeatedly sacked and pillaged by conquerors from the East *and* from the West for centuries. Yet despite that, Max saw some hesitantly welcoming smiles among the villagers whom he nodded to and greeted now.

Children walked beside the visitors' horses, looking up at them with round, serious brown eyes. Max smiled down at a black-haired little boy who trotted on foot beside him, so small that he had to hurry to keep up with the plodding pace of Max's tired mount.

Apparently reassured by this smile, the boy tentatively touched Max's booted foot and spoke. His high-pitched voice was imploring, and even Max, with his marginal Serbian vocabulary, understood what the boy said: "Please make them go away."

He wanted to promise he would. He wanted to swear with confidence to the child that he would end this horrible nightmare, and then everything would return to normal. But, in truth, he had no idea what he would be able to accomplish here. He was increasingly unnerved by his failures, and even his modest successes as a vampire hunter were marred by subsequent setbacks.

He looked down at that innocent, imploring face and felt unable to lie or give false hope. Least of all to a child.

So instead of making promises that stuck in his dry throat, he said to the boy, "Please inform the village elders that we are here." He could tell from the slight frown on the child's face that his foreign accent made the phrase difficult to understand. So he repeated it slowly, enunciating clearly. This time the boy nodded in understanding. Then he ran ahead of Max's retinue, calling for someone.

Finding the main square of the village was just a matter of following this street until it reached the heart of the community. The boy had done as asked, and five older men were gathering in the square to greet Max and his party, along with many of the other locals. The five men's faces were stern and grave. One of them was wounded, his arm cradled in an embroidered sling.

To Max's relief, there was also a modestly prosperous-looking younger man with the elders who spoke some German. This would make communication easier. Max's mother tongue was Czech, which he'd seldom had occasion to speak in recent years. German was among his strongest languages, along with English, Latin, Greek, and French.

The man who spoke German introduced himself as Aleksandar Bosko. He greeted Max and Lieutenant Hoffman, then introduced them to the village elders. Bosko invited them all into his home nearby, where they sat together in a sparsely furnished but comfortable room to talk, while the four soldiers who had come here under Hoffman's command patrolled the vicinity. Max accepted something to drink, but declined food—his stomach was still bothering him—and asked the elders to tell him their story. Bosko's role as interpreter was very useful; but Max had heard so many similar accounts since arriving in the Balkans in the spring of 1730 that he could follow some of the Serbian language in this account.

First, there was a mysterious disappearance, which was very unusual for the village—or at least it was when no foreign armies were marauding through the area. Within a few days, another villager went missing. Then people started dying. They would be found in the morning, white as chalk, their blood drained from their bodies, their corpses horribly mutilated—even partly eaten. Panic and hysteria spread through the village. Old grievances became fresh feuds, and private suspicions turned into public accusations, which soon escalated into violence and mayhem.

More people disappeared, and their families were increasingly too frightened to go out in search of them. Then someone finally saw one of the terrifying creatures that was preying on their village—and lived to tell the tale. That was when they began to understand what was happening to Medvegia.

"Now, Dr. Zadok," said Bosko, "one person is dead or missing out of every five in Medvegia. We huddle together in fear at night and are preyed on by fiendish monsters. The dead walk among us, and people we knew and loved have become murdering demons who thirst for our blood."

When the gruesome account was finished, Hoffman looked at Max. "Where shall we start?"

"The local cemetery," he said promptly. "Let's commence our work by making sure no *new* vampires rise from the grave here. We'll start with the most recent burials."

Opening graves and desecrating corpses was grisly, disturbing, and exhausting work. And, as usual, it was accompanied by an unwanted audience of protesting relatives and wailing women. Predictably, an angry Orthodox priest was also there, arguing that Max and his helpers were violating the repose of the faithful whom the church had buried.

"Not a very practical objection, considering the situation," Max said, his rebellious stomach churning while the stench of decay gradually permeated his nostrils, hair, and clothing.

The more obvious it became that prayer and religious rituals weren't protecting their flocks or preventing vampire attacks, the more defensive and rigid the village priests tended to become. They were usually men of humble background who had very little education and no previous experience with such matters. Max was sympathetic to the terrified panic he could see in their eyes, but increasingly impatient with their obstreperous behavior.

Among the local volunteers helping with the work this afternoon, there were also, as was often the case, one or two young men who seemed to enjoy these distasteful tasks more than Max thought was seemly.

As night fell and darkness crept across the graveyard, the work continued; but, fortunately, the distractions diminished. Whether the locals were interested in watching the vampire hunter at work or just wanted to shriek at him in protest when he beheaded or staked the bodies of their former neighbors and relatives, the villagers were emphatically not willing to remain at the cemetery after dark. They departed, fleeing to their homes before the creatures of the night emerged, leaving an eerily ominous silence in their wake.

When only two sturdy local volunteers remained, Bosko said, "It's very dark, Dr. Zadok. Perhaps we should go now."

"Yes, of course," Max said absently, noticing some disturbed earth on yet another grave. "By all means. Be vigilant on your way home."

"I meant that you and your companions should come, too," Bosko said.

Three of the soldiers were still digging. Hoffman and another soldier were patrolling the graveyard alertly, their weapons ready, their pace measured.

"No, we must remain and work." Max was still examining the grave which had attracted his attention. "Before you leave, may I ask when the burial in this plot occurred?"

"It's not safe for you to remain outside after dark," Bosko warned.

"Based on the elders' account, being inside isn't safe in Medvegia anymore, either."

"That's true," Bosko said sadly. "Still . . ."

"I've come to your village to hunt vampires," Max reminded him. "Therefore, it is advantageous for me to remain where I am likely to encounter them."

"Oh. Yes, of course. Well, then." Bosko cleared his throat. "I must remain here, too, in that case."

Max glanced at him. "That's brave, but very dangerous. I don't advise it. You would be wise to go home, sir."

"No, I will remain."

"He *is* a brave man," said one of the two local diggers, setting aside his shovel and making preparations to leave. "He has even slain one of the vampires."

"Have you?" Max said with interest, well able by now to follow Serbian phrases about killing vampires.

The other digger, also setting aside his shovel, said, "Tell him, Aleksandar!" He added to Max, "It's a good story."

"No, no," said Bosko. "I cannot speak of my deed to a *true* vampire hunter."

Max said in German, "Based on what your friends have just said, sir, I gather you *are* a true vampire hunter. The requirements of the vocation are quite simple, after all. It's *surviving* them that's complicated."

"Yes, surviving the vampire was . . . not simple." Bosko paused, then said, "If I may ask, Dr. Zadok, does your work make your wife very anxious?"

"Oh, she died some time ago." It had been more than twenty years; but, given his youthful appearance, he knew better than to say so.

"God rest her soul. I am also a widower." Seeing Max's inquisitive expression, Bosko shook his head. "No, not vampires. Childbirth."

"I see. I am sorry to hear that." It was a tragically common story. "God rest her soul."

The two diggers bade them farewell and departed, casting understandably nervous glances around the dark cemetery as they began walking home with long, quick strides

Max's attention returned to the burial plot that concerned him. "We need to open this grave."

"Oh, but this is the grave of Miliza Pavle," Bosko said in surprise. "She was a fine woman. Much admired."

"Alas, that is no protection against what I fear may have happened to her."

"But the diggers are gone."

"They have thoughtfully left their shovels." Max picked one up.

"Oh," Bosko said without enthusiasm. "Very well. I shall assist you."

"When was Miliza Pavle buried?"

Bosko suddenly lifted his head and turned it slightly, as if listening to something Max couldn't hear. After a moment, Max repeated his question. Bosko still didn't respond; his attention was obviously engaged by something else.

Max looked around the cemetery, now illuminated

only by several torches that the soldiers had posted when darkness fell. Near one of the torches, he saw Hoffman turn suddenly, his body poised alertly as he gazed out into the night. Then the lieutenant called softly over his shoulder to Max and the others, "Riders approaching."

"Yes." Bosko nodded. "How strange."

"Your hearing is most acute," Max noted, only now becoming aware of the faint thunder of hoofbeats in the distance. "Do you know who that is?"

"No," said the Serb. "But surely they must be strangers. No one here would make a journey after dark. Not anymore."

Leaning on his shovel, Max listened for another moment. "Well, I suppose we'll find out momentarily who they are. They're headed in this direction. It seems rather— Argh!"

The grave beneath his feet heaved violently, flinging him forward. He careened into Bosko and the two men fell down, hitting the ground together with a thud that knocked the wind out of Max's lungs.

"MwwwwarrrrgggGGGH!"

An undead woman who was presumably Miliza Pavle rose from the grave in a quick, powerful surge of motion, sending dirt flying everywhere as she issued another ear-splitting howl of bloodthirsty hunger.

"Oh, dear," Max gasped, wishing he hadn't let the shovel fly out of his hand when he fell.

Miliza staggered toward him, her decomposing arms outstretched, foamy saliva hanging from her cracked blue lips, her ravaged torso gaping open where she had received mortal wounds from a vampire while still alive. She gave off a terrible stench.

Bosko screamed and seized the shovel Max had dropped. He leaped to his feet and brandished it at the approaching vampire, shouting in Serbian.

Two shots were fired in close succession, and Max

heard shouts in German. One of the words he caught was, "Reload!"

If he lived through tonight, he would obviously need to remind his Austrian retinue that firearms didn't slay vampires and, unfortunately, seldom even slowed them down.

When Miliza dived for Bosko, who jumped out of reach, particles of dirt flew everywhere—including into Max's eyes.

"Perdition!" He scuttled backward on the ground, his eyes watering and stinging fiercely, his vision obscured. He needed his ax, which he'd left lying close at hand—or so he thought at the time. Now, disoriented from his fall and unable to see, he didn't know where the weapon was.

"Yarrrgggghhh!" Miliza roared nearby.

Bosko was still shouting in terror, so at least he was alive.

Another shot was fired, and Max heard the lead ball whiz right past his cheek, barely missing him.

"Hold your fire, man!" he cried, feeling around frantically on the ground for his ax, blinking hard as he tried to clear his vision.

The earth under his hands bulged violently, and then burst upward in an explosion of noise, movement, and fury as another vampire leaped forth from its grave.

"Gott im Himmel," Max gasped, rolling away from the emerging monster which instantly reached for him, growling and drooling with hunger.

His panicky, crawling retreat from the powerfully grasping hands brought him into unexpected contact with his ax—which he discovered by cutting his hand painfully on it. "Zounds!"

Reflexively cradling the injured hand against his body, he seized the ax with his other hand, rolled to his feet, and took a wild swing at the approaching vampire. He missed its head but did manage to lop off its hand as it spun away from the blow. The vampire bellowed with rage, as well as with what may or may not have been pain—after so many battles against them, Max still wasn't sure whether the creatures felt pain. In any case, loss of a hand was not a severe enough injury to disable a vampire, as he well knew. When the creature lunged at him an instant later, he danced to one side, holding his ax ready, seeking the opportunity to counterattack.

He heard the shrill whinny of a horse and was vaguely aware that the approaching hoofbeats were very close now. There were male voices, deep-throated shouts echoing through the night. He realized from the howls and screams he heard all around him that more vampires were rising. The epidemic here was even worse than he'd supposed upon hearing the elders' account. He had neutralized at least seven corpses before nightfall, and yet an alarming number of vampires were nonetheless bursting forth from the hallowed ground.

Then he saw yet another vampire emerging from the darkness, coming from somewhere behind the one he was fighting. He noticed it was approaching from *outside* the graveyard. Max circled his foe, and the change in his position brought more vampires into view. They weren't just *in* the graveyard, emerging from the soil, he realized with dawning horror; they were also attacking now from the woods beyond the cemetery. The victims had evidently fallen there in death and not yet been found or buried.

Max heard more shouting, unfamiliar voices, words he couldn't distinguish. He looked past the vampire he was fighting, and he saw strangers dismount their horses and run into the graveyard. Three men. One headed for Hoffman, who was frantically trying to reload his carbine while two vampires approached him from opposite directions.

These brave reinforcements gave Max a moment of hope. But then he realized the foolishness of that optimism. The living in this battle were badly outnumbered by the undead. A quick, frantic glance around the cemetery revealed a shocking number of vampires. And more were emerging from the darkness even as Max returned his full attention to trying to defeat the one he was combating before another one could attack him.

There were too many of them. There were just *too many* . . .

He took a deep breath and recognized that he would die in Medvegia.

Acceptance was best. Fear, panic, and vain protests against his fate would cloud his mind and make him more vulnerable to his adversaries. In this, his final battle, he wanted to fight well and take as many vampires to hell with him as he could.

He also, he realized with sick dread, did not want to *become* one of them.

Do not think about that. Think only of destroying these monsters.

Max feinted to the right. The vampire followed his lead. He whirled around, turning a complete circle to the left, and swung a true blow, connecting exactly as intended. The vampire's head flew off and rolled away. As the decapitated body fell toward him, Max took a step backward to avoid contact—and backed straight into the arms of another vampire.

Heart thundering in his chest, he struggled against the powerful arms that held him, pinning Max's own arms to his side. He felt blood dripping from his injured hand, making it slippery, making the ax handle difficult to hold onto—especially with his arms being squeezed ruthlessly against his body. The foul odor of the creature which held him was nauseating, and the way the thing snuffled hungrily at his flesh filled him with revulsion. He felt its grip tighten and its head move to sink its teeth into the back of his neck, where it would gnaw and tear, laboriously mauling his living tissue while he screamed in agony and struggled to survive . . .

And then he felt the vampire grunt in surprise as it was wrenched violently backward. Its arms flailed, releasing Max. He staggered away, then turned quickly—in time to see, to his utter astonishment, one of the newly arrived strangers turn the creature's head sharply in his bare hands and *rip* it off the body.

His blood roaring in his ears, Max just stared in open-mouthed shock.

After a moment, the tall, powerfully built, gray-haired man looked up and shouted something at him. Max didn't understand the language, but the urgency of the tone returned him to his senses. He lunged to the right as he whirled sharply, his ax ready for engagement. The vampire that was attacking him from behind howled in frustration and lunged for him again. Max heard a faint humming sound shoot past him, then he saw the vampire flinch as if in response to a blow. It staggered back a few steps and clutched its chest with both hands. Then it let out a horrible sound and fell down.

Max turned to see the stranger holding a crossbow still aimed at the vampire, which was when he recognized what had just happened. The stranger lowered the weapon, approached Max, and spoke tersely, still in that unfamiliar language. Max realized an instant later what he wanted; the man seized his ax as he strode past him, and he used it to behead the fallen creature.

Just beyond where the stranger was doing this, Max saw the vampire which had once been Miliza Pavle wrestle the shovel away from Bosko and strike him with it. The dazed Serb fell facedown, and the vampire raised the shovel for another blow, clearly intent on bludgeoning the back of Bosko's head with it.

"No! Fly from her!" Max shouted in Latin, pointing at the shovel, concentrating all his energy on the animative spell.

The shovel flew out of Miliza's hands and disappeared into the darkness.

The stranger saw this deed. He turned and met Max's gaze. His heavily lined face, like his gray hair, was a puzzling contrast to his speed, strength, and agility in combat.

He said to Max in Latin, "You are something out of the ordinary, aren't you?"

"So, it would seem, are you," Max said in the same language.

They continued staring at each other in puzzled curiosity for another moment.

Then the stranger's expression changed. "Get down!"

Max dropped to the ground as the man hurled the ax over Max's head. It connected with a heavy thud behind him. Even as Max was turning to see the attacking vampire fall backward, his ax now planted firmly in its chest, the stranger was already running past him to retrieve the weapon from its target and use it to decapitate the creature.

I might not die after all, Max realized in astonishment.

That glimmer of hope renewed his strength and infused him with the first sense of optimism he'd felt in quite some time. He caught his ax when the vampire-killer tossed it to him, and he re-entered the fray with vigor—well aware, from that point forward, that the three strangers who had arrived in the nick of time were doing the lion's share of the slaying.

The battle was over in a remarkably short period of time. And to Max's trembling relief, all five of the young soldiers who had accompanied him to Medvegia were still alive. Hoffman was babbling hysterically and seemed as if he might not be quite himself for a while, and another of the soldiers had a leg wound, but everyone had survived and would live to see the dawn.

Breathing hard with fatigue and limp with relief, Max cradled his injured hand against his chest as he watched the stranger who had saved his life give instructions in his unfamiliar language to the other two men who had arrived with him. They mounted their horses and rode off into the night.

"Where are they going?" Bosko asked, limping to Max's side.

"Are you all right?" Max was relieved to see the Serbian alive and in one piece.

"Miliza Pavle changed a great deal after death," he said seriously. "But I am well enough. And you?"

Max looked down at his blood-drenched hand. The cut made by the ax was long and deep. "This isn't serious, but it *is* messy. I need to wrap it in something."

Bosko made a strange gurgling noise. Max looked at him and, in the faint torchlight, saw that the Serb's gaze was wide-eyed now, fixed on his bloody hand.

"It's bleeding rather copiously, but it is just a cut," Max said reassuringly as he extended his hand to catch the wavering light and get a better look at it.

"Magician!" The vampire-slaying stranger called in Latin, crossing the graveyard and coming toward him. "I think that you and I have much to discuss."

"I agree," Max called back.

Bosko started to pant anxiously. Max looked at him again and saw that the man's gaze was still riveted on his bloody hand. The Serb's face was contorting into an awful expression.

"Does the sight of blood distress you?" It was an affliction Max had encountered before. He turned away, intending to conceal the injury from Bosko's gaze.

"No!" The man growled in his native language, stopping him with a rough tug on his shoulder. "Give *me!*"

Bosko seized Max's hand, dragged it up to his mouth, and sucked furiously on the bloody wound.

"Good God!" Max gasped, trying to pull his hand out of the man's powerful grasp—and away from that thirstily consuming mouth. "What are you *doing?*"

"Magician!" the stranger shouted.

As Max struggled for possession of his hand, Bosko

made obscene grunting noises of satisfaction, slurping and sucking messily, biting and scratching as Max tried to escape his clutches.

"Stop!" Max cried, caught off guard by the man's unexpected strength and bizarre behavior. "Release me!"

He heard rapidly thudding footsteps come up behind him, and then the stranger's harsh breathing was near his ear as a big fist shot past him and hit Bosko sharply in one exultantly closed eye. Bosko cried out in pain and staggered backward, his hand covering his eye and Max's blood staining his mouth and chin.

The stranger raised his crossbow.

"No!" Max shouted.

Bosko uttered an abortive squeal even as Max lunged for the stranger's weapon—too late.

Too late.

"No . . ."

The crossbow bolt sticking partway out of Bosko's forehead was still quivering as the Serb fell over dead.

Max turned on the stranger in horrified fury. "What have you *done?*"

"He was a vampire," the man said simply.

"No, he wasn't!"

"He was. And, based on the way he attacked you, he was not in control of himself. He would soon have become a killer, if he was not one already."

"You're mad!" He felt he could scarcely breathe as he looked again at the deceased Serb—a man whom he had rather liked.

"Do you imagine he was *tending* your bloody wound?"

Max looked down at his hand in an appalled daze. "He . . . he . . . I . . ." What had Bosko been *doing?*

"He was drinking your blood. Sating his hunger."

Revolted, enraged, and grieving over the murder of a good man, Max clung to the only rational thought he could find in his whirling confusion. "He was *not* undead! He was as alive as you and I are!"

"Yes, he was," the stranger agreed. "And he was also a vampire."

Max stared at him, dumbfounded.

"A *made* vampire," the man added. "That much is certain."

"A made . . ."

"Did you notice him exhibiting any symptoms?"

"What?"

"Heightened senses, for example? Did his hearing, vision, or sense of smell seem abnormally acute?"

"He . . ." Max drew in a sharp breath. "His hearing." His throat felt raw as he said, "He had unusually good hearing."

"And he let you notice." There was a touch of condescension in the stranger's voice. "That is typical of the made. Especially the newly made. They are unaccustomed to the superior senses of the vampire, and it often shows."

"The *made?* What on earth are you saying?"

"He was not born a vampire."

"Who is *ever* born a vampire?" Max demanded in frustrated bewilderment.

"He *became* one. Perhaps quite recently." The man looked around at the vampire corpses that littered the graveyard. "Certainly there seems to be no shortage of opportunity in this village, if one is so inclined."

"Opportunity?"

"Do you happen to know if he killed a vampire?"

Max blinked. "Er, yes. He did. How did you know?"

"That is presumably when he drank vampire blood. And thus became made as one."

"He became a vampire by drinking the blood of . . ." Max looked around at the odorous, decaying bodies of the undead which they had just fought and slain. His restless stomach roiled in revulsion. "Dear God! How *could* he?"

"He was presumably seeking heightened strength,

keener senses, and improved well-being. One who yearns for these gifts overcomes his disgust if only the undead are available. He did what was necessary to fulfill his desire."

"Necessary?" For a moment, as he imagined what Bosko must have done to become a vampire, Max thought he would vomit.

"He very likely did not anticipate the blood hunger he would experience. And when it came upon him tonight . . ."

Max's grief and anger returned. "You should not have *killed* him!"

"The made can be very dangerous. You obviously have no idea *how* dangerous. If they lack self-control, as he did, they must be executed." The tall, gray-haired stranger added, "This is precisely why my people rarely allow a vampire to be made."

"Your peo . . ." Max took a few breaths, trying to steady himself and martial his madly careening thoughts. "Who *are* your people? Who are *you*? Where did you come from?"

"My name is Jurgis Radvila. I have come from Vilnius."

"In Lithuania? *That* Vilnius?" Max blurted, still bewildered.

"Yes," said Radvila. "The journey was long. And I now realize that we should have come sooner."

"We . . ." Max's gaze returned to Bosko's corpse as he asked, "Where did your companions go?"

"They are patrolling."

"It's dark."

"We can see better by night than you can."

Images of the recent battle flooded Max's mind. "You possess some form of mystical power," he said slowly.

"So do you, magician."

"My name is Maximillian Zadok." He glanced at Radvila's crossbow. "Why are your crossbows more effective against the undead than our firearms?"

"The bolts we use are made from a special alloy. An ancient formula known only to us."

"Us?"

"Maximillian, the situation here has clearly passed the point of crisis and is now descending into all-out catastrophe," Radvila said. "Therefore, I believe we should forego wasting time and be candid with one another."

Although still appalled by the slaying of Bosko, Max recognized that Jurgis Radvila seemed far better equipped than he to combat the vampire epidemic. Therefore, cooperation was advisable—no, essential.

Max nodded in agreement. "Yes, by all means. Let us exercise candor."

"Very well. I should perhaps begin by telling you that my comrades and I are vampires."

Max flinched and fell back a step.

Having apparently expected that reaction, Radvila added, "Not made. And certainly not undead. We are *Lithuanian* vampires."

"Does that make a difference?"

"Of course. We are hereditary vampires."

"Hereditary?"

"And we have come here to halt this vampire epidemic."

Recalling that the three Lithuanian combatants had slain a veritable army of vampires tonight—whose stinking remains were now scattered all over the graveyard— Max said, "I don't yet understand what you're saying. But I suspect that, once I do, I shall be very grateful for your presence here."

"We must act quickly and decisively," said Radvila. "The Council of Gediminas is very concerned about the situation in this region."

"Who?" Max asked.

"The Council of Gediminas," Radvila repeated. "As I said before, you and I have much to discuss."

13

66 He told me they were an ancient council of hereditary vampires who governed, er, vampire matters," Max explained to me. "They also thwarted vampire epidemics by slaying the undead with prompt and merciless efficiency, as well as executing unruly made vampires."

A middle-aged woman strolling near us in Washington Square Park on this sunny Sunday afternoon heard this and gave us an odd look. She also noticed my black eye, scraped cheek, and ravaged neck—all of which had alarmed Max when I'd first arrived at his bookstore earlier—and obviously drew her own conclusions about us.

"Keep your voice down," I reminded Max as the woman deliberately changed direction to avoid us.

At some point during Max's account of his experiences as a vampire hunter in the Balkan provinces of the Habsburg empire, Nelli had made it known to us that she needed her walk—or, as Max called it, her habitual afternoon perambulation. (Much of Max's syntax was still living in the Habsburg era.) So after attaching Nelli's pink leather leash to her matching collar, we had brought her to the park while Max continued his story.

"All right, I follow how vampire victims became the

undead, bloodthirsty monsters that you hunted and killed. Um, slayed. Slew?" I said, reviewing the key elements of Max's terrible tale. "And based on what Jurgis Radvila told you, I also follow how a living person becomes a made vampire. And, by the way, how disgusting is *that*? No *way* am I ever drinking the blood of a stinking, drooling, decaying corpse just so I can have supersonic hearing or feel more robust!"

A passing jogger stumbled, stopped, and stared at me.

"I'm an actress," I said quickly to him. "We're running lines."

"Oh! *Oh.*" The young man's expression cleared. "Cool." He continued on his way.

Tugging gently on Nelli's leash to urge her away from the siren smell of some garbage that lay on the ground, Max noted, "You might want to keep your voice down, as well."

I did so as I said with disgust, "If Bosko wanted improved vigor, he should have tried eating right and exercising more, rather than sucking on the marrow of the undead."

"He lived in an impoverished village in eighteenth-century Serbia," Max pointed out. "Eating right was seldom an option. Exercise consisted mostly of backbreaking work, relieved by sporadic intervals of feuding with other locals or fleeing from invading armies."

"Well, yes, okay. I get that." I took Max's arm as we walked. I was stunned by the story he had told me. My considerable respect for what he had faced, endured, and conquered over the course of his long life had increased again today. "But what Bosko did was so extreme, Max. What was he *thinking?*"

"I never really had a chance to know him, obviously. And since we left Medvegia within two busy days of his demise, I also had little opportunity to learn much about him after his death. But it was obvious that he was respected and valued in the village. And I saw for myself that his friends were correct when they described him as a brave man. He stayed in the graveyard with me to battle the undead. He did not flee when attacked, nor even after we were outnumbered." Max sighed sadly. "I have always believed that Bosko did what he did because he sought to absorb vampire power so that he could more effectively combat the undead and protect his village from those creatures."

"At the cost of *becoming* a vampire?"

"He may have thought it was worth that sacrifice. Or perhaps he didn't fully understand what would happen to him—what the transformation would entail. Radvila believed the latter to be the case, and he may well have been right. The beliefs, superstitions, and apotropaics of the region in that era were a complex muddle of partially accurate folklore, desperate measures, and uselessly bizarre fiction."

Max stopped to let Nelli greet another dog, her tail wagging and her attitude playfully bouncy—which the other dog dealt with bravely, considering the difference in their sizes. This was apparently a friend whom she met regularly, since the other dog's owner acknowledged Nelli by name. In response to the woman's greeting to him, Max smiled and briefly lifted the white fedora he wore on his head. A chilly gust of wind whipped through the park, making his long duster flutter and flap in the breeze; the pale brown coat, a true relic of the Old West, had been bequeathed to him by a gunfighter.

As we continued walking again, he said, "Bosko must have learned—perhaps from a local wise woman or village elder, or possibly from remembered legends about a previous epidemic—that drinking vampire blood could enhance his physical prowess. He may have gone hunting a vampire with the goal of using its essence to turn himself into a more effective warrior. But I think it more likely that the decision was made on impulse after he managed to survive an attack and dispatch his adversary.

When he saw the creature's body lying at his feet . . . I think Bosko believed he could make a difference, if he could just steel himself to do what was necessary."

I heard remembered sorrow in Max's voice again, and I squeezed his arm. "Oh, how terrible." Realizing that the long-dead Serb deserved recognition as a fallen hero, I added, "It seems very cruel of Radvila to have killed him, if he had transformed himself so he could better protect the villagers."

"I would say ruthless rather than cruel," Max said. "I admired Radvila. I grew to like and trust him. I am proud to say that we became friends, though we never met again after signing the Treaty of Gediminas. But he was quite ruthless. Then again, it was his duty to be so. The council had put him in charge of eliminating the vampire epidemic that was spreading through Eastern Europe. He did not have the right—as he subsequently told me—to leave alive a made vampire who lacked self-control. A vampire who might start killing to feed his hunger."

Max made a little sound of regret and shook his head before he continued, "Bosko's fate was sealed the moment he attacked me. I don't believe he intended to hurt me, and I sincerely doubt he would have tried to kill me. His behavior in that moment was just instinctive. But once Radvila saw—*agh!*"

Max nearly fell over when Nelli, who weighed more than I did, suddenly lunged for the remains of a discarded hot dog that lay in the grass. As she gulped down her unsanitary treat, she pretended deafness, looking everywhere but at us and completely ignoring Max as he scolded her for her ill-mannered and ill-advised behavior.

Then Max smiled ruefully at me. "*Instinct.* Now that she has physical form, Nelli finds herself unable to control the canine impulses she experiences. After he transformed himself, Bosko also found himself unable to control his instinctual vampire cravings."

When I saw him absently rub his shoulder, which Nelli's sudden lunge had wrenched rather sharply, I said, "Here, give me the leash, Max. I'll hold her for a while."

I took the pink leash from him and gave Nelli a brisk tug, attempting to halt her frantic snuffling around in the grass as she searched for more processed-meat remains.

Watching her activities, Max said pensively, "Once the Lithuanian saw Bosko's behavior, there was nothing else to be done. I grew to understand that. Radvila would never allow sentiment to persuade him to let an unstable and dangerous vampire remain alive and at large."

"How dangerous was Bosko? Does vampirism turn the living into monsters, too?"

"Not necessarily, but it *is* a serious risk and an all too common problem with made vampires. Which is why making a vampire is only allowed if the Council of Gediminas permits it after considering a formal petition. And they very rarely *do* permit it, precisely because whether the made vampire becomes a responsible individual or, instead, a violent hazard to society depends on too many complex variables.

"Such as?"

"Oh, the character of the individual, the nature of his transformation, and the circumstances of the new vampire's life."

"*Nelli.* Come on." I gave the oversized familiar's leash another sharp tug. She lifted her head from the grass, wagging her tail as she gazed innocently at me, and we finally moved on. "Well, I agree that character is complex and often unpredictable, Max. And given that the nature of vampire transformation consists of dining on a ravaged corpse, I'd say—"

"Oh, it doesn't," Max said. "Not usually, that is. That does occasionally happen, as it did in Bosko's case. However, given how distasteful—indeed, almost unconquerably repulsive—imbibing from the undead is, it's more common to achieve living transformation by ingesting the blood of a made or hereditary vampire."

"By killing one?" I asked dubiously. Based on what Max had said about their strength and prowess in combat, that sounded suicidally risky.

"Well, one could, if one were so inclined—as well as heavily armed and very daring. But the more typical method is that the vampire voluntarily shares his or her blood. The practice is rigorously controlled by the Council of Gediminas, and the process is, I gather, very formal and ritualistic." After a pause, he added, "A vampire who ignores the rules might choose to share blood with someone as a personal, private, unregulated matter, but this is strictly prohibited and the penalties can be severe. Indeed, both parties might be executed. Did I mention that Lithuanians can be ruthless?"

"So this is your . . . your *thing* with Lithuanians?" I asked. "They're all vampires?"

"Oh, goodness, no! Have I given that impression? How careless of me! Oh, dear." He explained quickly, "No, no, vampirism is extremely rare among Lithuanians. And almost unknown among other peoples."

"It sure wasn't unknown among the Serbs," I pointed out.

"That was an epidemic, not a lifestyle. And those vampires were undead, not hereditary."

"All right, that's what I *don't* follow. What is a hereditary vampire?"

"Ah." His face brightened. "That's a rather interesting subject."

According to the legend that Radvila had recounted to Max long ago, hereditary vampirism in Lithuania dated back to the Middle Ages.

Gediminas, the great fourteenth-century warrior king who founded of the city of Vilnius, was out hunting in the woods one day. The king's favorite dog went missing, and Gediminas didn't want to return to the castle without it. So he went searching for it, and thus wound up staying out too long. Darkness fell, and a swarm of un-dead vampires attacked him. Gediminas defeated them singlehandedly in fierce combat, during the course of which he accidentally imbibed enough of their blood to become a made vampire.

"How much is enough?" I asked.

"A sip or two is certainly insufficient," Max said. "A more substantial quantity of vampire blood is required to effect transformation."

"How does someone *accidentally* imbibe that much blood?"

"Actually," Max said, "I find that part of the legend easier to believe than the claim that a normal man, even one very skilled in combat, singlehandedly vanquished multiple vampires who set upon him in a frenzy."

Well, what with warring factions in his own land, ma-rauding bands of unemployed knights from the south coming north to burn and loot in Lithuania, a land-hungry Polish kingdom on one side of him, and various Cossacks and Mongols on the other side, Gediminas re-ally had a lot on his plate. However, he soon found that his vampire transformation made it easier to cope with the heavy demands of being a beleaguered warrior king. Eventually, through energetic conquests (as well as shrewd alliances), he created an empire.

It occurred to him at some point along the way that it would be advantageous for the future of his kingdom and the success of his progeny if he could pass on his acquired gift of vampirism to his heirs. He consulted various scholars, magicians, physicians, and prophets, both foreign and domestic. After a number of disap-pointments, he finally found someone who subjected him to an effective mystical ritual which achieved his goal; the progeny he sired thereafter, with Mrs. Gedimi-nas and with other women, were born with the heredi-tary gift of his vampirism.

"The results, however, were probably not what Gediminas envisioned," Max said. "His various heirs fought over the throne, and his unified empire did not long survive his death."

"Figures." Feuding royal heirs seemed to be a common theme throughout history.

"Nonetheless, vampirism did, through Gediminas' efforts, become a hereditary trait among a very small percentage of Lithuanian males—"

"*Only* males?"

"Yes."

I frowned. "That's not fair."

"I agree. But Gediminas was interested in securing the succession and protecting his empire," Max explained. "Not gender equality."

"Hmph."

"Before dying, he founded the Council of Gediminas in Vilnius, which is still the regulatory body governing vampires to this day," he said. "Established by a ruler seeking to maintain political stability through vampirism, the object of the council has always been to ensure that hereditary vampires are valuable members of society, rather than bloodthirsty murderers. Thus the members of the council—and, indeed, Lithuanian vampires, in general—have occupied an utterly unique position in vampire phenomenology for centuries."

"They sound like the police force of the vampire world."

"Police, judge, jury, and executioner," said Max.

"Don't other vampires object to that?"

"There *aren't* many other vampires. Vampirism is only hereditary among Lithuanians. In all other instances worldwide, vampires are undead or made. The undead, for obvious reasons, must be fought and dispatched as soon as they emerge," he said. "Made vampires are very rare, and it's often necessary to execute them, as Radvila did, in order to prevent them from killing to quench their thirst."

"I suppose this is a trivial point, all things considered, but doesn't this mean that John Polidori and Bram Stoker could have based their suave, articulate vampires on Lithuanians?"

"No, the aristocratic vampires in their fiction are undead, as you may recall," Max said. "And that's just *one* of their irresponsible inaccuracies!"

"Forget I spoke. So let me make sure I've got this straight," I said. "There are three kinds of vampires: monsters, loose cannons, and Lithuanians."

"Correct."

"And Lithuanians are the responsible citizens of the vampire world, making sure that their dangerous relatives don't cause trouble."

"Precisely," he said. "The Lithuanian vampires I knew and fought beside in Serbia were honorable men who believed deeply in their moral duty to protect people from the undead and, er, loose cannons. But Radvila readily admitted that there were also practical reasons for their actions."

Nelli decided this was a propitious moment to roll on her back in the grass. Her long legs stuck up in the air and her big pink tongue hung out of the side of her mouth as she frolicked and made sounds of cheerful pleasure. It was impossible not to smile as we watched her.

Then Max continued, "Traditionally, the council policed vampirism within Lithuania, because if unruly vampires became a local pestilence, then the peaceful existence of law-abiding hereditary vampires would ultimately be threatened by mob hysteria."

"In other words, the council functioned like a neighborhood watch."

In a voice that was again filled with regrets, he said, "It was the Serbian vampire epidemic that convinced the council that their protection of the innocent must move beyond their borders and become international.

The Magnum Collegium and the Austrian government were unable to control the spread of the contagion. If vampirism menaced Europe on a large scale, the council realized, it was only a matter of time before all vampires everywhere—including law-abiding Lithuanian vampires who held government office, gave to charity, and had never harmed anyone—would be hunted and slaughtered like wild beasts."

"So the Lithuanians decided they had a stake in foreign vampires." I paused. "Sorry about that."

Nelli hopped to her feet, gave herself a thorough shake, and greeted a couple of passing children. Then she started sniffing purposefully around a nearby bush.

"Therefore, the council sent Radvila and his companions to the Balkans. More Lithuanians soon arrived in the region, and they were extraordinarily effective. But there were conditions for their involvement in ending the crisis. Conditions which they saw as essential to their own survival, and which I soon realized were realistic and reasonable. I had no authority to negotiate officially on behalf of the Austrian government or the Magnum Collegium, but Radvila and I made an unofficial agreement in good faith."

He continued, "Then as winter descended, the Lithuanians remained in the region, fighting vampires and ending the epidemic, while I returned to Vienna to propose Radvila's terms—the treaty terms of the Council of Gediminas—to the Austrian government and to my colleagues in the Collegium."

"This is the treaty you mentioned?" I asked. "The one that you and Radvila signed the last time you ever met?"

He nodded. "As it turned out, negotiating with government officials was almost as dreadful as battling vampires," Max said with a shudder. "Meanwhile, the Magnum Collegium was uneasy about the proposed terms and indecisive for some weeks, despite my exhortations. They didn't truly understand how dire conditions were in Serbia, and they were also uneasy about signing a treaty with vampires. So you see, I was asking both the Collegium and His Majesty's government to place a *great* deal of faith in my judgment."

"And did they?"

"More or less. In early spring, by which time the vampire epidemic had been conquered, I returned to Serbia with authorization to ratify the Treaty of Gediminas."

Having found a satisfactory spot, Nelli relieved herself. I scooped up her leavings with a plastic bag, which I carried over to a waste receptacle.

"Given the size and urgency of the problem," I said, "you'd think everyone would be relieved that the Lithuanians were there to solve it. I don't understand, Max. What was in this treaty that made it so controversial?"

"It stipulated that, from that day forward, all vampire matters, *wherever* they occurred, would come strictly under the authority of the Council of Gediminas. No other party to the treaty could intrude or interfere. Similarly, Lithuanian vampires undertook never to engage in or interfere with any non-vampire concerns of the other parties."

"They didn't want anyone's help with the next vampire epidemic?"

"The Lithuanians thought it was our fault that *this* one had become such a catastrophe. They felt we should just stay out of their way in future. They asserted that our failures—*my* failures—had indirectly put them at risk, and they couldn't allow that to happen again."

"That seems very unfair," I said loyally, "given what you were dealing with."

"No, their viewpoint had merit, Esther," Max said wearily. "Although I threw myself into my mission, I was not a particularly effective vampire hunter. I realized after seeing Lithuanians hunt and destroy the undead that it really was work best left to vampires."

"Was anyone else involved in the treaty?" I asked. "Were there other signatories?"

"No. Given the nature of the subject matter, it was something of a *secret* treaty," he said. "The Austrians and the Collegium both found it potentially embarrassing, albeit for different reasons."

"Ah." After a moment, I said, "But the Habsburg monarchy doesn't exist anymore. They fell from power and their empire crumbled at the end of World War One."

"True. The Magnum Collegium does still exist, however, as does the Council of Gediminas. And both parties continue to honor the treaty."

"Is this why you aren't supposed to have anything to do with Lithuanians, Max?" I asked. "Because of the treaty?"

"Yes. It's prohibited for Lithuanians—well, Lithuanian *vampires*, to be specific—to get involved in my work." He added a little anxiously, "Similarly, I cannot get directly involved in a vampire matter, Esther."

"Oh." I was at a loss for words. This possibility had never occurred to me.

"But I am very puzzled. Even alarmed," Max said. "Given that there have been three—possibly four—local murder victims whose blood has been drained, there should be a Lithuanian involved in this situation by now."

"Maybe there is, and I just haven't encountered him," I suggested.

"Perhaps," he conceded.

Nelli shoved her way between us, wriggling playfully as she sought some attention.

As I patted her head, a thought occurred to me. "This may be irresponsibly inaccurate, too," I said slowly, "but I've read that animals can detect vampires. Or are sensitive to their presence. Is that true?"

"Certainly in the case of the undead, it's true," Max said. "But I never observed any such phenomenon in relation to living vampires. In fact, Radvila was very good with horses. However . . ." He retrieved Nelli's leash from me as he gazed at her thoughtfully. "Nelli is only in the *form* of an animal. In reality, she is a mystical being. We have had previous experience—albeit, somewhat confusing at times—with her demonstrating sensitivity to other mystical entities. It *may* be that she could sense a living vampire if she encountered one."

Nelli noticed another dog approaching us, and she whined a little with friendly interest, her floppy ears perked alertly, and her long, bony tail whipped back and forth so furiously that it probably could have beheaded an unwary vampire.

I checked my watch. "I have to go to work, Max. Instead of waiting until performance time, why don't you come with me and bring Nelli? I don't think the undead would pass unnoticed at the Hamburg, not even among the vamparazzi, but it sounds as if a loose cannon could. If it wouldn't violate the Treaty of Gediminas, maybe you and Nelli could try to determine whether there's a vampire lurking around the theater?"

14

I soon discovered that I had drastically underestimated the vampysteria that would be unleashed by the ghoulish tabloid stories and Internet chatter about Angeline being murdered while dressed as Miss Jane Aubrey, the exsanguination (which the police had indeed, as Lopez predicted, been unable to keep quiet), and Daemon's involvement in the case.

Max disliked all forms of motorized transport, and the theater was within a few blocks of the park, so we walked there. I felt anxious about encountering the vamparazzi on foot; but today I was accompanied by a dog the size of a minivan, as well as a talented mage who had survived fighting real vampires. So, hah!—let the Janes just *try* to attack me now! Apart from sleeping with men like Daemon, it would prove to be the biggest mistake of their scantily clad lives.

However, though reckless, I wasn't stupid. I put on a pair of dark glasses and borrowed Max's fedora, hoping not to be recognized.

When we got within a block of the theater, though, I was flabbergasted by the size of the crowd, as well as alarmed by how unruly they were today.

The NYPD seemed to share my reaction. Even as

Max and I approached the first barricade, a police van pulled up to the curb and additional patrolmen started pouring out of the back of the vehicle, obviously summoned to assist with crowd control. A cop who looked as if he was considering changing professions was speaking into a megaphone, warning people to stay behind the police barricades, to refrain from pushing and shoving, and to keep all their clothes on—adding to someone in the seething throng, "Yes, that *does* include you, miss."

"Good heavens!" Max said. "This is extraordinary!"

"Yeah," I said. "You would think it's just too *chilly* for partial nudity."

Nelli was looking around with mingled interest and anxiety, panting a little with nervous excitement. Her long tail wagged in an uncertain rhythm, evincing her indecision about whether she found the noisy, swarming, strangely dressed crowds here friendly or menacing.

"Ow!" A woman behind us yelped when Nelli's lethal tail whipped against her. She wore the requisite black leather, goth makeup, elaborate hairstyle, and impractical heels.

"I do apologize!" Max said to her, unfazed by her appearance. Well, he'd seen the bloodthirsty undead, after all. "Nelli, please be more cautious."

"Is that a *dog?*" The woman's nasal voice and New Jersey accent rather spoiled the exotic effect of her outfit. "That's the biggest dog I've ever seen!"

Forcing my way through the dense crowd, I pulled Max along behind me, who in turn pulled Nelli. I kept going until my stomach was pressing against a police barricade. With some difficulty, I waved down a police officer and convinced him to get close enough for me to speak to him. Then I showed him my ID.

Pitching my voice for his hearing only, I said, "I'm in the cast. I need to get to the theater. I don't want to attract any atten—"

"Sergeant!" The cop lifted his head and shouted

down the street, loudly enough for the nearest hundred vamparazzi to hear, "This is Esther Diamond! She's in the cast! What do I do now?"

I sighed, removed Max's fedora (which was too big for my head, anyhow), and gave it back to him as people in the crowd started screaming, "Jane! It's Jane! *Jane!*"

"Thank you, officer," I said wearily. "You're very helpful."

"That's what we're here for, miss."

People in the crowd immediately started pressing in on me, pushing and shoving to get closer to me, grabbing at my clothes and arms. My sunglasses fell off, hit the ground, and were trampled. I cried out when I felt my hair being pulled. Nelli barked sharply, prancing around me in agitation as bodies smooshed up against both of us. She had obviously made up her mind about these people, now that they were shouting, shoving, and pawing at me. Whether or not Max's mystical familiar could identify a living vampire remained to be seen, but she certainly knew an unruly mob when she saw one.

I was clutching Max for balance now. He had a look of fierce concentration on his face and was muttering something in what sounded like Latin. A moment later, at least a dozen people around us suddenly flailed and flew backward, as if pushed by a large, unseen hand. Some of them staggered into the people behind them. Others fell on their butts. All of them looked utterly astonished.

Max looked around, clearly pleased with the results of his effort to protect me. "Oh, that was rather good. I wasn't sure it would work."

The stunned vamparazzi were jabbering in confusion, shrieking, or trying to catch their breath after being winded by that sudden fall. Cops nearby were rushing toward this area and blowing their whistles.

A thin, sallow Jane who was lying on the ground pointed at me. "She assaulted me. She *pushed* me! I want to press charges!"

"I never touched you," I snapped. "And that dress doesn't suit you at *all.*"

Max was trying to soothe Nelli, who was still barking in alarm.

"Miss Diamond?" One of the cops from the blocked-off portion of the street called, "If you'll move to the end of the barricade, we can let you through."

I doubtfully eyed the horde of vamparazzi whom I would have to push past to get to the spot he had indicated.

Then I heard another shrill whistle—made by an unaided human mouth this time—pierce through the sea of bodies that surrounded the people who were still picking themselves up off the sidewalk.

A deep male voice bellowed, "Coming through! Please make way! Miss, do *not* make me move you. Thank you! Coming through!"

Four tall men, moving together like a military unit, shoved their way through the crowd, then stepped over the people who were still sitting on the sidewalk with dazed expressions. The foursome stopped directly in front of me and Max.

The one whose voice I'd heard said, "Miss Diamond, how do you do? I'm Flame." He gestured to his three black-clad companions. "That's Treat, he's Casper, and this is Silent. We're your vampire posse."

"My what?"

"Your vampire posse, ma'am." He was a tall, burly man with long blond hair, a beard, and tattooed forearms. He wore no makeup, but he was in the usual black leather clothing, and he had a profusion of silver jewelry—chains, pins, earrings, and rings, all in the shapes of skulls, dragons, and daggers. "We will escort you safely to the stage door." He eyed Nelli, who was bristling at him. "And we'll protect you from this dog."

"She's with me. So is this gentleman." I was clinging to Max's arm. "Who sent you?"

"No one," said Flame. "We are strictly a voluntary force, ma'am."

"I see." I suspected that four total strangers offering to take charge of my safety was implicitly included in the things Lopez had instructed me to avoid. "I'm not sure . . ."

"The vampire community has decided we need to protect the cast members of this show from people who are conducting themselves in a way that reflects badly on vampires."

"Lithuanians, loose cannons, or the undead?"

"Even the undead aren't this unruly," Max said seriously.

Flame continued, "*Your* protection was deemed a matter of particular urgency, Miss Diamond, because you were assaulted last night."

"And also the night before," I added.

"Nothing like that will happen to you again. Not on *my* watch." Flame looked over my shoulder and raised his hand in friendly salute to the cops on the other side of the barricade. "Thank you for your vigilance, officers. We've got this covered now."

"Miss Diamond?" a cop called behind me.

I noticed that the vamparazzi were gradually backing off and calming down. Perhaps because Flame and his pals were their own kind, so to speak.

"My vampire posse, huh?"

"Yes, ma'am."

"Okay." I made my decision. "Please get me and my companions to the stage door without further incident."

"Absolutely. Right this way, ma'am."

I waved to the cops and, still holding onto Max's arm, proceeded through the crowd, surrounded by my bodyguards and followed so closely by Nelli that her paws kept scraping my heels. Her nails needed cutting.

My vampire posse moved through the crowd like a hot knife through butter, maintaining a steady pace, keeping people away from me, and sternly advising the vamparazzi to show courtesy and respect.

Several young women dressed like Jane were trying to get my autograph, which was certainly an improvement over punching and kicking me; but I was disinclined to risk stopping long enough to sign anything.

My protectors (except for Silent, who said nothing) tersely warned the Janes away, uttering phrases like, "Move out of Miss Diamond's perimeter *immediately* or you will be deemed a clear and present threat."

We also passed a long line of black-clad people carrying banners from Vampire Recovery (whose membership appeared to have tripled overnight). When they realized whom the posse was escorting, they all started screaming at me, "Run, Esther! *Run! Don't* do the show! He's too dangerous! Look what happened to Angeline! *Don't go anywhere near him!*"

"Well, that's certainly helped settle my distracted nerves right before a performance," I said. "Much appreciated, folks."

They were too busy shouting to notice that I had spoken.

Max leaned close to me. "Attempting to identify a vampire in this milieu will be more challenging than I anticipated."

"Indeed." Considering the insanity out here, as well as Nelli's agitation, I said, "You'd both better come inside with me."

I also saw Dr. Hal from the Society for the Scientific Study of Vampires. He was hopping up and down on the edge of my, er, perimeter. Today his picket sign said: VAMPIRE — OR JUST MURDERER?

I began to wonder how many people besides the cops thought Daemon was guilty.

Dr. Hal caught my eye and shouted, "Esther! We need to talk! Help us prove he's not a vampire!"

"Who is that?" Max asked curiously as Hal waved at me.

"Don't encourage him," I said.

My vampire posse escorted us to our destination without anyone laying a finger on me. Then, at my insistence, the police allowed them to pass through the barricade and go right up to the stage door with me. As I pointed out to the cops, I had been attacked on this very spot two nights in a row, *while* police were on duty there; so now I chose to bring my own security. I gave instructions that my vampire posse, who had done a better job of protecting me today than any of the police had done to date, were to be allowed to wait for me *right* outside the stage door after the show.

Once inside the theater, with the stage door closed firmly behind us, Max, Nelli, and I all let out identical sighs of relief.

"The Council of Gediminas," Max said, "will be more than a little vexed by how much negative attention this whole matter is attracting to vampirism."

I shrugged and led the way to my dressing room. "Who are they going to complain to?"

"*Complaining* is not their way," Max said ominously as he followed me. "Swift, decisive, comprehensive action—and, if they deem it necessary, *ruthless* action—is more in keeping with their methods."

"Oh. Good point."

"*You fucking bastard, Eric!*" Mad Rachel screeched. "*Go to hell, you SHITTY FUCKFACE!*"

Nelli flinched.

Max winced. "Good heavens! What is *that?*"

"My roommate." I sighed and pushed open the door to my dressing room.

Already in costume and makeup (she was punctual, if nothing else), Rachel was pacing the room with her cell phone pressed to her ear. As we entered, she emitted another volley of vicious obscenities at full volume. Despite living through 350 eventful years of confronting Evil, Max seemed shocked by her language.

Rachel looked annoyed by our intrusion. Then her gaze fixed on Nelli. An unfamiliar expression contorted her pretty face. It dawned on me that she might be afraid of dogs. Or allergic to them. Or just not like animals. And Nelli, in addition to her intimidating size, was neither the best behaved nor the most hygienic animal in the world—or, indeed, within any random two hundred-yard radius.

Perhaps it had been thoughtless of me to bring Nelli into this dressing room without asking.

I certainly *hoped* so.

"Rachel, this is my friend Max. And that's his canine companion, Nelli." Driven by a level of malice I would have said was beyond me, prior to sharing this space with Mad Rachel for the past six weeks, I added, "Max has come to see the show. Nelli will stay here in our room."

The contortion of Rachel's face grew more pronounced. She said into her phone, "I have to go now. Love you. Bye." She disconnected the call. "Nelli?"

Hearing her name, Nelli, whose nerves were recovering now, crossed the room to greet Rachel.

Eagerly anticipating Rachel's horrified reaction as Nelli approached her, I finally recognized the unfamiliar expression distorting her face. *Pleasure.*

I had never seen Mad Rachel look pleased before.

She reached out to pet and pat Nelli enthusiastically, then gave the canine familiar a big hug. "Ohhhh, who's a pwiddy widdle dog? Who's got the pwiddiest face in the whole wide world? Is it you, Nelli? Is it *you?* Oh, yes, who's a good girl? Who's a good gurrrrl?"

Nelli, the traitorous baggage, lapped it up. She wagged her lethal tail furiously, whined with delight, bounced around playfully (knocking over a chair), licked Rachel's face, and gently butted the actress in the stomach with her massive head.

I looked at Max in bemusement.

He beamed at me. "Nelli has such a way with people."

"Oh, there you are!" Leischneudel said from the doorway, still clean-faced and in his street clothes. He was pale and there were dark circles under his eyes. I recalled that he'd scarcely slept for the past two nights. "I was kind of worried. Those crowds out there . . ."

Nelli sneezed violently. Right on Rachel's dress.

I tensed, expecting a sudden (and noisy) shift in the prevailing wind. Rachel was so fastidious that she threw a tantrum if I happened to leave a used tissue lying on my side of our makeup counter.

But the actress just brushed casually at her gown and warbled, "Oh, somebody *sneezed!* Did Nelli sneeze? Was that you sneezing, Nelli?"

As if sensing her cue, Nelli sneezed again. And yet again.

"Oh, poor baby! Someone's got a widdle cold!"

Leischneudel was staring at Rachel as if she had grown a second head.

I said to him, "I guess she likes dogs."

He continued gaping at Rachel for a long moment, then gave himself a little shake. "I suppose, sooner or later, she was bound to like *something*."

I introduced Leischneudel to Max. They exchanged cordial greetings, then the actor's gaze shifted again to Rachel. She was cooing solicitously as she poured a drink of water for Nelli into an empty cookie tin that previous denizens of this room had left behind.

"I have a four-man vampire posse now," I told Leischneudel. "Do you have one, too?"

"I have the Caped Crusaders," he said. "Two guys in . . . capes. I was, oh, a little startled when they suddenly flanked me outside the theater today."

"I know the feeling."

"I guess they mean well, but they make me nervous."

"Go figure."

"Esther, something's up. There's a . . ." He glanced hesitantly at Max.

"Max is a trusted friend," I said. "You can speak freely in front of him."

And there were no worries about speaking in front of Rachel, who was still yakking chirpily to Nelli.

Leischneudel nodded and said, "Well, Daemon came to work early today. Trying to beat the crowd, I think."

"That's not like him," I noted.

Nelli sneezed. Rachel coddled her.

Leischneudel continued, "I got the impression from what Victor said—Victor's really in a *state*—that Daemon was worried about a negative reception from some of the fans. So he wanted to arrive well before he was expected and get inside quickly." He explained, "You see, Tarr filed a story about the murder that was released in the *Exposé*'s online edition a few hours ago. And it doesn't make Daemon look good."

"Well, what did Daemon expect?" I said dismissively. "Tarr's in this for himself, not for Daemon."

"Apparently that didn't really occur to Daemon until he saw today's story," said Leischneudel. "Anyhow, Tarr got here a few minutes after I did. As soon as they met, Daemon started shouting."

"I kind of regret missing *that*." I asked hopefully, "Is there any chance Daemon threw him out of the theater and told him never to darken our doorway again?"

"I think he might have been working up to that. He was really angry. But then they were interrupted. Detective Branson showed up and wanted to speak to Daemon right away."

"Who is Detective Branson?" Max asked.

I explained, then wondered, "Doesn't Branson ever sleep?"

"I guess Tarr got kicked out of the room then, because he . . ." Leischneudel stopped speaking and turned his head to look through the open door.

"What?" I prodded.

"Someone's coming," he said, obviously interested in seeing who it was.

I heard footsteps a moment later. Then I saw Detective Branson walking past my door. He noticed that it was open—and that Max, Leischneudel, and I were all looking at him. So he stopped to say hello.

"How are you today, Miss Diamond?"

"A little worse for the wear." I hadn't intended my voice to be quite so chilly, but I was recalling that he'd told Lopez he considered me a viable murder suspect. "And you, detective?"

He took in my appearance—the black eye, the welt on my neck, the abrasions on my cheek. "Have you seen a doctor?"

"I'm an actress. I can't afford a doctor," I said. "How is the investigation coming?"

"Well, it would be better for everyone if the tabloids would leave it alone, that's for sure."

"Fat chance," I said glumly.

"Yep." Branson left.

Keeping his voice low as the sound of Branson's footsteps faded away, Max asked Leischneudel, "Do you know why the detective came to see Mr. Ravel?"

Leischneudel shook his head and was about to say something, but we suddenly heard shouting coming from Daemon's dressing room. Without hesitation or delay, the three of us scurried into the hallway and stood there eavesdropping. Unfortunately, though, Daemon lacked Rachel's industrial-strength volume, so I couldn't tell what he was saying.

Victor was pacing anxiously right outside Daemon's door, so absorbed in his thoughts that he didn't notice us. However, I thought he probably *would* notice if, for example, I shoved him aside and pressed my ear directly to Daemon's door.

Listening with a faint frown of concentration to the

echoes of Daemon's angry voice floating down the hall, Leischneudel said, "Something about the girl didn't stay. She left after ten minutes . . . 'You *knew* that. I *told* you that' . . . He's asking why Tarr didn't write the truth."

I snorted. "Can Daemon really be that naive?"

Victor finally noticed our presence. He gave a wan little wave, then went back to pacing.

Now we could hear Tarr's voice. He was apparently trying to soothe Daemon.

"Tarr being soothing is peculiarly disturbing, isn't it?" I said.

Daemon stopped shouting after one more short, sharp outburst.

A few moments later, Leischneudel shook his head. "I can't make out anything else."

"Daemon certainly sounded agitated. Not at all like his usual self." I said to Max, "Reluctant though I am to subject myself to Tarr's prose, I wonder if we should read that article?"

"You can find it easily. It's all over the Internet," Leischneudel said. "And tomorrow's print edition of the *Exposé* will run an expanded and updated version on the front page."

"Give me a summary."

"Daemon lured the girl to his place and killed her in a fit of delusional bloodlust," Leischneudel said.

"Wow," I said. "No wonder he's angry."

"The article never actually *says* that, of course. It's all insinuation and innuendo, written with the pretense that the author considers Daemon innocent. But by the time you finish reading it, you're convinced he did it."

Even for a D-list celebrity who believed that no matter what was said, being talked about was always better than *not* being talked about, this probably crossed the line.

Leischneudel glanced at his watch. "I'm going to go get ready for the show. Oh, by the way, is Thack still coming?"

"Yes, as far as I know."

After Leischneudel left us, Max said to me, "Under the circumstances, perhaps our first step should be to attempt to determine whether Mr. Ravel is or is not what he claims to be."

I nodded. "I'll get Nelli."

I still didn't believe that the attention-seeking actor who secretly extracted his own blood in the course of conducting his elaborate charade was a vampire—either made *or* hereditary. But I agreed with Max that it made sense to try to find out for sure.

I went back into my dressing room, where I found Nelli still playing with Mad Rachel. I grabbed the dog's pink leash and ignored Rachel's whining objections as I led Nelli out of the room.

"I'm very disappointed in you," I said to Nelli in the hallway. "You like *her?*"

She panted cheerfully as I handed her leash to Max. We three proceeded down the hall to Daemon's dressing room, where I brushed off Victor's anxious protests as I knocked on the door. Then I opened it and entered without waiting to be invited in. My disdain for both of the men inside the room ensured that I really didn't care if I was interrupting a private conversation.

As it happened, though, Daemon looked relieved by the interruption, and Tarr was pleased to see me. I found the reporter's welcoming grin and warm greeting so disturbing that I momentarily forgot why I was there.

Then Tarr said, "Who's the old guy? And what is *that*—a hybrid dog-horse thing?"

Nelli sneezed again, quite forcefully.

I performed introductions.

"I'm allergic to dogs," Daemon said. "Could you please take her out of the room?"

"A creature of the night with allergies?" I said dubiously.

Daemon put his hand over his eyes and gave a watery sigh. I stared at him in surprise.

Nelli sneezed.

"Hey, I think that dog's allergic to *you*, Daemon!" Tarr guffawed at his own witticism.

"I think something in the theater is bothering her," I said, noticing that Nelli's eyes looked a bit irritated.

Dogs have very sensitive sinuses, and the backstage area of the Hamburg was redolent with dust, sawdust, industrial grime and commercial cleaning fluids, chemical residues and odors, and airborne particles from hairspray, starch, cosmetic powder, and the sweat of generations of actors. In addition to which, I realized, I was somewhat aromatic myself, having applied generous amounts of muscle liniment and antibiotic cream before leaving home today—though that hadn't bothered Nelli before, so I probably wasn't the cause of her irritated senses.

"Did you want something, Esther?" Daemon asked without enthusiasm.

Max and I both looked expectantly at Nelli. On previous occasions, she had become extremely agitated, even menacing, upon encountering dangerous mystical beings. Would that be her reaction to vampires?

Nelli sneezed again and gave a little groan.

I said her name with concern and stroked her head. She drooled a bit and gave a gentle wag of her tale.

Max and I looked at each other. Then we both looked at Daemon.

Noticing our intent expressions, the actor said, "Yes?"

Since our mystical familiar hadn't clarified things by treating Daemon as a threat, Max evidently decided to cut to the chase. "As an ardent student of vampire lore, sir, I would be very interested in hearing the story of your transformation."

Daemon made an inarticulate sound, closed his eyes, and rubbed his temples.

Tarr folded his arms and said cheerfully, "I have a feeling our boy may be rethinking that part of his bio just now."

"Don't call me your 'boy,'" Daemon snapped, still rubbing his temples.

Tarr shot back, "Who is Danny Ravinsky?"

Daemon opened his eyes at that. "Get out."

Nelli sneezed.

Tarr said to us, "That cop—Branson—showed up a little while ago. When our b . . . When Daemon tried to brush him off, Branson said he wanted to talk about Danny Ravinsky. And, whoa, *that* certainly attracted our friend's attention." He paused, then prodded, "So who is he, Daemon?"

As the obvious answer hit me, I blurted, "Another murder victim?"

Tarr seemed grotesquely entertained by this question.

Daemon scowled at me. *"No."*

There was a long, awkward silence.

Tarr broke it by saying, "You know, when I was in Hollywood, there was this *huge* star who—"

"Get out," Daemon said again. "I have to get ready for the show. *Leave.*"

"Okay, okay. I'll be back tomorrow. We still have a lot to talk about." Tarr looked at me. "You and me, too, toots."

"We don't have anything to discuss," I said firmly. "And don't call me 'toots.'"

He grinned and said, with what he evidently imagined was flirtatious charm, "I'm an interesting guy, when you really get to know me."

I was spared having to respond, since Daemon and Nelli both sneezed at the same time, startling everyone.

Daemon said, *"Please* take that dog out of here."

"Of course! My apologies, sir." Max said to me, "Nelli and I shall go, er, engage with the crowd. Now that all the actors are inside the theater, the situation may be less volatile outside."

"But there are so *many* people out there, Max."

Tarr said to Daemon, "What was I *just* saying? This thing is *exposure* for you."

"Why are you still here?" Daemon asked him coldly.

"Yeah, yeah." Tarr was still grinning. "Going, going."

"Our reconnaissance outside may turn out to be fruitless," Max said to me, "but that possibility should never be a deterrent in any endeavor."

"You'll miss the show," I pointed out.

"Lucky you," Tarr muttered as he passed Max on his way out the door and left.

Nelli sneezed.

"She's still here," Daemon noted tersely.

"Never mind, Max, I'll get you a ticket for another night," I said quickly.

"Excellent!" He paused in the doorway. "I shall rendezvous with you in your dressing room after the performance."

I nodded. Then I closed the door behind Max and Nelli, and I turned to face Daemon.

"And now *you're* still here," he grumbled.

I asked, "Who *is* Danny Ravinsky?"

"None of your business, Esther."

"Oh, come on, Daemon," I said. "Wise up! Whoever he is, do you honestly think it's a secret you can keep now that *Tarr* has heard the name? Now that he's heard a *cop* baiting you with it?"

To my surprise, Daemon suddenly looked like he was going to cry. "Oh, my God." He buried his head in his hands and heaved a horrible, half-sobbing sigh. "Oh, *God.*"

"Who is Danny Ravinksy?" I asked again. "Why are the cops interested in him?"

Daemon lifted his head and said wearily, "He's *me.*"

15

I blinked in surprise. "You?"

"Rather, he *was* me."

"Danny Ravinsky is your real name?" I guessed.

"No! Daemon Ravel is my real name!"

I had never actually believed *that*. So I stared at him, waiting for a more comprehensive answer.

He let out his breath on a gust. "I changed it. *Legally.* I'm Daemon Ravel now."

"Ah. I see. You *were* Danny Ravinsky." When he nodded, I said, "So what? I don't understand. Why is that such a big deal that Branson would . . ." Then it hit me. "Oh, good God, Daemon. When the cops were questioning you on suspicion of *murder,* did you *not* tell them your real name?"

"Daemon Ravel *is* my real name!"

"It didn't occur to you how suspicious that would look?" I said in exasperation. "Or how much it would annoy the cops when they found out you'd concealed your real name from them in—let's review—a *murder* investigation?"

He said doggedly, "Daemon Ravel is my real—"

"Fine, whatever. Ravinsky is your *given* name, then. The name you were born with. The name the cops were bound to find, you *idiot,* when they started looking into your past—which they were certainly going to do, since they think you killed Adele Olson."

"Who?"

"The murder victim!" I snapped. "Angeline—the girl you intended to have sex with two nights ago. Ring any bells *now,* Danny?"

He winced. "Don't *call* me that!"

Although it was beside the point, I said, "Daniel Ravinsky seems like a perfectly reasonable name. Why did you change it?"

"I . . ." He shook his head. "I didn't want to be that person anymore. I'm *not* that person anymore."

"Who was that person?" I gasped and asked, "Oh, my God, was he a con?"

Daemon—who had never worked for the *Crime and Punishment* empire, after all—looked puzzled. "A what?"

"A skell. A perp. A criminal. Was he—I mean, were *you*—in prison or something?"

"Oh, for God's sake, *no!*" Daemon jumped to his feet and paced the room in agitation. "I am *not* a killer! I *was* not a criminal! I've never been arrested. Until this girl got herself killed, I've never been in trouble with the law at *all.*"

"Got herself killed?" I repeated.

"This is a nightmare for me!" he cried.

I looked at him in appalled wonder, and I fervently hoped that this self-absorbed jackass wasn't a reflection of what Branson saw in *me.*

"Well, if you don't have a criminal record as Danny Ravinsky," I asked, "then what's the problem?"

"Like you said." He sagged into another chair. "The cops think it's suspicious that I didn't tell them who I used to be."

"Go figure."

"Look, *I* knew I didn't have a criminal past. So I didn't think my former identity was relevant."

"I'm pretty sure the cops like to be the ones who decide what's relevant in a murder investigation."

"And apparently the wheels of justice turn slowly," Daemon grumbled. "They've found out who I was, but they *haven't* yet determined that I have a clean past. Not to their satisfaction, anyhow. I gather that'll take a little longer."

"But if you're telling the truth about that—"

"I am!"

"—then they'll find out, and they'll drop it. So cheer up. It'll blow over."

"No, it won't," he said desperately. "Not now that Tarr has caught a whiff of this. You're absolutely right about that."

I didn't understand why this made Daemon look suicidal. "Okay. Tarr will print that you used to be a blameless guy named Danny Ravinsky. So what?"

He looked at me as if I were a pathetic half-wit. *"I'm Daemon Ravel."*

"Yes, I think you've established that."

"I am a vampire!"

"Oh, *please.*" I turned to leave the room.

"I'm a romantic prince of the night, a mysterious figure who walks the edge of darkness, an icon of erotic desire."

I turned back to him. "And because of that, I keep getting assaulted by your crazed fans!" I added, "I've meaning to kill you for that, by the way."

"I'm a symbol of modern society's craving for magic and wonder in their drab little lives," he insisted. "I'm a representative of man's struggle with his dark impulses and his quest to understand his primal nature."

"And *I'm* about to barf."

"I'm also a celebrity. The face of a national ad campaign. The star of my own TV show."

"Canceled."

"The title character in a sold-out off-Broadway play,"

he continued. "And the first choice for the lead role in an upcoming movie."

I blinked. "Really?"

"Yes! Plus," he added, "I own a nice loft in Manhattan."

Well, he had me there.

I said, "I gather none of this was true of Danny Ravinsky?"

"God, no." He leaned back in his chair and contemplated the ceiling. "Danny was a middle-class kid from Gary, Indiana, who studied acting at a state college and then spent years doing summer stock, school tours, and industrial training films."

"Well, that's an actor's life," I said with a shrug. "That's how most of us get started."

"It was *still* my life when I turned thirty."

"And I *still* don't understand your tragic tone," I said. "We become actors because we're driven to do this, Daemon. Because we can't stand *not* doing it. We get no guarantees about achieving success by a certain age—or *ever*. If you thought otherwise, then you were kidding yourself."

"Thirty years old, and still doing crap acting gigs for low pay," he said, ignoring me. "Still waiting tables most of the time, living in a low-rent apartment in Los Angeles, and driving a rusted-out death trap."

Then a girl he knew asked him to participate in a performance piece for a Halloween event, and in playing a vampire for the first time, Danny began to glimpse his true destiny.

"I had always been an also-ran, offstage and on," Daemon said with unprecedented candor. "Until that night. As a *vampire,* I stole the show! Sure, it was just a kitsch skit. But I'd never been a hit before. An audience had never *loved* my performance before. It's an amazing feeling! It's addictive."

"Yes," I agreed.

"It's better than sex."

"All too often," I admitted.

"And speaking of sex, a dozen women gave me their phone numbers after the performance. I had a three-some with a pair of them that same night."

"Too much information."

"And I thought, Why do this only on Halloween? Why not keep it going year round?"

So he created his own street-performance act. Before long, he was making enough money, by passing the hat as a vampire, to see the greater potential in this role. He began gradually evolving a whole persona in tandem with his act and eventually decided to reinvent himself. Danny dyed his hair black and replaced his entire ward-robe with "vampire" clothing. He consulted a plastic sur-geon, who made him look more like the mysterious gothic antihero he wanted to become. While healing from surgery, he changed his legal name to Daemon Ravel, shedding his old identity and embracing the new one he was creating. Then, intending to start his life all over as Daemon the vampire, he got on a plane for New York and never looked back.

"Once the tabloids get hold of this . . ." he said mo-rosely.

"Get hold of *what?*" I said impatiently. "You changed your name. Big deal. Surely no one besides your fans believes Daemon Ravel is your real name, anyhow."

Between gritted teeth, he said, "It *is* my real—"

"And you got some plastic surgery. Well, gosh, *there's* something no celebrity has ever done before." I shook my head. "You were a struggling actor who reinvented yourself in order to pursue success. So *what?*"

"You don't understand!"

"That much is clear."

"I *am* my image!"

"After the Ravinsky story breaks, you'll still be your image." And still nothing more substantial than an image.

"The vampire community has been so supportive of me ever since I came to New York," he said tragically. "My fans *believe* in me!"

"Once they are confronted with facts that contradict their beliefs, I have a shrewd suspicion that most of them will go *on* believing in you," I said. "After all, it's not as if your fan base is big on reason and logic."

"I buried Danny," Daemon said darkly. "I don't want him back in my life."

"You might want to make an effort to stop sounding as if you have multiple personality disorder," I said. "Daemon, I don't understand why you gave so much access to a tabloid reporter when you had secrets to keep."

"I have to keep my name in front of the public." His tone implied that this was so obvious as to be indisputable. "Tarr is an effective tool for that. He raised a lot of profiles during his years in Hollywood."

"I especially don't understand why you're *still* letting him hang around, all things considered."

"This story is in play now, whether I keep giving Tarr access or not," he said wearily. "So I'm better off with him as my friend than as my enemy."

Although it sounded like a shrewd strategy, I thought it virtually certain that it was a viewpoint that Tarr had talked Daemon into holding during their recent argument. And I was sure that the crafty reporter would benefit from it far more than the celebrity vampire would.

"There's something important I'd like to ask you," I said.

"Go on."

Since I had caught Daemon in an uncharacteristically candid mood, I decided to go for broke. "Are you Lithuanian?"

"Lithuanian?" He seemed startled by this bolt out of the blue. "Uh, no." After a bemused pause he asked, "Why? Are you?"

There was a knock at the door and the assistant stage

manager opened it. "Daemon, there's a—Whoa! Why aren't you people getting ready? Curtain is in twenty minutes!"

"What?" I exclaimed. "No, it can't be. Nothing's come over the intercom."

Daemon, who had already jumped out of his chair, was starting to take off his shirt. "I turned it down. I forgot."

"You *what?*"

"I've been a little preoccupied," he snapped.

"Christ, Esther," said the assistant stage manager. "Look at your face! Can you go on like that?"

"Yes. Makeup. Lots of makeup."

"Get it done in nineteen minutes."

I ran down the hall and into my dressing room. Mad Rachel was, as usual, yakking into her cell phone. She interrupted her conversation just long enough to ask if Nelli was coming back and to criticize me for running so late, then went back to ignoring me.

Luckily for me, while I was frantically stripping off my clothes, Bill announced a fifteen-minute delay over the intercom. Due to ticket holders having trouble getting through the unruly crowds, he was postponing the start of the show until all the audience members were in their seats.

It was a welcome reprieve, but I still needed to work quickly. I swallowed some ibuprofen and, well aware of my renewed aches and pains now, recklessly slathered myself in muscle liniment. Next I applied a generous layer of pain-relieving antibiotic ointment to my inflamed cheek and the tender welt on my neck. By using a veritable trowel to apply my stage makeup, I managed to conceal the bruising and discoloration, but I couldn't completely camouflage the bumpy texture of my abraded cheek.

Thanks to the delay Bill had announced, I made it to the stage in plenty of time to take my place before the curtain rose; and the opening of the show went fine. However, when Daemon went onstage on for his first scene, things started to go awry.

He was undoubtedly distracted by the events of the past twelve hours—and also, I realized, probably exhausted; while I had been sleeping, Daemon had been answering police questions. In any event, his performance was uneven and forced. Meanwhile, the audience, many of whom were perhaps also thinking more about the real-life murder scandal than about Lord Ruthven today, was unresponsive, neither laughing nor applauding in the usual places.

It was soon apparent that this lukewarm reception was throwing Daemon off, and his performance became even more unsteady—to the point of being awkward and distracted. He started forgetting some of his lines and ad-libbing with Aubrey and Ianthe. Leischneudel adjusted well, but Rachel just stared at Daemon in confusion, unable to recognize cues that she didn't hear phrased exactly as she expected to hear them. So there were some glaringly clunky moments during the first act.

At intermission, Daemon stormed into his dressing room, slammed the door, and refused to speak to Victor—who was the only person willing to try talking to him. Rachel, predictably, called Eric on her cell and complained loudly about how Daemon was ruining her performance.

By the time we started Act Two, audience members were restless—something we'd never before experienced in this show. People were coughing, riffling around in their purses or pockets, rustling candy wrappers, flipping through their program books, and whispering to each other. I had been in other shows where this happened, and I had learned to tune it out, as had Leischneudel. But Daemon clearly wasn't used to this (not since becoming the Vampire Ravel, anyhow), and it was rattling him so much that he even broke character a few times, turning to look at the audience with ragged exasperation.

During the scene where Ruthven proposed marriage to Jane, I noticed that Daemon's eyes were getting red and his nose was starting to look pink.

Dear God, I thought, *is he getting so unraveled that he's going to start* crying? *Here? Now?*

As the stage went dark, we exited into the wings, and Leischneudel took his place for the next scene, in which Aubrey had a fevered nightmare and Jane came to his room to calm him down.

Ruthven would enter the scene later, coming dramatically through the upstage French doors, accompanied by roiling mist, moonlight, and the sound of nocturnal predators baying for blood. Daemon normally made his way to that spot backstage as soon as we finished the marriage proposal scene. I always remained stage left, where we had just exited, and entered Aubrey's nightmare scene almost as soon as it began.

Tonight, though, instead of heading for his next entrance when we exited into the darkened wings, Daemon grabbed my arm and dragged me away from the stage with him.

"What are you doing?" I hissed. "I have to go right back on! Let go!"

"What is that stench?" he whispered.

"What?" I was still tugging against his grasp, aware that Leischneudel would start howling with nightmarish horror at any moment.

"I think I'm having an allergy attack."

Ah, *that* explained the red eyes and pink nose.

"Is it the dog?" I asked, thinking this was a delayed reaction.

"No, it's *you*," he snapped. "That *smell*. I'm allergic to something you're wearing!"

"Just how many allergies do you *have*?" I heard Leischneudel wailing in terror. "I have to go!"

Daemon sniffed and coughed a little. "What *is* that odor?"

"Antibiotic cream and muscle liniment." Well, yes, I *did* smell—at least, if someone got close enough to me. "Daemon, let me *go*."

I yanked myself out of his grasp so hard that he staggered sideways and somehow managed to bash his knee against a steel lighting pole. He grimaced in pain and made a horrible gurgling noise, his teeth clenched with the effort of trying to keep quiet.

I rushed onstage to awaken and comfort the howling Aubrey. From the corner of my eye, as I embraced and soothed my hysterical brother, I could see Daemon just offstage, hunched over and staggering around as he clutched his knee and mouthed silent outcries of pain.

Once Aubrey was calm, Jane proceeded to tell him that she had married Lord Ruthven that morning. Considering that her brother practically went into convulsions every time Jane mentioned Ruthven, I had struggled in rehearsal to understand why she announced this to him right now, when he was still gibbering from nightmares and mentally fragile. (The only real answer I ever came up with was that Jane was an idiot—which certainly accounted for her choice of husband, too.) Predictably, the nuptial news incited another bout of tormented raving from Aubrey, the content of which would trouble Jane as she embarked upon her fatal wedding night.

Having made Aubrey's day, I urged him to get some rest, and I exited stage left again. He promptly had a horrible half-waking nightmare in which Ianthe came back from the dead to accuse him of letting Lord Ruthven murder her. This guilt-ridden vision forced Aubrey to contemplate leaving his sickroom to warn his sister that she was about to go to bed with a supernatural serial killer. But then Ruthven made his dramatic entrance and yammered at Aubrey about his promise to keep silent, the meaning of honor, and so on.

Watching this scene now from the wings, I realized that the dialogue had awkward ramifications, given the current circumstances. Daemon seemed to realize it, too, and his performance grew increasingly awkward as he uttered flowery dialogue implying that he had a *right* to take lives without interference or consequences.

I didn't know whether he was feeling so self-conscious that he deliberately started omitting lines, or whether he was just so distracted that he was fumbling and forgetting them again but, either way, Daemon wound up skipping whole chunks of his dialogue. This shortened the scene so much that a startled Leischneudel had to leap over several emotional transitions that he usually played while Lord Ruthven blathered on, and he wound up simply diving straight into the catatonic stupor in which Ruthven left his new brother-in-law at the end of the scene.

Waiting in the wings for my final scene, I heard a woman in the audience say, "Oh, come *on*." And no one shushed her.

The hypnotic spell Daemon had held over the vamparazzi ever since opening night seemed to be crumbling.

It was during the wedding night scene that this abysmal performance of *The Vampyre* took an unexpected turn from gothic melodrama to farce.

As usual, Daemon and I began circling each other while exchanging our dialogue, gradually reducing the distance between us. A spark of Daemon's usual performance level started to return now, and the openly disenchanted audience actually began paying attention as the sexual tension built between Jane and Ruthven.

But then, as soon as he got within arm's reach of me, Daemon's reddened eyes started watering and his pink nose began running.

At the point where he was supposed to seize me by the shoulders, pull me backward against his chest, and start taking down my hair, Daemon instead backed away from me and turned upstage for a moment to sniff and wipe his nose.

After that, he wouldn't come near me. He just kept circling me while Jane gazed at him in wary but rapt fascination, and *I* wondered how we were going to perform the rest of the scene if he wouldn't touch me.

The audience began losing interest again, and I could hear their rustling, shuffling, and muttering. I didn't really blame them. Now that Ruthven wasn't pawing and seducing Jane, there was no concealing just how boring and pretentious his speech was. Obviously aware of this, Daemon suddenly walked over to a neoclassical statue of a half-naked woman that was part of the set décor, and he fondled it.

This created a wave of surprised laughter. Obviously not having expected amusement, Daemon froze and stared at the audience like a deer caught in headlights. That produced a burst of hilarity.

I kept gazing at him, my eyes trying to telegraph the message, *We have to get this scene back on track.*

Daemon pulled himself together enough to say his next few lines, twitching a bit as the audience continued giggling. I heard my next cue, but I really wasn't sure, under the circumstances, that I should say my line.

I stared at Daemon helplessly, willing him to understand my dilemma.

He finally looked at me, with his hand still planted on the statue's naked breast, and gave me an exasperated scowl.

So I uttered my dialogue: "You shouldn't touch me there."

The audience howled with laughter.

Daemon snatched his hand away from the stony breast as if he'd been burned. The audience laughed even harder.

"Why not?" he said. "After all, we were wed today."

Beyond Daemon, in the wings, I could see Mad Rachel gaping at us as if we'd both lost our minds.

Daemon scowled at me again, clearly waiting for me to say my next line.

I didn't *have* a next line. Normally, by now, Ruthven was boldly fondling Jane. Glaring at Daemon, I gave a deep moan of sexual arousal, which was what I always did at this point in Ruthven's yammering. Daemon looked startled.

More laughter.

Then I lifted my brows at him, indicating it was his turn to speak.

Remembering his next line, he fondled the statue again and said, "You like that, my pet?"

Still more laughter.

This would be terrific, if we were actually performing a comedy.

Enough already. I just wanted to get exsanguinated and get the hell out of here. And I didn't see how Daemon could possibly bite Jane and suck her blood if he wouldn't get within five feet of me.

I walked over to Ruthven, seized his hands, and hauled my heel-dragging groom over to my mark, where the white spotlight would find me when Jane died. Then I boldly put his hand on my breast. He gaped at me in astonishment, then gaped at my breast.

The audience found this so hilarious, it was a few moments before either of us could deliver more dialogue. By then, a surprised Daemon had adjusted to my taking charge of the scene. He seemed relieved to be back in a familiar position, and he said his next few lines with almost credible gravity, though his reddened eyes were tearing up and his nostrils were quivering.

I swooned in his arms, right on cue, more than ready by now to die. Daemon leaned over to place his mouth against my tender neck with ravenous ardor—and then he sneezed so violently that he dropped me.

I gasped and reflexively grabbed him to keep from falling. He kept sneezing convulsively—which was probably why he lost his footing and fell on top of me. We hit the hard stage floor with a resounding thud, accompanied by gales of laughter from the audience and a scattering of applause. With the wind knocked out of me by the fall and Daemon's weight on top of me, I couldn't catch my breath and was afraid I would black out.

From my prone position, I could see the curtain starting to come down. Actually, it was jerkily starting and stopping, as if the crew couldn't decide what to do.

Daemon rolled off me and sat up, sniffing and sneezing while the audience continued howling with merriment. I drew in a gulp of air. High overhead, I saw the lowering curtain stop again, hovering indecisively.

Oh, we might as well finish this.

"Ah, my lord!" I cried in mingled agony and ecstasy.

Despite not having been bitten or drained, I gave a noisy dying gurgle and a quick body-stiffening shudder of death throes, then I closed my eyes and went limp.

I heard the audience chuckling, but nothing else. I opened my upstage eye and saw Daemon staring at me in consternation. Frantically gesturing only with my eye, I tried to indicate that Leischneudel would enter any moment and they could finish the scene. However, my right eye was apparently not as self-explanatory as I hoped. Daemon just sat there wheezing as he gaped openmouthed at me, clearly dumbfounded.

Bill, however, was on the ball. He recognized what passed for my lighting cue in these unprecedented circumstances, and the white spotlight came on, glaring down on me with bloodless intensity. I shut my right eye and lay there dead, feeling relieved to effectively be out of this scene.

Leischneudel came on a moment later, and Daemon staggered to his feet to finish the performance, such as it was. I could hear the vampire sniffing and clearing his

irritated throat throughout the rest of the scene. Leischneudel did a creditable job, all things considered, but I
could tell he was making a heroic effort not to burst out
laughing. When he fell down dead, just outside the white
pool of my spotlight, I held my breath to conquer my
own impulse to start laughing. We both lay there in tense
silence, waiting for Daemon to finish his final
monologue—which he rushed through like a man desperate to finish the job and go find his private hoard of
Nocturne.

The stage went dark, the curtain came down, and a
wave of uncertain applause spread through the audience, as if they weren't quite sure the play was over. I let
out my breath on a relieved sigh, then Leischneudel and
I convulsed simultaneously with hysterical laughter.

"Get up!" Mad Rachel insisted. "Get *up,* you guys!"

I couldn't. I was laughing too hard.

"Come on, goddamn it!" Rachel, who *hadn't* just had
a spotlight shining against her eyelids, readily found me
lying on the darkened stage and started tugging on my
arm.

"Ow, that *hurts.*" That heavy fall to the stage a few
minutes ago, combined with my other injuries, ensured
that I was just one big ache by now.

"And where are *you* going?" Rachel cried.

I couldn't see yet, but I could hear Leischneudel still
laughing helplessly as he lay near me, so I knew Rachel
must be speaking to Daemon.

"I'm not taking a bow after *that,*" he said.

"No!" Rachel cried. "Stop!"

The curtain rose on me and Leischneudel still lying
on the stage, while Rachel clung desperately to Daemon's arm, her full body weight dragging on him as he
tried to make his escape. Leischneudel and I hopped to
our feet, and we all fell into line for our curtain call—
though Daemon declined to hold my hand this evening.

Half of the audience members were already out of

their seats and leaving, ignoring us as they gathered
their belongings and streamed toward the exits, talking
about where they would go for dinner—or perhaps
about how bizarre this show was. Some of the people
who were still in their seats applauded enthusiastically—
most of them, I noticed, were die-hard fans, dressed as
vampires, Janes, or bondage babes. The rest of the still-
seated crowd applauded politely, but their expressions
suggested they were thinking of asking for their money
back.

As soon as the curtain came down on what would
clearly be our only bow today, Rachel gave Daemon a
hard shove and cried, "You *ruined* the show!"

He ignored her and said angrily to me, "Don't you
ever wear that stuff onstage again!"

"Watch your tone!" I snapped back. I pointed to the
covered-up welt on my neck. "*You* did this to me, you
jerk!" I touched my injured cheek. "And you *encouraged
your fans* to do *this* to me! I am the walking wounded because of you! So don't you *dare* take that tone with me!"

Daemon sneezed and gave a little groan. "Oh, fine.
Whatever. Just don't wear it again."

"I won't," I said. "I certainly don't want to be stranded
onstage with you like that *again.*"

"Oh, I don't know," said Leischneudel. "That final
scene today was the first time I've ever liked this play."

"Fuck *all* of you." Rachel stormed off in search of her
cell phone.

Daemon stalked off to his dressing room, followed by
Victor, who was unwisely telling him the show hadn't
really been *that* bad.

Still laughing, Leischneudel and I staggered together
toward our dressing rooms.

When we reached his door, his eyes widened as he
said, "Oh, no! *That* was the performance Thack saw."

"Oh, God." I put my hand over my mouth. "He'll kill
me for making him sit through that."

"Well, I can kiss *that* opportunity good-bye." Leischneudel's smile faded.

"No, you were fine in the first act, and you rescued a couple of scenes as best you could in the second act. I'm sure Thack saw that," I said truthfully. "I'm sure he also recognized that *no one* could have rescued the final scene."

We both burst out laughing again.

"Esther?" a familiar voice called.

I looked over my shoulder to see Thack being escorted down the hallway by the house manager, who had brought him backstage.

Thackeray Shackleton was slim, blond, nice looking, always impeccably dressed, and (as I had found was so often the case with attractive, well-dressed men who loved the theater) gay. He thanked the house manager, greeted me warmly, and presented me with a bottle of champagne.

"I'm *so* glad you brought alcohol," I said honestly.

"After sitting through that play," Thack said, "I think I need something stronger than bubbly."

Although it wasn't the most propitious moment, I introduced him to Leischneudel.

"Congratulations," Thack said to him, "on being the only actor in the cast who can hold his head up after that performance."

"Oh, er . . . thank you, sir."

"Thack!" I said.

"Oh, you did as well as anyone possibly could, darling," Thack assured me. "But even *you* couldn't save yourself when you were stranded out there with a demented marionette puppet whose strings had snapped."

Leischneudel and I both laughed again.

"Tell me, is this show always quite that . . . odd?" Thack asked.

Daemon's door opened and he came out of his dressing room just in time to hear Thack say this.

He looked at us. We looked back.

I cleared my throat and introduced Thack to Daemon. Their civil greetings were followed by an awkward silence.

Thack broke it by saying, "I saw the show today. You offered your audience . . . a unique interpretation of the role. That's the hallmark of a great actor."

Nice save.

"Thanks," Daemon said morosely. "Does anyone know where Victor went?"

Leischneudel and I shook our heads. Daemon went back into his room and closed the door.

Without missing a beat, Thack said to Leischneudel, "I understand you're seeking representation?"

"Um, yes," Leischneudel said, obviously surprised that Thack was raising the subject after today's performance. "I am."

"Why don't you two talk while I change?" I suggested. "And Leischneudel can explain what happened out there today. That wasn't really our show. It was more like a crazed nightmare of our show."

They went into Leischneudel's dressing room. I went down the hall to my room, where I found Rachel raging into her cell phone about the performance while undressing and removing her makeup. I opened the champagne, then drank some of the lukewarm liquid straight from the bottle. I changed into my street clothes, cleaned off my makeup, and applied a fresh layer of antibiotic ointment to my cheek, pausing often to take more swigs from the champagne bottle. When Rachel left, still yammering into her phone, I sank into a chair and enjoyed the blessed silence as I drank warm bubbly.

I felt exhausted and in pain. Also overwhelmed, all things considered. I really wished we didn't have to do a show tomorrow. However, although most theaters were dark on Monday nights, the performance schedule for our eight-week run had been based on Daemon's schedule—and he'd had two longstanding commitments for public appearances on Tuesdays, related to his work for Nocturne. So our weekly day off on this show was Tuesday. At the moment that seemed very far away.

There was a knock at my door.

"Come in," I said wearily.

Max and Nelli entered the room. I blinked in surprise, having forgotten about them during the course of that disastrous performance.

"Welcome back," I said, as Max took a seat and Nelli lay down with a little sigh. I offered Max some tepid champagne, which he declined. I set aside the bottle as I asked, "Did you find any vampires out there?"

Max shook his head. "We encountered some interesting individuals. Also some rather alarming ones. As well as many friendly, er, vampire enthusiasts. I also spoke with a number of people who are very disturbed by the recent murder. But we did not discover any vampires. Or, rather, Nelli showed no unusual reaction to any of the hundreds of people we encountered. Well, apart from the ones who offered her food, obviously." He frowned. "Our lack of results could be because there wasn't a vampire out there."

Nelli sneezed twice and gave a little groan.

I looked at her with concern as I rose to pack my tote bag so we could leave. "Has she been doing that all evening?"

"No, she was fine outside." He reached down to stroke Nelli's head soothingly. "However, it also may be that, despite her sensitivity to certain phenomena, Nelli cannot actually recognize a made or hereditary vampire."

"Why are you trying to identify a made or hereditary vampire?" Thack asked sharply from the doorway.

We both flinched in surprise and turned to look at him. He was eyeing Max warily.

I said, "Er, we just, uh . . ."

Max studied Thack curiously. "We are concerned about the recent murders by exsanguination."

"Murders?" Thack said. "As in, plural?"

"Yes."

Thack frowned. "There was only one in the news."

"Max," I cautioned. What Lopez had told me about the other murders was confidential.

Still holding Thack's gaze, Max held up a hand to silence me. "There have been at least two others. Possibly three."

Thack entered the room and closed the door. "How do you know about this, given that it's not in the news?"

Nelli sneezed. I patted her head as she wheezed a little.

"I think a vampire may be responsible," Max said slowly. "What do you think, Mr. . . . ?"

"This is my agent, Thackeray Shackleton." I gestured to Max, wondering just how crazy he must sound to Thack. "Dr. Maximillian Zadok."

"Let me make sure I understand you," Thack said. "At least three recent murder victims—possibly four— have been exsanguinated, and you think a vampire is responsible?"

"Yes," said Max.

"Hey, Thack," I said. "After a performance like that, you probably just want to get out of here right away, and—"

"Does it mean anything to you, Dr. Zadok," Thack said slowly, his gaze still locked with Max's, "when I tell you that I'm . . . Lithuanian?"

16

I gasped and leaped backward, gaping at Thack. Nelli looked at me with mild curiosity.

Max made an elaborate gesture with his hands and said something in Latin.

"Oh, please don't bother with all that, Dr. Zadok." Thack took a seat as he waved his hand dismissively. "I'm not at *all* traditional—much to my family's dismay, I might add."

"Oh?" Max paused midgesture.

"No ritual greeting," Thack said. "I beg you."

"As you wish." Max asked, "Have you come here to deal with this matter?"

"God, no." Thack grimaced. "I came here because a client of whom I am very fond had a fit of insecurity and insisted I sit through this dreadful play."

"Thack!"

"I *told* you how I felt about this sort of thing," he said to me. "I loathe these revolting vampire stereotypes! Even so, I never suspected just how awful Daemon Ravel would be in his role. Leischneudel has explained why— sort of—but that's no excuse. The people who paid four hundred dollars to see Ravel's performance today must be feeling positively suicidal after sitting through it."

"That's what the scalpers are getting now?" I said in astonishment. "Four hundred dollars?"

"Never underestimate the commercial power of having your lead actor charged with murder," Thack said dryly.

"He hasn't been charged yet," I pointed out.

"After that performance," Thack said, "he certainly *ought* to be."

Nelli sneezed twice more, then she laid down on her side with a weary moan. Her eyes looked a little bloodshot.

Thack glanced at her. "Your . . . small horse seems to be ill."

"I think she's allergic to something in the theater," I said.

"And what happened to your *face?*" Thack asked, studying my colorful injuries with appalled concern, now that my heavy stage makeup had been removed. "Are you all right?"

"I'm fine. I'll explain later." I pulled myself together and stared at my agent in amazement. "Thack! You're a . . . a . . ." Though we were alone and behind a closed door, I lowered my voice. "A vampire?"

"*Not* a practicing one." He said to Max, "Since I get the impression you know something about these matters, Dr. Zadok—"

"Please call me Max."

"—let me state clearly that I lead a fully integrated life here in New York. I gladly shed all that Lithuanian business when I left home, and I am not equipped to deal with whatever may be happening here."

"What do you mean, 'not practicing'?" I demanded.

"Don't give me attitude, Esther. I happen to know that you only go to Temple twice a year—and only *then* if your mother nags you."

"You're saying it's voluntary?" I asked. "You can *choose* whether or not to be a vampire?"

"No, alas," Thack said. "Like being Jewish, it's something decided by birth. But *you* can at least convert. I, on the other hand, am stuck with being a vampire until I die."

"If I converted, my mother would die," I said. "Noisily."

"However, I can choose whether or not I *practice* vampirism," Thack said. "And like you, darling, I choose not to practice unless my family nags me enough on special occasions."

"Vampires have special occasions?" I blurted.

Thack seemed a little miffed by my question. "Everyone else has special occasions. You don't think *we're* entitled?"

"And on these special occasions you . . ."

"Drink human blood? Yes." Seeing my reaction, he sighed and said to Max, "You see? This is exactly why I never tell anyone about my family background."

"Shackleton is not a Lithuanian name," Max noted.

"As I said, I left all that behind me when I left Wisconsin."

"There are vampires in Wisconsin?" I gasped. "*I'm* from Wisconsin!"

Still lying on her side, Nelli wheezed a little. We all looked at her.

Then Thack said, "I legally changed my name when I came here. William Makepeace Thackeray and Sir Ernest Shackleton are two of my heroes. Isn't New York the place to reinvent oneself? I wanted to live unfettered by all that . . . vampire stuff. It is so not *me*."

"I always thought Thackeray Shackleton couldn't be your real name," I admitted.

"It *is* my real name," he said firmly. "Just not my given one."

"Well, you and Daemon Ravel certainly have something in common."

"Oh, *please*," Thack said in disgust. "If he's a vampire, then I'm Eleanor Roosevelt."

"Actually, I meant the name thing." I explained briefly about that. Then I noted, "You seem positive he's not a vampire. Can you sense other vampires? Can they sense you?"

He gave me an exasperated look. "No. And we don't wear secret code rings or special badges, either, Esther."

"I was only asking."

"But no way is Ravel a vampire! We do *not* call attention to ourselves—let alone alert the media," Thack said. "Even the most orthodox vampires keep a very low profile. It's how my family, for example, have survived for centuries as practicing vampires—including my two little nephews, whom my brother is raising traditionally, back in Wisconsin."

"Let me get this straight," I said. "Your family is originally from Lithuania?"

"Yes."

"So *vampires* immigrated here?"

"Is that a problem?" He looked insulted. "Everyone else gets to immigrate and pursue the American dream, but vampires should be kept out of the country?"

"Well . . ."

"This is why—this is *exactly* why!—I never talk about my background."

"I didn't mean to offend you," I said. "I'm just a little . . . never mind."

"Hmph." He frowned. "What were we just talking about?"

"Daemon Ravel."

"Oh, yes. What a ridiculous name," Thack sneered, blissfully unaware of the irony of his criticism. "But it certainly goes with his absurd pretensions."

"I agree he's absurd," I said. "But I don't believe he's the killer."

Thack said to Max, "You really think a vampire is the guilty party?"

"Having had time since this afternoon to contemplate our scant information, yes, I am inclined to think so," Max said.

"Where are you getting this scant information?" Thack asked curiously.

"A confidential source on the police force," I said.

"The same one whom Daemon Ravel's own personal tabloid menace is using?"

"No," I said with certainty.

"If this is vampire business, then what's your involvement?" Thack asked Max. "Zadok isn't a Lithuanian name, either."

"I am the local representative of the Magnum Collegium."

"Which means?"

"I deal with mystical problems."

Thack nodded. "Ah, that makes sense."

"Really?" I blurted.

Both men looked at me.

"Never mind."

"I also used to be a vampire hunter," Max said.

"But you're not a vampire?" When Max shook his head, Thack whistled, evidently impressed. Then he frowned and asked, "Is that even allowed?"

"Not anymore," Max said. "Based on my experiences, though, I am convinced that the killer is not undead."

Thack nodded. "Although I wasn't very attentive to my grandfather's teachings about these things, I think you must be right, Max. An undead monster would be noticed before long. They're not exactly stealthy, I gather."

"Moreover, an undead creature would inadvertently create more undead, at least in some instances. Which would also not go unnoticed," Max said. "I believe the murderer is a living vampire."

"Living vampires don't infect their victims with vampirism?" I asked.

Max shook his head. "The living create another vampire only by sharing their blood. When they prey upon people, the victims stay dead."

"Do you think the killer is an illegal made vampire?" Thack let out his breath in a rush. "That's a scary thought. Aren't they dangerously unstable?"

"They can be," Max said.

Nelli gave a little groan of discomfort.

"When you say 'illegal,' you mean not authorized by the Council of Gediminas?" I guessed, absently patting the dog's side as she lay by my feet.

"Yes," said Thack. "I've heard that getting a permit from the council to make a vampire is slightly harder than getting a papal dispensation from the Vatican. So if he is made, he's probably illegal."

"He?" I prodded.

"Legal or illegal, the vampire would have to be male," Max explained.

"Wait a *minute*," I said. "Are you telling me that in addition to hereditary vampirism being strictly a male gig, *only* males can become made? That is so unfair!"

"Don't look at me," Thack said. "I told you—I turned my back on all that. Apart from drinking a little blood to keep my family happy on the rare occasions when I visit them, this all has nothing to do with me."

Dragging the discussion back on topic, Max said, "We must also consider the possibility that the killer is a rogue Lithuanian."

"They have those?" I asked.

"Certainly," said Max. "It's the sort of problem the Council of Gediminas was founded to regulate."

"You really know your vampire history," Thack said, clearly impressed.

"What exactly is a rogue Lithuanian?" I asked Max.

He gestured courteously to Thack. "As the only vampire present, perhaps Thackeray would like to explain."

Thack grimaced. "It's sort of a power-mad addiction to blood that drives a vampire to kill—and keep killing."

"Aren't all vampires, by definition, addicted to blood?" I asked, hoping not to offend him again.

"No, of course, not." He added, "Ah, I mean, *hereditary* vampires aren't."

"Certainly the undead are," Max said to me, as if trying to encourage a slow student. "You are correct about that."

"And made vampires are addicted, too. Which is precisely why making one is so strictly regulated," Thack said. "When you make a vampire, you are, for all practical purposes, creating an addict. So it's just not a good idea."

"But the made don't have the same needs as the undead," I guessed—otherwise, Max's long-ago Serbian acquaintance Bosko would have been exposed as a vampire almost immediately upon becoming made.

"No, their need is typically much more moderate," said Thack. "I believe that feeding once every week or two can keep a made vampire sated. Is that correct, Max?"

"Yes. Unlike the undead, the made eat normal food and drink normal beverages, after all. Human blood sustains only their mystical aspect."

"And when they feed," Thack added, "the made don't need anywhere near the quantity of blood that the undead do. So if they become killers, it's mostly due to lack of discipline or lack of guidance."

"How much blood do they need?"

Looking to Max for confirmation, Thack estimated, "Perhaps the equivalent of a wineglass every week or so."

"Oh!" I said in surprise. "Well, that's not very much, is it? Even *I* kind of believed Daemon's claims that he was getting quantities like that from sexual partners."

"That ludicrous poseur is correct only in the sense that *real* adult vampires often do get their sustenance from an intimate partner." Thack added with disdain, "But it's not done as a sex sport between virtual strangers who then go around bragging about it."

"If you don't have fangs . . . Er, you *don't*, do you?" I peered into Thack's mouth, wondering if I could have somehow missed this during the three years I had known him.

"Oh, for God's sake." He opened wide to show me his excellent and perfectly normal dentition.

"She is not to blame," Max said to him. "I hold fiction writers responsible for such misconceptions."

"I blame Hollywood," Thack said darkly.

"And Van Helsing is not that similar to me," Max added to no one in particular. "Not his speech patterns, certainly."

"Without fangs," I said quickly, "how do you extract human blood?"

"Well, if you're modern and civilized, you do it with a hypodermic needle and a syringe." Thack shuddered with distaste as he continued, "But if you're a stubbornly orthodox family that cherishes all that self-aggrandizing guff about being descended directly from Gediminas himself, then you do it with a ritual vessel of some sort— usually silver or pewter—and a very sharp blade."

"Ouch."

Max said, "Mothers, sisters, wives, and friends of the family are the usual donors."

"Oh, great, men do the cutting and the drinking, and women get to be the donors," I said in disgust.

"Men can be donors, too," said Thack. "It's just that a woman can't be a—"

"Vampire. Uh-huh." I folded my arms and scowled at my companions.

"I didn't make the rules," Thack reminded me. "And the rules were made in the fourteenth century, after all."

"Hmph. Well, all I can say is, there must be a lot of anemic women in Lithuania. *And* Wisconsin."

"We really don't drink that much," Thack said.

"A wineglass every week or two is a lot of blood for a woman to—"

"Ah, that's for a made vampire," Max said. "And they're very rare, after all."

"Oh? So how much does a hereditary vampire drink?"

"It depends on how orthodox he is," Thack said. "I, for example, haven't had a drink of blood in about two years."

"You can survive that long without blood?" I asked in surprise.

"Hereditary vampirism isn't about *needing* blood," said Thack. "We don't wither and disintegrate like the undead or go into withdrawal and fall into a decline like the made if we don't get blood. We just lead normal human lives without it."

"Then why drink it?"

"Well, partly to honor the ancestors and keep the old traditions alive."

"Ah." Being Jewish, I knew something about that.

"And partly because drinking human blood enhances us. A vampire's metabolism transforms blood into mystical energy. By consuming it, we improve our strength, speed, and agility, and our senses become keener."

"That seems very desirable, Thack," I said. "Why don't you drink blood more often?"

"I live and work in Manhattan," he pointed out. "I don't *want* a keener sense of smell—in fact, in summer in New York, I'd pay real money to disable the ordinary sense of smell I've already got, thank you very much. And if my hearing got any better, I don't know how I'd manage to sleep in the city that never sleeps." Warming to his theme, Thack continued, "Since—much to my parents' disappointment—I did not choose a career as a hockey player or a Navy SEAL, I also don't feel a burning need for enhanced strength, speed, and agility. What am I going to do with *that,* for God's sake? Leap onto the roof of a subway train to catch a ride when the cars are all full? Tackle waiters and physically force them into submission when I want my check *now,* please?" He shook his head. "Look, I can see why a medieval warrior king might have wanted these 'gifts,' but I really think it's time to put all this stuff behind us. It's not the four-teenth century anymore, folks! Vampirism in the mod-ern world is like a Humvee in the suburbs—I mean, *please*. Are you taking the children to preschool or in-vading the Middle East?"

I shrewdly sensed that my innocent question had aroused longstanding grievances and incited a habitual rant.

"If a hereditary vampire doesn't need blood to sur-vive," I said, deliberately changing the subject, "then how does that power-mad murderous addiction that you mentioned occur?"

Thack took a deep breath and regrouped. "It usually happens when someone decides he *does* want to be a medieval warrior king, and there are no elders around to stop him."

"Pardon?"

"The individual in question," Max said, "may be in-herently bloodthirsty and lack guidance."

"Vampires can be bad seeds, just like anyone else," said Thack.

Max continued, "Or an individual may crave en-hancements and empowerment beyond what is normal among orthodox hereditary vampires."

"And for that, he needs a *lot* more blood than normal practices allow," Thack said. "More blood than a coop-erative donor can afford to lose. After killing donors who expected to live through the ritual, he'd move on to killing unwary strangers—including ambushing his prey, if need be."

"Eventually, the enhancements endowed by so much blood," Max added, "mean that only the classic methods of dispatch would be effective in stopping such a vam-pire."

"Fire or decapitation," I said faintly.

Thack nodded. "Me, you could kill any old way. But a hereditary vampire who, in defiance of all norms and values governing the community, has been drinking *liters* of blood from his victims?" His expression was grave. "Very hard to kill."

I looked at Max, my heart thudding in alarm. "In other words, a rogue Lithuanian is a *really bad* thing."

"So is a made vampire who's run amok," said Thack.

"No wonder the Council of Gediminas has been needed all these centuries." Battling the undead was just one of their crucial roles.

"If our theory is correct, then this individual, whether made or rogue, *must* be stopped," Max said. "This vampire will keep killing—and the rate of the murders will accelerate."

"Addiction," Thack said to me. "The more he drinks, the more he'll want."

Max said, "The most recent victim was the first to be fully exsanguinated. I suspect that indicates that the vampire's thirst is increasing."

"Oh, God, I *hate* this," Thack said with feeling. "I love theater. Art. Wine. French-Asian fusion cuisine. The Baroque composers. Cashmere and linen. Sondheim musicals and Shakespeare in the Park." He shook his head, his expression distressed. "Bloodthirsty murder does not belong in the same world with such wonderful things."

"No, it doesn't," Max agreed. "Yet here it is. And our duty is to eliminate it."

Thack said, "*Our* duty? Look, Max, I told you, *I* am not equipped—"

"You are a Lithuanian vampire whose heredity goes back centuries," Max said. "Given the current inexplicable absence of another of your kind, I implore you not to walk away from this situation while the innocent are unprotected and the killer is at large."

"Oh . . . *damn*." Thack obviously felt cornered by this supplication.

Really scared by their theory, I said, "Couldn't the killer be a homicidal mundane person who knows how to exsanguinate his victims?"

"Do you have any idea how much blood the human body contains?" Thack said. "It's a lot more than the tidy *demi-bouteille* you see on *Crime and Punishment*. If the killer isn't a vampire in an advanced stage of addiction, then what the hell is he *doing* with all that blood?" As he pulled out his cell phone, he added quickly, "And before you speak, that was strictly a rhetorical question. I'm freaked out enough already. I don't want *more* psychotic images entering my head."

"You're phoning someone?" I said incredulously. "Now?"

"I'm calling my Uncle Peter in Wisconsin. He's peripherally involved in council politics, and he's also done a little vampire hunting." Thack dialed the number, then held the phone to his ear as he met Max's gaze. "I'm way out of my depth here. We need help from someone who *is* equipped to deal with this before anyone else gets killed."

Max nodded. "Excellent."

There was a knock at the door.

Waiting for someone to answer his call, Thack said, "That must be Leischneudel. I told him we'd stop by his room to collect him. The poor kid must think we forgot and left without him!"

"Oh!" I flew to the door and flung it open.

Daemon was standing there.

Behind me, I heard Thack say into his phone, "Uncle Peter. Yes, it's me. Yeah. Fine. No. Listen, we have a *big* problem here."

"Hi," I said without enthusiasm to Daemon. "What do you want?"

"Just seeing who's still here," he said. "I . . ."

We heard sprightly footsteps coming this way, accompanied by the sound of cheerful humming. We both looked down the hallway—and I was surprised to see Bill approaching.

He was smiling and there was a lively bounce in his step. "Esther. Daemon." His smile became a delighted grin. "Great show today, guys! *Loved* it. If only every performance were that entertaining."

Daemon closed his eyes and lowered his head, looking like he might start weeping. I smiled wanly at Bill, who was still humming as he passed us and continued bounding down the hall.

"I think I prefer him when he's depressed," I said.

"What are you doing now?" Daemon asked. "I don't really feel like being alone."

Chilled by the implication that he thought *I* would spend time with him, I said, "You have a gazillion fans outside the stage door. Go hang out with them."

"Not tonight," he said tragically. "I really can't face . . . Some of them aren't very . . . Victor says there's grass-feet . . . grass . . . grass-fiti—"

I realized he was drunk. "Graffiti?"

"Thank you. On the side of the theater. Did you hear it with your own eyes?"

"Uh, no. And I'm busy right n—"

"Murderer." He swayed a little on his feet. "That's what it says. They think I killed that girl."

"Oh, only a few of them think that," I said dismissively. "The rest of them still love you. Go outside. You'll see."

I tried to close my door. He leaned against it, folding his arms as he continued morosely, "They think I could *kill* someone. Me! *I* was almost a vegetarian! Though, okay, that was really more about getting laid by—"

"I can't talk right now," I said, trying to nudge his body weight off my door so I could close it.

Behind me, I could hear Thack explaining the situation to his uncle. Nelli sneezed a couple of times. Max promised her they'd leave here momentarily.

"And that *performance*." A tall man, Daemon lowered his head to confide in me. I noticed that his breath stank of whiskey, not Nocturne. "*God.* I think my career could be over after that."

Since I was still aromatic with liniment and ointment, his irritated eyes started watering as soon as he got that close to me. I noticed that his pink nose was running and quivering, too. I took a couple of steps back, not wanting the romantic prince of the night to sneeze on me again.

"Well, we certainly shouldn't do it twice, but everybody has a disastrous performance once in a while. That's live theater." I shrugged. "It goes with the territory."

I could afford to be philosophical about it since, through no fault of mine, today's show had been a dismal flop well before I inadvertently triggered Daemon's allergies—and then, at least, we woke up the bored audience.

"The police think I killed her, too," Daemon said sadly. "But you don't think that, do you?"

"Not really. Is Victor still here? He should probably help you get home. You seem a little—"

"Hey, there are visitors in your room!" Daemon said, cheering up. "Introduce me."

"No, you've already met—"

Daemon sneezed messily as he shoved his way past me and entered my dressing room. He greeted Max and spoke earnestly to Thack, evidently not noticing that the agent was on the phone. Then Daemon sat down near Nelli—and sneezed again. As he wiped his nose with his black silk sleeve, I recalled that the dog was another of his allergies.

Thack gave me an exasperated look. I shrugged and spread my hands, indicating that I had *tried* to get rid of our unwelcome visitor.

Daemon launched into a long, rambling monologue about how misunderstood (and also how wonderful,

caring, and special) he was, punctuated by sneezes and
sniffles, while Nelli lay nearby, occasionally wheezing.
Max and I ignored Daemon and waited for Thack to finish his call. He stood with his back turned to everyone
and was talking in a low voice.

When he was done, he turned to face us, started to
speak, then gave Daemon a doubtful stare.

The actor broke the expectant silence. "I need to go
out somewhere. I feel suffocated here."

"That's because you apparently can't breathe," Thack
noted, eyeing Daemon's red-rimmed eyes and runny nose.

"Hey, we should *all* go out together!" Daemon exclaimed. "Wanna go out somewhere?"

Seeing a chance to get rid of him, I said, "Good idea.
Go get ready."

"I'll tell Victor to have the brought car round." He
paused, evidently realizing that hadn't come out quite
right. "To have the round car br . . ."

"Yeah, I get it." I hauled him out of his chair and
steered him toward to the door. "Go do that."

As soon as he was gone, I turned back to Thack. "Well?"

"My uncle will call Vilnius right away. It's some un-
godly hour early tomorrow morning there, I guess. But
there's an emergency number that's answered around
the clock, for obvious reasons. He'll get back to me later,
after he talks to them." Thack continued, "Uncle Peter
agrees it sounds like there should be a vampire hunter
on the scene. He says that an exsanguination murder is
bad enough, but now that it's tabloid fodder—well, the
council will be shitting kittens."

"And there's an image I don't want in *my* head," I
said.

"He also said, Max, that you need to back away from
this and go home," Thack said apologetically. "Something about the Treaty of Gediminas? He said that since
you're in the Magnum Collegium, you'd know what the
means."

Max sighed deeply. His expression was troubled, but he nodded his head. "Yes. Of course. I understand."

"*I* don't," said Thack.

"It's a long story," I said.

My eyes met Max's, and I nodded. I would call him later and let him know whatever Thack found out.

Max wanted to honor the treaty, and he knew better than anyone why its terms had been negotiated this way. But, in the absence of a Lithuanian vampire hunter taking charge of this situation, he couldn't bear to stand by idly while Evil menaced the people of New York.

"Nelli is physically distressed here," Max said, rising to his feet. As if to back him up, the familiar sneezed again. "We should go home."

I gave Max a hug, promising casually to talk to him soon. Thack shook his hand, expressed pleasure at having met him, and ruefully acknowledged that Max had placed Thack in the unusual position of doing something that would make his family proud.

Leischneudel appeared in the doorway just as Max was departing. He greeted Max and Nelli—who sneezed.

"I think your dog is sick," Leischneudel said with concern.

"I'm taking her home now," said Max.

"I think I'm going to go home, too," Leischneudel said apologetically to me and Thack. His pallor and the dark circles under his eyes were noticeable as he explained, "I've scarcely slept the past two nights, and I think I'll collapse facedown in my dinner if I go out now." He added happily to Thack, "I'll see you at your office for my appointment later this week."

"I'll see you then," Thack said. "Nice performance today—despite everything."

"Thank you." Reminded of that farce, Leischneudel covered his face with one hand and started laughing helplessly again. I realized he *did* seem overtired.

I also recalled that the vamparazzi would still be outside in force, since Daemon hadn't yet left the theater. So I suggested that Max and Nelli walk Leischneudel to his cab, along with the Caped Crusaders who would be waiting outside the stage door for him. Obviously grateful for the company, since I wasn't going with him, Leischneudel was chatting pleasantly with Max as they left.

I turned to Thack. "So I guess it's just you and me for dinner."

"No, I'm afraid we're doing to have to . . ." He swallowed and continued with obvious difficulty, "To accept Mr. Ravel's invitation to join him."

"What? No! Why?" I had never spent any of my personal time with *The Vampyre*'s star, and I didn't intend to start now.

"Uncle Peter says that since the cops and the media seem to think Daemon is the killer, he wants me to stick to him like a burr until we have instructions from Vilnius." Thack sighed unhappily. "So that's what I'll do. My uncle isn't really the sort of person you argue with."

"Oh. I see. All right." My own course of action was obvious to me. "You know, Thack, I'm quite tired, too. If you don't mind, I think I'll just go home and—"

"Oh, no, you don't," Thack said sternly. "You and your friend got me into this, Esther. So you're coming, too. I will *not* spend the evening on my own with that appallingly clichéd— Ah, Daemon!" Without missing a beat, Thack smiled as the Vampire Ravel appeared in my doorway. "There you are! Are we all ready to leave? Good, good. Where we shall go?"

17

"**M**y God," Thack muttered, gesturing to our surroundings. "This place looks like a bad marriage between a Tim Burton film and a French bordello."

"I thought there would be food," I complained. "I'm hungry."

Thack said to Daemon, "You're not eating those, are you?"

Without waiting for an answer, he plucked a little bowl of nuts off Daemon's end of the table and put it in front of me. The celebrity vampire, still red-eyed and pink-nosed, was sitting as far away from me as he could get while still remaining part of our merry little trio.

"I want dinner," I said as I accepted the nuts. I had already eaten a bowl of pretzels.

"I need another cosmopolitan," Thack said. "Where is that tastelessly dressed waitress of ours?"

Daemon, whose attention now seemed fully occupied with the vampire girl sitting on his lap, had chosen the venue for our evening out. We were in his (enviably luxurious) car by then, and Thack felt honor-bound to remain by his side until Uncle Peter called again. So when Daemon announced we were going to a club called the

Vampire Cave ("where they love me"), we hadn't put up nearly as much of a struggle as I now realized we *should* have put up.

For one thing, there was no food here other than generic bar snacks and, as was usually the case after a performance, I was ravenous. There were some choices on the specialty drinks menu which I might have found amusing under other circumstances, but all things considered, I just felt my gorge rise at the thought of drinking a Bloodsucker, Jugular Juicer, or Carotid Cooler. In any case, right after the show, I had swilled about one-third of a bottle of lukewarm champagne on an empty stomach, so I had decided I'd better stick to club soda here.

I was rethinking that decision at the moment, actually, since the Vampire Cave wasn't sort of place where I particularly wanted to be sober, if I had to be here at all. Down a steep flight of steps, situated underneath a leather-gear novelty shop, this club was decorated pretty much as Thack had described. The customers were a cross-section of self-proclaimed vampires, vampire groupies, vampire lifestylers, psychic vampires, donors, and people hoping to (as Leischneudel would put it) meet a vampire. There were enough other customers dressed in ordinary street clothing that I didn't look out of place (though Thack, in his Brooks Brothers suit, certainly did), but vampire-goth was the most prevalent style choice among the clientele.

Thack glanced at his watch. "You would think," he said, "that these people might have some place else to be this late on a Sunday night."

"Such as home in bed?" Which was where I wanted to be. I gave in briefly to fantasizing about eating my favorite Chinese carry-out food in bed while watching TV, and then sleeping undisturbed for at least eight hours.

"Do you suppose that vampire hunting is always this

demeaning?" Thack wondered, as Daemon and Vampire Girl pawed each other at our table. Several people in flowing black capes greeted the two of them while walking past us. "Or are we just lucky?"

Daemon was obviously well-known here, and he had told us he'd been a regular at this club ever since coming to New York. A number of people had greeted him since our arrival a half hour ago. They spoke to him as friendly admirers, rather than with the hysterical adulation displayed by fans outside the theater. And the woman currently occupying his attention wasn't even the first one to sit in his lap since we'd arrived; indeed, he seemed to have *several* friends-with-benefits among the club's clientele tonight.

Nonetheless, I noticed he was also getting some censorious looks from this crowd. I wasn't sure whether some of the people giving him dark glances thought he was a murderer, or whether they just thought he shouldn't be out partying and pawing so soon after the murder, all things considered. (Or maybe they just didn't like him bringing a scowling yuppie in a Brooks Brothers suit to the club, as well as a hungry actress who was eating all the bar snacks.)

When I used the ladies' room a little while later, though, I discovered another possible reason for the chilly glances. While I was out of sight in one of the two wooden bathroom stalls, a couple of girls were touching up their elaborate makeup at the sink. I wound up hovering in my stall and listening with mild interest as they talked about how Daemon had "gone commercial" and "sold out." He also gave people the wrong impression of vampires, they said, which was bad for the vampire community.

"I mean, most vampires don't even drink blood at *all*," one of the girls said. "But he makes it such a *thing*."

"God, I know! And that whole 'sunlight must not touch me' attitude," said the other girl. "Puh-lease. How corny can you *get*?" She suddenly inhaled sharply. "Oh!"

"What is it?"

"Mmm." She gave an ecstatic little moan. "I'm getting a psychic embrace from Rafael."

"Oh, *wow.*"

I flushed the toilet and exited my stall.

As I was returning to my table, I paused to give a little finger wave to half of my vampire posse. The four guys had met us outside the stage door and had insisted on following Daemon's car here, riding on a couple of motorcycles, two men per bike. After we got here, Flame and Casper stayed outside with the bikes. Treat and Silent entered the club with us, though they sat unobtrusively at a separate table and didn't intrude on our evening, such as it was.

Flame had instructed Treat and Silent, "Keep eyeballs on Miss Diamond at all times."

The Vampire Cave was small enough that my half-posse could easily monitor my trips to the bathroom and the bar without even leaving their table. And, fortunately, I had managed to convince Silent that coming *inside* the ladies' room with me would make the two of us much closer than we really wanted to be.

Daemon was canoodling with yet another goth girl when I sat back down at our table. I could tell from his unfocused, heavy-lidded eyes and slurred speech that he was very drunk by now. I gathered that, to top off the pleasures of my evening, my vampire host in this fine establishment had decided to go on a real bender.

Ignoring our companions, Thack said to me, "I mean it as an observation, not a criticism, when I say that, although you are normally an attractive woman, tonight you look like a boxer who recently lost a brutal match and you smell like a pharmacy. What on earth happened to you?"

I wearily recounted my misadventures with lust-maddened Janes.

Thack shook his head in disgust. "I should never have

let you audition for this show. I had a bad feeling from the moment you told me about it."

"Your bad feeling had nothing to do with the show," I pointed out, "and everything to do with the chip on your shoulder about, er, cultural stereotypes."

"But you insisted I get you the audition, and *now* look where we are," he said grimly. "In a vampire night-club with a drunken poseur who I fear may wind up having sex on our table before Uncle Peter calls me back."

"Oh, come on, Thack, I've got a supporting role in a sold-out off-Broadway show. That's a *good* thing."

"Jane is not a part worthy of your talent, darling."

"Speaking of which," I said, "I need some auditions. This show closes in two weeks."

"Oh!" He made a rueful face. "Sorry. I should have said something sooner. A murderous vampire menacing New York kind of distracted me." Thack added wearily, "And talking to my relatives always rattles me."

"Should have said what?" I prodded.

"I was going to tell you over dinner. I got you an audition for next week. It's for another new play. *Not* a gothic revival this time."

"Really?" When he nodded, smiling at me, I gave him a hug. "That's great!"

"Geraldo will call you in a day or two with the details," he said. Geraldo was Thack's assistant. "And I've been talking with the *Crime and Punishment* people. They thought you did very well in *D-Thirty,* and they said you were really a good sport on the set. So they felt bad that they wound up having to cut your role so much in that episode. The upshot is they'd like you to come in soon and read for a guest spot on *Criminal Motive.*"

While *The Dirty Thirty* was the grittiest and most controversial series in *C&P*'s spin-off empire, *Criminal Motive* was considered the brainiest.

"Suddenly, I feel so much better! Good news is like

an antidote," I said cheerfully. "Now I can scarcely even tell that I was beaten almost to a pulp last night."

"Did something happen?" Daemon asked us blearily.

"No, go back to your fondling," I said to him. Then I smiled at Thack. "Now I can look forward to life after *The Vampyre*."

Gesturing to my injuries, Thack said, "I'll certainly be relieved when you're done with this show. You look as if a third assault could put you in the hospital."

"Fannish hysteria is a dangerous thing," I noted. "And it's not even as if they're *my* fans."

"*Vampire* hysteria is a dangerous thing," said Thack. "I had to make my way through that crowd today to get to the theater. The effort made me better acquainted with Daemon's fans than I had any desire to be. Which is how I know that, despite his being suspected of murdering his most recent pick-up, half the women in that crowd still want to sleep with him—as do some of the men. That doesn't just run contrary to reason and good taste, it also defies any healthy sense of self-preservation."

I thought back to something Leischneudel had said yesterday, on the way to work, about how the fans romanticized Lord Ruthven's murder of his bride. "Maybe they think it would be worth dying to be possessed by Daemon in the final embrace."

"Are you *trying* to make me nauseated?" Thack asked.

"Or maybe they fantasize that he'd turn them, and they'd become his undead true love."

"I'm warning you, this evening has descended to such an unprecedented nadir that I am quite capable of tossing my cookies in public." Thack glanced at our canoodling companions. "Possibly all over our preening pal and his giggly goth girlfriend."

He'd spoken a little too loudly. The girl finally noticed us, and she looked offended. That was predictable, given what Thack had said; but I thought she could have easily avoided the insult by declining to give Daemon a lap dance in public.

"Who are your friends?" she asked him with a sour expression.

"Hmmm?" Daemon looked blearily at me. "I . . . work with her." His gaze moved to Thack. "Who are you again?"

Thack asked me, "Should I risk a third cosmopolitan? The first two *were* pretty weak, after all."

"I haven't seen our waitress in ages," I said.

"There is a sense in which that can only be a blessing."

Goth girl stuck her tongue in Daemon's ear, then said, "Why don't you and I go back to your place and give your coffin a workout?" She uttered what I gathered she intended to be an alluringly wicked giggle.

"Oh, good God!" Thack exclaimed. "A coffin? A *coffin?*"

"Oops, I think the damn just burst," I told the dreary couple.

"Is there no limit to your tasteless banality?" Thack cried.

"Oh, wait, you came with Esther, didn't you?" Daemon said to Thack, as if starting to recognize him now.

"You sleep in a *coffin?*" Thack demanded.

"No, I don't *sleep* in it," said Daemon. "Do you have any idea how claus . . . claus . . ."

"Claustrophobic?" I guessed.

"Thank you." Daemon nodded at me, then concluded, "How what-she-said a coffin is? Really tight squeeze, man."

"Not to mention that it's intended for the departed and should therefore be treated with respect. Not used as a PR gimmick, let alone as a venue for—for . . ." Thack concluded with discreet disdain, "Fun and games."

The girl looked at Thack's well-tailored suit, and her

puzzled expression cleared. "Oh, I get it! You're an undertaker?"

"Vampires do *not* sleep in coffins," Thack said tersely.

"I remember now," Daemon said to Thack. "You were in the car with us, right?"

"Vampires *particularly* do not sleep in coffins filled with the soil of their native land," Thack said in aggravation, getting it all off his chest now. "If we have any attachment to our native soil, it's purely sentimental! Though, I, for one, was delighted to shake the dust of Wisconsin off my feet. But I had family issues, so that's beside the point."

"What is the point?" Daemon asked in confusion.

"As for all this claptrap about being immortal . . . Where does that even *come* from?" Thack demanded.

"The undead?" I guessed. "Though I suppose Max would say they're not immortal, they're just mystically animated by—"

"Someone living for hundreds of years? It's idiotic!" Thack raged.

I kept my mouth shut.

He added to Daemon, "And how, by the way, were you planning to fake *immortality?* Plastic surgery can only take you so far, after all."

Daemon's jaw dropped and he gave me a look of horrified betrayal. "You *told* him?"

"Told him what?" I asked blankly.

"About . . ." Daemon made a vague gesture.

"Oh! About your plastic surgery?" I said, realizing what he meant. "No. Why would I tell him? Why would I tell *anyone?*"

The girl looked at him. "You had surgery?"

"Childhood accident," he said quickly, slurring the words.

I had no doubt that Tarr would soon sniff out who Danny Ravinsky was, as well as the fact that he had altered his appearance when becoming Daemon Ravel. And then *everyone* would know. But since celebrities getting plastic surgery had by now become as common as my mother getting brisket and matzo, I still didn't see what the big fat hairy deal was.

Thack, meanwhile, was really on a roll now.

"You know what *else?* The only vampire who requires an *invitation* to enter your home is a well-raised one with good manners." His voice was rising, along with his temper. "A gauche lout of a vampire can burst through your front door whenever he feels like it—no invitation needed, folks!"

Thack's outburst was starting to attract some attention.

From my posse's nearby table, Treat said, "Yeah, dude, I hear you. Like, I can go anywhere without an invitation. I *don't*. But I *can*."

Silent nodded his head in agreement with this.

Thack stared at them in consternation and said to me, "They think they're vampires, too?"

"Well, they *are* my vampire posse," I said.

"You know what *else* is complete nonsense?" Thack said, returning to venting his spleen on Daemon and the girl. "Vampires who cringe at the sight of Christian crosses and melt when someone sprinkles them with holy water. Lithuania is mostly Roman Catholic—and that means, so are *we!*"

"Lithuania?" Daemon repeated with a bewildered expression.

The girl asked, "Who's she?"

"Do you go to Mass every week?" I asked Thack curiously, thinking about Lopez.

"No, just once in a while. Easter. Christmas. Before the Obie Awards," he said. "The usual."

"Look," Daemon's lap girl said to Thack. "You are totally free to practice vampirism the way you want to, and that's cool. But I totally think you should stop trying to tell everyone *else* how to be a vampire. Let them be vampires in their own way."

"Let it go," I told Thack. "You're wasting your breath."

He sighed and let his posture sag. "Totally."

Now that Thack had raised the subject, though, I had a question about vampires which I had been pondering for some time. "As long as we seem to be rooted to this spot until Uncle Peter phones back . . ."

"Who?" Daemon asked.

"Tell me," I said to him and his cuddly friend. "What is the sexual appeal of vampires? I mean, I understand why someone would be attracted to the idea of *being* one. There are perks, after all. Immortality, superhuman strength, psychic powers, shape-shifting abilities—"

"Oh, for God's sake." Thack folded his arms on the table and lay his head on them.

"But given that we're talking about a murderous creature with fangs who feasts on human blood—why does anyone want to *sleep* with a vampire?"

The girl snorted. "If you have to ask that, then you *obviously* haven't slept with one."

"Oh, neither have *you*," Thack said without lifting head.

Daemon's red-rimmed eyes focused a little with interest, and I realized this must be a subject he'd thought about often in the years since he had first played a vampire and discovered the erotic power of the role.

"Well, it's sexy stuff, isn't it?" he said. "All that piercing and sucking and biting. The rich, sensual flow of blood. The intimacy of being fed on."

It didn't come out of his liquor-soaked mouth quite that clearly, but that was the gist of it.

"Yeah, I get the metaphors," I said. "And in performance, I play those metaphors. In fact, I practically beat them to death. But as a sexual fantasy—let alone a dating strategy—I really don't get it. The logistics keep getting in the way."

"Huh?"

"Have you ever actually been bitten by something with fangs or sharp canines?" I asked.

"A dog," Daemon said.

"A snake," the girl said. "I was posing nude with it, and—"

"That's all the information we need," Thack said, still facedown on the table.

"And I've been bitten by a cat, two dogs, and a ferret," I said. "Also by Daemon."

"Wow," the girl said.

"I lead a thrilling life." I continued, "And being bitten *hurts.* Once those sharp teeth sink in, break the skin, and draw blood, your nerves scream with pain. Sex is the very *last* thing on your mind."

Thack lifted his head. "I hope you people are listening to her."

"Now imagine someone doing that to a major vein or artery." I was gaining momentum. "The piercing of your jugular vein would be eye-crossingly painful and also dangerous—quite possibly life threatening."

Thack said, "Call me old-fashioned, but I'm not interested in sex that involves a visit to the ER."

"And piercing the carotid artery?" I said, really finding my stride now. "Do you have any idea how *messy* that would be? You wouldn't get an artistic trickle of ruby liquid sliding down your neck," I told the girl. "You'd get a geyser of bright red arterial blood that would turn the bed into a gory mess. And your vampire lover would be covered in the stuff spraying from your neck, not tidily wiping a few drops of it from his lips."

I had spent three days playing an ER nurse on the popular medical soap opera *Our Restless Hearts.* I knew my stuff.

"You should be taking notes," Thack said to the girl, who looked increasingly appalled.

Daemon was staring at me with fierce concentration—

which was certainly more attention than he ever paid to my words when he was sober.

"And *you*," I said to him, "would need an industrial cleaning team to keep up with the mess, if you were doing this on a regular basis. You'd have to throw out all your sheets and pillows every time. You'd go through mattresses pretty fast, too. You also might need your walls and floors thoroughly scrubbed after every—"

"God, you're sick!" The girl looked at me as if I had just urinated in her drink.

"*I'm* not the one who proposed having sex in a coffin a few minutes ago," I replied.

"I do *not* like your friends, Daemon." She slid off his lap and stomped away, ignoring his belated suggestion that maybe she could go get us some more drinks.

Daemon shrugged, then looked at me. "You're foka too much on the milkall deals."

I frowned. "What?"

"You're focused too much on the medical details," Thack translated.

"Oh." I was surprised that Daemon had followed my rant well enough to have an opinion.

I touched the welt on my neck. "*This* was not a sexy experience for me, even if your fans enjoyed it."

"A vampire lover," he said seriously, making a noticeable effort to articulate clearly, "is powerful, mysterious, experienced. He dominates your will. He lives outside the rules. He is ruthless, but can be tender if—"

"He also probably has skin like ice," I said, as the ramifications of an "undead" lover occurred to me. "I mean, he's not alive, right? Not in the normal, mortal sense of the word."

"So his skin wouldn't be the *only* cold thing you'd notice about him," Thack said with a startled laugh.

"You're right!" My eyes widened. "Daemon, I can assure you, after the first time you've had a cold gynecological instrument shoved up your—"

"Please rephrase that thought," Thack said.

"Well, suffice it to say, there are certain body parts that aren't coming anywhere *near* me if they're cold," I said firmly. "Plus—cold kisses? A cold tongue? Blegh! Wouldn't it be like kissing a reptile?"

"Thank you for yet another image that will be haunting me late into the night," Thack said.

"I'm just not seeing it," I said to Daemon, who was staring at me dumbfounded. "Sure, I get the metaphor. But once you really start thinking about this stuff—a vampire lover is about as erotic as serving dinner in a morgue that needs cleaning."

"And the imagery keeps right on coming." Thack pulled his cell phone out of his pocket.

"Ohhh . . ." Daemon hunched over a little and covered his mouth with one hand. "I don't feel so good."

"It's just barely possible," I said without sympathy, "that you've have too much to drink."

"I'm calling my uncle." Thack flipped open the phone. "I can't take much more of . . . Oh, for God's sake. Of course. *That's* what's taking so long."

"What?" I asked.

"I'm not getting a signal down here."

"Ungh." Daemon clutched his stomach. "I think I'm going to . . . to . . ."

"You just need some air," Thack said to him. "Let's get out of here so I can call Wisconsin."

"Good idea." I was already out of my chair. "Oh, what'll we do about the bill?"

Thack eyed Daemon, who was groaning and making alarming faces. "He's a regular here. Let's tell them to put the drinks on his tab. He did most of the drinking, after all."

I nodded. "Our waitress is still AWOL, so I'll go tell the bartender. You take the prince of night outside before he makes a mess on the floor."

Thack nodded, then took a firm hold of Daemon's elbow and guided the groaning actor toward the stairs. I told Treat and Silent the plan. Since they were on duty, so to speak, they'd only had soft drinks; so rather than search fruitlessly for the waitress, they just threw some cash on their table and went to wait by the stairs, keeping their eyes fixed on me as I made my way to the bar. I elbowed my way through the crowd, found the bartender, and explained the situation. She said it was no problem. I got the impression that despite Daemon's character flaws, he was a reliable customer who could be trusted to cover his debts.

Eager to get outside and learn if there was any news from Vilnius yet, I quickly turned to go—and walked *right* into our long-absent waitress. She was carrying a platter loaded with dirty empties back to the bar, and she seemed to be in a hurry, too. We collided fast and hard, staggered sideways together, tripped over an empty chair, and went flying. The two of us landed in a noisy, painful clatter of breaking glass, startled shouts, and bone-cracking collision with the hard floor.

I lay there winded and in pain, thinking about how much I wished I had defied Thack and just gone home to bed. When helpful hands grasped my arms and shoulders to help me off the floor, I protested. I didn't want to get up. I just wanted to lie here until someone brought a stretcher, put me on it, and took me home.

Then someone said, "She's bleeding!"

I became aware of the stinging in my left hand, previously unnoticed because everything *else* hurt so much. I turned my head to look at it. I saw that, when landing in this painful heap, I had cut the heel of my palm on a wineglass that had shattered into large, sharp pieces.

"Oy." I held up my quivering hand and studied it. I was lucky. If the cut had been just a half-inch lower, the broken glass would have driven into the soft tissue of my wrist and I'd need a paramedic. I groaned, cradling my hand, and let Treat and Silent haul me off the floor.

I apologized to the waitress, who was disheveled and grimacing but didn't seem to be seriously hurt. She blamed me for the accident—and was so vocally angry at me that Treat wound up speaking firmly to her while Silent folded his arms and gave her a hard stare.

While they were doing that, I looked down at my hand and realized it was really bleeding. "Damn."

I grabbed a couple of red-and-black cocktail napkins off the bar to press against the cut.

Then I looked around and realized that I was far from the door, in an underground cellar, surrounded by strangers who self-identified as vampires; and I was *bleeding*.

"We need to go," I said to my posse. "*Now*."

I turned and headed for the door, feeling all eyes upon me. Quickening my footsteps, I heard my two bodyguards right behind me—and felt uncomfortably aware that they, too, considered themselves vampires.

I sure hoped those girls in the bathroom had been right about most of the "vampire community" not drinking blood. As the club's clientele all watched me make my dash for the door, my heart pounded with anxiety and I prayed that no one would try to snack on my hand.

I dashed up the steep, dark steps to exit the Vampire Cave, unnerved by the thudding footsteps of the two vamparazzi right behind me. When I emerged onto the sidewalk, I panted with relief.

Shaking a little with reaction from my painful fall, my nasty cut, and my subsequent anxiety attack, I looked around to get my bearings. Daemon was leaning against the side of the building, close to the window where the leather-gear novelty shop displayed its wares. He was clutching his stomach with one hand and his head with the other. Thack was pacing up and down the sidewalk, talking into his cell phone. Flame and Casper, hanging out by their bikes, approached when they saw me emerge from the club.

Flame immediately noticed my injured hand. "What happened, Miss Diamond?"

"I fell and cut myself."

He looked sternly at Treat and Silent. "You allowed Miss Diamond to be injured? On *our watch?*"

"It was an accident," I said. "I bumped into—"

"Miss Diamond's safety is our responsibility!" Flame admonished his crew. "If we can't protect her in a low-risk environment like the Vampire Cave, how will we protect her against a real threat?"

"Actually, I just fell and—"

"If Miss Diamond falls down again, we need to be there *breaking* the fall!" Flame declared. "Do I make myself clear?"

"Yes," said Casper.

"Yes," said Treat. "I won't fail again."

Silent nodded.

"Oh, it's just a cut, fellows." Actually, in the dim light of the street lamps, I could see that the blood was seeping through the bar napkin. "Uh, has anyone got a hanky or something?"

I had left my tote bag locked inside Daemon's car with his chauffeur, rather than haul it into the club. And it only contained a few tissues, anyhow; I could tell that I needed something more substantial for this cut.

The men searched their pockets, then apologized profusely for coming up empty-handed.

"That's okay. I'll ask Thack," I said. "Um, at ease, men."

I walked over to my agent. His eyes widened when he saw my disheveled appearance and injured hand.

"Just a minute, Uncle Peter." He held the phone against his chest. "What on earth has happened to you *now?*"

"Never mind. What's the news from Vilnius?"

"There *was* a vampire hunter here. A guy called Benas Novicki. Apparently he was an old hand. Very experienced."

"And?"

"He's missing," Thack said gravely.

"Missing?" I repeated. "For how long?"

"They're not sure. The last time they heard from him was about three months ago, when he reported that he was closing in on someone he'd been hunting for a while."

"That's it? No more contact after that?"

"None."

"They didn't think that was strange?"

"Not for a while," Thack said. "Apparently hunters are better at killing vampires than they are at staying in touch with the council. Anyhow, they finally started trying to reach him couple of weeks ago. No response. He's missing." Thack sighed and added, "Now that we've related what's happening here, he's also presumed dead. The council is sure he wouldn't drop the ball on *this*."

"Well, isn't there another vampire hunter in town? A back-up guy?" When Thack shook his head, I demanded, "What kind of shoddy operation *is* this?"

"A fourteenth-century one," Thack said. "And it's not as if vampire hunters are thick on the ground, Esther. Only some vampires are hunters. And there are only a few thousand vampires, after all, in a world of six billion people, so—"

"Okay, okay, I get it. Well, what are we supposed to do now?"

"That's what I'm finding out."

Seeing that he was about to put the phone to his ear again, I said, "Wait! Do you have a handkerchief?"

He patted his breast pocket then shook his head. "Sorry."

Thack went back to talking to his uncle, and I went over to where Daemon was leaning against the building in a stupor. I asked if he had a hanky. Lost in the throes of booze-induced dizziness and nausea, he didn't seem to hear me.

"Where's your car, Daemon? Can you call the driver?" I prodded.

He wheezed, and his eyes started watering.

"Can you hear me?" I asked. "I want my bag. And it's time to go."

To my surprise, as I stood there trying to communicate with the inebriated actor, a police squad car pulled up to the curb. I was even more surprised when Lopez got out of the car's backseat.

He gave me an exasperated look, then leaned down to the driver's window to speak to the officers in the vehicle.

He was clean-shaven today but otherwise still looked disreputable, and his clothes were even more unexpected than last night's grubby ensemble. He was wearing waders, the sort of things that fishermen or utility workers sometimes wore: rubber boots that turned into trousers that came up to his waist, held up by suspenders.

Lopez finished speaking to the cops, then turned and came toward the spot on the sidewalk where I stood with an actor who was threatening to puke.

As a chilly breeze swept across the street, I got a distinct whiff of sewage. "What is *that?*"

Daemon sneezed, then groaned again. "My allergies. You're standing too close to me!"

"Oh. Sorry."

I stepped away—and bumped into Lopez. He caught me by the shoulders and turned me to face him.

That's when I realized where that odor was coming from. "Oh, my God, that's *you?*"

He said tersely, in a low voice, "What part of 'stay away from him' didn't you understand when we talked about this?"

"What is that *smell?*" Daemon moaned.

"*Fine*, I'll get farther away from you," I said to him.

His hands still on my shoulders, Lopez said, "You aren't supposed to be near him in the first place!"

"No, not you," Daemon said, his speech slurred, his half-closed eyes red and tearing. "It's like . . . ugh, what *is* that?"

Lopez's impatient expression changed to mingled surprise and alarm when he got a good look at Daemon. "I'll stand downwind of you," he volunteered quickly.

"Oh, no . . ." Daemon hunched over. "I think I'm go-ing to—*Bweegggh!*"

Lopez had been wise to wear waders.

18

"**J**esus, Mary, and Joseph!" Hauling me with him, Lopez leaped back as the liquid contents of Daemon's stomach hit the sidewalk in messy splatter. "What in God's name have you two been *doing?*"

"He's been drowning his sorrows," I said, taking another step back as Daemon did an encore. "Now his sorrows are fighting back."

"What are *you* doing here with him? And at a vampire club, for God's sake?"

"Miss Diamond?" Flame and Casper joined us, looking sternly at Lopez. "Do you need assistance?"

"Oh! No thanks, guys. This is a friend of mine." I glanced at Lopez. "Are you still going by Hector Sousa?"

He said to them, "I'd like a few minutes alone with Miss Diamond."

I saw Flame's skeptical expression and assured him it was okay. He nodded, gave Lopez a hard glance, and stated that he and the others would be within earshot and visual range at all times. Then he and Casper turned away and rejoined Treat and Silent near the motorcycles.

"Who are *they?*" Lopez asked me.

"My vampire posse," I said, still cradling my injured hand against my chest.

"Your what?" He drew in a sharp breath when he got a good look at my battered face and my general dishevelment. "Holy shit, what's *happened* to you?"

"I am never working with vampires again," I said seriously.

Daemon finally seemed to be finished with his stomach's rebellious response to the evening's festivities. He gave a despairing groan and sank down into a sitting position on the sidewalk, his back resting against the building, a prudent distance away from the mess he had just made.

"Hey, are you all right?" Lopez asked him distractedly, still looking at me.

"Urngh."

"It's been a rather trying evening, but I was safe," I assured Lopez. "I have my vampire posse to protect me now."

"Vampire posse? You know, somehow, that seems just . . . *perfect.*" He rubbed his forehead. "I was having a lovely evening wading through a sewage mishap underground while searching for the murder scene. I would have been happy to stay there all night—or at least until the methane gas made me pass out. But then I got a message saying that *you* were *here* with *him.*" He glanced at Daemon, who was holding his head in his hands and muttering that he felt like hell. "At first, I thought, no, it must be the *other* actress from the show, because Esther and I talked about this—exactly *this*—and there's no way she'd do something that crazy . . ." He sighed and glared at me. "But then I realized, no, if anyone was going to be that crazy, it would definitely be you. So I asked a squad car to bring me straight here."

"Ah, so that's why you smell, um, the way you do." I asked, "But how did you find us? I mean, who sent that message?"

"Daemon's a murder suspect in a high profile case," he said in a low voice. "Who do you *think* contacted me?"

My eyes widened in surprise. "The police are tailing him?" I whispered.

"Plainclothes cops, unmarked car. They followed him here from the theater." Still keeping his voice low, he added, "And since the investigating team knows that I'm worried you're at risk, they contacted me when they saw you in his company. I got the message a little while ago, when I came topside for some air."

"Oh." I felt bad about disrupting his work.

"What are you *doing* here?" he asked in exasperation.

I tried to remember. "Actually, I was keeping my agent company."

Lopez glanced over his shoulder at Thack, who was some distance away, with his back to us all, as he continued his conversation with Uncle Peter.

"That's who the other man is?" he asked in surprise. "Your agent?"

"Yes. Thackeray Shackleton."

"Oh, right. You've mentioned him before." Lopez added, "That can't be his real name. Speaking of which . . ." He turned his gaze back to Daemon with a sigh. "I only came here to get you. But we can't just leave him here like this."

"We can't?" I said in disappointment.

After all, Daemon had a cell phone, a personal assistant at his beck and call, and a chauffeur-driven limo somewhere around here. He was also indirectly responsible for all my injuries. So I was perfectly willing to leave him alone, drunk, and vomiting on the sidewalk.

"Well, *I* can't," Lopez said apologetically. "You know—that whole 'protect and serve' thing."

"Oh, right," I said. "Bummer."

Daemon's nose was swollen and runny, and he was drooling a little. Some vomit had gotten on his black silk shirt and his leather coat.

"This has been the worst day of my life," the celebrity vampire moaned.

"All things considered," Lopez said as he looked at how the mightily self-absorbed had fallen, "this is almost enough to make me believe in a just god."

"You don't?" I asked. "A churchgoer like you?"

"If I hadn't already had doubts," he said, "then being a cop would certainly have brought them on."

Daemon sneezed violently, twice in a row, then glared at us through glassy, red-rimmed eyes. "For fuck's sake, will the two of you get *away* from me?" he said, his speech noticeably less slurred now.

"Are you sobering up?" I asked hopefully.

"I can't *believe* the week I'm having," Daemon moaned.

Gazing at him, Lopez shook his head. "I just don't get it. How does *this* guy get so many women?"

I shrugged. "It's a mystery to me."

Daemon snapped, "It helps that I don't smell of sewage."

"He looks pretty rocky," Lopez said. "I wonder if he needs to go to a hospital. How much has he had to drink?"

I shrugged. "Other than *plenty*, I don't really know."

"I *don't* need a hospital," Daemon insisted.

"In that case," said Lopez, "we need to get you home, Danny."

Daemon flinched. "Don't *call* me that!"

Lopez asked, "You came in your own car, right? Where is it now?"

"My car," Daemon said wistfully. "Yes. I want it right *now.* I want to go home."

"And I want my stuff." I added to Lopez, "My tote bag is in his car."

"My car . . ." Daemon squinted at Lopez. "Do I know you?"

"No."

I went out into the street so I could look up and down the block. I spotted the limo double-parked, halfway down the street, shining darkly beneath the streetlamps. With my injured hand cradled against my midriff, I stepped into a pool of light and waved my good hand overhead, hoping to attract the driver's attention. It worked. The headlights came on, illuminating me as I gestured for the car to come collect us.

Nearby, Lopez was again speaking to the cops in the squad car. Then he joined me in the street, a regrettable aroma wafting around him, and put his hand under my elbow, tugging me back toward the sidewalk as Daemon's car pulled to a stop near me.

"I need to get into the car," I said. "My stuff—"

"The officers will get your bag and keep it in the squad car until you're ready to go. They're taking you home," he said as he dragged me back to the sidewalk.

"Oh?"

"Yes. *After* they help the Vampire Ravel get into his car without passing out." He turned to face me. "As long as I'm here, I wanted to make sure . . . What's wrong?"

I had been trying not to grimace. Apparently I was not successful. "Could you stand downwind of me?"

He sighed. "Fine. Whatever." We switched places. "I wanted to check . . ." Now *he* made a face. "What do *you* smell of?"

"Antibiotic ointment and muscle liniment."

"Oh. Of course."

"You were saying?"

"I wanted to make sure you . . ." Lopez stopped speaking and looked over my shoulder with some consternation.

"Now what?" I glanced in the same direction and saw my four-man posse all staring at us.

"If this is what it's like to have an audience," he said, "I don't understand the attraction."

"No, I think this is what it's like to have bodyguards." I admitted, "It takes some getting used to."

Lopez held their unwavering quadruple stare for another moment, then gave up. "This is distracting. Let's go around the corner and talk for a minute."

I waved and reassured my posse that all was well, then I let Lopez lead me around the corner of the building. This being late Sunday night, the street was quiet, with no cars or pedestrians in our immediate vicinity.

"Jesus, what *else* happened to you?" Lopez asked with concern, noticing the way I was cradling my injured hand. He gently took it in both of his hands, palm up, and examined it while I explained. The cut was still bleeding. "This looks deep, Esther. I think you might need stitches."

"I can't afford stitches. Do you have a handkerchief or something?"

"Oh, um, here, use this." He reached for the cotton bandana that was keeping his long hair out of his eyes, pulled it off, and shook it out.

While he folded it into a neat square, I threw the bloody, crumpled cocktail napkins on the ground. I was normally a conscientious citizen who despised polluters, but I was much too tired to go look for a garbage can in the dark.

As Lopez took my hand in his again, I asked him, "Do you really think I need stitches?"

I was fretting about the cost. As a city employee, he might have a medical plan that would cover something like this, but I certainly didn't.

"I don't know." He brought my hand a little closer to his face and bent his head over it, trying to get a good look in the dim light. "Does it hurt very much?"

"Not that much." In fact, I was mostly aware of the feel of my hand lying in his warm palm, his fingers clasping me gently. "Uh, just stings, I guess."

He absently stroked the side of my hand with his thumb, sending tingles through my solar plexus. "I guess it'll be all right if you . . . take care of it."

His voice was a little husky now.

"Oh. Good." So was mine.

"But I'm not a . . ." He swallowed.

"A . . ." I breathed.

"Not a doctor," he murmured.

My chest hurt. My throat felt tight. I was pretty sure he noticed that I was breathing too fast. But then so was he.

It wasn't a good idea for us to stand so close together. Touching. One of us should move away.

I tried and found that I couldn't. My feet felt like they were weighted down. I realized the hand he was holding was starting to tremble.

His black hair gleamed like onyx beneath the rays of light flowing down from a nearby street lamp. I felt his warm breath wafting softly across my palm. I swallowed and curled the fingers of my other hand into a fist, aware of a desire to stroke his hair.

A delicate trickle of blood started to run down my wrist.

He hesitated for a moment, then lowered his head. I gasped when he caught the ruby trickle of blood with his tongue. He went still, aware of my startled reaction. I didn't move a muscle, just stood there with my hand in his hand, staring at his bent head while his warm mouth hovered over my skin.

My heart started pounding, and I felt a quiver in my pelvis. His rapid breathing tickled me as it danced across my tender flesh. I leaned a little closer to him, feeling hypnotized by the moment. Captured by the damp, trembling touch of his lips.

"Let's find out," he whispered, his breath stroking my wrist, "what's so great about . . ."

I closed my eyes when his warm, wet mouth moved over the base of my palm. He licked delicately at my recent wound, then closed his lips on my skin and began sucking gently, drawing my blood into his mouth.

Although the night was chilly, I started to feel warm

all over and then, in certain places, wickedly hot. A brisk wind swept down the dark street, and the contrast between the cold air on my skin and the hot mouth sucking more insistently on me now drew a voluptuous sigh from me. I tilted my head back, spiraling into the mindless sensation that spread through me from the nerves that were thrillingly alive beneath that stroking tongue.

Ramping up his game, he nipped my sensitive skin, making me flinch me a little. I gave a helpless moan and leaned against him as my knees sagged, shakily seeking something to hold me upright. I felt the delicate flutter of his eyelashes brushing my skin and the teasing caress of his thick hair as his tongue and mouth continued working rhythmically, taking what wanted. Sucking with increasing intensity now. Feeding on me.

Hot. Wet. Hungry . . .

Clinging to him for balance as my heart thundered, I looked down at his head, bent over my hand, his breathing getting harsh now, and I brushed aside his black hair and sank my teeth into the back of his neck, biting him hard enough to hurt a little—in that *good* way.

He drew in a sharp, startled breath and went very still for a moment—then sucked more fervently on my wound, drawing my life force into his hot mouth, massaging me with his agile tongue, and nibbling—

"Detective?"

I uttered a gurgling shriek and staggered backward—which is what saved me from getting a bloody nose when Lopez lifted his head and sprang bolt upright, moving as if he'd received an electric shock.

I clapped my good hand over my mouth and gaped with horrified embarrassment at the patrolman who had come around the corner and caught us in the act.

Lopez's chest was heaving as he stared at the cop in consternation.

The policeman looked a little bemused at our reaction. "Oops. Sorry," he said casually.

I realized that *my* chest was heaving, too. I tried to get control of myself. And of my thoughts. It was dawning on me that nothing in the cop's face suggested that he realized he had just interrupted . . . *that.*

Huddled together in the dark, a dozen feet away, and glimpsed for only a second or two, I realized we had probably looked like we were just embracing, not . . . not . . .

Whoa, I can't believe we just did that.

Lopez cleared his throat. "Yes, officer?"

"We put the vampire guy in his car and sent him home. Four bikers and a guy in a suit are all asking for Miss Diamond." The cop concluded, "And we're ready to take her home as soon as you're done with her, detective." Perhaps realizing how that sounded, in the circumstances, he added, "Er, I mean, as soon as you're done talking with her."

"Thank you. We're almost done now. I mean, we're almost done talking. Well, I mean . . ." Lopez said in defeat, "Jesus, go away, would you?"

"Yes, detective."

The cop disappeared around the corner. Lopez took a deep breath. Then another. The wind blew this way again, and I caught a whiff of sewage.

I hadn't noticed the smell at *all* when he was sucking my blood. I hadn't noticed *anything* but the way he . . .

Wow.

And *then* when he . . . Well, I doubted I would have noticed a nearby rocket launch at that point.

Oh, man.

"You're really *not* the altar boy you pretend to be, are you?" I said on a puff of mingled embarrassment, surprise, and lingering arousal.

He laughed a little, obviously embarrassed, too. Then he asked, "Are you okay?"

"Of course," I said.

"So . . . I guess that's blood play, huh?"

I felt my face flush. "I guess so."

"I, uh . . ." He looked away, still a little self-conscious. "I think I get it now."

"Uh-huh." With my good hand, I fiddled with my hair. "It's, uh . . . Yeah."

"I mean . . ." He took another breath, then met my gaze again. Shedding his self-consciousness now, he said with candid directness, "I liked that."

"You *are* a dark horse," I said.

He smiled. "Only in the right company." Then he added, "But, God, I really don't think I could . . . you know . . . *cut* you to play around like that."

"Good to know." I looked down at my throbbing hand.

"Oh! Here. I think you need this."

Without coming any closer, he extended his arm to offer me the folded cotton bandana. Also without getting any closer, I accepted it with thanks, being careful not to let our fingers touch when I took it from him.

Still feeling self-conscious, I started to laugh. "Oh, God, do I have to take back everything I just said to Daemon a little while ago about how disgusting I thought this sort of thing was?"

"Nah, don't give that guy any ideas." He brushed his hair out of his eyes.

"I was wrong," I said ruefully. "There's definitely . . . something about it."

But only in the right company.

I didn't say it aloud. And I wasn't going to.

"Yeah," he said. "There is."

My nightmares still haunted me. As did the waking memory of how close Lopez had come to dying—*twice*—because of me. Sure, I might have been quivering pre-orgasmically in the middle of a public street a minute ago, but that was unexpected (to say the least), and it certainly didn't mean I had changed my mind about what was right. Or what I could live with.

"Be honest with yourself, Esther," the killer had said to me that night, having left Lopez to die alone in the dark. *"Would he be lying in agonized paralysis awaiting his death now if not for* you?"

I couldn't live with *that.*

Pressing the folded bandana to my injured hand and trying to stifle the blood flow, I forced myself to pull my thoughts together. "What did you want to ask me?"

"Huh?" He seemed startled by the question.

"Didn't you want to ask me something?"

He looked at me like a deer caught in the headlights.

"Lopez?" I prodded.

"Well . . . yeah, I do want to ask you something."

In the silence that followed, I recalled that during sexual arousal, a man's blood flowed *away* from his brain. I was wondering just how long it would take *this* man's brain to start functioning again, when he spoke.

"I'm wondering . . ."

"Yes?" I said encouragingly.

He let out his breath slowly. "Am I being punished?"

"What?"

"It feels like I'm being punished."

I stared at him in blank bemusement.

Confronted by my bewildered silence, he said, "I wasn't going to bring this up. I swear. Well, not until we had the killer in custody, anyhow. I didn't want to make things awkward." He made a gesture indicating the two of us. "Between you and me. Or *for* you, with me," he added quickly. "I wanted you—I *still* want you—to feel comfortable calling me if anything weird happens or you see anyone suspicious. I don't want you to hesitate to ask for my help because of . . . personal things."

"I didn't need help tonight," I reassured him. "Everything was—"

"No, I don't mean that. I mean . . ." He stopped, regrouped, and started over. "After what just happened . . ." His vague gesture indicated our brief bout of vampire sex. "I know I'm the one who started it, but you didn't seem like you were . . . just being polite."

I felt my face flush again. "No. I wasn't being polite." I couldn't imagine the circumstances in which I would passionately bite a man's neck, while he sucked my blood, in order to be *polite* to him. It occurred to me ask, "Are you okay? Did I hurt you when I, uh . . . ?" I gestured awkwardly to his neck.

"I'm fine. But since we just got, um, pretty personal, and you seemed to be . . . into it . . ."

"Go on."

"Am I being punished because I dumped you? Is that why you wouldn't even talk to me after that night in Harlem?"

"Dumped me?" I repeated, a little miffed. "I thought you gave me up."

"I did." He shrugged. "But you felt dumped. You told me so. And then, later, when I wanted to talk . . ."

"Oh. I see." I shook my head. "No, you're not being punished for dumping me."

"You're sure?"

"Yes. I don't play games, Lopez. Not like that."

"I know. I didn't mean you were playing games. I meant . . " He made a frustrated sound. "I don't know. Women are hard to figure out. You, especially. So I had to ask. Because this *feels* like punishment."

"I'm not punishing you." In an attempt to prove it to him, I asked, "What did you want to talk about? If you say it now, I'll listen."

"I didn't have a speech ready, Esther. I thought, you know, we'd *both* talk. And then . . ."

"And then we'd try dating again, and everything would be different this time? Because things went so *well* between us when we saw each other in summer?"

There was a long silence.

I finally asked, "Was that the talk, then? Did we just have it?"

"I think so."

"How did it go?"

"Oh, it was a lot like talking to myself for the past couple of months."

Another silence.

"So we're okay now?" I asked.

"Yeah, I guess we are." He sounded perplexed.

My heart and body were screaming about how much they had missed him, demanding to be heard. But I kept my head in command of things this time, and I reminded my unruly organs that the two very worst experiences of my entire life were the two times that this man was targeted with death because of me.

And the second attempt had come *so* close.

Much, much too close.

Lopez saw the shiver I couldn't control. "Are you cold?"

"A little." I pulled my jacket more tightly around me; but I was shivering because of my memories of a stormy night in August, not because of the November wind.

"Come on." He nodded in the direction of the people who were waiting for us. "The cops will take you home."

We walked back that way together, keeping a sensible distance between us now. As soon as I saw Thack, pacing impatiently with his hands in his pockets while he waited for me, it hit me.

"The first victim," I said suddenly to Lopez, stopping in my tracks. "I mean, the remains that were found underground which you think might be this killer's first victim."

"Yeah?"

"Male or female?"

"Male," he replied. "Why?"

"Have you identified him?"

"No."

"When was he killed?"

Looking at me with mingled interest and suspicion

now—a familiar combination in his attitude to me—he said, "Probably mid-August."

I went still. "A little less than three months ago."

He nodded, studying my expression. "Now tell me why you're asking about this."

I took a steadying breath, my heart thudding. "I think the victim might be a Lithuanian named Benas Novicki."

"How do *you* know who the victim might be?" he demanded.

"Benas Novicki was kind of an acquaintance of Thack's distant—*very* distant—relatives in Vilnius." I nodded toward my agent, who was making exasperated gestures at me, indicating that he was more than ready to blow this popsicle stand. "Benas disappeared about three months ago in New York."

Lopez was frowning. "That's not a name I've seen in any missing persons reports that have been cross-referenced with the murder case."

"Nobody reported him missing."

"Why not?"

"I guess they weren't that close," I tried.

"Esther."

"Okay. Here it is." I knew this wouldn't go over well, but I might as well just tell him. "Benas was a vampire hunter. Before he disappeared, he was hot on the trail of a vampire he'd been pursuing for a while."

"Okay," Lopez said wearily, "I obviously inhaled *way* too much methane gas in the tunnels earlier tonight. In fact, I think we can safely say that *all* of my behavior since I arrived here has been pointing to that conclusion. And *now*, I could swear I just heard you say that the first victim was a vampire hunter. Probably I should go seek treatment."

"There's no need to be sarcastic," I said. "Look at it this way—"

"A vampire hunter? *Esther.*" His facial expression suggested that our very brief chat tonight about our relationship had been right on the money.

"Look, *he* thought of himself as a vampire hunter," I said patiently. "Which means that if he knew about a killer who exsanguinated his victims . . ."

There was a pause.

"Oh, *Jesus.* Point taken." Lopez nodded, his expression turning somber. "He'd have gone after him, and that's how he wound up dead."

"Now that you have a name, can you identify the remains?" I asked.

"Maybe. If so, it'll take time, though. There's definitely not enough of him left for a visual ID."

I wondered if Lithuanian vampire hunters still used crossbows. "Were there any personal possessions found with the remains?"

"No, nothing." Lopez brushed his hair out of his eyes. "Benas told someone he was on the trail of a killer?"

"Yes. Someone back in Lithuania."

"If he was right about that, it might mean he wasn't the first victim," Lopez mused. "He's just the first one we know about."

"Oh! Of course." After a moment, I asked, "You've been over the case file for Adele Olson by now. Was she killed by the same person as the other victims?"

"In my opinion, yes. Branson is . . ." Lopez made a waggling gesture with his hand. "Starting to lean my way. His partner, though, is stuck on good old Danny Ravinsky for Angeline's murder. And, by the way, just *how* stupid is that guy? He didn't give the cops his real name in a *murder* investigation?"

"Don't even get me started," I said.

I assumed Branson's partner was the woman detective who had questioned Daemon. Her theory of the case was wrong, but I found it easy to understand how several hours of interviewing Daemon made her desperate to see him behind bars.

"Have I got the, uh, vampire hunter's name right?

Benas Novicki?" When I nodded, Lopez said, "Okay, I'm going to look into it."

"Good." I waved to Thack to indicate I was ready to leave.

He opened his arms to the heavens, as if to say, *Finally!*

"Oh, wait, one more thing," Lopez said as Thack headed this way. "I remember what I was going to ask you. Have you had that door sealed?"

"What?" I said blankly.

"The door I showed you, leading into the tunnel system."

"Oh! *Damn.*" I covered my eyes with my good hand.

"I gather that means no?"

"We're going now, right?" Thack asked. "I'm *so* ready to leave."

"I forgot," I said to Lopez.

"How could you forget? I thought it was pretty memorable, Esther."

"A lot happened right after that!" I said defensively. "And a lot *keeps* happening."

Thack said, "Esther, *please.*"

"Oh, who dragged me here in the first place?" I snapped at Thack.

"Who got me involved in this?" he snapped back.

"In what?" Lopez asked.

"*Nothing,*" we said in unison.

Looking as if maybe he *had* inhaled too much methane tonight, Lopez said to me, "Remember the door tomorrow. Okay?"

"Okay."

My vampire posse joined us.

Flame asked, "Are we leaving, Miss Diamond?"

"Miss Diamond is being escorted home by the police, who will see her safely inside her apartment," Lopez said. "You're dismissed for the night."

Flame looked at me for confirmation, which I gave. He made arrangements to meet me near the theater to-morrow, "beyond the perimeter" of where trouble could be expected. Then he, Treat, Casper, and Silent left, roaring away on their two motorcycles.

"Can we go *now?*" Thack asked.

"Yes."

"Wait," Lopez said. "One more thing."

"*Now* what?" Thack asked wearily.

"It's personal," Lopez said to him.

Thack said to me, "On the way home, you're going to tell me who he is, right?"

"No, she's not," Lopez said.

"Get in the car," I urged Thack. "I'll be with you in a second." Once he was out of earshot, I asked Lopez, "Who exactly are you tonight? I'm so confused!"

"I'm pretty confused tonight, too," he said. "So just don't talk about me at all. All right?"

"Sure," I said. "Was that the 'one more thing'?"

"No." He hesitated.

"Well?"

"This is a little awkward. I don't want you to be of-fended."

"What is it?"

"Well, um, considering what I did back there . . ." He made a gesture indicating the spot around the corner where we had played with fire. "You'd tell me if there was something I needed to know, right?"

"Something you . . . Oh! *Oh.*" I realized what he meant. I wasn't offended. It was a fair question, coming from someone who'd just drunk my blood. "There's nothing to tell. *Nothing,*" I assured him.

"Okay." His gaze shifted to the squad car. "You'd bet-ter go. I see that Shackleton's chomping at the bit to set off on this expedition."

19

At my insistence, Leischneudel and I arrived at the theater unusually early the next evening. I was determined to be ready for the curtain tonight in *plenty* of time, without any of the panic-stricken rushing I'd wound up doing last night. I also wanted additional time to concentrate on my makeup, given that I was still black, blue, pink, and mottled.

My injured hand was a little stiff and sore, but I thought I would get by without needing stitches, as long as I was careful with it. I'd gone shopping today and found a brand of sturdy adhesive bandages that matched my skin tone; and the cut was on my palm, after all. So, although the bandage was anachronistic for a Regency-era play, very few audience members would see it.

Mindful of Daemon's allergies, I had also purchased hypoallergenic antibiotic ointment and muscle balm. They were too expensive, but spending the money was certainly better than living through a repeat of yesterday's performance.

Leischneudel was a wreck by the time we got inside the theater, and I was very grateful for the protection of the Caped Crusaders and my vampire posse. They hadn't been sufficient, though. We had also needed several policemen to help our cab get through the agitated crowds, as well as several more to deal with unruly vamparazzi while we made a mad dash from the taxi to the stage door, surrounded by our vampire bodyguards.

Now, as planned, I was all made-up and dressed, well ahead of curtain time. This had a calming effect on my nerves, which was a blessing, all things considered. I was almost ready to go ask Leischneudel to lace me up when there was a knock at my door.

"Come in."

Tarr entered the dressing room. I ground my teeth together and wished I had bothered going to the door, so I could have kept him out of the room. He waltzed in now and flung himself into a chair as if he were a regular and welcome visitor here.

"I heard you got here early today," he said. "You look great. I love that dress."

I tugged the neckline up, unsuccessfully trying to minimize the way it exposed my breasts to his gaze. "What do you want?"

"Man, those crowds are *crazy* today, aren't they? It's insane out there! I really think they might start rioting when Daemon gets here."

I glared at him. "Gosh, and who do we think might be responsible for *that*, Al?"

"What?" he asked innocently. "You think this is *my* fault?"

"You've certainly stirred the pot."

"Hey, just doing my job," he said cheerfully.

I shook my head and continued putting the finishing touches on my hair, ignoring the reporter.

I loathed Daemon, and even *I* was appalled by Tarr's treatment of him in the "updated and expanded" account of the murder that was in today's *Exposé*. Oozing with sleazy innuendo and unfounded speculation, it created the emphatic impression that Daemon had murdered Angeline, and it barely stopped short of calling on fans to commit vigilante justice before he killed again.

I thought that Daemon ought to sue Tarr and the *Exposé*. Thack had also read the piece and agreed that they damn well deserved to be sued; but he said he suspected a lawsuit might be fruitless. He thought the article was so shrewdly written that the *Exposé*'s lawyers had probably approved it. Besides, the story was selling so many copies of the rag and getting so much exposure, the *Exposé* might even, Thack suggested cynically, have run a profit-and-loss calculation and decided that paying Daemon a settlement would be worth what they gained from smearing him like this.

Thack hadn't called me to gossip about the tabloids, though—all of which were spewing variations on the depiction of Daemon Ravel as a vampire gone bad. He had called to update me on the Lithuanian situation.

The Council of Gediminas, convinced that Benas Novicki had fallen in battle against a rogue vampire, was sending a crack specialist from Vilnius to clean up the mess here.

"I gather they rousted him out of bed for a briefing right after hearing from my uncle and then put him on the first available flight out of Vilnius. His name is Edvardas Froese," Thack had said when we talked earlier today. "It sounds as if he's a combination of Dirty Harry, D'Artagnan, and the Terminator, all rolled into one Lithuanian vampire hunter."

However, the Dirty D'Artagnanator, as I thought of him, had one slight handicap: He didn't speak English. So Uncle Peter was flying in from Wisconsin and would meet him at JFK Airport, acting as his guide and interpreter in our fair city.

"And then I guess we'll get our next update," Thack said.

I had relayed the information to Max. That was several hours earlier, and we were still awaiting more news.

Now that the *Exposé* was encouraging vigilante violence and the natives were restless, the Vilnius vampire hunter couldn't arrive soon enough, as far as I was concerned.

Although many things under heaven would have been a welcome distraction from my thoughts at the moment, Tarr's speaking again was not one of them.

Especially not when he said: "You smell really good."

"I'm not supposed to smell at *all*," I said prosaically. "I'm wearing all hypoallergenic stuff today."

Tarr's nostrils flared. "*I* think you smell good."

"Hmph. I'll need to see Daemon as soon as he gets in. If he can smell this stuff, I might have to wash it all off." That would be quite a setback to my whole "be ready early" strategy today.

"*If* he gets in." Tarr grinned wolfishly. "Sure, I know, half the babes out there still want to sleep with him—even after everything that's happened. What *is* it about that guy? Me, I just don't see it. But by now, the other half of the loonies out there are ready to tear him apart."

Based on the volatile behavior of the crowd when Leischneudel and I had arrived, I thought Tarr was right—the vamparazzi might well go berserk when Daemon got here.

I was repelled by the way the reporter was gloating about it; and even more revolted when I realized he was delighted that his "work" was playing a significant role in inciting the mob.

I said, "I really don't think *this* is what Thomas Jefferson envisioned when he argued in favor of a free press, Al."

"Spin is a beautiful thing." Tarr ogled my back, where my gown flapped open. "And so are you, kiddo."

"Don't call me—never mind. Why are you here, Al?" Realizing that gave him an opening to ask me out again, I hastily amended, "I mean, at the Hamburg? You shouldn't be here when Daemon arrives. All things considered, the sight of you today might *actually* turn him into a murderer. Are you willing to be strangled just for the sake of another headline?"

"I found out who Danny Ravinsky is." Tarr's toothy grin broadened. "I thought he might want to talk about it before I file my story." When I didn't rise to the bait, he prodded, "Aren't you curious?"

"No. And I'd like you to leave me alone now so I can—"

There was another knock on the door, which Tarr had left open. My gaze flew eagerly to the doorway. Attila the Hun would be a welcome visitor now, if it meant I wouldn't be alone with Tarr anymore.

"Victor!" I said, seeing the bald, anxious assistant hovering there. "Come in. I'm glad you're here." Aware of Tarr's eyes following me everywhere, I said, "Could you lace me up?"

"Pardon?"

Tarr said, "Hey, I'll do that."

"*No*, Victor's got it." I presented my half-naked back to the befuddled assistant. "It pretty much works like shoelaces."

"I'm wondering whether to phone Daemon," Victor said anxiously as he started working on my laces. "What do you think, Esther? The mood of the crowd out there is so ugly, I feel I should warn him. But at the same time, I don't want to distress him unnecessarily. And, after all, it's not as if he can skip work tonight. The show must go on."

"Well, he'll have to come through that crowd, any-how, Victor. So maybe telling him about it ahead of time won't help or change anything." As the assistant finished tying my laces, I added doubtfully, "Though if he wanted to avoid attention tonight, I suppose he could try com-ing through the fire exit on the other side of the stage."

"The way he left," Tarr said with an amused snicker, "when the cops hauled him away for questioning."

"There's not as much police presence near that door," I said, "but there usually aren't many vamparazzi hang-ing out around there, either."

"Vampa-what?" Victor asked.

Tarr guffawed. "I get it! Good one!"

"That door doesn't open from the outside," Victor said.

"So wait by the door and let him in when he pounds on it, genius," Tarr said rudely.

I gave Tarr a cold glance. "It might not be such a good idea, after all, Victor."

"No, I think it is. I'll call Daemon and suggest it." Victor pulled out his cell and hit the speed dial. "He can phone me as his car pulls up, and I can be waiting right by the door to let him in." He held the phone to his ear, then said a moment later in disappointment, "It's going to voice mail." He glanced at me. "Well, I'll leave you to finish preparing. Thank you, Esther."

"No, don't go," I said to his retreating back, unwilling to be abandoned alone with Tarr.

Victor didn't hear me. He was leaving a message for Daemon, suggesting my plan.

"That guy gives me the creeps," Tarr said to me. "No life of his own at all. Just exists to cater to Daemon's every whim, twenty-four-seven, and is *grateful* for the 'privilege.' I swear, I think he's in love with Daemon." Tarr leaned forward and confided, "Between you and me, I think Victor leans the other way, you know what I mean?"

"Your keen insight into human nature is always a revelation, Al," I said coldly.

"God, I love your zingers!" he said with a chuckle.

I sighed. Why me?

I went back to my makeup table, privately considering Tarr's comment more seriously than I was willing to let him see. If Angeline's killer was someone obsessed with Daemon, that didn't preclude the person being someone Daemon knew—even someone close to him. Where *was* Victor when the girl had been murdered? I had no idea. No one had ever said.

Admittedly, I found it difficult to picture the high-strung, effeminate assistant as a rogue vampire prowling through the dirty, dark, spooky tunnels beneath the city, preying on other victims and also slaying an experienced vampire hunter in combat.

Then again, what did *I* know about rogue vampires? I supposed if you were endowed with mystical power and driven by your homicidal blood addiction, being high-strung and effeminate were probably just minor eccentricities.

"Oh, my God, I can't believe what it's like out there today!" Mad Rachel boomed, coming into the dressing room. "I swear it took me twenty minutes for my cab to get from the corner to the theater! People aren't even staying behind the police barricades anymore!"

I was packing up my makeup. Tarr was watching me. A moment of blessed silence descended on the room.

Then Rachel said, "What am I, *invisible?* Are you two even listening to me?"

We both looked at her in surprise. My jaw dropped when I realized that she had been speaking to *us*.

Tarr voiced my thoughts. "Where's your phone, Rachel?"

"In my bag. Why?" She dumped her hold-all on the counter and continued, "The cops have *not* got that situation under control. Something bad is going to happen out there. I can feel it!" Noticing that I was still staring openmouthed at her, she said, "What?"

"I'm just not used to seeing you without a phone glued to your ear," I admitted.

"Me, neither," said Tarr.

"What*ever*. Oh! I read your story today, Al," Rachel said. "And I'm *so glad* you're here."

"You are?" I blurted.

"I have a *lot* of questions." She pulled up a chair and sat down close to Tarr, which obviously startled him. "Do you really think we're working with a killer? Because if Daemon's murdered someone, then I'm calling

Equity. I don't think I should have to share the stage with him, do you?"

I noticed the open, partially empty bottle of champagne I had left sitting here the night before, and I seized on it as an excuse to flee the room. "I have to go put this in Daemon's fridge. Bye!"

Tarr said, "Wait a minute, toots. I wanted to—"

"I'll be right back," I lied.

I made my escape, pleased to realize I wouldn't have to go back in there before intermission, when I'd need to do a quick touch-up to my face. For now, my make up, hair, and costume were all ready. I'd go wait in Daemon's room until he arrived, when I'd ask him to sniff my hypoallergenic self and make sure we were good to go. Then I'd go hang out in Leischneudel's room until curtain. This strategy would also have the advantage of making it harder for Fiona to find me, if she were around. She hadn't cornered me yet about the stain on my hem, and she might make the effort tonight.

Halfway down the hall, I realized I had left my cell in my dressing room, which meant that I wouldn't be able to check for an update from Thack. Oh, well. I certainly didn't want to go back in *there* to fetch it. Besides, I should be thinking about the show for the next few hours. The latest update on the Lithuanian connection could wait until I was finished with work.

I saw Bill approaching from the other direction, looking frazzled. I remembered my promise to Lopez and decided I'd better speak to the stage manager now about that door that led into the tunnel system.

"Um, Bill, I have kind of a strange—"

"It is a madhouse outside," he said heavily. "I swear, it's gone from crazy to dangerous."

"I know. It's pretty bad tonight. Listen, there's something I need to—"

"The cops really have their hands full. And I don't know *how* we're going to manage to open the house and get people seated," Bill continued morosely. "The house manager says they're about to have a riot in the lobby."

I frowned. "Seriously?"

"People are trying to *break in* to the theater out front," he said. "And, actually, I think people *have* broken in back here. I've just called the cops and told them we need some of them inside tonight. We might have intruders backstage."

"What? *How?*"

Bill held up a finger as his cell phone rang. "Just a minute, Esther."

I thought through the possibilities while he answered his call, which seemed to be a follow-up on his request for assistance inside the building. The only ways into the backstage area were through the front-of-house, which was still closed (but apparently under siege); via the unloading area, which was always securely locked if the crew wasn't moving sets and equipment; via the backstage fire exit, which could only be opened from the inside; and the stage door, which was guarded.

My stomach sank as I realized there was one more way to get in here—via the underground tunnels.

Oh, *no.* Had I waited too long to follow Lopez's instructions? Had the killer infiltrated the theater from below? Was he stalking the cast and crew even now, preparing to pounce, slay, and feast?

Bill ended the call with a demoralized sigh. "The cops understand our concern about the intruders, but they can't spare anyone from duty outside the theater. Things are too out of hand out there, as it is. They're going to try to shift more officers from other duties to the Hamburg, but that'll take a while."

"Somebody has broken in backstage?" I prodded in alarm. "From the basement?"

"The basement?" he repeated with a puzzled frown. "No, I think someone's come in through the roof."

"The roof?"

"There's an old ventilation shaft way at the back of the stage. We've just found a couple of rappelling ropes dangling down from it. They weren't there when we re-set the show last night, I know that much."

"Whoa." The ceiling there must be thirty feet high. "You're saying that someone climbed onto the roof and rappelled down to the stage?"

"I know. Even for these people, it's crazy, isn't it?"

"How did they get up there?" I wondered.

"I have no idea. But it's been dark for well over an hour, so I guess they were able to do it without being spotted." Bill added, "That's a long fall to the floor if someone doesn't really know what they're doing. I hope they chickened out and went away after dropping the ropes down."

"So do I."

"But I'll feel better when we get a cop or two patrolling back here."

"Me, too."

Bill said, "Look, if you see Daemon before I do, please warn him about this. If someone has broken in, then he's bound to be the person they're trying to see—or to harass."

"Of course." I started to add, "By the way, there is another way to get into . . ." But Bill was already halfway down the hall—and much too busy and stressed for me to show him the tunnel door right now, anyhow.

Hoping that Daemon would get here soon, I walked to his door, opened it, entered the room—and came to a surprised halt when I saw Leischneudel standing in front of Daemon's little refrigerator, with the door open, revealing its empty interior. He was drinking a bottle of ruby red liquid.

He flinched guiltily, lowered the bottle, and gaped at me in openmouthed alarm.

My first thought was that he was so stressed-out by the hysterical vamparazzi tonight that he was filching Daemon's last bottle of Nocturne, despite being a nondrinker. I started to hold up my open bottle of luke-warm, flat champagne, to offer it as an alternative . . .

But then I realized that wasn't a Nocturne bottle he was now trying to conceal behind his back. It was one of the decorative little bottles in which Daemon kept his own blood.

I also saw, with a horrified chill that raced straight to the pit of my stomach, that the sticky red liquid clinging to Leischneudel's lips and teeth wasn't wine cooler.

"Oh, my God!" I dropped my champagne bottle as I gaped at him. It hit the floor with a heavy thud and spilled tepid bubbly all around my feet.

"It's not what you think," he said quickly.

His mouth was bright red with blood. I uttered a hor-rified gurgle of disgusted fear when he unconsciously licked and smacked his lips while staring at me in quiv-ering, guilt-ridden anxiety and trying to think of what to say.

"You're a *vampire?*" I cried.

"Oh." Leischneudel blinked. "Well. Yes, then maybe it *is* what you think."

"A vampire?"

"Keep your voice down," he said anxiously. He set down the bottled blood and glanced into the hall to see if anyone had heard me. "Close the door."

Taking all factors into account, I let out a bloodcur-dling scream—which stuck ineffectually in my terror-constricted throat—and turned to flee. I slipped on the spilled champagne and flailed madly in the doorway, try-ing to get traction.

"Esther!" He was on me in flash, his arms around me as he dragged me back into the room, faster and stron-ger than I had expected.

"No!" I screeched. *"No!"*

Leischneudel slammed the dressing room door, shoved me against it, and pinned my arms to my sides when I tried to fight him.

"Esther! Listen! *Listen* to me."

I looked at his reddened lips and teeth, and I screwed up my face in disgust. "Oh, my *God!* You're the killer! *You* murdered that girl! It's you! How *could* . . . umph nnng!" My voice was reduced to panicky grunting when he covered my mouth with his hand and pressed hard, trying to silence me.

"The *killer?*" he blurted, clearly horrified. "Oh, my God! How could you think *that?*"

Panting frantically through my nose, I grunted out my answer beneath the pressure of his hand.

"Well, yes, I'm a vampire," he said. "But I'm not a *psychopath*. All right, I have to drink a little blood now and then. But I certainly don't go around *killing* people."

I stared at him, my heart pounding, caught off guard by how normal he seemed—well, except for the blood on his mouth. I grunted inquisitively.

"No, of course not! How could you *possibly* . . ." His expression was shocked and hurt. "I don't even kill spiders! *You* know that . . . Well, okay, there was that one time—but it was really big and hairy, and it was in my tub, and it scared me."

I was still breathing hard, torn between frightened suspicion of this newly exposed vampire and a desire to believe my friend. "Ung oong imayay?"

"What? Oh. Sorry." He removed his hand from my mouth. "I guess I freaked out for a minute there. I was afraid you were going to run all over the theater screaming that I'm a vampire."

"Well, I was." I winced and touched my cheek, which was still tender and slightly inflamed beneath my makeup.

"Oh, I'm sorry. Did I hurt you?" He leaned closer to inspect my skin.

"Stay back!" I snapped, seeing that bloody mouth coming within range of my jugular vein. "Don't come near me!"

His eyes misted with tears. "See? This is exactly why I never tell anyone."

"Where were you on the night of the murder?"

"I was with *you* until four o'clock," he said.

"Oh. Right. And *then?*"

"You know where I was! Home in bed. Mimi woke me at six thirty, and we were at the twenty-four-hour clinic by seven. You can call and ask them!"

I stared at him in consternation. "Are you Lithuanian?"

"No." His eyes widened. "You *know* about Lithuanians?"

"You're made, then?"

Based on what I had learned from Max about made vampires, I now recalled various revealing moments during the three months I had known Leischneudel—none of which had ever before struck me as noteworthy. In particular, I thought of his uncannily acute hearing.

He hesitated to answer my question, then let out his breath and nodded. "Yes, I'm a made vampire. And if you know about Lithuanians, then you know you mustn't tell anyone, Esther! It's very dangerous. They'd *kill* me!"

"You didn't get a permit?" When he shook his head, I said, "What were you *thinking?*"

"*I* didn't know what was going to happen!" he said defensively.

"What *did* happen?" I demanded.

He gave a weary sigh. "Well . . . you remember my telling you that I was very sickly growing up, right?"

"Yes." I put a hand over my pounding heart and tried to steady my breathing.

"I was born with a congenital immunodeficiency disease. And the older I got, the more things went wrong with me. In college, I couldn't even complete the second semester of my sophomore year. I wound up dropping out of out school. I even broke up with Mary Ann. It was a very dark time for me, Esther." He glanced hungrily at the bottle of blood on the other side of the room, and said, "And I began . . . experimenting."

"With vampirism?"

"*No*, with alcohol. Cigarettes. Marijuana. I even tried . . ." Shamefaced, he blurted, "Magic mushrooms."

"Leischneudel!" I said in surprise.

"I know it's no excuse, but I was very depressed and angry. Anyhow, one night, I got really drunk with this guy I hardly knew, and one thing led to another . . ."

He looked so uncomfortable, I decided to just say it for him. "And you had sex."

"*No*, he convinced me to drink some of his blood."

"Oh!"

"He told me it would heal me. Change me. Make me strong, and healthy. He was . . . very persuasive." Leischneudel paused. "You know how some things seem like a really good idea when you've had *way* too much to drink, but then you wake up the next day and wonder what you could *possibly* have been thinking?"

"Oh, *that's* never happened to *me.*"

"At the time, I was just worried about AIDS," he said. "It wasn't until a couple of weeks later, when I noticed I had become obsessed with *everybody's* blood, not just the blood I had drunk, that I realized something weird was happening to me. So I knew I had to face this guy again and find out exactly what he had done to me."

"Was he Lithuanian?"

Leischneudel nodded. "It turned out he was even more appalled than I was the morning after, when he woke up sober and realized what he had done. He was also terrified. He told me he wasn't allowed to do this without special dispensation, and if anyone found out, we'd *both* be killed."

"Oh, Leischneudel," I said in sympathy.

"I was really shaken up at first," he admitted. "Almost suicidal. But, of course, as soon as I went to Mary Ann in despair and confessed everything, she straightened me out."

"Oh?" How did a girl straighten out her boyfriend after finding out he had just accidentally become a *vampire?*

"She made me see what was important. What actually mattered."

"Which was?"

"The transformation *did* heal me!" he said. "It did make me strong and healthy. It completely changed my life! I got back together with Mary Ann and could be a real boyfriend to her. I also returned to college, finished my degree, graduated, and moved to New York to become an actor. I'll be able to marry Mary Ann, be a good father to her children, and grow old with her while I spend my senior years doing character roles."

Leischneudel's blood-sticky smile was glowing with grateful happiness as he recognized his blessings anew. "And *now* I've got a major role in a sold-out Broadway show. Okay, it's a show about an evil vampire who kills people, which is a little disturbing for me . . . And we're mauled nightly by vamparazzi, which I find a pretty stressful."

"Uh-huh."

"But I think of myself as the luckiest guy in the world!" he said. "And if the price for all this is that I have to drink a glass of blood every week or two, I think that's a fair bargain, even if I didn't originally know what I was getting into."

I glanced at the bottle he had pilfered from Daemon's refrigerator. "Leischneudel, before you started stealing blood from Daemon's stash, how did you get your—"

"I didn't!" He flushed guiltily and amended. "Well, just this once. I shouldn't have done it. But when you opened that bottle the other night and I smelled his blood, even before you took a sip—"

"You knew it was *his* blood?" I blurted.

"Oh, of course. It smells just like him." Seeing my expression, he added, "Well, to a vampire, anyhow."

"You could have *told* me," I said irritably. "I was worried all night that—"

"I know. I wanted to tell you. Just like I wanted to tell the cops that the blood in those bottles was Daemon's, not the murder victim's. But then I would have to explain how I knew . . . And, well, how could I?" He gave me an apologetic look, then continued, "Anyhow, when I realized those bottles really did have blood in them, I stole one."

I recalled that he had been transfixed for a few moments by the site of the stuff spilling onto the carpet, his eyes wide, his nostrils quivering. At the time, I thought he was just shocked, as I was, by our discovery.

"It was very wrong of me," he said. "I was just so *hungry*. Mary Ann and I originally thought she'd visit this weekend, and she had left enough blood at my place to last until then."

"Ah, so Mary Ann is your source," I said.

"Of course! We . . . we, uh . . ." He blushed furiously.

"It's part of your sex life?" I guessed.

He nodded, too embarrassed to say more.

Thinking of Lopez, I said, "Man, you straight arrow guys are full of surprises."

He sighed. "She was really stressing out about this research paper she's got to finish, and I knew I wouldn't be able to spend much time with her if she came here, anyhow . . . So I lied and told her I still had some of her blood left over, and I'd be fine if she didn't come."

"That didn't work out so well, I gather?"

"Daemon's refrigerator was just too tempting," he said. "Those bottles of blood right *there*. I thought Daemon wouldn't notice if just *one* was missing. So that night, while he was onstage and no one was around, I snuck into his dressing room and stole this bottle."

"I don't understand," I said. "If you stole it then, what are you doing here now?"

"That was the same night the police came—and confiscated the remaining bottles. So I was terrified after that. I had stolen something the police were treating as evidence in a murder case." He admitted to me, "That's why I couldn't sleep that night, and why I called Mary Ann so early Sunday morning. I didn't know what to do."

"What did Mary Ann say?"

"She was very disappointed in me," he said sadly. "I had *lied* to her, and I had *stolen*. We had a pretty serious talk."

"I'll bet."

"We decided there would be too many complications for me if I turned the bottle over to the police."

"True."

"But Mary Ann didn't think I should drink *stolen* blood. So I promised I would return it to Daemon's refrigerator as soon as I could find an opportunity."

I looked at the open bottle I had caught him drinking. "I guess you had a crisis of willpower at the very last ditch?"

"I'm just so *hungry*," he said again. "And Mary Ann won't be here until the weekend."

"Then for God's sake, Leischneudel, finish the bottle."

His eyes widened. "You really think I should?"

"Yes. Quickly, too, before Daemon gets here. Go on. Start drinking."

"*Now?* With you here?"

"Yes." I decided not to spoil his appetite by telling him that a crack Lithuanian vampire hunter was headed our way. I'd wait until he was done drinking. "You should never have brought that bottle back here. You should have drunk the blood and disposed of the evidence. Mary Ann is admirably moral and obviously very supportive, but she's not very pragmatic."

Leischneudel took several greedy glugs of the bottle, then sighed luxuriantly through blood-soaked lips. "Oh, *God*, I was hungry."

"There's something that still doesn't add up." I frowned, thinking it over. "There should have been more bottles when the cops confiscated them."

He paused before his next sip. "I thought so, too. There were four bottles left when I took this one. I remember because, well, to be perfectly honest, that was *why* I took only one. I thought more than that would be noticed."

"And you never stole a bottle before that?" I asked.

He shook his head. "Mary Ann and I always, um, extract enough blood for me to get by between her visits. This weekend was just . . . a mistake. One I won't make again."

"When he caught me drinking his blood," I said, remembering now, "Daemon said something about how his supply was being pilfered."

"You mean you weren't the first person to raid Daemon's fridge?" Leischneudel asked.

"And you weren't the *last* one to raid it before the cops got here and took what was left."

Our eyes met.

"Esther . . ." Leischneudel said slowly. "Are we saying there's another vampire in this building besides *me?*"

20

I used Leischneudel's cell phone to call Max and explain our suspicions.

"I have a theory, too," said the mage. "I observed the phenomenon *twice* yesterday that soon after we entered the theater, Nelli experienced what appeared to be an allergic reaction and soon after we exited, she reverted to a state of robust good health. You and I assumed that something in the theater was troubling her senses."

"Uh-huh."

I made an exasperated gesture at Leischneudel, who was listening intently to my conversation, urging him to *drink faster.* Daemon could arrive at any moment, and we were still in his dressing room—since I thought we might be noticed if we left the room with half a bottle of blood in our possession. Besides, I didn't want to bump into Tarr or Fiona, if I could avoid it.

Max continued, "I now postulate that, since Nelli is a mystical being, what irritated her senses yesterday was—"

"A vampire?" I guessed. "Or, rather, vampires." Thack and Leischneudel had both been here, after all.

"Yes. I think it possible," Max said, "that we *were* getting an affirmative reaction from Nelli. We just didn't recognize it."

"Because we were looking for something identical to her reactions to mystical threats on previous occasions," I said.

"Precisely. A living vampire—as you now know from your friendships with two of them—is not inherently threatening or evil. That's a matter of character and circumstances. Ergo, Nelli does not respond to vampirism as a threat. But I now suspect she *does* respond to it as an irritant to her delicate senses."

I exercised tact and did not mention that Max's delicately sensitive mystical familiar regularly gulped down discarded garbage during her habitual perambulations.

"The question is, Max, if I'm right and there is an unknown vampire wandering around here, can Nelli's senses pinpoint him?"

"We can only ascertain that by making the attempt."

"Can you bring her to the theater right away? Since the vampire hunter is coming to New York—"

"What?" Leischneudel blurted.

"I'll tell you in a minute," I whispered. Then I continued saying to Max, "We might be able to help narrow his search and end this nightmare faster if Nelli can identify the rogue vampire."

"Nelli and I shall come to the Hamburg forthwith," Max said. "However, under the terms of the treaty, if any representative of the council asks me to leave or wants Nelli to stand down—"

"Yes, I understand," I said. "I'll make sure someone knows at the stage door to let you in."

As I ended the call, Leischneudel said, "A *vampire hunter* is coming here?"

"Yes. I didn't want to spoil your dinner, so I was saving the news for afterward. Drink *up*, by the way."

He pursed his bloody lips and cradled the mostly empty bottle against his chest, rocking back and forth a little. "I think I've lost my appetite. A *Lithuanian* vampire hunter?"

"You should keep a low profile while he's here."

"Oh, you *think?*" he snapped.

I realized he was very upset.

"There's no need to panic," I lied, recalling what Max had said about the ruthlessness of Lithuanian vampire hunters. "We can get through this."

There was a sharp, heavy knock at the door. We both flinched, looked at it, and froze. A moment later, someone flung open the door.

Leischneudel hastily wiped his mouth with his hand. I glanced at him and saw with dismay that all that did was smear the blood around, making it even more noticeable.

A total stranger stood in the doorway. He was an older man, gray-haired and heavyset. He had a ruddy complexion and a pug nose, and he wore sensible clothing: a plaid flannel shirt, an anorak, khaki trousers, and sturdy shoes.

What I mostly noticed, though, was the crossbow in his hand.

He said, "I'm looking for Daemon Rav . . ." His blue eyes fixed on Leischneudel, who was frantically smearing blood across his mouth. *"Vampire!"*

The stranger raised his crossbow and took aim.

"No!" I leaped to my feet.

"Wait!" Leischneudel howled, diving sideways.

The vampire hunter shifted his crossbow to track Leischneudel's evasive move. He stepped further in the room to corner his quarry—and slipped on the champagne I had spilled by the door. His eyes bulged as he cried out and sailed up into the air, where he seemed to hover for a moment like a cartoon character, then he crashed heavily to the floor, banging his head against the doorjamb as he fell.

I knelt down next to him and felt for a pulse.

Leischneudel peeked out from behind the chair he was hiding behind. "What did you *do*, Esther?"

I said, "He's still alive."

"Also trigger-happy!"

"Quite." I took away the crossbow. "Do you think we should tie him up?"

"*Yes.*" Apparently too shaken to stand upright, Leischneudel crawled over to the stranger. "Let's do that right now."

I closed the door, since I shrewdly suspected that some of our colleagues might question our intentions if they saw us tying up an unconscious stranger.

Leischneudel, who was still in his street clothes, removed his belt and bound the stranger's hands behind his back. Then he rooted around the room searching for something equally strong to use on the legs.

"I'm a little disappointed," I said.

"What, that he didn't *kill* me?"

"Calm down. I just mean *this* is the Dirty D'Artagnanator, sent all the way from Vilnius to slay our rogue vampire? He's not quite what I expected."

Leischneudel, who had found an electrical extension cord, started binding the man's ankles with it. "What *were* you expecting?"

"Well, not a chubby old guy who immediately knocked himself out so we could tie him up." Then I realized what else I hadn't expected. "Wait a *minute.*"

I knelt beside the unconscious man and started fishing around in his pockets.

"What are you looking for?" Leischneudel asked as he finished his task.

"His ID. This man sounded American when he spoke. The vampire hunter who's coming to New York doesn't even speak English . . . Ah-hah! Here it is." I found his wallet, opened it, and pulled out the driver's license.

"Who is he?" Leischneudel asked.

I frowned, puzzled. "He's Peter Simkus of Oshkosh, Wisconsin." After a moment, it hit me. "Oh, *crap.* I need your phone again."

Leischneudel handed it over.

I called Thack's cell. He didn't pick up, so I left a message on his voice mail. "Your Uncle Peter just tried to kill Leischneudel. We've knocked him out and tied him up in Daemon's dressing room. I think you should come to the theater and talk to him. *Right away*."

"Thack sent his *uncle* to kill me?" Leischneudel said shrilly. "I thought Thack liked me!"

"No, Uncle Peter was supposed to be the interpreter for the vampire hunter," I said. "Thack mentioned that his uncle had done a little vampire hunting; but since he's managed to be captured by *us*, I'd say he's pretty rusty. I'm guessing he got a little too excited about being back in action and overstepped his mark."

"*Overstepped?*" Leischneudel repeated. "Esther, he pointed a *crossbow* at my *head!*"

"We have the crossbow now," I said reassuringly, waving it at him. "And he's tied up."

"Who let a stranger with a weapon into the building?" Leischneudel demanded.

"That's a good question." I knew the cops were overwhelmed, but I found it hard to believe they'd been distracted enough to let someone waltz past them with a crossbow. "And if Uncle Peter is here, then where is—"

Leischneudel and I clutched each other in panic as the door flew open without warning. Daemon stalked into the room.

He slipped on the spilled champagne and cursed as he righted himself. He tripped on Uncle Peter and gave the unconscious man an irritable kick before he stepped over him.

I quickly closed the door while Daemon flung himself into a chair.

"My God, I thought *yesterday* was the worst day of my life!" he said in an aggrieved tone, still looking hungover and wrung out from last night's bender. "I now look back on yesterday as an innocent time of unspoiled pleasures and youthful dalliance. Do you know *why?*"

"Why?" Leischneudel asked, perhaps too accustomed to playing Aubrey to Daemon's Ruthven.

"Because *now* I am living through today," Daemon declared. "Do you have any fucking idea what has happened to me *today*?"

I said, "You're not even curious, are you, about why we have an unconscious hostage and a crossbow in your dressing room?"

"Nocturne is threatening to fire me!" Daemon shouted. "I am the *face* and *voice* of Nocturne, and they're talking about dumping me!"

"Oh! Because of the whole . . ." Leischneudel made a vague gesture. "The tabloids are just *awful* today."

"You know what *else*? My movie deal is *this* close to being canceled!" Daemon held his thumb and forefinger a millimeter apart.

"You have a movie deal?" Leischneudel asked in surprise.

"Princeling of Darkness," Daemon replied.

"Feature film?" I asked.

"Cable TV," Daemon said darkly. "It's about a vampire who proves he's innocent of murder by hunting down the fiend who actually exsanguinated his lover.

"Wow, and they might not want *you* for that anymore?" I said. "Go figure."

"*And* when I came to work just now, I was spat on, insulted, and pelted with garbage outside the theater by people who were my devoted fans before the tabloids tried to turn me into a demented killer!"

"Did you sneak in through the fire exit, like Victor suggested?" I asked,

Daemon looked blank. "When did Victor suggest that?"

"I think he left it on your voice mail."

"Oh, I've had my phone turned off for hours. You would not *believe* the calls I'm getting! How do these people *get* my number, anyhow?" Daemon rubbed his forehead. "Where *is* Victor? Has he deserted me, too?"

"No, I think he's probably waiting for you by the fire exit. Victor said . . ." My eyes met Leischneudel's. *"Victor."*

Leischneudel looked at me inquisitively.

"Who has the most access to this dressing room besides Daemon? Who can come and go without being noticed?" I gestured to the fridge, from which bottles of blood had been quietly disappearing. "Who can take things *out* of this room without being stopped or questioned?"

Leischneudel's eyes widened and he gasped. "Victor!"

"What *about* Victor?" Daemon asked irritably.

"Where was he when Adele Olson was killed?"

"Who?" Daemon was absently fishing around in his pockets for something.

I whacked him upside the head. "The murder victim, you jackass!"

"Ow! Jesus, calm down, would you?" he said. "*I'm* the one having my life destroyed by this, not you."

"Where was Victor when the murder was committed?"

"How should *I* know? I'm more interested in where he is *now.* I need something for my stomach. And my head. And I need to use his phone. I don't want to turn mine on."

"You really think Victor is . . ." Leischneudel wiggled his brows meaningfully at me.

Looking at him with a puzzled frown, Daemon said, "Gay? Probably. But I don't ask about his personal life."

"Tarr says he doesn't have a personal life," I mused.

How twisted might that make a person? Or a vampire?

"*Tarr.* Is *he* here?" Daemon stood up, swayed briefly, then pulled himself together. "I want a word with him. No! I want five minutes alone in a room with him, no rules, no referee."

As he headed for the door, I said, "Don't trip—"

Daemon tripped.

"—on Uncle Peter."

Looking down at Thack's uncle, Daemon said, "All right. Fine. I'll bite. Why *is* there an unconscious man tied up on the floor of my dressing room?"

"No one really knows," Leischneudel said.

"Here's something else we don't know." I joined them in gazing down at Uncle Peter, who looked peaceful and was snoring a little now. "Where is the vampire hunter who was supposed to be with him? Did his airplane not take off from Vilnius? Did the guy never get here? Where . . . *Oh, my God.*"

"What?" Leischneudel said. *"What?"*

"He's here," I said with certainty. "The vampire hunter is in the building."

"No!" Leischneudel dived behind a chair again, taking cover.

"*That's* how they got in here with weapons," I said. "They climbed up to the roof after dark, then rappelled down via old air shaft." I looked down at Uncle Peter with more respect now. Sure, he was rusty, but he still had the right stuff. "*Two* ropes hanging down. Edvardas Froese is here, too."

"For God's sake," Daemon said. "They couldn't just buy tickets from a scalper, like everyone else?"

"They're not here to see the show," I snapped. "They're vampire hunters. Uncle Peter probably came in here to interview you. While Edvardas is doing recon or something. Who knows? The only stories I've heard about vampire hunting are from eighteenth-century Serbia, and they were slaying the undead. Edvardas has a whole different sort of quarry to hunt down."

From behind his chair, Leischneudel wailed.

"Just keep a low profile," I said to him. "I'm going to go see if I can find Edvardas. A total stranger carrying a crossbow and speaking only Lithuanian probably stands

out, even around *here.* I'll see if I can get through to him
with pantomime gestures or something. Don't untie Uncle Peter until I get back. We want to make sure he
knows not to kill you before we let him loose."

Leischneudel grunted an affirmative.

"And I," said Daemon through gritted teeth, "am going to find Tarr and kill him with my bare hands!"

He flung open the door to march through it.

We came face-to-face with a tall, slim, powerfully
built man with a neatly trimmed beard who had his pale
blond hair tied back in a ponytail. He wore a long suede
coat, old boots, and leather pants, and he carried a crossbow.

Now this is more like it.

"Edvardas Froese," I said with certainty.

He glanced at me and lifted one brow. He looked at
Daemon, and his eyes narrowed in recognition. Perhaps
he'd had a case file to study on his transatlantic journey.

Then he saw Uncle Peter lying on the floor behind
me, unconscious and securely bound. In a split second,
he raised his crossbow and pointed it at Daemon.

"Vampyras!" Edvardas cried in a deep baritone voice.

I didn't need to speak Lithuanian to understand *that.*

"Whoa." Daemon raised his hands. "What the hell
are you *doing,* man?"

"He doesn't speak English," I said.

Daemon looked at me. "You *know* this guy?"

"Not exactly."

Edvardas spoke coldly to Daemon. I didn't understand the words, but the intent certainly came across as,
"I'll see you in hell!"

"Wait! No!" With no idea what else to do, I raised
Uncle Peter's crossbow, which I was still holding, and
pointed it at Edvardas.

Keeping his eyes on Daemon, he said something dismissive to me.

"I'll shoot!" I warned.

Daemon sighed. "Look, I don't know what language this guy is speaking. But I'm pretty sure he's telling you that thing isn't loaded."

"What?" I looked down at my weapon. "How can you tell?"

Edvardas snickered.

"Oh, *shit*," I said. "Uncle Peter's even rustier than we thought."

"The old man was pointing an empty weapon at me?" Leischneudel blurted from his hiding place inside the dressing room.

On our left, Bill was running down the hall toward us. "What the hell is going on here?" he shouted. "Esther! Daemon! Who *is* that?"

Somewhere to our right, Mad Rachel starting screaming, "They're coming in! They're coming *in!*"

The combination of stimuli was enough to distract even a seasoned vampire hunter. Edvardas looked around, perhaps thinking he was being ambushed from multiple directions. I realized we had to disarm him to prevent a potential fatality before his interpreter woke up and could be convinced to tell him not to kill us. So I flung myself at him while he was off his guard, and the two of us went flying into the far wall together.

I heard a short, soft, menacing sound that I didn't recognize, immediately followed by Daemon shouting, "Jesus! That nearly hit me!"

I realized the crossbow had misfired when Edvardas stumbled into the wall with me. He flung me aside with one muscular arm as easily as if I were a paper napkin. I reeled backward and fell down as he launched himself at Daemon, who was shrieking, "I'm an actor! I'm an actor!"

Leischneudel appeared in the doorway, his lips quivering, his eyes glassy with fear. But he was a hero, deep down. When he saw what was happening, he joined Bill in jumping on top of the vampire hunter and pummeling him.

Edvardas was darned impressive, I had to admit. He fought three men at once (well, two, anyhow—Daemon was mostly cowering and shrieking over and over that he was an actor), and he seemed to be winning.

Down the hallway, I could hear Mad Rachel screaming, "Here they come! What do we do?"

I noticed a crossbow lying on the floor near me while Edvardas fought his adversaries. He had his hands around Daemon's neck now, and he looked like he was trying to rip his head off, exactly as Jurgis Radvila had done with an undead vampire in a Serbian cemetery long ago. Acting on instinct, I picked up the crossbow, rose to my feet, and walloped Edvardas over the head with it as hard as I could.

He cried out, swayed unsteadily on his feet for a minute, then collapsed.

Daemon was choking and gagging, red-faced, with tears streaming from his eyes.

"Oh, my *God*," Leischneudel said, panting with panic and exertion. "What do we do now?"

Bill was breathing hard, too. "I came back here to tell you the lobby has been breached. The crowds are pouring into the house. They've gone insane!"

I was also panting. "Crazy crowds rioting inside the theater? Two homicidal vampire hunters backstage, one of whom doesn't understand English?" I looked at my companions. "I say we run for it!"

"Good plan," said Leischneudel.

"I like it!" Bill seemed bizarrely cheerful.

Daemon was waving his arms feebly, indicating he needed help to stand up. Bill and Leischneudel hauled him off the floor. He was swaying dizzily in their arms as we all turned in the direction of the stage door to make our escape.

"Run for your lives!" Mad Rachel screamed.

I stared dumbfounded as Tarr and Rachel—who was in full costume and makeup—ran straight toward us from that direction, shouting their heads off. Then I heard the rising din of voices behind them, angry shouts, the roar of the crowd.

"They're coming through the stage door!" Tarr shouted. "The cops can't hold them off! Why do we *even* pay taxes in this city?"

Pelting down the hall behind them, I saw six men: my vampire posse and Leischneudel's Caped Crusaders.

When Flame saw me, he shouted, "The perimeter has been breached! Our position has been flanked! Man overboard!"

Silent shouted at him, "Oh, shut *up!*" Then to me: "Esther, run! We'll hold them off until you're gone!"

Then he laughed exultantly and turned to confront the sea of costumed, wing-wearing, befanged, goth-painted, Jane-look-alike, and mad-scientist vamparazzi piling through the stage door and flooding the hallway.

I saw Treat and Casper knock down Dr. Hal (whose picket sign today said: IMMORTAL LIFE IN PRISON!) while he was shouting, "No prisoners!" Then they high-fived each other.

The two Caped Crusaders leaped into the oncoming sea of people, swirling their capes with gusto and shouting, "Bam! Pow! Zam!" as they shoved and hit people.

A gaggle of Janes, unable to get past the bottleneck my posse was creating in the hall, were screeching, "Daemon! Daemon! *Please.*" Some of them were weeping with lust-maddened hysteria.

"Fire exit!" Daemon choked out, his nose running and his eyes still streaming. "Didn't you say something about the fire exit?"

"Hah! Yes!" Bill laughed maniacally as he and Leischneudel grabbed Daemon and started half-carrying, half-dragging him. "Fire exit! Stay together, everyone!"

As he passed Edvardas' prone body, Tarr asked me, "What is *that?*"

"A Lithuanian vampire hunter."

"Yeah, that's what I thought."

Mad Rachel started bawling her eyes out, making her makeup run as she wailed, "I want Eric! I want my mamma!"

"Come *on*," I said, dragging her by the arm. "Didn't you hear Bill? Stay together!"

We all ran toward the darkened wings, through them, and then across the stage. The curtain was down, and the working-lights for the crew offered enough illumination to ensure we didn't trip over the furniture in our mad dash to escape. The house of the Hamburg, directly on the other side of the curtain, sounded like the Roman Coliseum in some epic gladiator film. As the others kept running (except for Daemon, who was staggering while being dragged), I paused to peek through the curtain, wondering if there was any possibility of escaping unseen via the fire exit in the house.

"Good God!" I blurted.

There were dozens of people rampaging through the theater, with still more pouring through the doors at the back.

"Come on, come on!" Tarr grabbed my arm and dragged me away from the curtain, hauling me the rest of the way across the stage with him. "That is *not* your audience anymore, kiddo!"

"Don't call me that," I snarled at him and jerked my arm out of his grasp. "This is all your fault!"

"Hey, Daemon wanted to be noticed," Tarr said with a nasty sneer. "Well, now he's been noticed."

"Run! *Turn back! RUNNNNNNNN!*"

Emerging from the darkened wings at this end of the stage, Victor collided with Bill, Leischneudel, and Daemon. The four men all fell down, tumbling across the stage like billiard balls.

Rachel ignored them all and kept running forward, disappearing beyond the wings.

Victor was babbling as he hauled himself off the

stage, and then scooped Daemon up. "I was waiting for you. By the door. Like I said I would! There was a knock. I thought it was you!"

"You opened the fire door?" I guessed.

Rachel screamed in terror and came running back this way.

Tarr said, "Yep, he opened the fire door."

"And they came *pouring* in," Victor wailed. "Dozens of them! What do we *do?*"

"No, no, no!" Daemon shouted. "How can this be happening to me?"

"Oh, for God's sake," I said.

Bill pointed at the curtain. Beyond it, the decibel level of the seething horde was still rising. "There's a fire exit that way, if we can get to it."

I shook my head. "Not a chance. I looked."

Bill was practically jumping up and down with excitement as he said, "Stage door, no. Fire exit, no. House, no."

"Are you saying we're trapped?" Leischneudel asked in horror.

"We all going to *die!*" Rachel howled while runny mascara streaked down her face.

"I know another way out!" I said suddenly. "If we can get to it." There might be time, if we move fast enough. "This way!"

I ran toward the rear of the backstage area, near where Bill had found the rappelling ropes earlier. I went past the spot where Lopez and I had sat talking two nights ago, and down the hallway where he had then led me, into the alcove where the basement door was.

"No, this is a dead end," Leischneudel protested.

"It's not! Who has a flashlight?" I asked.

Bill pulled one out of his work belt. "I do."

Victor, who was hauling Daemon now, said, "I have a small one on my key chain."

"Me, too." Tarr added to me, as if I might care, "I like gadgets."

I opened the basement door.

"No!" Rachel howled. "We'll be trapped like rats!"

"There's an underground tunnel," I said. "Abandoned old water mains. We can escape this way. Hurry! Before anyone realizes where we've gone."

I lifted up my Regency skirts and started descending the stairs, the adrenaline of terror making me unusually swift and agile. I heard my colleagues stampeding behind me, and then the heavy basement door, already high above my head now, thudded shut behind us.

"Get out your flashlights," I said. "Bill, shut off the overhead light." When the vamparazzi got as far as that dead-end alcove, there was less chance they'd look for us down here if the basement was dark.

By then, I hoped, we'd be long gone, anyhow. Lopez had said there were other exits from the tunnel. It shouldn't be too hard to find one.

As soon as the lights went out, Rachel wailed, "This place is scary! I want Eric!"

"Shut *up,*" Tarr and I said in unison.

In the faint illumination provided by one large and two very small flashlights, I led them all across the basement, behind the rusted-out machinery and forgotten junk, and down the slick old steps to the heavy door in the wall.

Bill was laughing with delight. "What *is* this place? Esther, this is amazing!"

"You ain't seen nothing yet. Come on."

We entered the tunnel that ran under the street and connected the Hamburg to the old underground access chamber below Eighth Avenue. I was halfway to it when Victor, at the end of our queue, called out to me, "Uh, Esther? Problem."

Daemon's voice was raspy as he said, "Leischneudel, come *on.* What's the hold-up?"

"Uh, I'll wait here," Leischneudel said. "No one will look this far away for me. And the cops will have things under control in a while."

I said to Bill, "You take the lead. The access chamber is right ahead of you. When you get there, open the old iron door under the spiral stairs. It's very stiff, but it opens. That's the tunnel. From there you can get to an exit. A manhole or something like that."

"What about you?"

"I'll be right behind you with Leischneudel."

"Esther!"

"You guys go ahead. I know where I'm going." I added, "And whatever's wrong with Leischneudel, I can bring him around. *Go.*"

As they proceeded toward the access chamber, I started making my way back through this tunnel, passing my colleagues. When I reached Tarr, I realized I'd need a flashlight, and I took his without apology as I said, "Give me that. You can follow Bill."

As I passed Victor and Daemon, I remembered with a sudden chill that I suspected Victor of being the rogue vampire.

He said something to me, but I didn't hear what it was. The tunnel was reverberating with the echo of Mad Rachel's wails.

When I reached the door to the basement, where Leischneudel stood wringing his hands, trembling and sweating, it was pretty easy to guess what was troubling him. "Claustrophobia?"

He nodded. "I don't have too many problems in ordinary daily life, but an underground tunnel? I can't. Esther, I *can't.*"

I tried to convince him that we could do this as if it were a trust exercise in acting class, where he'd close his eyes and just let me lead him. But his nerves were shot to hell, and he was too frantic and panicky to be talked into this.

As we stood arguing, the lights suddenly came blazing on throughout the cellar, making us blink and squint. We heard the basement door slam in the distance, and then we heard two men's voices. After a moment, we realized *whose* voice it was and why we couldn't understand what he was saying.

"The vampire hunters!" Leischneudel whispered in terror.

"My God, those guys are tough," I said with reluctant admiration.

Leischneudel grabbed my arm, pulled me inside the dark tunnel with him, and quietly closed the heavy door behind us.

"Come on, come *on*," he whispered. "Let's go."

"I thought you were claustrophobic?"

"I am. It turns out I'm just *more* phobic about vampire hunters."

We proceeded through the dark, uneven tunnel with fast, fear-fueled steps. When we emerged into the access chamber, our colleagues had already pried opened the door and entered the tunnel. We were alone in the chamber. Leischneudel paused and looked around at the nineteenth-century construction and the crumbling spiral staircase that led to nowhere.

"Wow, this is amazing!" he said. "If I weren't terrified out of my mind, I think I'd enjoy this."

We heard shouts behind us in Lithuanian.

"Holy shit! Get in the tunnel," I said. *"Now."*

We ran through the iron door, sloshing into the thin layer of water there and slipping a little on the tunnel's old curved floor.

"Should we close it behind us?" Leischneudel reached for the rusty door and tugged. It screeched a little.

Something whizzed past us with deadly speed. A crossbow bolt!

"Uncle Peter!" I cried. "Edvardas! Stop this *now!*"

The next crossbow bolt came so close to me it brushed my arm. Startled, I nearly dropped Tarr's key-chain light. Then I turned it off, realizing what a good target it made me. I hastily stuffed the thing inside my corset so I wouldn't lose it. As my eyes adjusted to the complete, opaque blackness underground, I saw the dancing lights of the Lithuanians' flashlights flicker through the open doorway and bounce around the brick wall.

"Let's go," I whispered. "We'll have to lose them in the tunnels."

"Right."

I turned and ran. So did he.

Terrified, confused, and functioning in pitch darkness in a strange place, it was a few seconds before we each realized we weren't running in the *same* direction.

"Esther!"

"Leischneudel!" I took a step in his direction, then stopped abruptly when I heard two crossbow bolts fly through the door directly between us and clatter violently against the curved brick wall.

I instinctively backed up a step—then shrieked when something snakelike touched me, hanging down from the ceiling.

"Esther!" Leischneudel shouted.

"I'm all right!" I realized in that instant what it was. *Tree roots.* Hanging down through the ceiling. I remembered Lopez showing this to me. "Leischneudel, there are stalactites hanging down near you. *Be careful.* Now run! You'll come to an exit! You *will.* Go!"

"Esther, no, I won't leave you—"

"I'm not a vampire, and they know it. They won't kill me." I hoped I was right about that. "I'm going to try to reason with them. Go!"

"No, Esther—"

"*Go!*" Some brick dust fell on my head and into my eyes. I couldn't see anyhow, but the stinging was painful and distracting, and it made my eyes water. As some bits of mortar fell on my head, I remembered Lopez telling me that intruding tree roots could cause structural instability in these old underground tunnels.

I heard Leischneudel's footsteps sloshing through the

water as he fled into the dark. The tree root brushed me again, making me jump and gasp in frightened revulsion a second time. I backed well away from it, not wanting it to touch me again.

I heard the Lithuanian voices getting closer.

"Uncle Peter, can you hear me?" I called.

"Who *is* that?" the old man called.

I heard something all around me that sounded like sliding pebbles. I backed up a step further, my heart pounding with instinctive fear.

"I'm a friend of Thack's! *Do not shoot me.*"

"Friend of *who?*"

I heard rumbling like thunder, followed by cracking.

"Your nephew! Thackeray Shackleton!"

"Oh—that ridiculous name! What *was* the boy thinking?"

"Do *not* come into the tunnel." My chest was pounding with anxiety. "I think it's in danger of caving in!"

I moved forward, feeling my way along the wall. Something big fell in front of me, plummeting from the ceiling and hitting the water with a heavy thud and a splash. Pebbles hit me in the head.

"Young woman! Come *out* of there!" The voice was frightened, not threatening.

"I'm try—"

Somewhere behind me, from the far, dark reaches of this long-abandoned tunnel, a woman screamed in bloodcurdling terror.

The echo reverberated through the darkness and seemed to trigger the cave-in in earnest. The whole ceiling collapsed above me, and I threw myself backward just in time to avoid being buried by it. The long, echoing, thundering crash was deafening as the tunnel shook and I scrambled around in stygian darkness, screaming in blind, panic-stricken fear. I was coughing, holding my hand over my nose and mouth as I crawled through the water on my hands and knees, struggling to move in this ridiculous Regency costume while trying to escape from plummeting rocks and debris.

When the bricks finally stopped falling and I stopped screaming in hysterical terror, I was alone, in the dark, with the exit to the Hamburg sealed off by an immense pile of ruined masonry.

Behind me, trapped somewhere else in this tunnel with me, she screamed again.

21

For a moment, lying in absolute darkness, dazed, coughing, my head still reeling from the noise of the cave-in, and utterly alone except for those mad, terrified screams bouncing off the curved brick walls all around me, I thought I had died and gone to hell.

Then I started to pull myself together.

I felt something sharp poking me painfully in my breast, and I remembered that I had stuffed Tarr's little key-chain flashlight into my bodice. I pulled it out, flicked the switch—and could have wept with relief when it worked. As soon as the tunnel was illuminated, my surroundings—though eerie—started to settle into a normal, prosaic pattern.

Being able to *see* again calmed me down enough to start thinking rationally about other things.

I realized that Mad Rachel must be the woman I'd heard screaming—and, knowing her, she was simply having a hysterical reaction to the frightening, implosive thunder of the cave-in.

If she was up ahead in this tunnel, then so were my other colleagues. I just needed to catch up to them. And then we would find an exit.

Now that I had survived the cave-in, the thick barrier

of brick, rock, mortar, dirt, and sediment behind me mostly meant that I didn't have to keep running from vamparazzi or vampire hunters now. And getting away from them had been the point of coming down here, after all.

So I felt calm, collected, and optimistic as I painfully scraped myself off the wet tunnel floor and examined myself for injuries. I was scraped and bleeding in a few places, and feeling twinges of pain in others; but there was no serious damage.

Well, not to *me*. My costume was another matter. No amount of cleaning and ironing would ever make this dress presentable again. It was utterly filthy and in tatters.

I felt some anxiety about Fiona's reaction when she saw it; but, after all, it wasn't as if I had *planned* to be caught in an underground cave-in while wearing my costume. Sometimes these things just happen.

To me, anyhow.

Poor Leischneudel! He didn't have a flashlight, he must be all alone wherever he was, *and* he was claustrophobic. I needed to get out of here quickly so I could call Lopez. He seemed to know this underground area well, so he'd come up with a good search strategy if Leischneudel hadn't emerged by then. We needed to get him *out* of the tunnels.

I started walking ahead, relieved that my limbs were in good working order. Still, I wouldn't catch up to my colleagues unless I sprinted, so I'd better see if I could get them to wait for me.

"Hello?" I called. Then louder. *"Hello?"*

Rachel screamed her head off. For the first time since meeting her, I found that a reassuring sound.

"Esther!" she shrieked. *"Esther!* Is that you?"

I waited for the echo to stop bouncing off the walls. Then I responded.

"Yes! Can you guys wait for me?"

"Esther!" she screamed. *"He's mrgh vrungh oong!"*

"What?"

"Esther?" Tarr called. "Are you okay? Did you *hear* that before?"

More bouncing echoes.

"Cave-in!" I called. "I'm fine, but Leischneudel and I got separated! Wait up! I'm coming!"

"Okay!"

"Esther!" Rachel screamed. *"Hurry!"*

Yeah, yeah, whatever.

Since I was sloshing through water, on uneven ground, in shoes that were never intended for this sort of thing, it seemed as if I walked a long way, though it was probably not more than two hundred yards.

Mad Rachel was weeping and wailing hysterically now, howling inarticulate pleas, and babbling nonsense syllables. The noise floated and echoed eerily through the dark tunnel as my feeble little light guided me through the murky gloom of this old, abandoned, forgotten place . . . until I reached what seemed to be some sort of underground intersection.

There was a wide, high-ceilinged chamber, and the tunnel I was emerging from was one of three that met here, all coming from different directions. I smelled dirty water, wet old brick and cement, rotting garbage, a hint of sulfur . . . and also a strong whiff of sewage.

I choked a little, hoping the air quality wouldn't get any worse before we found a way out of this system.

I flashed my little light around, wondering which way to go from here. Rachel's sobbing seemed very close now, almost as if I should be able to reach out and touch her. I was about to call out to my colleagues when I was startled to see Rachel appear in the beam of my light.

What was she doing weeping here alone in the dark? Had the men *abandoned* her? I could understand the temptation, but it didn't seem likely.

She was sitting on a stony protrusion that had been

worn smooth and shiny with time and erosion. Her gown was wet and filthy, though not as tattered as mine. Her eye makeup had turned into dark, thick, ugly streaks that flowed down her puffy, weeping face. She rocked back and forth, sobbing brokenheartedly, her eyes squeezed shut, apparently not even aware that I had emerged from the tunnel and was shining my light on her face.

Unnerved by the sight of her huddled alone in the stygian darkness, wailing inconsolably, I flicked my light around the room—and fell back a step and gasped when I saw Tarr, standing perfectly still just a few feet away from me in the dark, staring at me in silence.

"Jesus, you scared me!" I snapped.

"Esther!" Rachel stood up and stumbled through the water, which was deeper here than it had been in the tunnel, to reach me. She flung herself against me, making me stagger, shrieking and sobbing.

Trying to hold Rachel away with one hand, I shone the feeble light around the chamber, looking for Victor, Daemon, and Bill. There was no sign of them. Which explained why mine was the only light here.

Raising my voice to be heard above Rachel's noisy sobbing as she clung insistently to me, I asked Tarr, "Where's everyone else?"

"They went the other way." He nodded in the direction from which I had just come.

I didn't understand. "Why did you guys split up?"

"I came this way on my own." He shook his head and looked at Rachel in exasperation. "She followed me. I didn't ask her to."

Rachel howled louder.

Oh, great. I was stuck down here with the only two people I knew who could make me think fondly of Daemon's company, by comparison. He, Bill, Victor, and Leischneudel were probably all discovering an exit and going topside right now, even as I remained lost underground with Rachel weeping hysterically on my shoulder and Tarr—I could have sworn it—ogling my tattered neckline.

I was about to suggest we proceed and search for a way out of here when Tarr suddenly grabbed Rachel by the hair, *yanked* her away from me while she howled in pain and clutched her head, and then *threw* her across the chamber. With much more raw strength than I would have suspected he possessed.

Rachel screamed loudly, then started crawling through the water on her hands and knees, scrambling to get farther away from Tarr.

I shouted at him, "Have you gone *insane?*"

"She's just so *noisy*," he said wearily.

Rachel screeched, "He's going to kill us!"

"Shut the fuck *up!*" Tarr's shout startled me so much I nearly dropped the light.

Rachel curled up into a ball and started rocking back and forth again, sobbing with her eyes squeezed shut.

"All right, you need to calm down," I said sharply to Tarr, horrified by his behavior—and more than a little scared.

"I'm hungry," he said casually. "It's making me cranky."

"It's making you *nuts*," I snapped. "Don't touch her again!"

"You *are* a tough one," he said with admiration. "I've liked that about you since we met."

"Let's get out of here," I said coldly.

"He's gonna kill us!" Rachel shrieked at me. "Don't you *get* it? He's going to kill us!"

"Of course he's not," I said firmly to her. I looked at Al again. "Er, right?"

"Well, *her* I'm going to kill," he said matter-of-factly. "But you and me . . . we could work something out."

I studied his face to see if this was another of his tasteless jokes—gone *way* too far in this case. But he wasn't grinning now. His shadowed face was relaxed but humorless.

"What do you *mean* you're going to kill her?" I demanded.

"I didn't ask her to come. In fact, I told her not to. But she followed me instead of going with them." He shrugged. "I could eat."

My head was spinning. I wondered if a rock had hit it during the cave-in and I just didn't realize it. My eyes were stinging from the foul air, and my throat was starting to itch. There was a disgusting taste in my mouth.

"Oh, my God," I said slowly, feeling cold shoot through my bones. "*You* killed Angeline."

"I don't really want to kill *you*," he said. "I like you."

"I'm *so* flattered."

"You and me, we could have some fun together."

"No, we couldn't."

"I thought for sure you'd stick with the others. I didn't expect to see you here. And I don't really *want* to drink you." He grinned. "Well, okay, maybe I want it a *little.*"

"A vampire lurking at the Hamburg," I said, trying not to let him see how much his words frightened me. "And plenty of access to Daemon's dressing room. You've been pilfering his blood supply since you started hanging around."

I also realized now why Nelli had sneezed so much in Daemon's room; Tarr had been there.

"You know, it's funny—even Daemon's *blood* tastes phony." Tarr guffawed and added, "Oh, this is even funnier. He's so stuck on himself, he thought the blood was disappearing because the cast and crew were sneaking 'personal mementos' of working with him. What an *asshole.*"

I thought it would be unwise to comment on the irony of Tarr's assessment. I said, "You know your way around underground, so you thought you could get away from the vampire hunters once we came down here tonight."

"Hey, you really impressed me with that one, Esther." He sounded almost flirtatious. "I mean, whoa! I had no *idea* that entrance was there! This whole area here is new to me."

"You turned the opposite way and tried to go off on your own when everyone entered this tunnel because you know what a Lithuanian vampire hunter is—what he's capable of," I said. "You knew he'd recover, track us, and catch up. And you didn't want to be with the rest of us when he did."

"You don't mess around with a vampire hunter, toots," he said. "They're serious business."

"I'm told they also err on the side of thoroughness. Let's say Edvardas does kill Daemon, just to be on the safe side, since you've worked so hard to smear him for Angeline's death," I said. "Do you really think a *vampire hunter* will just get on a plane and go back to Vilnius then? Come on, Al. Do you imagine he'll be gullible enough to believe that *Daemon* killed Benas Novicki?"

Certainly not after the way Daemon had cowered, flailed, and wailed "I'm an actor" in response to Edvardas' attack.

Tarr drew in a sharp breath. "How the fuck do you know about Novicki?"

My supposition was now certainty. "I know that Novicki was murdered by the same vampire who killed Angeline and two local urban explorers."

"Hey, what's with that tone, kiddo?" he said in a cajoling voice. "I'm just following the natural instincts of a predator. No reason to go all judgmental on me."

"*Al*," I said in exasperation. "You're a *murderer!* In fact, you're a serial killer!" And I was trapped underground with him, and nobody knew it.

"Oh, come on," Tarr said. "People wander around beneath the city in tunnels and vaults that haven't been used in a hundred years. What do they *think* is gonna happen to them?"

"Probably they *weren't* thinking they'd be eaten by a vampire," I said coldly.

"They got what they deserved."

"And what did Angeline deserve?" I said angrily.

"Don't try to pretend you're grieving for *her,*" he said.

"Why did you kill her?" I demanded.

"I was hungry." His tone suggested I was slow on the uptake. "Look, she bothered me at work around four in the morning to tell me she had a hot scoop about Daemon, so I met her—"

"Why haven't the cops traced that?"

"Prepaid cell. I got rid of it."

Four in the morning. Dead time. No one knew Tarr had left the *Exposé* building, and no one saw him or Angeline.

He said with disgust, "Her 'scoop' just turned out to be some time-wasting bullshit she was making up as she went along because she was mad that Daemon kicked her out."

So that's what happened after she was last seen by witnesses. Following through on her threat to Daemon to 'expose' him, she connected with Tarr, the nosy tabloid reporter she'd met in Daemon's car. "Jesus, Al, she didn't deserve to die for wasting your time!"

"She didn't die for *that.* She died because I'm a vampire, and it's what I *do,* baby."

"You were doing this in Hollywood, too, weren't you?" I blurted as the realization hit me.

"Things got a little hot there. It was time to leave. That jerk Novicki followed me here. *Persistent* bastard, but I took care of him." He grinned, and it was disturbing to see that familiar, cheesy, tabloid reporter's grin on this brutally amoral killer's face.

"How did you become a vampire?" I asked, wondering if he was an example of why the council was so stingy with permits.

"Born that way. Really didn't get into it that much

until I turned forty, though." He added with a guffaw, "What is that? A mid-unlife crisis?"

Rachel continued wailing loudly as I said, "Can I just say, Al? A vampire becomes a tabloid writer? And here I thought *Daemon* was a walking cliché!"

"Just going with my strengths." He said with nauseating enthusiasm, "Hey, as long as you know about Novicki, which is something I don't really get to talk about, can I just say? Killing a *vampire hunter*? What a rush! And the blood? *Amazing*." He added after a pause, "To be honest, though, once was enough. They're tough guys to kill. So I'd prefer if this one would just go back to Vilnius without bothering me. But if not . . . we'll see what happens."

"Do you think you can keep doing this and the Council of Gediminas will just *allow* it?" I said incredulously. "You've made it worth their while to *end* you."

"Hey, you do know a lot!" he said cheerfully. "That could be good. You know, it could be some common ground for us. Something for us to talk about."

"And do you think the *cops* will just walk away from this?" I said.

"The cops think Daemon did it," he said dismissively.

"Not all of them," I said. "And *none* of them think he killed the other victims."

Tarr went still. "What?"

"They're connecting the dots, Al. *Maybe,* if you got really lucky, you could've pinned *one* murder on some attention-seeking celebrity vampire."

"Did I ever tell you how much I really didn't want this assignment? *Me,* covering that phony jerk *pretending* to be a vampire?"

"But the cat's out of the bag, and you're not clever enough to smear *all* your murders on Daemon."

"You not making that up? The cops really know about the others? Shit."

"Game over," I said triumphantly.

"Not yet," he pointed out. "I've still got my double-tasty treat to finish down here before I get the hell out of Dodge."

"Your double-tasty . . . Oh, dear God."

Rachel heard this exchange and responded accordingly. "We're gonna *die!* No, no, *no!*" The echoes bounced all over the chamber.

I started backing away from Tarr. "Or you could just flee now, Al. Killing two more people would slow you down. Is that really a good idea? After all, there are vampire hunters *and* a whole team of cops after you—"

"The cops got no idea about me, and no idea where you are," Tarr said, his faintly illuminated expression eerily amused as he watched me sloshing backward, trying to put distance between us. "And the vampire hunters are gonna be slowed down for a while, with the cave-in down here and the stampeding vamparazzi everywhere else." He chuckled. "Hey, I *love* that word, by the way. You're fun, Esther. I'll miss you."

"Because you're getting out the hell of Dodge and we won't meet again?" I prodded, hoping for the best.

"I like you," he said kindly. "So I'll try to make this quick."

I was shocked by how fast he moved. One moment, he was about ten feet away; the next, his arms were wrapped tightly around me and he was breathing in my ear. The chamber went pitch black as my light fell out of my hand and into the water at my feet.

Rachel started screaming her head off. All out of other ideas, so did I. Trapped underground in total darkness, wrapped in the deadly embrace of someone who was a blood-addicted, murdering vampire *and* a tabloid leech, I pitched my screams with the deliberate intention of shattering Tarr's supersonic eardrums.

His whole short, stocky body stiffened, and for a moment, I thought maybe the combined screaming of two hysterically terrified women was more powerful than I had seriously hoped. But then he clamped a hand over my mouth, trying to shut me up, and I realized from his alert posture that he was listening to something.

"What the fuck *is* that?" He snapped at Rachel, "Shut up!" This had no effect of course. She kept screaming and wailing.

Since he evidently wanted us to be quiet, I—naturally—wanted to be as noisy as possible. He intended to kill me anyhow, so *not annoying* him seemed pretty pointless. I bit down as hard as I could on his hand, and although blood addiction had made him enhanced and powerful, it had not, I was pleased to discover, made him completely impervious to pain. He yelped and snatched his hand away. I started screaming again.

Tarr picked me up as easily as if I were a paperweight and threw me across the chamber. I flew through the dark, bounced hard off a stone wall, and then hit the cement floor of the tunnel with a lung-emptying thud. The filthy water didn't do much to break my fall, and I laid there, disoriented and gasping with pain, trying to figure out if anything was broken.

A moment later, Rachel's entire body weight fell on top of me with unerring accuracy, nearly making me pass out. That was when I realized that seeing in the dark was one of Tarr's enhancements.

I also realized I saw faint streams of light flashing through this chamber and, even above Rachel's shrieking, I heard voices echoing through the tunnels.

"Someone's down here!" I gasped, shoving at Rachel, trying to get her weight off me. "On this side of the cave-in. Someone's here! Help! *Help!*"

"Esther! Is that *you?*" called a blessedly familiar voice.

I was climbing to my feet in the dark, dragging Rachel with me. I couldn't see a thing except for the lights flashing around the chamber.

"Lopez!" I cried with relief. "Yes! I'm here! I'm *here!*"

I clamped my hand over Rachel's mouth to stifle the noise of her wailing. "Lopez!

"I'm coming! Stay right where you are!"

He wasn't alone. Multiple lights were flashing into this chamber now, and I could hear a number of voices echoing along the tunnel where his voice came from.

I was huddling in terror with Rachel, expecting Tarr to pounce on us at any moment. But as the beams of light got stronger and the voices drew near, I realized that he must have decided to flee rather than stand and fight. And he could disappear much more quickly down here *without* dragging along a noisy hostage or two.

Emboldened by my conviction that our vampire captor had run off without us, I dragged Rachel with me and stepped into the beams of light now pouring into the chamber. I squinted and raised my hand to shield my stinging eyes as the flashlights shone directly on me. Sobbing, Rachel clutched me and huddled against me.

"Esther!"

Lopez ran the final length of the tunnel he was in, then sloshed quickly through the water of this chamber, his headlamp beaming in my face. With Rachel still clinging to me, I staggered into his arms, and—by default—he embraced us both. I clutched him tightly, digging my fingers into the fabric of the sweater he wore.

"Are you okay?" he asked against my hair.

I nodded, feeling too emotional to speak for a moment. *That was really,* really *close.*

I had nearly been the next exsanguination victim.

Four more men entered the chamber. I lifted my head and took a look at them. They were uniformed cops, carrying flashlights.

I found my voice. "Oh, thank God."

Rachel switched from clinging to me to clinging to Lopez. She sobbed against his chest and hugged him tightly around the waist—elbowing me out of her way to get a better grip.

"Do I know her?" Lopez asked me uncertainly.

"Mad Rachel."

"Whoa." Apparently he hadn't recognized her. Given her horror-movie appearance right now, and the fact that they'd only met once before, that was understandable. "What *happened* to you two? What are you doing here?"

"What are *you* doing here?" His presence seemed miraculous.

"I heard what's happening at the Hamburg. *Everybody* heard. The whole block is a madhouse above ground," he said. "I thought we could get inside faster and help out if I brought in a few cops through the basement—since you haven't had that door sealed yet, Esther."

"Is this really the time to criticize me for that?" I said shrilly.

He grinned and hugged me again—using the arm Rachel had left free. "Since you made your escape that way, I stand corrected."

"We didn't just escape," I said urgently. "We wound up as hostages!"

He looked bemused. "What?"

"Al Tarr is the killer! He was just here! I think he ran off a minute ago when he heard you coming."

"Tarr's *here?*" Lopez quickly set aside Rachel, ignoring her shrieks of protest and fervent attempt to cling to him, and handed her over to an officer who accepted her with noticeable reluctance. "Where is he?"

"I don't know."

Lopez took my shoulders and spoke calmly. "There are only two tunnels here besides the one we just came in. Did you see which way— Oh, no, of course not. Were you able to *hear* which way he went?"

"No, I didn't." I was panting with a riot of agitated emotions. But his firm hold on my shoulders and his calm voice brought my careening thoughts into focus. "Wait! I think I know. The tunnel that goes near the theater caved in a little while ago. Almost on top of me, actually."

"Jesus." His grip tightened.

"Tarr knows that. He wouldn't go that way. It's a trap now."

Lopez gave my shoulders a squeeze, then said to the four men. "We've got him. He must have gone that way." He gestured to the remaining tunnel. "And it's a dead end."

"What?" I blurted. "You're sure?"

"Yep. Sealed off a long time ago." He pointed at two of the men—including the one already burdened with Rachel. "You two, get these ladies out of here. And you two—" He gestured to the other two. "On me. Let's bring this guy in."

"No! Wait!" I grabbed him. "Lopez, he's very dangerous!"

"I know." He firmly set me away from him. "It'll be all right, Esther. Go with the officers now."

"No, you don't know! *Really* dangerous! No! Don't go! *No!"*

I spiraled into hysterics at the prospect of Lopez confronting a cornered rogue vampire.

The cop who'd been assigned to escort me out of here was, in fact, forcibly restraining me and dragging me through the exit tunnel as Lopez and two cops went after Tarr down the dead-end tunnel.

"No! You don't know what you're dealing with!" Bullets wouldn't work. Lopez didn't know that! While being dragged to safety, I kept screaming, "Fire or decapitation! Nothing else will work! Fire or decapitation!"

"Miss, you must calm down!" said the beleaguered cop who was restraining me.

Oh, must I?

Realizing there was no other choice, I went limp in his arms.

Fire or decapitation.

The cop relaxed and said in a relieved voice, "Thank you, miss. Now let's get you out of here, and— Agh!"

I poked him in the eye—just enough to disorient him. Then I grabbed his flashlight, saying, "Sorry, sorry, sorry!" I ran back down the tunnel, tripping on my long skirts, and re-entered the chamber he'd dragged me out of moments ago.

Fire or decapitation.

I had no idea how we could manage either of those things now, down here, without a vampire hunter; but I at least had to warn Lopez that nothing else would work.

I ran across the main chamber, sloshing through the water, my long skirts dragging on me. Then I entered the dead-end tunnel, which curved around and turned a corner up ahead. Even with a good flashlight in my hand now, I couldn't see any of the men who were somewhere up ahead of me. I staggered forward as fast as I could move, slipping on the damp brick floor in my flimsy, ruined shoes, my legs tangling with my long, wet skirts.

I heard two shots fired and a lot of shouting coming from farther down this tunnel. There was a horrible roaring sound, like an explosion. I paused, and then I heard Lopez's voice—heading back in this direction.

"Move!" he shouted. *"Move!"*

A bright glow emerged ahead of me—and Lopez and the two cops appeared, all racing straight toward me, trying to outrun the wall of fire that was right behind them, spreading fast in this direction.

A wall of fire.

I stopped in my tracks and stared, dumbfounded.

"Run! Go! *Go!*" Lopez was shouting at me.

I turned to run back the way I had come, my wet skirts a burden, my slippers sliding on the bricks. Then something heavy hit me like a speeding train, and I went flying headfirst into the central chamber, where I landed facedown in the water . . . with Lopez's entire body weight on top of me as he shielded me from the fiery blast that roared into the chamber over our heads and then withdrew.

Lopez rolled off me and hauled my head and shoulders out of the filthy water we had plunged into. I immediately looked over my shoulder. The tunnel behind us was smoking and a little charred, but the fire was gone.

"Are you all right?" he asked me frantically, breathing hard.

"Yes," I choked out. I still had the wind knocked out of me.

"Are you *sure?*"

"Yes."

"You're all right?"

"Yes."

"Good." He seized me by the shoulders and shook me. *Hard.* "When I tell you to go to safety, *go to safety!*"

"Is he dead?" I croaked.

"Are you *listening* to me?"

Fire or decapitation.

"Is he dead?" I asked again.

One of the cops said. "Oh, yeah. He's dead. *Oh*, yeah. *Dead.*"

Lopez's gaze dropped to my chest. He drew in a sharp breath as his eyes widened, and he grabbed me again, this time to turn me away from the other two cops. He grimaced anxiously and made a frantic gesture with his hand. I looked down and saw that I had fallen out of my precarious neckline during that headlong dive into the chamber to escape the fire. I tucked myself in, tugged the filthy and tattered neckline upward as best I could, then looked over my shoulder at the cops.

"You're *sure* he's dead?" I asked again.

"In that explosion? Burned to a crispy critter," said the younger of the two uniformed cops. "Sorry, miss. Sorry. But, yes, he's dead, all right. Oh, yeah."

In the light of Lopez's headlamp, the young officer's

face was wide-eyed with shock as he continued babbling. "I shot him. I know I shot him. I could *swear* I shot him. And then he took my gun away. Just took it away! And grabbed me like a rag doll—my *God,* he was strong. He was about to kill me! He was going to rip my head off! I *know* it. I saw it in his eyes. He took my head and . . . And then . . . Jesus, that explosion. *Jesus.*" He looked at Lopez. "How did *we* get out of there alive?"

The other cop asked, "How *did* we get out there alive, detective?"

Lopez looked at me. "And you wonder why I go to Mass every week."

22

We emerged from the tunnels by ascending through a manhole in a street that was only a few blocks away from the theater. I was surprised; while underground, I had felt as if we were so much farther away than that. The dark, chilly night was wonderfully breezy and fresh. The city's familiar skyline glowed glamorously against the endlessly high vault of the open sky. I decided I wasn't even going into a *subway* tunnel for quite some time to come. After tonight's experiences, I was strictly an above-ground person for the foreseeable future.

My injuries were all superficial, but Lopez insisted I let a paramedic examine me. This turned out to be a good idea, since the guy had very nice painkillers and was generous with them. He also insisted on giving me a shot of antibiotics, since I'd been wandering around in filthy water with cuts and scrapes. This was less fun than the painkillers, but nonetheless appreciated.

Mad Rachel was resilient, if nothing else. She got someone to loan her a cell phone barely ten minutes after we emerged into the chilly November night; and a mere ten minutes after *that,* she was screaming into the borrowed phone, "Goddamn you, Eric, you fucking *bas-*

tard!" So all was well there. Lopez predicted wedding bells.

I was worried about Leischneudel, Bill, Victor, and even Daemon, as well as Thack and Max—who were each on their way to the Hamburg, at my request, when the riot broke out. So Lopez agreed to take me back to the theater—where, according to the information he was receiving now, order had been restored.

The crowds around the Hamburg were still being dispersed, but the atmosphere was subdued now. The cops who drove us to the stage door told me and Lopez that a lot of people had been arrested, but very few were injured—and none seriously. There was some property damage, but the immediate post-riot estimate was that it wasn't serious, either. The theater would re-open within a few days, and *The Vampyre* would complete its run.

The cop riding shotgun said, "Seems like the whole thing was more like a block party for nerds that got out of control for about an hour rather than a riot."

But I, for one, would not readily forget the sight of lust-crazed Janes and lunatic vamparazzi stampeding directly toward me while Dr. Hal screamed, "No prisoners!" and the Caped Crusaders provided their own captions while battling the wannabe undead. All of it accompanied by Lithuanian vampire hunters shooting crossbow bolts at me.

"I guess you had to be there," I said wanly to the cops.

Lopez squeezed my hand.

While our squad car rolled slowly through the crowded but no longer chaotically crazy streets, he explained to me that he'd entered the tunnels knowing—or, at least, feeling convinced—that Tarr was the killer.

"I started with the name you gave me last night, Benas Novicki. I tracked his movements. He was in LA for a few months before he came to New York. So I checked with LAPD, and they had an open case file." He paused.

"Several murders with one unusual feature in common. A detail that was never released to the public."

"Exsanguination," I said, wishing I could see his facial expression, but the car was too dark.

He nodded. "The last one was in July. None since then. Then your friend Novicki, who thinks he's chasing a vampire—"

"He wasn't my friend," I said. "I never met him."

"—leaves LA and winds up dead here sometime in August. After which, several murders occur here, similar to the LA file." He shrugged. "So I started looking for a match between someone who'd been in LA until this summer, and someone Adele Olson had contact with on her final night."

I gasped. "'When I was out in Hollywood . . .'"

"Huh?"

"All of Tarr's anecdotes began that way. He talked all the time about his glory days in Hollywood. I didn't know him or his work, and I vaguely assumed it was a few years ago. But I guess it was recent?"

"Yep. He resigned from his job in LA in June and got hired by the *Exposé* when he came here in July—the rag was glad to get him. I gather he had what passed for a great résumé in that line of work." Lopez added, "He's another one who wasn't using his real name, like the Vampire Ravel and—don't tell me I'm wrong on this one?—Sir Shackleton."

"What was his real name?"

"Algis Taurus."

"That sounds Lithuanian." Of course. He said he'd been born a vampire.

Lopez mused. "I don't understand why he didn't use it. It's more interesting than 'Al Tarr,' don't you think?"

"I guess this clears Daemon of the murder?" I asked.

"Yeah. And it closes my case, too. Thank God. I was starting to feel like a troll in a bad fairy tale, living underground and lurking in damp, murky places."

"Speaking of which, what exactly happened in the damp murky place that caught *fire?*" I asked. "That cop's account was . . . a little confusing."

"I get the impression he might decide police work isn't for him," Lopez said tactfully.

"Well?" I said. "What happened?"

"I think it was a methane gas explosion."

"Seriously?"

"You smelled the sewage, right?"

"Thank you for reminding me."

"It builds up methane gas, which is volatile stuff. If it isn't safely released, it can go boom."

"Which just *happened* to take out a lunatic killer while leaving the three of you alive?" I said. "A murderer who was, at that moment, about to kill a young cop in your care?"

"The kid wasn't in my *care*, Esther," Lopez said. "I just recruited him to . . ." He cleared his throat. "Well, as it turned out, to chase a dangerous serial killer into an exploding sewage chamber."

I decided not to press further. I had my own suspicions about what had happened. My theory about this was still as murky as those dark, dank tunnels; but I thought it significant—and I felt certain Max would, too—that at a moment when Tarr was about to kill a young cop for whom Lopez felt responsible, fire had consumed him.

Fire or decapitation.

If Lopez did have some sort of unusual gift he wasn't even aware of, then I silently thanked all the mystical powers that he'd gone into that dead-end tunnel with a weapon, however unwitting, that was a match for the murderous rogue vampire that lurked in wait there.

"By the way," Lopez said as the squad car halted near the stage door. "The cop you assaulted has decided to let bygones be bygones."

"I didn't *assault* him, I—"

"You poked him in the eye and stole his flashlight in the dark."

One of the cops in the front seat blurted, "You did *what?*"

Lopez added, "And, Esther, when I tell you to go to safety and let me handle something—"

"Look! We're at the stage door," I said brightly. "Are you coming in?"

"No, I have to go write my reports," he said. "And talk to Branson. And explain the death of a cornered felon to my superiors."

Nonetheless, he got out of the car and came around to my side to open the door and help me out of my seat. Which I appreciated, since I was stiff, bruised, and still in some pain, and my filthy, smelly, tattered gown was still damp and heavy.

"You and Rachel will need to give formal statements," he said. "Branson will call you about that."

There was an awkward pause.

Then he said, "So you and me . . . We haven't changed our minds about dumping each other?"

He was filthy and looked exhausted. He needed a shave again, and he smelled of gases, pollutants, and biowaste. And I wanted to take him in my arms and kiss him until the sun rose.

But I was haunted by nightmares I couldn't bear to live with if they came to pass for real next time.

So I said, "Are you sure you don't want to come inside? There are probably three genuine Lithuanian vampires backstage right now, as well as a made vampire—which is a pretty rare phenomenon. He was made without a permit from the Council of Gediminas, so I think we're going to have some controversy before the night is over. Max could explain it to you, if you're interested, since he battled the undead in the Serbian vampire epidemic, alongside vampire hunters who demanded, in exchange for their help, that he sign a treaty which—"

"Okay," Lopez said loudly. "Leaving now."

"You're sure? I can probably find a bottle of Nocturne we could share."

"Good night, Esther." He started to get back in the squad car, then turned to look at me. I could see his expression in the glow of the streetlights—a mingling of wry amusement, exasperation, and something that I suspected was affection. "When you give your statement to Branson, don't mention any of that."

"Of course not."

"And try to get along with him?"

"Well, we'll see. Good night, Lopez."

Our eyes held for a minute after he got into the car, and then it pulled away and he was gone.

I gave a little sigh and hugged myself as I watched the car go down the street and disappear around the corner.

Then I recalled that my other suitor lately was a tabloid sleaze and—oh, incidentally—a maniacal rogue vampire.

Yes, I should definitely put romance on the shelf for a while. Or perhaps lock it away in an armored vault.

Four tall men quietly approached me and surrounded me, their attitudes protective, their clothing torn and disheveled, their faces bruised and a little bloodied.

"Guys!" I exclaimed, turning in a circle to review the condition of my vampire posse. "Are you okay? The last time I saw you, you were fighting off the invading horde."

Flame sighed. "It was a great night, Miss Diamond."

"A *great* night," Treat agreed, grinning.

Silent nodded.

"How are *you,* Miss Diamond? You look like you had a rough trip out of the theater. One of your friends was kind enough to come outside a little while ago and let us know that you were safe and under police protection.

He said something about you . . . being pulled out of the sewers?"

"Yes," I said. "Hence the aroma you may have noticed."

"Shall we escort you to the door, ma'am?" Flame suggested.

"Thank you." At the stage door, I turned to them before going inside and said, "I appreciate your courage in the face of daunting odds tonight, gentlemen."

Flame shrugged. "It's our way, Miss Diamond. We're vampires."

"Of course." I thanked them again and went inside.

Leischneudel came running down the corridor. "Esther! Oh, thank God! I was so worried!"

"Leischneudel! Are you okay?"

We embraced, then looked each other over. Both of us looked like the survivors of an all-out apocalyptic battle. But *survivors* was the key word. Thrilled to be alive, we hugged again, laughing now.

He had stopped running, upon hearing the rumbling implosion and crash of the cave-in, and had come back and tried to dig through the rubble, frantic to find out whether I was alive. The vampire hunters were there and had insisted he stop in his fruitless task—especially given that moving any of the rubble might cause additional collapse.

The hunters decided to abandon their quarry—Daemon—whom they could certainly find again, given what a disgusting spectacle he made of himself. The thing to do *now,* obviously, was to go back upstairs, break through the rioting vamparazzi, and request help from emergency services in case I was indeed trapped under rubble.

"But it turns out that getting help is pretty complicated in the middle of a riot," Leischneudel said as he followed me into my dressing room. "So it's just as well you didn't need rescuing."

"I did," I said. "Just not *that* kind of rescuing."

Leischneudel was shocked and horrified as I told him everything that had happened.

"I never suspected Tarr," Leischneudel said in amazement. "He was so openly awful, it never occurred to me he was hiding even *more* awfulness."

"Indeed." I asked, "Where is everyone?"

"Bill's here," Leischneudel said. "He's got his hands full getting things back in order."

Bill, Daemon, and Victor had proceeded some way down the tunnel before realizing that Tarr and Rachel weren't with them. It didn't take them long to find an exit—by which time they also realized that Leischneudel and I wouldn't be joining them. Once they were above ground and safe, Bill decided he had to return to the theater to be ready to take charge backstage once the police got things under control and to try to find out what had happened to the rest of us.

Running ever true to form, Daemon had gone home to look after himself; and Victor had gone with him to help with that crucial task.

It almost made me sorry that Tarr's article about Danny Ravinsky would never be finished, filed, or published.

I realized then that Daemon would get a reprieve on all fronts now. He was not only cleared of Angeline's murder, but he would instantly become the object of guilt and sympathy, since the *actual* killer had used the power of the press (so to speak) to smear and discredit him, and more than a few people had fallen for it. I thought there was no way Nocturne would risk firing him now, and his movie deal would probably come through, too.

Not for the first time, I reflected on what an intrinsically unfair and unjust place the world was.

Leischneudel told me, "After the police got the vamparazzi under control—more or less—Max and Thack turned up. None of us could really think about anything but you, until we finally found out you were all right. After that . . ."

"Yes?"

"Thack and Max went into my dressing room with Uncle Peter and Edvardas Froese to . . . discuss things."

I gasped. "Are they talking about you?"

Leischneudel said, "I asked Thack and Max to see what they could do. After tonight, I've realized that I can't live in fear of the council or vampire hunters. I don't want Mary Ann to wind up as a widow with father-less children because I didn't sort out this problem before I took on those responsibilities." He squared his shoulders as he added, "I didn't ask to become a vam-pire, but now that I am one—I'm glad to be a vampire, and I think I'm a very responsible one. There's no reason the council can't give me some sort of . . . certificate or something. And I'm willing to work to prove that I de-serve it!"

"Good for you!" I said. "Excellent decision. I support this completely."

And I dearly hoped that Edvardas and Uncle Peter weren't about to come barreling down the hall, cross-bows blazing, now that they knew Leischneudel was an unauthorized made vampire.

He may have had the same thought, since he said anxiously, "Will you come with me to see how it's go-ing?"

"Of course." I really wanted to get out of my filthy, shredded, stinking gown but that could wait.

We went down the hall, knocked on Leischneudel's door, and entered when invited to do so.

"Ah, here are the young people now," Uncle Peter said, smiling jovially at us.

"*Esther!*"

"Oh, *here* you are! Thank God!"

Thack embraced me, Max embraced me, and Nelli

sneezed on me. Uncle Peter assured me there were no hard feelings about the fact that I had tied him up and held him hostage after he passed out. The Dirty D'Artagnanator, via his interpreter, apologized for trying to kill me and assured me it was business, not personal.

Keeping the details to a minimum, I explained that Al Tarr a.k.a. Algis Taurus was the rogue vampire whom Benas Novicki had pursued, and that the NYPD had dispatched him tonight, using fire. I gave Max a significant glance at that point, and he nodded, acknowledging that we'd discuss the details later, in private.

Leischneudel was by now practically vibrating with anxiety, so I boldly asked the men, "And now that we've wrapped up the business of the rogue vampire, gentlemen, I want to know what fair and reasonable measures the Council of Gediminas is prepared to take in support of my friend Leischneudel Drysdale, who is a good man and a discreet, responsible vampire. After all, I think if the case of Algis Taurus—who was a hereditary vampire—confirms anything, it's that character matters more than birth."

"And where is that sentiment *more* true, gentlemen," Max added, "than here in the New World, where old rules are remade to suit a better vision of whom each of us can be?"

Uncle Peter said, "Edvardas has agreed to present Leischneudel's request for legal recognition to the council, along with his personal recommendation that it be granted. I am recommending a trial period, which is fair, since none of us knows this young man."

"Yes, that's fair," Leischneudel agreed.

"My nephew," said Uncle Peter, eyeing Thack and declining to use his name, "will be in charge of monitoring Leischneudel during the trial period."

"Oh!" Leischneudel looked eagerly at Thack. "Is that all right with you?"

"All things considered," Thack said, "if it will get my family off my back for a while, then I am delighted to be of service."

"Thank you!"

"And now, if you'll excuse us . . ." Uncle Peter rose from his seat, as did Edvardas and Thack. "It's late." Edvardas added something which Uncle Peter translated as, "Especially for a man who's on Vilnius time."

"Ah, speaking of which . . ." Max rose, too.

Beside him, Nelli sneezed violently. Twice.

Max reached into his coat pocket and pulled out a simple wooden cross, elegant and sturdy, about five inches long.

He asked Uncle Peter to translate for him, then said, "Would you be so kind, when you return to Vilnius, to leave this on the grave of someone whose memory I should like to honor with this simple token of my esteem? He, too, was a vampire hunter. Jurgis Radvila. I was told he died in 1744."

Edvardas graciously agreed to carry out this deed for Max, and he accepted the cross from him. Then he bade us all farewell and headed out of the room.

Uncle Peter paused to pat Leischneudel on the cheek. "Don't worry, my boy. We Lithuanians are not nearly so rigid as you have been led to believe."

"Oh, what 'we'? You're second-generation *American,* Uncle Peter. Give it a rest." Thack kissed me on the cheek. "Since those two are staying at my place, God help me, I guess this means I'm leaving, too. Leischneudel, I'll see you at my office later this week. Good night, all!"

When they were gone, Leischneudel let out his breath in a big gust and sank into a chair. "Thank you, Max!"

The old mage beamed at him. "Don't mention it. They really were much more reasonable than I had anticipated." He added to me, "I suppose times have changed."

"Indeed." I sank into a chair, too. "I'm just glad it

worked out. And *really* glad that the rogue vampire has been slain." My gaze met Max's again. I could tell he was curious to hear the details, at a more appropriate time.

Nelli sneezed and gave a little groan.

"Oh, dear," Max said. "We should probably be leaving, too."

He shook hands with Leischneudel, then embraced me and once again expressed his relief at seeing me safe and sound.

After he and Nelli left, I said to Leischneudel, "I'm starving. Want to get a pizza on the way home?"

"Absolutely."

Bill stuck his head in the door. "Leischneudel, is Esther back ye— Oh, Esther! There you are." Like the others, he expressed his relief and pleasure at seeing me. Then he said, "Your mother's left four messages at the box office today. She says she's seen the tabloids, you haven't answered your cell, and she's worried."

I thanked Bill, said good night to him, then gave an anxious sigh. "I might as well get this over with."

"Are you okay?" Leischneudel asked.

"Yes. Viewed in its proper perspective, after all, talking with my mother isn't nearly as daunting as battling the undead in a Serbian vampire epidemic."

"Pardon?"

I shook my head with a wry smile. "Long story."

And one which, based on the mist which had clouded Max's eyes as he placed the cross in Edvardas' hands, I was proud that he had chosen to share with me.

Epilogue

Kisilova, 1732

The glowing sun descended gracefully toward the far horizon and the late autumn chill nipped his cheeks as Max sat on a hilltop overlooking Kisilova where, last night, he and the Lithuanians had slain the last of the undead vampires menacing the village. Tonight, for the first time in a long time, the people who lived here could sleep in peace and security.

Well, until the next war between land-hungry empires brought soldiers, mercenaries, and raiders stampeding through the Balkans on yet another destructive rampage. But such mundane disasters were the responsibility of the mundane authorities. For those who dealt with Evil of a more esoteric nature, the work in Kisilova was done.

While he sat admiring the dramatic colors streaking across the sky, thanks to a setting sun that created no looming sense of dread this evening, he saw Radvila appear on the ridge below him. The Lithuanian waved to him and continued climbing to this spot, moving with an agility that belied his (as Max had learned) sixty-four years. The vigorous constitution of a vampire was a remarkable thing. Max could understand how one might be tempted to become made—if one weren't thoroughly dissuaded by the dietary requirements.

As Radvila reached his side, not even breathing hard from his climb to this elevated spot, a chill wind whipped across the hilltop, making Max shiver a little.

"Winter is coming," said Radvila, sitting down beside him on an old log.

"But now the people of Kisilova don't need to fear the nights growing longer."

"Indeed."

Max caught a strong whiff of alcohol and eyed his friend. The village was planning to spend the evening celebrating the end of the vampire epidemic here. Based on Radvila's interesting scent, Max guessed that the festivities had already begun—and that Radvila had been imbibing the local brew.

"This is quite a view," the vampire said, gazing across the landscape.

Max nodded. "I feel almost as if I can see into the future from this spot."

"And what do you see, magician?"

"I believe I see the vampire epidemic ending before long."

They had made a great deal of progress in the months since the Lithuanians had entered the fight. Many areas of the region were now entirely rid of the undead.

"I could have told you that without climbing this hill," Radvila grumbled. "I see the epidemic ending before you return in the spring."

"Why *did* you climb this hill?"

"The celebration has begun." Radvila gestured to the village below. "I have been tasked with finding you so that the people may honor you."

Having been through such festivities in several other villages by now, Max said wryly, "If I attend another celebration, my stomach may return to being ill-humored." His digestive problems had gradually disappeared after hope had returned in the war against the undead; but he feared that yet another robust village soirée might cause a setback. "Perhaps I'll remain here."

"My comrades have informed me they will not endure this test of strength alone," Radvila said gravely. "They say you *must* come. It would be unfair for you to escape this, since you're leaving for Vienna tomorrow. Whereas we will remain in Serbia through the winter to fight more of the undead and will probably have to be honored several more times before our work is done."

"Oh, very well," said Max. "But you must not let me eat and drink too much this time, or my horse shall have to drag me on a litter tomorrow."

"Hmph."

They sat in companionable silence for a few moments, watching the setting sun.

Then Radvila asked, "How far is the journey to Vienna?"

"Well, not nearly as far as Vilnius," Max said. "Nor is the journey as hazardous. But it is far enough." He thought of the glittering imperial capital and mused, "It will be like a different world after my sojourn here. I imagine I shall feel very strange there, at first, though I know the city well."

"I would like to see Vienna," Radvila said. "I would have liked to travel more. My father sent me to study in Warsaw when I was young, and I once went to Stockholm with a cousin who traded amber and silver. But I have not otherwise been out of Lithuania. Not until I came here." He added, "And this has certainly not been a journey of personal enrichment—apart from your friendship, Maximillian."

"Thank you," Max said, touched.

"Yes, I would have liked to travel more," Radvila repeated as the wind toyed with his gray hair. "One always thinks there will be more time, but the years pass so quickly. Life goes by and, before you know it, you're an old man, and the things you might do one day have become the things you never did." He shook his head. "You're too young to understand this yet."

"Oh, not really," Max said, guiltily aware that he had already lived longer than Radvila, and that he would, if he continued surviving his adversaries, have many more years—perhaps centuries, for all he knew—to learn, to travel, and to enrich his life with new friendships. "I think I understand."

"I have no regrets." Radvila gazed reflectively at the setting sun. "I have a fine family and a good place in the world, and I was born a vampire. It's enough for one man." He smiled. "But I would have liked to see Vienna."

"Perhaps you shall," Max replied. "Perhaps you will come visit me there."

Radvila shook his head. "The time for that has passed. I have too many responsibilities at home, and I'll be gone from there until our work here is done and you return with a delegation to sign the treaty." He added ruefully, "Also, I am getting old. This journey has been hard on me."

"Perhaps it is nightly battling the undead which has been hard on you," Max suggested.

"That, too," Radvila agreed. "But I think this will be my last journey. And my last campaign against the undead. The time fast approaches for me to leave this work to those who are younger than I. My old bones are complaining about the physical conditions of a vampire hunter's life."

"Even my bones are complaining," Max said. "I am not sorry to bid farewell to my days—and nights—as a vampire hunter."

"What will you do next? After we meet in Belgrade, that is. After this is all over."

"I don't know," Max said, surprised to realize he hadn't thought about the future yet. Ever since coming to Serbia, he had grown used to thinking he probably didn't have one.

"Perhaps you will do the traveling that I did not,"

Radvila said, the alcohol on his breath evidently fueling an uncharacteristic bout of whimsy. "I believe you will venture farther than I ever dreamed of going—farther even than *you* dream."

"What makes you say that?" Max asked curiously.

"You seem like a man with a restless thirst for knowledge. As if you are on a quest to gain worldly wisdom."

"I have my quest," Max said. "Confronting Evil."

"I can see into the future from this hilltop, too, you know." Radvila nudged him with an elbow. "And I see that you will live long, help many people, and travel far. Who knows . . . perhaps you shall even travel all the way to the New World one day—whose wonders even vampires in Vilnius have heard about."

"The New World?" Max repeated with a smile, wondering just how much Radvila had been drinking. "That *is* far."

"It's another place I would very much have liked to see, if I had more than just this one life to live." Radvila said wistfully, "Think about it, Maximillian. The *New* World. How exciting that sounds!"

"Yes." Someday, perhaps . . . Feeling a little whimsical, too, he asked, "Do you suppose they have Evil there?"

"Ah, my friend," said the grizzled vampire. "I suspect they have Evil everywhere."

Author's Note

The vampire epidemics of Eastern Europe in the eighteenth century are a documented historic event, though I have added fictional dimensions (i.e. actual vampires) in this novel. In reality, the problem was serious enough to require official government investigations just as, in this story, it requires the intervention of Dr. Maximillian Zadok and Lithuanian vampire hunters.

But why (I hear you ask) was there a sudden outbreak of rampant vampirism?

Actually, such incidents had probably been occurring for centuries in that region. But by the early eighteenth century, imperial wars and treaties resulted in the Ottoman Empire losing much of its Eastern European territory to the Habsburg monarchy of Austria. Upon hearing about vampire epidemics for the first time, a few years after taking over control of the region, the Austrian government's reaction was (I paraphrase): "Whoa, they're doing *what* in those provinces?" Followed by: "We need to send someone to investigate this and find out what's going on."

Two particular vampire cases of that era created considerable interest in their time and are generally credited with introducing Eastern European vampire folklore to Western European culture: the separate and unrelated cases of Peter Plogojowitz and Arnod Paole. After each man died, in their respective Serbian villages of Kisilova and Medvegia, the local mortality rate increased. As a result, Plogojowitz and Paole were accused (in absentia) of being vampires and starting vampire epidemics. Panic and paranoia quickly spread—as did gruesome antivampire activities.

In the early 1730s, the authorities who were assigned to investigate these incidents wrote detailed accounts of strange phenomena for which they had no explanation. And thus the folklore of Slavic villages took hold of the imagination of Western Europe—including that of Dr. John Polidori, who wrote "The Vampyre" almost a century later. However, Polidori's suavely seductive Lord Ruthven is wholly unlike the grotesque, mindless creatures of folklore—the same creatures which Max encountered during his sojourn as a vampire hunter.

So what really happened in Serbia—and other provinces experiencing vampire outbreaks—all those years ago?

The two typical features of historical vampire epidemics were (1) a rash of mysterious deaths and (2) the exhumation of corpses that looked ruddy and well-fed, and which often had blood dribbling from their mouths.

Well, a wave of unexplained deaths in peasant villages wasn't actually mysterious if you consider the conditions in those communities. Disease was spreading through a vulnerable population that didn't understand epidemiology. Various fatal contagions, including the plague, were often blamed on vampires in the good old days. (For example, tuberculosis is considered the likely culprit of a vampire scare in New England in the nineteenth century.)

And the hysteria provoked by digging up plump, ruddy-looking corpses with bloody lips was based entirely on not understanding the stages of decomposition. As were all the other "classic" signs of vampirism, such as clawlike fingernails and strange noises coming from the corpses. What the living were seeing in those unearthed graves was, unbeknownst to them, the normal appearance of the decomposing dead. (For an explicit example, see a fascinating National Geographic documentary called *Forensic Vampires*. My fervent advice: Don't watch it while you're eating.)

Moreover, even well-trained doctors (which some of the Austrian investigators were) in the eighteenth century had a level of medical knowledge that wouldn't earn them so much as a Boy Scout merit badge today. Although the written reports of the Austrian officials demonstrate an ability (and, indeed, a Teutonic determination) to observe, investigate, and record strange phenomena with precision and detachment, they simply didn't understand what they were encountering in their vampire investigations.

This misunderstanding of disease and decomposition was at the heart of Eastern European vampire folklore, and also at the heart of Western Europe's fascination with it for generations before novelist Bram Stoker created his own enduringly iconic version of the undead.

Meanwhile, on another subject, there are indeed miles of tunnels, drains, chambers, and interesting structures beneath the streets of New York City (though the tunnel which connects to the Hamburg is, like the theater itself, strictly an invention of this novel). In fact, I used to eat regularly at a Chinese restaurant in Manhattan wherein the bathroom was accessed via a tunnel that ran underneath the street.

I also once spent a night with a group of urban explorers in some of New York's most famous underground tunnels and chambers. I was invited out one evening (*I* thought we were going to dinner), and before I knew it, I was being outfitted with rubber boots and a headlamp, and walking through the Bronx's Van Cortlandt Park at night (which was just as stupid of me as you might suppose). Upon reaching our destination somewhere in the dark, we shimmied beneath a large, rusty metal door, via a wet gutter full of used syringes and entered the famous Croton Aqueduct, the abandoned underground tunnel system that was built in 1842 to supply Manhattan with water from upstate. We explored the tunnels and caverns most of the night, saw amazing wonders, and bumped into another group of explorers doing the same thing. It was one of the most unforgettable experiences of my life, and I knew then that someday I'd have to use New York's underground world in a book.

To learn more about vampirism or urban exploration, check out the Research Library on my Web site at www .LauraResnick.com.

Having survived vampires and vamparazzi, as well as sewage and other hazards, Esther Diamond, her friends, and her nemeses will return soon for their next misadventure in *Polterheist*.

—Laura Resnick

Laura Resnick

The Esther Diamond Novels

"Resnick introduces a colorful cast of gangsters and their associates as she spins a witty, fast-paced mystery around her convincingly self-absorbed chorus-girl heroine. Sexy interludes raise the tension as she juggles magical assailants, her perennially distracted agent, her meddling mother, and wiseguys both friendly and threatening in a well-crafted, rollicking mystery."   —*Publishers Weekly*

"Esther Diamond is the Stephanie Plum of urban fantasy! Unplug the phone and settle down for a fast and funny read!"   —Mary Jo Putney

DOPPELGANGSTER
978-0-7564-0595-3

UNSYMPATHETIC MAGIC
978-0-7564-0635-6

VAMPARAZZI
978-0-7564-0687-5

To Order Call: 1-800-788-6262
www.dawbooks.com

Celia Jerome
The Willow Tate *Novels*

"Readers will love the first Willow Tate book. Willow is funny, brave and open to possibilities most people would not have even considered as she meets her perfect foil in Thaddeus Grant, a British agent assigned to look over the strange occurrences following Willow like a shadow. Together they make a wonderful pair and readers will love their unconventional courtship." —*RT Book Review*

TROLLS IN THE HAMPTONS
978-0-7564-0630-1

NIGHT MARES IN THE HAMPTONS
978-0-7564-0663-9

FIRE WORKS IN THE HAMPTONS
978-0-7564-0688-2
(available November 2011)

To Order Call: 1-800-788-6262
www.dawbooks.com

Gini Koch
The Alien *Novels*

"This delightful romp has many interesting twists and
turns as it glances at racism, politics, and religion en route.
Darned amusing." —*Booklist* (starred review)

"Amusing and interesting...a hilarious romp in the vein of
'Men in Black' or 'Ghostbusters'." —*Voya*

TOUCHED BY AN ALIEN
978-0-7564-0600-4

ALIEN TANGO
978-0-7564-0632-5

ALIEN IN THE FAMILY
978-0-7564-0668-4

ALIEN PROLIFERATION
978-0-7564-0697-4
(Available December 2011)

To Order Call: 1-800-788-6262
www.dawbooks.com

DAW 160

Diana Rowland

Secrets of the Demon

978-0-7564-0652-3

"Rowland's hot streak continues as she gives her fans another big helping of urban fantasy goodness! The plot twists are plentiful and the action is hard-edged. Another great entry in this compelling series." —*RT Book Review*

"This is an excellent police procedural urban fantasy that like its two previous arcane forensic investigations stars a terrific lead protagonist... Kara is fabulous as the focus of the case and of relationships with the Fed and with the demon as the Bayou heats up with another magical mystery tour that will take readers away from the mundane to the enjoyable world of Diana Rowland."

—*Midwest Book Reviews*

And don't miss:
Sins of the Demon
(January 2012)   978-0-7564-0705-6

To Order Call: 1-800-788-6262
www.dawbooks.com

DAW 176